Royal Street

TOR®

A TOM DOHERTY ASSOCIATES BOOK

NEW YORK

Suzanne Johnson

Royal Street

ROYAL STREET

Design by Ellen Cipriano

A Tor Book
Published by Tom Doherty Associates, LLC
175 Fifth Avenue
New York, NY 10010

www.tor-forge.com

Tor® is a registered trademark of Tom Doherty Associates, LLC.

Library of Congress Cataloging-in-Publication Data

Johnson, Suzanne, 1956–
    Royal street / Suzanne Johnson.—1st ed.
        p. cm.
    ISBN 978-0-7653-2779-6
    1. Wizards—Fiction.   2. Serial murderers—Fiction.   3. Voodooism—
Fiction.   4. New Orleans (La.)—Fiction.   I. Title.
PS3610.O38335R69 2012
813'.6—dc22   2011025187

First Edition: April 2012

Printed in the United States of America

10   9   8   7   6   5   4   3   2   1

*To my much-loved friends in New Orleans and
southeast Louisiana, who've endured so much and yet
live so large, no matter what life throws your way*

ACKNOWLEDGMENTS

Deepest thanks to my editor, Stacy Hague-Hill, who saw potential in my jumble of a book and knew what it needed: You rock! And to agent extraordinaire Marlene Stringer, for faith, tenacity, and endless patience: You rock, too.

To Dianne, my alpha reader, who keeps me real; to Debbie, my staunch advocate, who keeps me sane; to Larry, without whose encouragement DJ would never have seen daylight; to Susan, creator of mojo bags and one fine writer; to Mom, whose willingness to take on the "varmints" allowed me time to write; and to all those who read this in various stages of disarray and still speak to me: Nancy, Stella, Lauri, Amanda, Jennifer, Delaine, Pete, Matt K., Shawn, Matt L., and Meg.

Any mistakes in this book are mine, especially regarding the legendary people and places with whom I took great liberties.

ROYAL STREET

FRIDAY, AUGUST 26, 2005 "Once [Tropical Storm Katrina] moved over the gulf today, it was expected to wheel north, pick up speed and hit the Florida Panhandle on Sunday."

—THE NEW YORK TIMES

CHAPTER 1

A secluded Louisiana bayou. A sexy pirate. Seduction and deceit. My Friday afternoon had the makings of a great romantic adventure, at least in theory.

In practice, angry mosquitoes were using me for target practice, humidity had ruined any prayer of a good hair day, and the pirate in question—the infamous Jean Lafitte—was two hundred years old, armed, and carrying a six-pack of Paradise condoms in assorted fruit flavors.

I wasn't sure what unnerved me more—the fact that the historical undead had discovered modern prophylactics, or that Lafitte felt the need to practice safe sex.

Nothing about the pirate looked safe. Tall and broad-shouldered, he had dark-blue eyes and a smile twitching at the corners of his mouth as he watched me set two glasses and a bottle of dark rum on a rickety wooden table. A tanned, muscular chest peeked from his open collar, and shaggy dark hair framed a clean-shaven face. A jagged scar across his jaw reminded me the so-called gentleman pirate also had his ruthless side.

He'd arrived by way of a stolen boat at this isolated cabin

near Delacroix, a half hour outside New Orleans, to pursue two of the world's most timeless pleasures: sex and money. I'd met him here to play the role of a gullible young wizard falling under the spell of the legendary pirate, at least for a while. Then I'd do my duty as deputy sentinel and send his swashbuckling hide back to the Beyond, where he could rub shoulders with other undead legends and preternatural creatures unfit for polite human company.

My hand shook as I poured the rum, sloshing a few drops of amber liquid over the side of the glass. I'd finally been given a serious assignment, and I needed it to go without a hitch.

Lafitte's fingers brushed mine as he took the drink, sending an unexpected rush of energy up my arm. "*Merci,* Mademoiselle Jaco—or may I address you as Drusilla?"

Actually, I'd prefer he didn't address me at all. Despite his obvious hopes for the evening, this wasn't a date. "Most people call me DJ."

"Bah," he said, taking a sip of rum. "Those are alphabet letters, not a name."

From beneath the red sash that accented his waist, Lafitte pulled a modern semiautomatic handgun and set it on the table next to the rum bottle. I knew how he'd gotten it—he'd rolled the Tulane student who summoned him, lifted the kid's wallet and iPod, rode the streetcar to a Canal Street pawnshop, and made a trade for the gun. Enterprising guy, Lafitte.

I pondered the odd spike of energy I'd gotten from his hand. Touching increases the emotional crap I absorb from people as an empath, but Lafitte was technically a dead guy. Still, I'd like to say if he touched me again, I'd demand double pay from the wizards' Congress of Elders. Triple if it involved lips.

But who was I kidding? My bargaining position was nonexistent. My boss, Gerry, only sent me on this run because he had something else to do and thought Lafitte might respond to my questionable seduction skills.

I'd pulled my unruly blond hair out of its usual ponytail for the occasion, loaded on some makeup to play up my teal eyes, and poured myself into a little black skirt, short enough to show off my legs while not offending Lafitte's nineteenth-century sensibilities.

It must have worked, because the pirate was giving me that head-to-toe appraisal guys do on instinct, like they're assessing a juicy slab of beef and deciding whether they want it rare, medium, or well-done.

"You really are lovely, Drusilla." The timbre of Lafitte's voice shivered down my spine, and I fought the urge to check out the biceps underneath that linen shirt.

Holy crap. This was just wrong. I should *not* be absorbing his lust.

I forced myself to take a step back and put a few inches of distance between us. He was at least six-two and I had to crane my neck to make eye contact. Plus, distance was good. "Shouldn't we discuss business first, Captain Lafitte?"

He took another sip of rum. "Very well. Business then, *Jolie*. After all, you are the first sentinel to realize how beneficial a relationship with me could be."

"You've tried doing business with my boss?" That conversation should have been entertaining. Gerry had probably zapped him back to the Beyond faster than he could say *walk the plank*.

"Gerald St. Simon is an arrogant man who exaggerates his own importance," Lafitte said, and if that wasn't a case of a pot and a black kettle I'd never heard one. Although it did make me wonder how often he'd met Gerry.

"Present-day businessmen such as your antique merchants

would profit greatly by selling goods from the Beyond," he continued. "And an experienced trader like myself could procure valuable items from the past. As my business partner, you would of course receive a generous percentage without having to involve your Elders."

I swallowed hard as he shortened the gap between us again. "And you and I could forge a most enjoyable personal partnership as well."

He regarded me with a slow smile, and I found myself smiling back, heart pounding. My damned eyes were probably twinkling as my gaze lingered first on his mouth and then the fine line of his jaw. I wondered if the scar would feel rough under my fingertips . . .

Good grief.

I've spent most of my twenty-five years learning to manage my empathic abilities, to guard against emotions I don't want and channel the rest into my magic. I hadn't performed my grounding ritual today because, really, who'd expect to absorb emotions from a dead guy? Yet Lafitte's lust and anticipation shimmered across my skin. Touching ramped the empathy to warp speed.

He stepped close enough for me to feel the heat from his body and answer that age-old question: No, the historical undead, powered by the magic of memory, did not have cold skin like vampires.

Setting his glass on the table with one hand, he used the other to lift a stray curl from my cheek and tuck it behind my ear. His breath heated my neck as he leaned over and swept a soft kiss just below my jaw, and another across my lips.

I closed my eyes and returned the kiss—until some kernel of sanity finally reminded me to reach in my skirt pocket and finger the slim packet of herbs Gerry calls my mojo bag. Basically, it's a magic-infused ruby for emotional protection plus a blend of acacia and hyssop to clear my mind in an emergency, which this definitely was.

My pulse slowed as the warmth from my hand released the calming energy, and in a few seconds I felt only my own chagrin and a blush creeping up my cheeks that had nothing to do with the hellish temperature.

Maybe I'd ask for that bonus after all. Gerry liked that I could harness outside emotion to fuel my magic, but if I had to let myself be pawed by the undead, he would by God pay for it.

I stepped back, handed Lafitte his glass again, and offered a vague toast: "To our mutual satisfaction."

He tossed back the rest of his rum in one swallow, and I pretended to sip. I should have sprung for something better than the cheapest rum on Winn-Dixie's shelves, but the Elders are tightwads when it comes to reimbursable expenses.

I gazed off the porch of this ramshackle cabin near the edge of Bayou Lery. Lafitte hoped to establish his headquarters here once we consummated our partnership, so to speak. The orange-gold sunset illuminated a pair of white egrets splashing around the murky water and accentuated the fierce, wild beauty of the place. Here, surrounded by marshes and alligators, it would be easy to forget metro New Orleans lay only a few miles away.

Lafitte poured himself another drink and relaxed in one of two old wooden chairs we'd retrieved from the cabin's dusty interior. "I know you don't want to betray your mentor, *Jolie,* but . . ."

He frowned and set the wine glass on the table, flexing his fingers and looking at them as though they belonged on someone else's hands. "Something is amiss," he muttered, and cast a suspicious glance at me.

I stepped away from his chair, just in case he could still move when he figured out *Jolie* had caused his sudden loss of dexterity.

Within seconds, he'd lost use of his hands and feet. He stared at me in outrage. "You . . . You . . ."

A word rhyming with *witch* was probably about to roll off his tongue, but he stopped mid-sentence, eyes widening as he realized his body had frozen in place. He did the only thing he could unless I came within biting range—bombard me with a torrent of French most likely filled with expletives. Glad I couldn't understand a word of it.

Note to self: Next time you make an immobilization potion, add an accelerant and a silencer.

I knelt and retrieved my silver dagger from its sheath inside my boot, avoiding eye contact.

He lapsed into English. "Damnable wizard, treating me with such treachery when I come to you in good faith. You will rue the day you crossed me."

Definitely add the silencer next time.

"I have to admit you made a tempting case for yourself, Captain Lafitte, but I'm a licensed sentinel and I've trained under Gerald St. Simon since childhood. I'd never betray him or the Elders."

As I talked, I cleared the area around Lafitte's chair, kicking aside branches and leaves to ensure ample space on all sides. I prodded a tiny brown lizard back into the swamp with the toe of my boot. Better for him to stay here in Delacroix, munching mosquitoes.

From the bag I'd used to bring the rum and glasses, I retrieved a small syringe of mercury and a half-pint mason jar of sea salt. "You know, this is all Johnny Depp's fault," I told Lafitte, glancing around to see if he was still listening. "People summon you thinking they're going to get this loveable movie pirate, and you show up."

Anger darkened his eyes till they were almost black, and the energy coming off him sent a warm tingle across my scalp. "I do not know this Depp." He spat the words. "But there is always someone in *Louisiane* who wants to meet the famous privateer Jean Lafitte. When I am summoned to the modern world again I will find you."

Terrific. Something to look forward to. While Lafitte ranted, I formed a triangle of salt around his chair, leaving a gap of about six inches. I considered throwing another pinch in his smirking face for good measure, but unrefined sea salt is too expensive to waste.

"Drusilla," he said, his voice sliding from anger to sarcasm. "Why must you use your magic to bind me like a prisoner, and make your silly little figures on the ground? Your Gerald simply points a finger at me and sends me back to the Beyond."

One corner of his mouth edged upward in a sly smile. "You must be a very poor wizard. That is a good thing to remember when we next meet."

Big undead jerk.

"I'm just a different kind of wizard." I stopped working and treated him to a saccharine smile. "Besides, if I were so weak, you wouldn't be stuck in that chair like a big old Jean Lafitte statue, would you?"

That earned me another spate of name-calling, in Spanish this time. Couldn't understand that, either.

"You might as well calm down," I said. "I don't have to send you back to Old Orleans, after all. I'm sure the vampires would enjoy a nice pirate snack after they played with you a while. Or I could send you to the elves."

He narrowed his eyes and shifted his gaze back toward the swamp. At least he was fuming in silence. He didn't even look when I lifted the handgun from the table with two fingers and eased it into my bag. I raised my hand to toss the condoms in the water, thought about the ecological implications, and threw them in my bag as well.

I drew a triangle in the air over the pirate's head with my dagger and used more salt to close the one around his chair. Finally, I used the syringe to release small beads of mercury at three points along the triangle. The air shimmered as the third drop of mercury fell, and I released a small burst of magic along with it. With a final glare in my direction, Jean Lafitte disappeared.

My limbs felt heavy and the headache started within seconds—part adrenaline drain, part the cost of physical magic. Green Congress wizards like myself, who specialize in rituals and spellwork, can muster enough juice to do summoning and dispatches, but it takes a toll. I was tempted to rest on the porch awhile and watch the egrets, but dark had begun to settle in and I didn't want to be gator bait.

On the porch outside the triangle lay a gold doubloon, an unintended souvenir from Lafitte. I picked it up for Gerry's antiques collection, thinking it might butter him up for better assignments. More jobs like Lafitte and fewer crap jobs like pixie retrievals and research.

Today was a turning point—I could feel it. Lafitte had been dispatched as planned, despite the little lust problem, and it would prove to Gerry I could handle myself.

"Yo-ho-ho," I muttered, smudging a break in the triangle with my boot. The air solidified, and I retrieved my cell phone from my bag, punching in Gerry's speed dial.

"Ahoy, matey." He sounded chipper. Whatever his mystery job had been, it must have gone well.

"Ahoy to you, too. All's done on this end, and I'm on my way back."

"No problems with the dispatch?"

"Strictly textbook," I assured him. "But did you realize I'd be able to absorb Lafitte's emotions?"

"No, I didn't." Protracted silence. "Interesting. Meet me at

Sid-Mar's and you can regale me with the ghastly details over dinner. Oh, and pick up a case of bottled water, would you? Looks like we might be in for a little hurricane after all."

In Gerry's British accent the word sounded like "herrikin," even after almost thirty years in New Orleans.

I tried to remember the last report I'd heard on the storm, which was so small it barely rated a name. "It's not supposed to come here, is it? This morning, the weather guys said it was headed for Florida."

I loaded my bag in the back of my dusty red Pathfinder, phone tucked between shoulder and chin, and paused before climbing in. "What's it called, anyway? Kitty? Koko? Kelly?"

"Just as bad," Gerry said. "Katrina. Not exactly a name that inspires fear, is it?"

CHAPTER 2

Two hours later, Gerry and I relaxed on the wooden deck behind Sid-Mar's, reviewing the Lafitte job and gorging on stuffed artichokes and fried oysters. The restaurant filled a small wooden house in Bucktown, which had been an isolated fishing village on the south shore of Lake Pontchartrain before the railway line connected it to New Orleans and jerked it into the nineteenth century. Now it was a suburb clinging to its colorful history.

A hot breeze blew off the lake as we crunched spicy oysters and used our teeth to scrape savory stuffing off the artichoke leaves. The food took the edge off my post-magic malaise. Until recently, we'd done these recaps after every job—a way, Gerry said, of helping me learn the mysterious ins and outs of sentinel work. Lately, he'd been putting off the reviews of his jobs, and mine weren't worth talking about. Well, until today.

I plucked a French fry off his plate and sprinkled it with Louisiana Hot Sauce. "Lafitte made it sound like he's tried talking you into a business deal before." I left out the part about him calling Gerry arrogant.

"Only every time he's summoned," Gerry said, chuckling. "I had another appointment today, so I thought we'd try something different. Obviously, it worked."

"Yeah, except he swears he's going to hunt me down and get even." I flagged down the waiter and ordered a refill on my soda. "I think he took the whole fake seduction personally. What made you think he'd fall for it?"

When Gerry came up with the idea of having me lure the pirate to a swampy tryst, I'd thought he was certifiable. Lafitte was famous for many things, but not naïveté.

Gerry gave me a bemused smile. "You've really no idea, do you?"

"What?"

"Well, let's just think about it. Why would a ladies' man like Lafitte want to venture into a secluded spot with a young woman, especially one whose magical skills he doubted?" He shook his head, still laughing. "All he wanted from me was a business deal, DJ."

Of all the arrogant, pigheaded, Neanderthal attitudes. "Meaning?"

"You've grown into a lovely young woman, and that gives you a certain power. You can use it to your advantage."

I stabbed a plump oyster with my fork. It was one thing for Lafitte to belittle my abilities as a wizard, but another to hear such dismissive talk from Gerry. Like most sentinels, he was a Red Congress wizard, skilled in physical magic. He could blast the fangs off a vampire at fifty yards.

Green Congress wizards were the geeks of the magical world, hell on rituals and potions but always last to get picked for wizard dodgeball, so to speak. I'd have to immobilize the vampire, saw off his fangs, and dissolve them in an herbal potion while muttering some obscure incantation. We had no flair.

I sighed, struggling against Gerry's logic. I wasn't strong in physical magic, but I did have skills. Maybe he'd take me more seriously if I started packing heat.

Speaking of which. "Remind me to give you Lafitte's pistol later," I said. "You can have his condoms too, if you want them. Fruit-flavored."

Gerry choked on an oyster, coughing till his face turned pink. "Please tell me you're joking."

Prurient curiosity made me itch to ask Gerry if the historical undead could really do the deed, but it didn't seem appropriate dinner conversation. Lafitte sure didn't seem to think sex would be a problem. I'd do like any other self-respecting young wizard of the world. I'd look it up on the Elders' secure website when I got home.

I had to bring up the empathy problem, though. "Why do you think I was able to take in emotions from Lafitte? I didn't go through my shielding ritual beforehand because I wasn't expecting it to be an issue."

"You could feed off his anger. Wouldn't that strengthen your magic?"

I rolled my eyes. "By the time he got angry I had it under control, thanks to my grounding herbs. No, what I picked up from Mr. Lafitte was lust."

The more I thought about it, the more outraged I got. "Lust, Gerry. Which I absorbed. If it weren't for my mojo bag, we'd be out in the swamp doing God only knows what. And this was all your idea, remember?"

"Oh my." Gerry took a sip of his beer, trying to fight back laughter without much success. He was getting way too much enjoyment out of this.

"I'm sorry, love." He wiped away tears. "I had no idea. I guess it makes sense. I understand empaths can sometimes pick up emotions from vampires because they were once human.

Apparently the same thing works with the historical undead. Maybe zombies, too."

Great. Other things I had to shield myself from.

I changed the subject, hoping to squelch Gerry's laughter. "Heard any more about the storm? I couldn't find anything on the radio driving back from Delacroix, but lots of people were talking about it when I came in the restaurant." Worry hung over the place like a dark mist.

Gerry tugged his thick silver hair into a short ponytail to keep it out of his face and regarded me thoughtfully.

"Every time the weather service updates its forecast, projected landfall has shifted farther west, and now they aren't sure if it will make that curve into Florida. If it doesn't, it's coming straight for us. Unless something changes overnight, you'll have to evacuate."

I snorted. "Yeah, right. I tried leaving before Hurricane Ivan a couple of years ago, remember? For three hours, I sat in traffic that would give Mother Teresa road rage and still hadn't made it out of downtown. I finally did a U-turn and went home. We never even lost power."

I shook a few drops of red, peppery hot sauce in a small bowl, mixed in some ketchup and horseradish, and stirred it into a cocktail sauce for my oysters. No New Orleans restaurant worth beans offered its patrons bottled cocktail sauce.

"Besides," I said, "the weather guys always freak everybody out and then the storms pass us by."

I still held a grudge against one TV forecaster who had an on-air meltdown a few years back and urged everyone within hearing to hustle out and buy an ax. We'd need it, he said, to hack through our roofs ahead of rampaging floodwaters. Instead, we got a quarter-inch of rain that drained in ten minutes. I'd since dubbed that forecaster the Drama King.

"You sound like a regular native," Gerry said. "But I've a bad feeling about this one. You need to plan on going while I tend to things here."

I settled back in my chair, looking at the dark waters of Lake Pontchartrain as a family of ducks waddled past, snapping up the bits of bread diners tossed their way and quacking at a stray cat. I rubbed my throbbing temples with my fingers and willed my aching muscles to hold out a little longer. It was going to take a few hours of sleep to slough off the energy drain from sending Lafitte and his wandering lips back into the Beyond. The last thing I wanted to think about was packing up and running from a hurricane that would end up going somewhere else.

A gust of wind blew out the small candle on our table, and Gerry touched the wick, casually shooting enough magical energy from his fingertip to relight the flame. I looked around to see if anyone had noticed, and shook my head.

He laughed at my reaction. "Do you really think the Elders are going to swoop down on us because I lit a candle in a restaurant?" He scanned the other diners as they talked, laughed, paid no attention to us. "Besides, it would do ordinary humans good to learn there's still a bit of magic in the world. They've put all their faith in science and damned near lost their souls in the process."

I started to argue but bit my tongue. I was too tired to get into a philosophical chess match with Gerry. I had more immediate concerns. My mind went back to his motives for sending me after Lafitte. I was better at this job than he gave me credit for, damn it.

Gerry studied me, traces of a laugh still playing on his face. "You aren't even going to argue? You're no fun tonight."

We could keep dancing around the problem till doomsday, but my dancing skills sucked.

"I don't want to hear about how you think the Elders are mishandling the magical world," I said. "I want to talk about my job, and why you think I can only handle an assignment when you're too busy to take it or when I can use something like sex to make it work."

He leaned back in his chair, crossing his arms over his chest and squinting at me. "Very well, then. Speak your mind."

"It was nice to go out on a real assignment today. Don't you think it's time to let me out of the minor league and start giving me better things to do than handle runaway pixies and immobilized mutts?"

I put my fork down, the better to avoid stabbing him with it. "I can handle this job, Gerry. I might not be an al-freaking-mighty Red Congress wizard, but I'm better than what you give me credit for."

He twitched his mouth in a faint smile. "Admit it. You enjoyed the dog job."

Two weeks ago a low-level wizard had grown so annoyed with his hyperactive Jack Russell that he immobilized the dog, then needed help getting it unfrozen. Welcome to my life—savior of the magically inept.

Gerry looked away, taking in the lights along the water's edge. "You'll have everything you want soon enough, DJ. Don't be impatient."

Whatever that meant. "I'm never going to be able to advance from deputy status if I don't get bigger cases, Gerry."

His gaze remained fixed on the water. "Do you really think you're ready? You're still learning to control your empathic skills, and emotions and magic make dangerous companions. You consider it a liability right now, but it can be an asset when you learn to use it. And you have some physical magic we need to explore. Until then, you'd need to learn a weapon."

He turned from the water and looked at me, arching an

eyebrow. "I'll set you up with shooting lessons, if that will make you feel better. You can use Jean Lafitte's gun."

"Fine, I'll do that." I took a deep breath and bit back the urge to keep arguing. It was obvious I wouldn't get anywhere with him tonight. I'd have to dissect Gerry's psyche later, when my head didn't ache with fatigue and a hurricane wasn't looming.

"Okay, back to Katrina," I said, and Gerry looked relieved. "I'll come to your house and we'll have a hurricane party like we did when I was a kid. You know, sit outside and grill after the rain blows through and the electricity's off? Or better still, come to my place Uptown. We've never ridden out a storm there."

Gerry's house in Lakeview, the one I'd lived in since I was seven, sat about ten city blocks south of us, with a steeply sloping backyard that edged up to the 17th Street Canal. A high concrete floodwall sat atop the canal's levee, designed to keep Lake Pontchartrain from spilling its guts into the city during a storm surge. It always made me feel safe. My own house was in an older part of town that spanned the strip of land along the east bank of the Mississippi River. Either place would work.

Gerry sipped his beer, the breeze rippling the rolled-up sleeves of his shirt. "Don't make too many plans. I think you're going to have to evacuate this time unless something changes overnight. I don't have to tell you why."

"Yeah, yeah, I know." One of us had to keep an eye on the Beyond during the storm. The other had to leave and be ready to return quickly should all hell break loose in New Orleans— literally. Sentinels were in short supply, and the Congress of Elders couldn't afford to lose both of us. I knew the drill.

"Theoretically, I should be the one to stay since I'm more expendable," I said, knowing he'd never go for it.

"You're not more expendable to me." The breeze blew out the candle again, and he didn't bother relighting it. "Besides, I'll enjoy the quiet time while the city is shut down for a day.

Maybe even two or three days—this is feeling like a real storm to me."

I had to agree. Despite the fluff-ball name and my own desire to avoid evacuation, Katrina felt ominous somehow. Maybe it was the way dry heat hung in the wind blowing around us, or just the stray bits of disquiet I kept picking up from the people sitting nearby. It strummed across my skin like fingers across guitar strings. I'd stay and ride it out if Katrina began making an early turn toward Pensacola or Mobile. Otherwise, I'd have to suck it up and go.

I tipped my diet soda in his direction and tapped the edge of his beer bottle. My taste of cheap rum with Lafitte had soured me on alcohol for the day, but there was time for one more toast. "Here's to postponing a decision till tomorrow, then," I said.

Gerry smiled. "To tomorrow."

SUNDAY, AUGUST 28, 2005 "Katrina could turn out to be the perfect hurricane, much to the dismay of south Louisiana residents."

—THE TIMES–PICAYUNE

CHAPTER 3

I stared into the hatch of the Pathfinder, ruminating. What should a wizard pack when fleeing a hurricane? It sounded like the opening line of a bad joke.

The suggested packing list from the morning newspaper included three days' change of clothes, my laptop, insurance papers (even wizards need a good hazard policy), and a box of photos. My backpack of magical gear occupied one corner, along with a cooler of perishable herbs and potions in case the electricity died, some personal spellbooks and journals, and a fifty-five-hour unabridged audio CD of *The Lord of the Rings*. Frodo and Sam would probably stumble halfway to Mordor before I cleared the Louisiana state line.

Saturday had been spent hurricane-proofing my house. I lugged pots of herbs and flowers inside from the front porch and lined them along the kitchen wall, propped the patio table against the side of the house, and dragged the chairs inside. All my perishable food went in the trash—two eggs, a block of cheese, three frozen pizzas, and a green-tinged pack of sandwich meat. So I'm not Julia Child. At least I wouldn't come back to a fridge full of rotten food.

Finally, I unplugged everything and carefully coated all my windows with a paste of ground bay leaves and purified water shot with a quick infusion of magic. It looked gross and smelled like a pot of soup, but it would make the glass unbreakable for two or three days. By then, Katrina would be a memory.

I slammed the hatch and climbed in, pausing to look around before I left. The dry, scorching wind that had persisted the last couple of days rustled the leaves of the ancient live oaks lining the avenue beside my house, a Victorian camelback in a neighborhood straddling the line between commercial and residential. The result was an eclectic mix of private homes like mine and funky boutiques whose owners often lived above their businesses.

Everybody was scattering. My neighbor Eugenie Dupre, who ran a hair salon named Shear Luck across the street and lived on her second floor, had evacuated yesterday to wait out the storm with relatives in Shreveport. I'd helped bolster her windows with big Xs of masking tape, which probably wouldn't do any good but made her feel better, then lied and told her Uncle Gerry would tape mine later. Eugenie doesn't know about magic.

Gerry's girlfriend, Letitia Newman, had left for Houston a few hours ago. A Green Congress wizard who'd spent almost as much time with me as Gerry, Tish had taught me herbs and minerals and potions. We'd talked about evacuating together, but the hurricane provided a good excuse for me to visit my grandmother in Alabama. I hadn't seen her since last Christmas. I'd probably have to make an appearance with my dad, too.

Light traffic hustled along Magazine Street in front of my house. Like all New Orleans thoroughfares, its pavement rippled with ruts and bumps wrought by the unholy trinity of soft soil, a high water table, and ambivalent city government. My truck creaked and groaned from too many years driving on it.

Around me I heard the staccato *rat-a-tat* of hammers as neighbors with more do-it-yourself skills than I possessed nailed plywood over their windows. Early-morning light from a gloomy sky cast halfhearted shadows on the row of pastel century-old houses with their ornate gingerbread molding. I rejected the notion that all this might be gone tomorrow, no matter what the forecasters said.

I called Gerry on my cell as I wound through mostly empty streets toward the interstate. "Remind me again why I'm evacuating and you're at home reading the paper?" I could imagine him on his deck, cup of Jamaica Blue Mountain in hand, fighting to keep the panic-driven headlines of the *Times–Picayune* from ruffling in the wind. Today, in type so large it took up half the front page, screamed two words: "Ground Zero."

He laughed. "Because the Congress of Elders ordered you to and they pay your salary. You chose to drive, remember? They offered to set up a transport for you to Las Cruces, or you could have gone to Houston with Tish."

The sentinel in Las Cruces, New Mexico, was a self-absorbed, Elder-wannabe asshat monkey. I'd walk to my grandmother's before I'd voluntarily spend time with him.

I assumed a sour expression and kept driving, taking a shortcut through the run-down and razor-wired neighborhoods of Central City. Plywood covered almost every storefront window, and an air of nervous anticipation hung in the air.

"Wait and see," Gerry said. "The fickle Katrina will probably curve north before she gets this far. But if by chance she does knock the electricity off a few days, you'll be glad you left. New Orleans in August without air conditioning will be as miserable as one of Dante's circles of hell."

"Yeah, well, I hope you enjoy the inferno." I'd take on a little fire and brimstone to avoid a heaping helping of relatives.

I knew the real danger from the storm had nothing to do with heat and sweat. The fluctuating barometric pressure of a strong hurricane could wreak havoc on the energy fields between this world and the Beyond, opening the door for any old monster to stroll through. Hurricane Andrew had led to such an explosion in the vampire population of south Florida back in 1992 the Elders had been forced to bring in sentinels from Europe to contain it.

"Do you think we'll have the same problems as Miami?" I'd only been twelve and had been hustled to Gran's, but Gerry had been one of the sentinels sent down to help, at least till Andrew reentered the Gulf and headed toward Louisiana.

"Probably not," he said. "Although it wouldn't necessarily be a bad thing for a few new species to move in, stir things up a bit."

Oh, God. Back to that old tune.

"Look, I'm almost to the interstate," I said. "If it gets bad, use the transport we set up between your house and my grandmother's—you and Sebastian both. Gran would be glad to see you." I'd finally talked him into setting up an open transport so he and his cranky, cross-eyed Siamese cat could get out if they needed to, or I could get back quickly. I'd establish my end of the transport when I got to my grandmother's.

He was still laughing at the idea of Gran being happy to see him when I ended the call. She might have foisted me off on Gerry when I was seven, but she didn't like him. She'd deny any animosity till she turned blue, but it's hard to hide emotion from an empath. She'd be happier to see the cat, and she disapproved of house pets on principle.

I had reached the interstate on-ramp quickly. Maybe this wouldn't be so bad. Then I actually *saw* the interstate. Even at seven a.m. it looked like a mega-mall parking lot on Black Friday: an ocean of cars, little movement, lots of tension.

I gritted my teeth and invoked the law of the urban jungle—any vehicle smaller than mine was fair game. I waved an apology as I nosed in front of a blue sedan with two harried-looking adults in the front, at least four kids in the back, and two dogs hanging their heads out the rear windows. They all gave me the finger, except the dogs. They barked.

New Orleans ain't the city of brotherly love, at least not when a storm's brewing and traffic's creeping at less than two miles an hour on the I-10.

It took more than ninety minutes to drive the ten miles to New Orleans East and another hour to inch over the five-mile Twin Span bridges that crossed the eastern edge of Lake Pontchartrain. As I sat on the eastbound bridge, I had plenty of time to watch the whitecaps chop and foam on the lake and try to ignore the ominous mountain of clouds building around me.

Katrina was turning into one nasty storm. I tried to concentrate on the audiobook and calm the fingers of panic that scrabbled around the edge of my brain, looking for a way in.

I knew most of the day would be spent on the road, surrounded by other cars full of nervous people. If normal hurricane frenzy ranked five on a scale of one to ten, Katrina hysteria had ratcheted up to fifty in the past twenty-four hours. Friday, it had been a minor storm headed for Florida. Now, it was a monster hurtling straight for us. Without a miracle, the City That Care Forgot (or, as we liked to call it, the City That Forgot to Care) would be in trouble.

So I'd gotten up early enough to go through my most effective grounding ritual, part meditation, part magic. Aromatics in a room hydrator, Pachelbel on the iPod, both hands holding magic-infused rubies washed in holy water for emotional protection, eyes closed, mind focused on precisely nothing. Works every time.

And, just in case, I had put fresh herbs in my mojo bag.

I edged the Pathfinder up another three feet and wondered: If enough wizards turned their powers toward it, could they change the path of a hurricane? Of course, doing so would violate magical law. The Congress of Elders keeps the magical community on a tight leash, and despite his doubts about the system, Gerry had taught me every *thou-shalt-not* in the book, including the one about interfering with nature.

Bottom line: I couldn't do anything about this storm, which really ticked me off. I just crept along and started hour three of the audiobook. Bill the Pony could make better time in this traffic.

Whenever I stopped to stretch my legs, I found people gathered around radios, fear mirrored from one face to the next. My emotional shields were holding so far, which was a good thing. My own skittering nerves were bad enough. Add any more stress and I'd be sitting on the side of the interstate gibbering like a chimpanzee when the storm hit.

"Most of the area will be uninhabitable for weeks, perhaps longer," warned a National Hurricane Center spokesman, his voice vibrating out of someone's car radio at a rest stop. The NHC guy used phrases like "catastrophic structural failure" and "human suffering incredible by modern standards," sending a palpable tremor through everyone within earshot. The feds were putting the Drama King to shame.

I still couldn't accept it. We'd had too many close calls. Hurricanes headed our way, the weather prophets spouted doom and gloom, and the storms either took sharp last-second turns or fizzled out before landfall. We had an unwritten belief system: God watches out for fools and New Orleanians. I'd clock anyone who said that phrase was redundant.

Waiting my turn at a gas station outside Meridian, Mississippi, I heard people talking about fuel shortages along the evacuation routes. I bit my lip, thinking. Maybe I could do something to help, at least on a small scale. Let the Elders track down my happy evacuating backside if they didn't like it.

I jumped out of the Pathfinder and dug through my backpack full of potions and charms arranged in neatly labeled vials and bottles. I finally found the one I wanted: a replenishing potion made from a simple blend of ground hawthorn and geranium in my usual base of magic-infused olive oil. I stuck it in my pocket and went to lean against the nearest pump, half-listening as evacuees from Biloxi and Gulfport exchanged horror stories about the scarcity of hotel rooms.

A red-faced man in a white polo shirt that failed to camouflage the evidence of a few too many Budweisers ranted to nobody in particular. "I heard there's over a million people running from this dadburned storm."

He had to be from Mississippi. Nobody from Southeast Louisiana says "dadburned."

A white-haired woman in wrinkled shorts and a pink visor nodded at him from the next pump. "Heck, I just talked with my cousin Luanne. She left Yscloskey last night with three babies and a dog, and they couldn't find no place to stay. Spent the night on the floor of a motel up near Jackson."

Okay, maybe I wouldn't diss my family. At least I had a place to go.

I strolled around the gas pumps, looking for the circular cover that led to the underground fuel storage tanks. I finally found it and knelt, pretending to tie my shoe while I pried off the lid and looked at the hatch. The tanker-truck drivers probably had a special wrench to open it, but I had something faster: magic. Using a tiny bit of magical energy, I managed to get it open enough to pour the replenishing potion inside. This set of pumps, at least, wouldn't run out of fuel for another six or eight hours.

"Take that, Gerry," I said, replacing the cover and returning the empty potion vial to my pocket. Red Congress wizards might fight better, but they were downright dangerous when it came to electronics, fuels, or explosives. If Gerry had tried that stunt, we wouldn't have to worry about a hurricane. We'd be so deep-fried you could roll us in powdered sugar and sell us as beignets.

The beginnings of a headache rewarded me for my efforts. After filling my own tank and buying a giant coffee with enough caffeine to keep a narcoleptic awake, I wedged the Pathfinder back into traffic and snaked up the I-59 into Alabama, stopping to magically replenish fuel storage tanks along the way as long as my premade potions lasted. Always, I was surrounded by drivers whose faces grew incrementally more worried. A series of back roads out of Tuscaloosa eventually led to my grandmother's house in the tiny northwest Alabama cotton mill town of Winfield.

I'd spent the first seven years of my life here, not all of them particularly happy. I prayed it wouldn't turn out to be the only home I had left.

MONDAY, AUGUST 29, 2005 "Superdome becomes last resort for thousands unable to leave. New Orleans braces for nightmare of the Big One."

—THE TIMES-PICAYUNE

CHAPTER 4

As Katrina grew to monstrous Category Five status and started her last slow march toward land, I'd spent Sunday night frozen in front of the TV in my grandmother's living room with no more eloquent prayer on my lips than "please."

Please let this storm die out. Please take care of those people who couldn't leave. Please help my home survive. Please help Gerry. If nothing else, help him make it through this.

I drifted into an exhausted sleep around four a.m., then awoke to the news that Katrina had weakened just before landfall and taken a last-second jog to the east. It had avoided the direct hit, socking New Orleans with a blow from its weaker, westerly side. Relief rolled through me, relaxing muscles I hadn't realized were bunched. News hadn't come in from the Louisiana and Mississippi coastal areas east of New Orleans, but it would be bad.

I was still trying to process it when Gran, wearing her pink housecoat and fuzzy slippers, wandered in to tell me coffee was ready. "Looks like it didn't amount to much in New Orleans," she said in her slow drawl as we watched TV news teams wander around the French Quarter. The reporters seemed torn between relief at their own safety and disappointment that the big story was happening to the east, where Katrina was probably making mincemeat of St. Bernard and Plaquemines parishes and the Mississippi coast.

"I don't know what I would've done if it had hit us head-on." I watched as camera crews captured the palm trees on Canal Street bending under 140-mph gusts. Hundreds of windows on the Hyatt Regency had exploded, but the building stood. An old storefront downtown had collapsed on a car, but no one was hurt. There would be a lot of wind damage, but it wouldn't be catastrophic. New Orleans would survive.

"Well, you'd have moved back here, I reckon," Gran said. "Wouldn'a been the end of the world. Come get breakfast." A woman of few words and highly understated compassion, my grandmother.

As soon as I'd arrived Sunday night, I'd moved my late grandfather's old Pontiac out of the garage and created the other end of the transport in case Gerry needed it. We'd talked by phone, made sure the two portals were connected, and then I'd locked myself in the bathroom and retraced the steps of my grounding ritual. I'd learned the hard way that Gran and I got along better if I didn't know what she really felt behind that stiff upper lip.

I wandered into the kitchen, slid a biscuit and piece of ham onto a plate, and poured some coffee.

"Is Gerry coming here?" Gran sat at the kitchen table scanning the Birmingham newspaper, reading glasses perched on the end of her nose and every strand of silvery-blond hair in place. "You gonna see your daddy while you're here?"

I sighed. Two loaded questions.

"I don't guess Gerry will have to come after all," I said, sitting opposite her at the table. "And do you really think Dad wants to see me?"

My father, Peter Jaco, had dumped me on my grandparents' doorstep when I was six, shortly after my mom died of an aneurysm. She'd been on borrowed time her whole life and didn't know it. Dad had worked at the conveyor belt plant, a solid and quiet man. My mom had given up her magic to marry him and live a normal life just like Gran had done with my grandfather. But with Mom gone, Peter Jaco hadn't wanted the stress of a six-year-old kid with magic skills. Maybe it wasn't that simple, but that's how it looked from my end of things.

"Well, of course your daddy would want to see you. What a question." Gran rattled her paper and turned the page, ending the discussion.

I ate silently, trying to think of an excuse not to visit him. Really, though, he'd done no worse by me than my grandparents. They'd kept me less than a year before driving me to New Orleans and leaving me with Gerry, a complete stranger. I don't think I was a bad kid, just one with a lot of untrained magic. I tried not to blame them. Sometimes I even succeeded.

I poured the last of my coffee into the sink, then placed my mug in the dishwasher. "I'll see Dad before I head back home."

"When you going?"

What was the old saying about fish and houseguests stinking after three days? "In a day or two, unless Gerry needs me sooner."

"Stay as long as you want to, Drusilla Jane. This is your home too." Her face was hidden behind the newspaper, and I decided to give her the benefit of the doubt. One of these days, I was going to have to come to terms with the fact that Gran and Dad were my closest family members whether or not they approved of the life I'd chosen. But not today.

Back in the living room, the cable news reporter had left the French Quarter and stood in the New Orleans Central Business District, the CBD, looking perplexed.

"We're getting reports of rising water in different parts of town, but we haven't been able to confirm more than this." He pointed the camera's focus toward his shoes, which were immersed in a half inch of water. "This wasn't here an hour ago."

I frowned and returned to the sofa, my dysfunctional family forgotten as I listened to new reports filtering in. Storm surge had caused levee breaches that were dumping tons of water into the Lower Ninth Ward and St. Bernard Parish. The Lower Nine was a predominantly black neighborhood a few miles east of the French Quarter; St. Bernard was predominantly white and just east of the Lower Nine. Other breaches in the area's broad levee system had reportedly flooded New Orleans East, but the media couldn't confirm it—only that 9-1-1 calls had come in before the phone lines went down. No one knew where the water downtown was coming from.

I scrambled in my jeans pocket for my cell phone and called Gerry.

He answered on the first ring. "I thought it was about time you called. You're such a mother hen."

"Are you getting any news?" I said. He sounded relaxed, even cheerful. Maybe nothing was wrong after all.

"No, the electricity went out early this morning, but I'd say the worst of it missed—" He stopped talking, and I heard him moving around. "Damn."

"Gerry? The levees are failing. Get in the transport."

He didn't answer, but I heard him calling Sebastian. "There's water coming in the first floor. I think the floodwall—"

The phone's tiny gray screen blinked CALL ENDED. Hitting redial got me nothing but silence.

I raced through the kitchen to the garage, passing Gran along the way. "Something's wrong." My voice sounded calmer than I felt. "I'm going to try to bring Gerry here."

I knelt beside the interlocking circle and triangle I'd drawn in chalk on the concrete floor. Lighting two small candles from my backpack, I set one on each end of the transport and laid small chunks of green amber at each point of the triangle. I warmed the largest piece of green amber in my hands, placed it carefully on the circle, and shot a tiny bit of energy inside it. The power of the transport caught like an ember bursting into flame. Gerry should be able to come through.

Nothing happened.

"TV just said the Lakeview levee broke."

I started, unaware that Gran had come into the garage and was standing behind me.

A thrill of fear shot through me. "You're sure it was Lakeview?"

She nodded. "They say the whole place'll fill up like a soup bowl. They had no business buildin' a city below sea level in the first place."

I bit back a retort and did some mental calculations. The foundation of Gerry's house sat about twelve or fourteen feet below the levee. If New Orleans really did fill up, his first floor would be underwater, but he should be able to go upstairs unless the force of the water pushed the whole house off its foundation. It would depend on how close he was to the breach.

Retrieving the large piece of amber, I warmed it in my hands again. "Gerry established his transport in his upstairs study," I said. "I'm going to try to go there and see if he's okay."

I stepped inside the transport and knelt again, placing the green amber on the line of the circle and willing a small amount of energy into it.

Pressure squeezed me from all sides, and I waited for the transport to begin. Then it dissipated. Gerry's side of the transport wasn't working. It had been disconnected, or destroyed.

TUESDAY, AUGUST 30, 2005 "Catastrophic: Storm surge swamps 9th Ward, St. Bernard; Lakeview levee breach threatens to inundate city."

—THE TIMES–PICAYUNE

CHAPTER 5

Several hours of frantic transport attempts and aborted phone calls passed before I thought of trying to locate Gerry by less-conventional means. The Elders had outlawed unauthorized hydromancy and other forms of divination years ago because they were too easy to abuse, but like most young wizards I'd tried a few times just to see if they worked. Want to see what the cute boy down the street's up to? Hydromancy is a teenage girl's dream.

Sometimes you have to break rules to get things done in an emergency, and I thought a hurricane probably qualified. Besides, I'd run out of other ideas. I'd even checked with Tish, staying at her cousin's house in Houston, and she hadn't been able to reach Gerry either.

My energy was flagging from the transport attempts by the time I headed to the Winfield Walmart in search of makeshift hydromancy tools. A headache nudged at my temples, and my muscles ached as I prowled the aisles looking for an acceptable substitute for a dark marble bowl. I found a smoke-brown Pyrex dish that should work, and purified water to substitute for holy water. Alabama was Bible Belt. Methodists and Baptists do casseroles, not holy water.

Back at Gran's, I pulled a small gardening table into the backyard to take advantage of energy from the full moon, and set up the ritual. Faux-holy water in the bowl. Something of Gerry's—a book I had borrowed. Patchouli incense from Walmart. I really needed mimosa leaves to burn, but patchouli would have to do. I lit the incense sticks and tried to relax while the ashes collected in the mason jar I was using as an incense burner. Finally, I added the ashes to the bowl of water.

I rested one hand on Gerry's book and dipped the other hand in the water, concentrating on Gerry and tapping my dwindling reserves of magic. A minute passed, then two, and a cloudy image reflected on the water's surface.

Thank God. It had been almost four frantic hours since our phone conversation, but at least I knew Gerry was alive. He sat at the desk in his upstairs study, writing by candlelight and looking hot and sweaty and miserable. But alive. I closed my eyes and my heart rate slowed. I couldn't imagine my life without Gerry. I might share blood ties with my dad and Gran, but Gerry was my family. I'd stop complaining about my assignments. I'd appreciate what I had. I'd trust Gerry to bring my skills along the way he thought best.

※

I spent the next two weeks glued to the TV news channels, watching as my beautiful city died an ugly death, broadcast around the world 24/7. Thousands of people were stranded without help because they'd been too poor to leave, or too sick, or too old and frail, or too sure nothing bad could happen. If Gerry and the Elders hadn't forced me to leave, I would have been one of them.

International media and private rescue groups swarmed the city immediately, but it took almost a week for squabbling officials to send even such basics as bottled water. In the meantime, people drowned in the eighty percent of the city that flooded, and died on the streets in the twenty percent that didn't.

A report on what looked like a voodoo ritual killing of a National Guardsman trying to secure one of the neighborhoods finally propelled me off the sofa. The camera crews raced to a partially flooded Central City area and showed a black-draped form on a patch of high ground next to a boarded-up nail salon. A strange symbol had been drawn on the side of the building in white paint, and reporters speculated that a voodoo practitioner had sacrificed the soldier in some misguided plea to save the city.

Enough. I had to do something, but I couldn't go home without blustering my way past jumpy soldiers and breaking the mandatory evacuation order. Gerry's side of our transport remained inoperable for some reason. No phone calls to the 504 area code would go through. My options were limited.

On Thursday, almost two weeks after the storm, I finally broke down and visited my father—Gran had told me it was his off-day. I didn't feel too badly about waiting so long. The roads worked in both directions, and he hadn't come to see me, either.

I pulled up to his neat redbrick ranch house, about a ten-minute drive from Gran's. The lawn was green and the flower beds well-tended. A black Ford pickup sat in the driveway. Like every place here, it seemed eerily quiet. My life was filled with sirens and horns and streetcars and crowds, with a constant backdrop of music.

The front door opened before I cleared the small brick porch, and Dad stepped back to let me in. "Wondered when you were gonna come by here," he said, smiling and pulling me into a quick hug. He was always smaller than I remembered. In my mind, Peter Jaco was a tall bear of a man, I guess because in most of my memories, I was a kid. This Peter Jaco was just a middle-aged man in a navy polo shirt and khakis, thinning on top and thickening in the middle.

"Sorry it took me so long," I said, following him into the bright kitchen with its floral wallpaper and white curtains. "I've been trying to follow what's going on at home, and, well . . ."

"Yeah, it's a shame. Your house all right?"

He'd never come to see it, but at least he asked. "I don't know. I heard the spots along the river didn't flood so maybe it's okay. I'm hoping they'll start letting us go home next week when it drains a little more."

Dad held up a Diet Dr Pepper. "You still drink these?"

I smiled and took it. "Where's Martha this morning?" Dad had remarried when I was ten, but never had more children. Probably just as well.

"Always gets her hair done on Thursdays," he said. "She'll be sorry she missed you. You talk to Gerry since the storm?"

I followed him into the neat den and took a seat on the end of the plush sofa nearest his favorite armchair. "I haven't really gotten to talk to him, but I know he's okay. His house was about eight blocks from one of the worst levee breaches."

At first, I'd used hydromancy to check on Gerry every night but finally decided he was fine. He'd always been reading, writing at his desk, pacing. Once or twice I'd seen him talking to someone outside my field of vision—a trapped neighbor, probably, or one of the rescuers going around in boats.

Dad didn't ask how I knew Gerry was okay. The whole idea of magic made him antsy so neither of us mentioned it anymore. "Gerry will be fine," he said. "He always lands on his feet."

I was about to ask what he meant when Fats Domino started belting out "Walking to New Orleans" from deep inside my purse.

Dad chuckled. "Your bag is singing."

I smiled and dug in the oversize satchel. "I have a five-oh-four area code and no one's been able to call since the storm," I said, pulling out a chocolate bar, some keys, and a notebook, but no phone. "Maybe this means the cell towers are working again."

By the time I'd excavated it from the tangle of stuff that purses always seem to collect, the caller had hung up. I checked the call log and choked on my soda. *Congress of Elders.* No phone number, but the message icon blinked.

"Uh, I need to check this."

"You go on," Dad said, heading for the kitchen. "I'm gonna get me some coffee."

My hand shook as I punched in my PIN. Pixie retrieval did not put one on the Elders' radar. I'd never seen an Elder, much less talked to one. The highest I'd ever rated on the wizarding scale of importance was a certificate showing I'd passed my sentinel exam four years ago and the nifty badge that came with it.

A deep, rich voice boomed out a short message: *Gerald St. Simon is missing. Return to New Orleans immediately.*

CHAPTER 6

Alarm signals went off in my head. I automatically reached in my pocket and grabbed my mojo bag, willing my tightening muscles to relax as I inhaled the sweet, minty scents of acacia and hyssop. Gerry couldn't be missing. I'd been keeping tabs on him until a couple of days ago. But Katrina had already taught me the world could change in much less time than that.

I stuck the phone in my pocket and returned to the kitchen. "Dad, I'm sorry, but something's going on in New Orleans. I need to go."

He set down the coffee cup and frowned at me. "Don't go down there and let those people drag you into nothin' dangerous."

I didn't have to ask who *those people* were. Gerry. Elders. Those people. People like me.

Still, he'd at least expressed concern, so I poured the rest of my soda down the sink and surprised both of us by hugging him. It took a couple of heartbeats, but his arms circled me and held me tight before we both pulled away.

"You look just like your mama, you know that?"

We smiled at each other, and suddenly I wished I could stay here and talk to him. Really talk. Maybe if we could sit down, just the two of us, he could tell me why he made the decisions he did and I could be at peace with it.

But first I had to talk to those people.

I drove back to Gran's and went straight to the garage, grabbing a bottle of purified water and my backpack along the way.

Hydromancy should be done at night to pull on the aura of the moon, but a dark garage was the best I could do on a sunny Saturday. I grabbed a folding TV tray to use as a table and shut the door behind me, setting up my work space next to an ancient Maytag deep freeze filled with homegrown tomatoes, peppers, and corn. While the incense burned, I lit an unscented candle and worked on relaxing, settling my thoughts, and focusing on Gerry. Finally, I stirred the incense ash into the water and turned off the lights. Kneeling in front of the tray, I placed one hand on the book and the other in the water, projecting a surge of magic into the bowl.

The water clouded for a few seconds, swirled, then cleared. Nothing. I tried twice more. Still nothing.

I blew a frustrated breath between my clenched teeth and tried again, this time focusing on Gerry's upstairs study instead of Gerry himself. Within a few seconds an image appeared, hazier than my moonlight images but still recognizable. Sebastian curled like a bristly brown ball on Gerry's favorite armchair. No sign of Gerry.

One by one, I looked in the other upstairs rooms, even the bathroom. Finally, I tried the first floor. The floodwater should have receded enough for him to go downstairs. A chaotic assortment of furniture and inky sludge showed up in the living room, but no wizard. Outside, his vintage BMW remained in his driveway, upside down and sideways, covered in mud. Still no Gerry.

Blowing out the candle, I sat in the dark a minute, feeling the familiar achy aftermath of using magic. Where was he? How long had he been missing—an hour? A day? Two days? It couldn't be longer.

I pulled myself to my feet and returned to the kitchen. The sun pushing through the open curtains blinded me after the darkness of the garage, and I squinted against it. Gran puttered around outside, the water faucet squeaking as she turned it on, followed by the hiss of the garden hose.

I dug the phone out of my pocket and scrolled through the tiny screen's menu. Gerry once told me the Elders could contact any wizard at will, but I'd always envisioned something more along the lines of a glowing crystal ball or a bolt of lightning, not a silly little camera phone. Gerry kept up with activity from the Beyond through a large wall-mounted screen in his study, but I wasn't sure how he communicated away from home. By phone, maybe.

I scrolled to *Congress of Elders* in the missed-call log, punched the send button even though no number was listed, and heard the static pause of a call going through.

The voice on the other end sounded like the one on the message. Deep, melodious, British accent. "Yes, Drusilla Jaco? Are your instructions unclear?"

I flinched. First impressions counted, so I should try to impress this guy with my rapier wit and keen intelligence. My mind blanked, and a prong of pain started behind my right eye. The Elders would think I was a moron.

"May I ask to whom I'm speaking?" Maybe they'd think I was polite, if not particularly bright. I sat hard on a kitchen chair.

"I am the Speaker of the Congress of Elders. And *you*"—he paused for effect—"must return to New Orleans as soon as pos-

sible." Like many outsiders, the Speaker mispronounced the city
New Or-leens, but correcting him seemed like a bad idea.

"What happened to Gerry?"

The Speaker hesitated. "We have been unable to locate the
sentinel for the past twenty-four hours."

I frowned. Travel in Lakeview still required a boat, but I had
seen Gerry talking to someone outside his window. "Maybe
he rode out with one of the rescuers. He might even have gone
to my house—I don't think it flooded." He might have left
Sebastian, knowing the cat would be okay alone for a few days.

"He is not in New Orleans, I can assure you," the Speaker
said, his tone implying that he did, indeed, consider me a
moron.

Gerry might be a closet anarchist, but he took his sentinel
duties seriously. "He wouldn't have left New Orleans unpro-
tected." I avoided the other options—that he'd left New Orleans involuntarily, or something bad had happened to him.

The Speaker's voice softened. "We cannot detect his unique
energy field, which is how we locate wizards with whom we
wish to communicate. We should be able to find him anywhere
in the world. Of course, we are investigating, but in the meantime we need you to go back. We're shorthanded, and although
you aren't Red Congress, you know the city and have been the
deputy sentinel several years."

I took a deep breath. "This doesn't make any sense. I know
Gerry was fine two days ago."

"How do you know that? We were in contact with him ourselves until yesterday, and he said the two of you hadn't spoken."

I might as well fess up. Surely the Elders wouldn't arrest me
for a tiny bit of illegal magic if they were shorthanded. "When I
couldn't reach him after the flooding started and the transport
we'd set up didn't work, I used hydromancy to make sure he was
okay."

"I see." Two short words, dripping with disapproval. "Well then, I assume as soon as you received my message you tried to scry him again." He didn't wait for me to answer before adding, "Did you see anything out of the ordinary?"

Huh. Did that mean the Elders couldn't do hydromancy, or that they were too law-abiding to try it? I took a deep breath. The alligators were halfway up to my ass. Might as well let 'em keep climbing.

"He isn't anywhere in his house," I said. "His car is in the drive, but it's totaled. I've been keeping an eye on him since the storm hit, though, and he's been fine. Disappearing at this point doesn't make sense."

"We'll keep investigating," the Speaker said. "In the meantime, you need to go back. Today if you can, but certainly by tomorrow. The storm weakened the temporal fabric between the mundane world and the Beyond, and breaches are showing up all along the U.S. Gulf Coast. Because of its age and supernatural history, New Orleans is particularly vulnerable."

No kidding. You couldn't walk down the street without tripping over a ghost story, and most were true.

The speaker continued. "Of course, the Elders could have overestimated your abilities. If you wish to stay where you are, I'm sure our New Mexico sentinel would be willing to step in temporarily."

What a jerk. The Elders would not give my job to the asshat monkey, even if I had to walk back to New Orleans.

"I can handle things just fine, sir. I need to make a few preparations and will head back early tomorrow." Preparations like a nice, long grounding ritual to help me emotionally survive a city filled with grief and anger and death. And maybe a bag of Cheetos.

"Fine," the Speaker said. "It will take a while for us to repair the damage between the Now and the Beyond. It's complex magic, and there are not many wizards able to do such spell-work. In the meantime, I don't have to tell you how important it is that we monitor anyone from the Beyond who tries to come into New Orleans."

I tried to wrap my brain around the situation, pushing thoughts of Gerry aside for the moment. He'd always told me to keep my emotions in a compartment that could be shut off till later, when there was time to deal with them. I did it now, focusing on the immediate problem and shutting away the part of me that wanted to have a meltdown.

"Any ideas on how I can best get into the city?" I asked. "The mandatory evacuation is still in effect and my transport to Gerry's house doesn't work." It would take at least eight hours to drive down, and I didn't know what kind of roadblocks I'd run into.

"You're obviously a resourceful wizard," he said. "Just get there. And we'll look past the hydromancy this time, given the circumstances. But don't do it again."

I opened my mouth to answer but the void on the phone told me that, for the Speaker at least, the conversation was over. I got a whiff of why Gerry usually referred to the Elders as "arrogant old gits."

I leaned back in my chair, flexing my shoulders to stretch out the kinks and trying to think where Gerry might be. If he wasn't showing up on the Elders' version of magical radar, it could mean he'd discovered a way to move around undetected, although I wasn't sure why he'd want to. Gerry was no dumb bunny. Did they think he was dead?

My heart did a flip-flop. I wouldn't even go there.

I walked to the window and saw Gran on her knees in front of the flower bed, pruning her hybrid roses for one last bloom before autumn. She was tall and thin, her every movement deliberate and controlled. She didn't laugh often. I had a few fading images of her and my mom giggling as they baked cookies in this kitchen and pretended to let me help, but most of my memories came afterward, when Dad sent me to live here. She said and did the right things, but I couldn't control my empathic skills so I knew she missed my mom every time she looked at me. And I knew my magic scared her, which I never understood because she'd had her own magic when she was young. Within a year, they'd foisted me off on Gerry.

Gran stood up and looked back at the house. I motioned her inside, and at the sight of my face, she laid down her shears and headed toward the back door, pulling off her heavy gardening gloves.

"It's Gerry," I said as she opened the door, eyebrows raised. "He's missing."

Gran frowned and steered me toward the worn wooden table in the center of the kitchen. "How do you know?" She pulled two green vintage Fiesta mugs from the old Hoosier cabinet and rummaged in a drawer for tea infusers.

I told her about my close encounter of the Elder kind, and she trained beady, suspicious eyes on me.

"You're being awfully calm about this, Drusilla Jane." Gran never called me DJ. I think some small part of her still hoped I'd abandon my magical ways and turn into a normal, baby-producing granddaughter. Fat chance.

"I'm calm because I don't believe anything is really wrong. It's some kind of misunderstanding. I need to get back down there as early as possible tomorrow and see if I can sort it out."

I caught myself tearing a paper napkin into a pile of tiny shreds. I wadded it up and stuck the evidence in my pocket while Gran's back was turned. So much for calm.

She handed me a cup of herbal tea, one of her special blends that wafted traces of ginger and bergamot. Her instinct for herbs was all the magic she'd retained after giving it up to marry my granddad.

"Did you ever wonder why your grandfather and I sent you to live with Gerry?" she asked. "I mean, why Gerry in particular?"

"Sure. Gerry always said it was because he knew how to work around empaths," I said. "You never seemed to really like him, though, and I always wondered why." I was surprised she'd even broached the subject.

Gran paused as if trying to decide whether or not to acknowledge her animosity. "Gerry is a good enough man, I guess. Your grandfather and I just hoped you'd do like me and your mama, that you'd give up on the magic and be normal. The Elders chose Gerry for you to live with."

I didn't want to go down the normal-versus-magic road. "Why Gerry?"

She looked out the window and took a slow sip of tea. "You developed your magic real young, not just your ritual magic. You had that empathy thing too, and some physical magic—I didn't know how to deal with it all."

I frowned at her. "I don't really have much physical magic. What made you think I did?"

She looked at her teacup a moment, then picked it up and took it to the sink. "You could move things around a little—just enough so we were afraid you'd hurt yourself, or us. Those people, the Elders, said you'd do better with somebody like Gerry, who knew more about it."

Those people again. As the hot tea warmed my throat and settled my nerves, I found myself wishing, for the second time today, that I could stay a little longer and hash things out, maybe put to rest some of the questions and hurt I'd avoided dealing with all these years.

It would have to wait. For the past eighteen years, Gerry had been the one who was there for me. Now it was my turn.

FRIDAY, SEPTEMBER 16, 2005 "New Orleans is now occupied by two armies: the military troops who are restoring order, and the TV crews bent on broadcasting the destruction and rebirth of an American city."

—THE TIMES-PICAYUNE

CHAPTER 7

The return to New Orleans took me on a roundabout path, literally over the river and through the woods, except the woods were full of buffed-up guys with short hair and in uniforms. The interstate was heavily policed, and all the bridges across Lake Pontchartrain were either destroyed or closed to non-military traffic. I had to loop around and approach the city from the west along the narrow two-lane highway that skirts the Mississippi River.

At the Orleans Parish line, a young National Guardsman yawned as he glanced at my driver's license, taking in my green doctor's scrubs from the Winfield Walmart and my hastily constructed fake hospital badge. I'd used a basic illusion charm to make the laminated card look like it came straight from Tulane Hospital.

"You be careful, doctor. Most of the major streets have been cleared but there's still lots of debris and power lines around. Some places still got flooding, so stick to Uptown and the Quarter."

I hadn't liked the idea of lying my way back into town, but

using serious magic seemed like overkill and I wasn't sure how the emotional aura of the city would affect me. I'd gone through my grounding ritual once last night and again this morning. I might be aware of the sadness and desperation around me but wouldn't absorb it. I hoped.

The soldier waved me through and motioned to the pickup behind me, which pulled a small boat. Dozens of vehicles lined River Road, all of us ready to march into the debris and assess what was left of our lives, never mind the evacuation order still in effect. Obviously, this soldier thought we had the right to be here. He wasn't turning anyone away.

My back ached from the long drive, but I took a northerly detour to see if I could get anywhere near Gerry's house. A manned roadblock stopped me before I got a half mile from Lakeview, and a sunburned soldier about my age gave me a blank stare when I tried to convince him of my high standing in the New Orleans medical community.

"Come back with a boat, doctor, and we'll talk," he said. Was it paranoia, or did he really look doubtful I'd ever been within a mile of a stethoscope?

I'd figure out a way to get into Gerry's neighborhood to-morrow. Only a couple of hours remained before the dusk-to-dawn curfew kicked in.

I made a U-turn and navigated through Mid-City toward home, sticking to the major streets. Even with my mojo bag on a cord around my neck, I had to blink back tears. The TV cameras hadn't begun to capture the devastation; all around me were vignettes of horror I knew would haunt me. Mile after mile after mile of them.

Watermarks rose like brown bathtub rings on every building. Huge oaks lay on their sides, massive root systems exposed to the blistering sun. Cars coated with dried mud filled the neutral grounds—thousands of them. Head-high piles of tree limbs and trash had been shoved out of the roadways to line every street.

Only it wasn't trash, not really. I stopped at an intersection and stared at a muddy picture frame lying in one of the tangled piles of tree branches. A little girl looked out from her class photo, her grin revealing a gap where a front tooth used to be, her school uniform pressed and neat.

As I drove deeper into the city, the watermarks grew higher till they reached roof level. Houses leaned to the south where the wind had howled in from the north and threatened to blow them off their brick and concrete piers. A few had collapsed, but most tilted drunkenly. Jagged holes gaped in rooftops where people had hacked their way out, waiting for escape. The Drama King had been right about the ax.

I felt like Alice, but I'd slid down the rabbit hole past Wonderland and straight into hell.

As I approached St. Charles Avenue, I hit the lucky twenty percent of the city—the part that hadn't flooded.

The elegant old mansions stood like sentries guarding the entrance to the narrow sliver of land beyond. This slender thread of high ground on either side of the Mississippi River snaked like a single artery through town, trying to pump lifeblood back into a patient barely hanging on. There was damage here, but it was from wind, not water.

Traffic picked up, mostly military or police vehicles. I slammed on my brakes to avoid a fender bender as a black Humvee crunched into an Army-drab Jeep in the middle of the intersection in front of me. With no working traffic lights and only a few handmade stop signs, this was going to be a colossal mess as more people returned.

I edged around the two vehicles filled with soldiers arguing in the broiling sun and passed through two more checkpoints.

So far, my fake ID had aroused no suspicion. Two sentries even told me where to find the nearest makeshift medical clinic so I could go to work.

I bit my lip and sucked in a deep breath of relief when the burgundy clapboard of my house came into view. The sixty-foot cedar that consumed most of my tiny backyard tilted against the chimney, and pieces of heavy gray roofing slate lay cracked and broken on the ground. Otherwise, nothing looked out of place, and the cedar didn't look as if it had caused any structural damage.

The old house sat squarely on its brick piers, oozing the comfort and stability of home. I remembered trying to decide between buying this house and one near Gerry in Lakeview. This one had been overpriced and poorly maintained, but I'd felt drawn to its air of faded Victorian gentility. Lots of high ceilings and old millwork. If I had made a different choice, I'd be homeless now, and I wasn't sure how to feel about that. Grateful, definitely. But also guilty. Those few of us in the unflooded twenty percent weren't better or more deserving. Just lucky.

Pulling into the drive behind the house, I fingered my little bag of herbs and thought of Gerry, wondering how things had gone so wrong in two weeks, praying this would all prove to be some big, stupid mistake.

Unloading the Pathfinder could come later. For now, I grabbed my backpack and walked around front. On the sidewalk lay *The Times–Picayune* from August 28, the last day it had been delivered. The headline screamed from the musty-smelling, heavy paper, still muddy and waterlogged. I shook my head at the irony and threw it back to the ground. The edge of a hurricane blew through and a flood brought a major city to its knees, but the newspaper hadn't moved.

I unlocked the door and stepped into the large double parlor that served as a giant living room. Other than a little dust and a stale, moldy smell, everything seemed normal—in a sauna-like way. Hot, humid weather had persisted since the hurricane, and two weeks without AC made the house feel like the inside of a pressure cooker.

I peeled off the doctor's scrubs, socks, and Nikes in the middle of the parlor, threw them on one of the sofas, and dug a black sports bra and shorts out of my backpack. Tucking my mojo bag into my pocket, I walked around the first floor in bare feet and opened windows, hoping for a breeze and looking at the ceiling fan with longing. A Red Congress wizard like Gerry could use an easy shot of physical magic to start the motor, as long as he didn't overdo it and ignite a fire. I could direct magic at the thing until I died of heatstroke and it still wouldn't turn.

I frowned and looked around the parlor, realizing I'd been so preoccupied with storm damage I hadn't noticed the absence of my security wards. Closing my eyes, I concentrated on the air around me, reaching out with my empathic skills. It wasn't an exact science, but I could usually detect another magical presence if I put some effort into it. A slight pressure of energy flitted across my skin, just a whisper, like what might be left if my wards had been dismantled by the storm.

Or by a visitor. Only Gerry knew how to disarm them.

"Gerry? Are you here?" I shouted into the silence, my voice absorbed by a quiet so deep I could almost hear my heart beating. Disappointed, I wiped the back of my neck with the hospital scrubs, wondering if it would be irresponsible to waste one of my bottles of water by pouring it over my head. Probably.

Before nightfall, I'd need to reestablish my security wards in case any preternatural creepy-crawlies showed up. The wards would be useless in the face of the looters I'd been reading about online at Gran's. For them, I had Jean Lafitte's pistol in my kitchen junk drawer. I'd just have to pull the trigger and hope I didn't shoot myself.

Even under these conditions, it felt good to be home. Tired as I was, I decided to take a quick look through the rest of the house for roof leaks or other damage.

The parlor was definitely intact. Twin sofas with a deep red and gold fleur-de-lis print bracketed an oversize ottoman-style coffee table that still held a soda can and candy wrapper from before the storm. The old tongue-and-groove oak floor had a fine coating of dust, but no damage, and I hadn't seen any signs of damage to the doors or windows.

I grabbed the can and wrapper, heading for the kitchen. A small crack ran through one of the panes in the kitchen window, but it hadn't shattered and it didn't look like any water had leaked in. My potted herbs and plants had suffered a dry and dusty death.

A door to the right of the parlor opened into a small office/ guest room and half bath. A stairwell to the second floor branched off the back corner.

A faint smell tickled my nose as I opened the office door and headed for the stairs. Cinnamon, maybe. Along with a sitting room and my bedroom, my library was upstairs, home to all my herbs and stones and magical gear. One of the spice jars must have broken.

I climbed the stairs, rounded the corner into the sitting room, and stopped short. It wasn't the sofa and chairs of deep crimson and chocolate brown that took me by surprise. And it wasn't mold, although the man certainly qualified as moldy.

Jean Lafitte sat in my favorite recliner, black-booted feet propped up, drinking from the bottle of cheap Winn-Dixie rum he'd no doubt stolen from my kitchen cabinet. He smiled at me and raised the bottle in salute.

I wondered if he'd found his gun.

CHAPTER 8

I'm delighted to see you again, *Jolie*. You have a lovely home."
How very polite. I wondered how long he'd been enjoying my nonhospitality.

Lafitte looked none the worse since I'd immobilized him and sent him back into the Beyond. In fact, if he hadn't been dead and holding a grudge, he'd look pretty good, with black pants tucked into boots and a simple indigo shirt open to halfmast. He'd stuck a matched pair of long-handled pistols beneath the sash around his waist, and the curved blade strapped to his thigh would have added to the sexy bad-boy look except I figured he'd worn it in my honor.

He might be delighted to see me again, but I was two steps shy of panicked. My protective wards had failed, all my premade potions were in the truck, and I was flashing way too much skin. Maybe I'd just die of a heart attack now and save Lafitte the trouble of killing me.

"So, hi there," I said, edging along the wall toward my library. "Who summoned you this time? I bet it was the mayor.

He's been showing signs of post-traumatic stress." When in doubt, distract them with babble.

I needed something to defend myself with, like a blinding potion or an itching curse. Too bad the Elders outlawed black magic. The silver dagger from my backpack would be nice, or even a stick of chalk so I could draw a protective circle and crawl inside it. As long as I was wishing, shoes and a shirt would be nice.

Lafitte released the footrest on the recliner, letting his boots hit the floor with a thud. "I no longer need to be summoned, Drusilla. The hurricane opened the borders to the Beyond, and introduced me to many potential business partners more willing to cooperate than you. *Oui,* and certainly much more truthful than you."

"That's great! You should probably be off meeting with them," I said, all cheerful bravado. "Nice seeing you. Thanks for stopping by."

I'd made it halfway to the library when Lafitte sprang from the chair with a speed that would do a vampire proud and leaned against the wall between me and the library door. So much for distracting him with chitchat.

He moved to within a few inches of me, and I froze. At least it was easy to avoid eye contact this close because of the difference in our heights, and he had a nice chest. The edge of his cutlass scraped across my bare leg as he inched closer, and I felt a sharp sting from the tip of the curved blade. A trickle of blood started a path toward my foot.

I eased my hand in the right pocket of my shorts and fingered my mojo bag. Whatever Lafitte was feeling, I didn't want to share.

"Just tell me what you want and we can work something out." I started backing up again, trying to mentally sort through my options. I couldn't think of any. I'm a pragmatist, if nothing else, and since my experience in face-to-face combat is non-existent, my best solution seemed to be flying down the stairs and running like hell. I might be a chicken, but I'd be a live chicken.

I retreated toward the staircase, my back shifting along the wall. My head bumped against the *Be Nice and Leave* painting I'd bought from local artist Dr. Bob at JazzFest a few years ago, and it crashed to the floor. Nice sentiment, but Jean Lafitte wasn't being nice, and I didn't think he planned on leaving.

I decided to try the dumb-chick gambit, mentally apologizing to every woman I'd ever met.

"You don't have to make deals with anyone now, you know." I tried to pass a grimace off as a smile. "Gerald St. Simon is gone, New Orleans is on its knees, and I'm only a woman. I'm out of my depth here. I'm nobody. I'll just head on downstairs and get in the truck and leave."

He could *have* my truck if he'd just let me ease on over to the stairwell. I'd grovel as I went just to make it more satisfying for him.

Lafitte remained quiet, watching me with a half smile and moving a step closer for each one I took away. He was playing with me, stalking me like a tiger after a stupid, whining deer.

"It is too late to pretend helplessness, *Jolie*. I do not make the same mistake twice." His smile widened into a grin. "You are as weak as the alligators we fought in Barataria in the old days. We liked to toy with them for a while, then we would feast on them."

Guess that *I'm only a woman* thing hadn't worked. "I ate gator once." My voice sounded high-pitched and breathless. "It tasted like chicken."

He prowled closer as I backed up, his dark-blue eyes fixed on my face. I tried to avoid direct eye contact and block out as much of his emotion as I could.

He smiled and whispered, "I want to play first."

I still had about three feet to go before I reached the stairs, so I turned and ran, or at least I tried. Something shiny whizzed across my field of vision and I found myself nose-to-blade with a dagger that now protruded firmly from the plaster wall. If I lived long enough, I'd have to figure out the thrust needed to throw a knife into plaster. But escape now, physics later.

From the corner of my eye I saw Lafitte pull one of the pistols from his belt, and I flattened myself to the wall, hyper-ventilating. What a wimp. I should go down in a blaze of glory, not shaking against the wall. Actually, I should have kept running.

He raised the bulky muzzle-loader and pointed it at me as he moved to block my path to the stairwell. "Perhaps this will change your mind, little one. Let us enjoy each other's company a bit, and see if you can convince me not to kill you."

I could do better than this. I was a wizard, damn it, albeit an unarmed Green Congress wizard. I scanned the room in search of a makeshift weapon. Finally, I hefted a bulky wrought-iron candlestick from a side table, launched it at Lafitte's head, and made a beeline for the library.

The big pistol discharged with a booming shot that knocked out the hearing in my right ear but went wide, tearing another chunk of plaster from the wall. I shook my head, trying to settle my eardrum back in place, and saw the pirate rubbing his right temple. Damn straight, *monsieur*. I can wield a candlestick like a champ.

Lafitte's hand came away bloody. He grimaced, making the scar on his jawline more pronounced, and his pupils dilated as he headed toward me. He looked pissed. I slammed the library door in his face and locked it.

My library is my favorite room, even with an irate pirate banging on the door. It's long and narrow, with deep crown molding along the ceiling and wide-sashed windows stretching along the outside wall. The copper-colored curtains were open, and late-afternoon sun cast shadows on the pale-teal walls, making a surreal backdrop to Lafitte's thumping and banging.

He was shouting French obscenities again and, from the sound of it, battering the door with his boot. They made good doors in 1873, solid and heavy. And since I kept magic stuff in here, it had a modern heavy-duty dead bolt. The historical undead didn't gain super-strength like vampires and weres, so I'd bought myself a little time.

I walked along the inside wall, scanning the floor-to-ceiling shelves that held the stuff of ritual magic. Glass bottles in all shapes, sizes, and colors were labeled with the herbs or elixirs inside. Bins of clear glass held mineral compounds and different gemstones. Tools filled other spaces: mortars and pestles, silver knives, bits of iron and other metals. Candles of every size and color had been crammed in any gaps, along with magical reference books galore.

The library door gave an alarming rattle, then everything went quiet. The quiet was scarier. I kept scanning the shelves. Ritual magic was a meticulous art. Powerful, yes. Quick, no. Did I want something to hurt him or protect myself? The black arts were a capital offense in the magical world and, besides that, I didn't know any serious curses that could be turned on a dime. Self-protection it was.

I grabbed a bottle of potassium nitrate and pulled some sugar and baking soda from a cabinet. Using my worktable, I quickly eyeballed the right ratios into an aluminum pan, my shaking hands the only sign I heard Lafitte fiddling with the door lock.

I pushed the pan aside and scrutinized the shelves again as he failed in his attempt to pick the lock and began another stream of curses. Italian, perhaps? The man knew his languages. I'd have to give him credit.

I'd just pulled out a small vial of ground monkshood root, or wolfsbane, and stuck it in my left pocket when a blast splintered the door. He'd shot out the lock with his bigass pistol, and the blast had made the floor shake. I knew, because as soon as the splintering began I'd crouched behind my worktable. I peered around the corner as Lafitte's hand slipped through the hole he'd blown in my door and flipped the thumb latch.

That SOB had destroyed my 132-year-old cypress door. Game on.

I watched from behind the table as he walked in and paused, looking around and reloading his pistol. My heart hammered hard enough to make my body vibrate.

"Now, *Jolie,* what were we discussing when you tried to wound me so terribly?" He leaned over and squinted at me through the table legs. So much for hiding. Why did he sound so hurt that I'd tried to injure him when it seemed perfectly acceptable for him to kill me? Undead double standard.

He smiled. "Why don't you see if you can convince me to at least kill you quickly, Drusilla?"

Well, there was an offer I hated to pass up. I stood up and walked toward him slowly. I only knew one way to get him turned around so I'd be between him and the door.

He watched me approach and raised an eyebrow as I reached out to stroke his arm.

"How can I convince you not to kill me at all, Captain?"

His mouth twitched slightly, and I shivered as I absorbed a little of his feelings, one part lust, three parts anger. Lust was gaining, though, and it sure wasn't mine.

The pirate slid an arm around my waist, strong fingers hot on my overexposed skin, and pulled me against him.

"Much better, *Jolie,*" he whispered, locking his mouth on mine in a hard, rough kiss. He smelled of sweet tobacco and tasted of cinnamon. And I kissed him back, wrapping my arms around his waist and maneuvering him around slowly till my back was to the library door. Maybe I was getting better at this seduction stuff. It wasn't because I enjoyed kissing him, even though it seemed I'd been doing a lot of it lately. Absolutely not.

I even let his hands do a bit of wandering as I slowly reached to grasp the aluminum pan on the worktable beside us and began to release little bursts of magical energy into it. I couldn't produce enough juice to start a fire, but I could heat the pan enough to—

Ouch. Okay, wandering hands were one thing. A pinch on the ass called for action.

I backed away and flung the pan at his feet. He was still looking at it when a plume of thick white smoke burst from it and blocked him from my view.

Just a slightly enhanced smoke bomb. It wouldn't burn anything and wouldn't hurt him but I figured if I couldn't see him, he couldn't see me either. Time to run.

CHAPTER 9

I bolted out of the library, crossed the sitting room, and caught a toe on the banister as I rounded the top of the stairs. I half-ran, half-fell down them, picking up a couple of splinters along the way. I should have carpeted those stairs a long time ago. I should have kept my shoes on. And a shirt.

Lafitte wasn't far behind me, his heavy boots pounding down the stairs as I crossed the office and raced into the parlor. I got halfway through the room before a knife went flying past my ear (again) and shattered the beautiful old stained glass panes set into my front door.

I should have kept running. A smart Green Congress wizard would have zipped outside and barreled down the street till she found a nice soldier to help her. But damn it, that stained glass was half as old as Lafitte himself, and he'd already trashed my library door. I whirled to face him, furious. Did he have any idea how much I had to pay for this house? I would be ready for the old wizards' home by the time it was paid for.

Gerry always said my temper would probably do me in. Part of my brain acknowledged that I was acting on emotion, doing the very thing he always said kept me from being ready to take big, dangerous jobs like fighting pirates. But I loved that old stained glass and my cypress library door and my plaster walls. They were among the reasons I'd bought the blasted house in the first place.

"Do you know how old that glass was, you son of a—"

Lafitte pulled a modern semiautomatic on me. Guess he'd found his gun in my kitchen drawer after all.

I dove behind one of the overstuffed armchairs, pulling it in front of me like a shield while I backed toward the door on my knees. The chair back blocked my view, so I popped my head over it, ready to duck fast if the pirate was still aiming at me. Instead, dark-blue eyes met mine over the back of the chair. We were practically nose to nose. I might as well be sitting in his freaking lap. He didn't need the gun and he knew it.

He was smiling again, but not in amusement. More like the gloat of a terrier after it has finally trapped a troublesome rat.

He pushed the chair aside, grabbing my arm as I tried to spin away. When he drew me closer, I bent my head and sank my teeth as deeply into his forearm as they'd go. It was his right arm, his shooting arm, and I hoped it hurt.

He hissed and pulled away, giving me time to lunge toward the door. I spit out a mouthful of blood along the way, the taste salty and metallic. At least it was his blood and not mine. Score one for the home team. I hoped he carried the mark of my teeth on his forearm the rest of his miserable life. Considering he was virtually immortal, that would be a really long time.

I would have made it to the door if I'd been quicker, or he'd been slower, and if he hadn't managed to grab me around the ankle and send me sprawling facedown a few feet short of freedom. My cheek bounced off the floor and I had a quick, close-up view of the wood grain before Lafitte flipped me on my back and began pulling me toward him.

I gritted my teeth and scrabbled around with my hands, trying to find something to hold onto. The broken stained glass sliced into my palms and thighs as I slid. I might never wear shorts or go barefoot again, assuming I lived long enough to ever worry about wardrobe choice. But the pain helped me focus as I reached in my pocket for the wolfsbane.

I managed to thumb off the top of the vial one-handed and fling the contents at Lafitte. It wasn't the deadly form of wolfsbane—just a mild variety that would numb his skin and blur his vision. He shifted his head at the last second but still got an eyeful.

Any remaining trace of good humor disappeared. He snarled and released me, swiping at both eyes to try and clear his vision. I pushed away from him and had crawled half the distance to the front door when the room seemed to explode.

I instinctively rolled into a fetal position and wrapped my arms around my head. I hadn't seen the pirate pull his gun. Both his hands had been busy rubbing his eyes. Maybe his gun had gone off accidentally. Maybe it killed him. If his own gun killed him, it wouldn't be my fault. Of course, he wouldn't really be dead, either, but he'd fade back to the Beyond for a while.

It was quiet, too quiet. I conducted a quick mental self-inventory to see if any body parts were missing or maimed. My shorts and stomach were spattered with blood and my kicking foot was coated in red, but it didn't seem to be my blood. My legs and feet hurt from the glass cuts, I had a wooden splinter in my knee, my cheek was throbbing where it had hit the floor, and my head pounded from the magic I'd used. I couldn't sense any other injuries, and I didn't seem to be dead. If I was dead and this was the afterlife, I was going to be ticked.

A rasping noise near my feet broke the silence, and I sat up. Lafitte lay on the floor wearing the same startled, angry look he'd had after I immobilized him in the swamp. His hands covered a spot in the center of his chest, where dark blood seeped through his fingers. Our eyes met a moment before he quit breathing. What the hell had happened?

I gave a girly squeal of surprise as someone grabbed me under the arms from behind and pulled me to my feet. I should've known not to let my guard down, but how many times in one day should a woman expect to be assaulted in her own home?

I grabbed a shard of glass and spun around, brandishing it in front of me. It was a pretty, stippled blue piece, nice and sharp.

"Hold on, tiger. I give up."

A bear of a man stood in front of me, hands raised in mock surrender—well, except for the shotgun in his right hand. He towered well over six feet and was shaped like a linebacker, one who'd gone a little too long between haircuts. Dark curls hugged the collar of a basic black T-shirt that almost camouflaged a black shoulder holster holding some type of nasty-looking black handgun. It all matched his black jeans and boots. He looked like the poster child for an upscale *GQ* mercenary. The only shred of color on him was his eyes, and they were dark brown. Mr. Monochromatic.

He laid the shotgun on the table near the door and stepped back, hands up, watching me from beneath hooded lids.

A lesser woman would have noticed the thick muscles moving under his tanned skin when he raised his arms, or the T-shirt that fit just snugly enough to send a girl's thoughts to the Promised Land. Good thing I don't notice stuff like that.

"If you want to search me for more weapons, I'm game."

My eyes shot back to his, and I felt my cheeks flush, hot and bothered on the way to angry.

Leave it to a guy to open his mouth and ruin a perfectly good moment.

I'm not sure my fight with Lafitte would have ended well, but I'd finally gained an upper hand with the wolfsbane, and it infuriated me for some ripped Romeo with a gun to come in and blast him. For one thing, it broke magical treaties. These days, even the undead have legal rights in the preternatural community.

For another, regular bullets don't faze the undead, which meant this guy was packing special ammunition. You can't really kill the historical undead anyway—you simply send them back to the Beyond so they'll be truly and righteously irate next time they come across. There is always a next time for someone as resourceful as Jean Lafitte.

Finally, deep down, I didn't think Lafitte planned to kill me. He might have an eighteenth-century view of women and a nasty temper but, by all accounts, he was a shrewd and practical man. He'd eventually have realized hurting me wouldn't be worth the trouble it would cause with the Elders. If he'd really wanted me dead, I would be. His aim wasn't that bad.

I tried to convey all this in my glare. "Who are you, anyway?" I had an annoying urge to straighten my hair and wipe the plaster dust off my cheeks. And find more substantial clothes.

"Don't bowl me over with gratitude," he said in a baritone drawl, relaxing his posture.

He was awfully sure I wouldn't snatch up the shotgun and blast his arrogant, black-clad self all the way to St. Bernard Parish. If he laughed at me, I might try. At close range, I'd at least clip an arm or leg. It would be a pity to mar such beauty but sometimes sacrifices are called for.

Instead, I chose the moral high road. "Thank you. Now, who are you? How did you know what kind of ammunition to use?"

He stepped around me to examine Lafitte's body, which had turned translucent on its way to disappearing. With a few more seconds and a soft whisper of energy, the pirate disappeared back into the Beyond along with his original weapons, leaving only an evaporating puddle of ectoplasm and the gun.

I'd have to find a better hiding place for the gun next time, and there would be a next time. Jean Lafitte knew where I lived now, and eventually he'd return for round three. I sighed, wondering if he'd left me any cheap rum.

The Man in Black didn't seem disconcerted by the body's disappearance, another clue that he knew his way around the magical block. He picked up Lafitte's gun, popped the clip out, and laid it on the table next to the shotgun.

I was tired, bloody, my legs hurt, and my magic-hangover was pounding the back of my eyeballs like a woodpecker. "Last time, Terminator. Talk to me. Otherwise, you can leave—with my undying gratitude, of course."

One corner of his mouth curved up as he reached in his pocket and tossed a small leather case in my direction. Black, of course. I felt it hit the floor by my feet, but I didn't break my stare. We weren't playing charades.

Give the man two points for reading body language. He finally broke the stalemate, walking around the parlor and peering out windows and inside bookshelves and cabinets while he talked. Snooping, in other words. "I'm Alexander Warin, and I came here to find Drusilla Jaco, also known as DJ. I assume that's you."

He looked back at me, raising one dark eyebrow. "Of course, no one told me what to expect from my new partner. I read your file, but without photos I was expecting the robe, the wand. You know: more Merlin, less Glinda the Good Witch."

I gritted my teeth, trying to decide what needed addressing first: *partner* or *file* or *witch*. Best to stay on the moral high road—he was trying to push my buttons with the witch wisecrack.

"What's this partner business? What file? Who sent you?"

"I hear you're an empath. Can't you tell?"

Body of an Adonis, brain of an anchovy. "I'm an empath, not a psychic or telepath. I can tell what an arrogant letch you are but I can't read your flipping mind."

For some reason, I also couldn't read his emotions very well, a little detail he didn't need to know. Either he was a soulless freak or my mojo bag had kicked into overdrive.

He jerked his head at the leather case on the floor, turned his back, and unclipped what looked like a small cell phone from his belt. As he strolled around the parlor and stuck his head in the kitchen and office, he held it out in front of him.

Whatever else he might be, Alexander Warin was insufferable.

I snatched the case off the floor and flipped it open. It had two sections. The first held a badge, much like mine from the Green Congress, only this one said CONGRESS OF ELDERS. I stared at the interloper's broad back, frowning.

I sent out my empathic senses, trying to feel any buzz of magic coming from him. There was still a tingle in the air that wasn't wizard's magic, but it was probably left over from Jean Lafitte. So he wasn't a wizard, and he didn't look old enough to be an Elder. I studied the badge, flipping it over. The back of mine identified me as a licensed sentinel. His read, simply, ENFORCER.

Good Lord, he *was* a terminator.

The second compartment of the case held a badge identifying Alexander Warin as a field agent with the FBI office in Jackson, Mississippi. The woodpecker in my head began a frantic cadence.

I threw the badge on the coffee table and scrambled to remember anything I'd heard about enforcers, because I'd certainly never met one. They did the Elders' dirty work, took out the preternatural trash, made problems disappear. If an enforcer showed up at your door, you might disappear, too. Enforcers didn't have partners.

By the time I looked back at him, he had finished his inspection of my downstairs and stood with his arms crossed, watching me. I think he'd grown a couple of inches while I wasn't looking.

"Why are you here? What's an enforcer doing in New Orleans?"

He gave me a predatory smile, even more carnivorous than the one I'd seen on the face of Jean Lafitte. "Congratulations, DJ. You're the new sentinel of the New Orleans region, and I'm your partner—at least through the probationary period. You can call me Alex."

CHAPTER 10

I really wanted to hit something.

"Why would the Elders send you? We don't need an enforcer in this region. Do you have any magical skills, or do you just shoot people? How are you going to be a sentinel if you can't do magic?"

He cocked his head. "If you don't understand why you need an enforcer, you should replay that little scene with your pirate buddy. You might have gotten the upper hand temporarily, but he was going to win that fight. You were about thirty seconds away from getting to know Jean Lafitte *really* well."

His jaw clenched. "In fact, you owe me some serious gratitude—unless you *wanted* him."

God help me. I fought the urge to pick up a heavy vase and chunk it at his head. It had worked on Lafitte, but something told me this guy would probably catch it and bean me with it. "The fight wasn't over," I said through gritted teeth. "I'd have won it." Probably.

"Right," he said. "And something just flew past your window. It was oinking."

Words failed me, so he kept talking. "Look, the Elders want an enforcer here because of the breaches caused by the hurricane. They don't know what to expect from the Beyond, and I have ties to both local law enforcement and the were community."

Alex slipped out of his shoulder holster. "Did Jean Lafitte get summoned, or did he just show up?"

If the Elders thought New Orleans needed an enforcer with police and werewolf ties more than a Red Congress sentinel, the breaches must be serious. Blunt force might be trumping preternatural diplomacy. Gerry said the Elders always talked first and fought as a last resort. Well, the last resort had just unsnapped a knife sheath from his belt and laid it on my sofa table next to his guns.

I tried to remember the exact words the pirate had used when I found him in my La-Z-Boy. "Lafitte came on his own, but he also hinted about having new business partners. He'd tried to work smuggling deals with Gerry and me in the past."

I squinted at Alex. "Of course we can't ask him any specifics because you shot him. It will take a while for him to be strong enough to come back."

"The Elders don't know who or what is going to come across," he said, ignoring the Lafitte situation. "You're the first line of defense with your"—he waved a hand in the air—"magic tricks. If that doesn't work, I finish the job."

I had a few magic tricks I'd like to show him. "So you're the backup plan."

He retrieved his badge from the table and stuck it in his back pocket, then picked up Lafitte's gun again. "Let's just say the Elders don't want the borders to break down either because we're outnumbered or some of us are too inexperienced."

Ouch. That hurt. I might not be the world's most experienced wizard but at least I *was* a wizard and not just a bundle of testosterone with legs and opposable thumbs.

One part of his argument made sense, though. If too many pretes flocked across the border at a faster rate than we could send them back, the system would collapse. Some of the more organized and ambitious groups, such as the vampires and the fae, resented the wizards' control of the borders.

"You said you have ties to the were community," I said. "Does that mean they're already out of the Beyond?"

He didn't look up from his examination of Lafitte's pistol. "Most are mainstreamed, except a few like the loup-garou— rogue werewolves who live in the Beyond. A lot of enforcers are lycanthropes."

Holy cow. I didn't know that, and I should have. Did Gerry not know, or did Gerry not tell me?

"Are you a werewolf?" I studied his dark shaggy hair and powerful build, wondering how that big body could be condensed into a four-legged canine.

"I'm not a were-anything," he said. "Next full moon, I'll look the same as now."

Too bad. A werewolf partner might have been interesting.

"So, who reports to whom?" I asked. "And how exactly do you see this partnership thing working? I'll tell you right now— my first priority is finding Gerry St. Simon, at which point you can go back to Jackson or wherever you came from."

"We both report to the Elders, and we'll both be looking for Gerry. Day to day, we'll play it by ear. If a prete comes across, we'll try it your way, with your little spells and potions. As you said, I'm backup if your magic doesn't work or if we get too many things to handle at once. I'm already working on a potential case."

"What kind of case? Finding Gerry is our case."

He strode to the front door, crunching over my broken stained glass and grabbing a briefcase from the porch. He'd shown up at my door with a shotgun and a freaking briefcase. In what universe was that normal?

He set the case on the coffee table and opened it, pulling out a file.

I craned my neck to see what an enforcer might carry in his briefcase. I couldn't help myself.

He handed me a sheet of paper containing a rough sketch of a decorated cross atop two wide, shallow rectangles. Two boxes shaped like sarcophagi sat to either side of it. Stars and squiggles came off the figures at different points.

I'd seen that symbol before, on TV. "There was a murder right after Katrina hit. Wasn't this drawn on a building at the murder scene?"

"Good memory. Do you know what it means?"

I looked at it again and shook my head. "No idea."

"Me either, but it's been at both crime scenes."

I handed the paper back to him. "Crime *scenes*—as in plural?"

He nodded. "There was another one last night, down in . . ." He grabbed the file again and opened it. "An area called Faubourg Marigny—you know where that is?"

"Sure, it's just east of the French Quarter. One of the un-flooded areas." I sat on the arm of a chair, exhausted and beginning to feel rubbery as the adrenaline drained from my system. "How does this involve us?"

Good grief, what was I saying? There was no *us.* "How does this involve *you?*"

Alex shrugged. "I just wanted to see if you recognized the symbol—the Elders have us on high alert for pretes right now, and I'm in a good position to look. The NOPD is shorthanded so they're willing to let the feds come in and help. I'm consulting on both cases."

No kidding. The local cops were not only shorthanded. They also were stressed-out and jumpy. "You think it's something supernatural? The Elders didn't mention it."

Alex stuck the folder back in his briefcase, keeping it turned so I couldn't see inside. "Nothing to indicate the supernatural is involved, not yet," he said. "But according to police reports, there were voodoo ritual items at both crime scenes—black candles, dead roosters. It might be supernatural, or it might be a plain-vanilla serial killer." He locked the case. "Just something for us to keep an eye on."

Seemed too paranoid to me. We had enough problems without looking for more. "You go ahead and work with your police cases. I'll look for Gerry."

He propped the briefcase against the wall next to the fireplace. "We'll both work on it if it turns out to be related to the breaches with the Beyond, and we'll both look for Gerry. By the way, what do you shoot?"

He might as well have asked what planet I'd hailed from. "I'm a Green Congress wizard," I said. "We don't shoot."

"You'll need to learn. I'll teach you as we have time." He pulled the handgun out of his shoulder holster on the table and looked at it, then at me.

"Let me see your hand." He held out his own.

"Why?" I stared at his outstretched hand, which looked roughly the size of a catcher's mitt.

He grasped my arm and pulled it toward him. "I won't bite. I want to see how big a gun you need."

Thumbing a chip of plaster off my knuckles, he spread out my clenched fist using fingers that looked strong enough to choke a horse. Or a wizard.

I snatched my hand away. "I don't need a gun."

A whisper of a smile crossed his face. "My gun would be too big for you, so I'll find something that's a better fit. And Lafitte's needs to be checked out before it's used again."

He turned back to the table and began pulling other lethal objects off his person, having apparently confirmed that he needed no protection from me. He raised the bottom of his shirt—revealing an alarming set of abs, not that I noticed—and unstrapped a double-bladed silver knife from a sheath around his waist. I bit my tongue as he propped a black boot on one of my upholstered chairs and pulled out another knife and hand-gun. With a quirk of a smile in my direction, he reached for another clip on his belt and unhooked what looked like a small grenade.

"Do you think you brought enough firepower?" Talk about overkill. He could take down a small third-world country.

He looked at the stash and shook his head. "I didn't expect trouble today, except maybe with you. I was told you could be, ah, hard to handle." He gave me a slow once-over. "Might be more fun than I thought, but you sure do need a shower."

That did it. This day felt like it had lasted a month. I got up and wiped blood and plaster dust off my face with the doctor's scrubs still piled on the sofa, and walked over to look at my door, or what was left of it. "Here's the deal, Alexander Warin," I said as I studied the shattered panes. About two-thirds were broken but the wooden framework was intact so it could be saved. "I'm too tired to even think about this right now, and I sure don't want to play *flirt with the enforcer*."

I turned to face him. "Let's set a few ground rules. First, turn the sexist crap down a notch. Make that two notches. I'm sure lots of simpering women fall for your tall-dark-and-dangerous routine, so save it for the next simpering woman you see. It isn't me.

"If we have to be coworkers, fine—at least until we find Gerry. But if you think I won't report you for sexual harassment, think again." Of course, first I'd have to find someone to report it to. Somehow, I doubted the Elders would care.

No response.

"Second, if you're going to be the cosentinel, we decide together the approach to take with interlopers like Jean Lafitte.

You didn't need to shoot him, and because you did, he's going to come back looking for revenge, and I'll be the one that has to deal with him, not you."

His mouth twitched.

"Finally, can you keep the arsenal out of here? Especially grenades." I shuddered. What kind of person walked around with a grenade clipped to his belt?

He gave me a tight smile. "Here's the deal. I'll follow your lead on cases until you need me to step in, and I'll decide when that is. The guns stay. A grenade's the best thing to use on a zombie and this is New Orleans, after all, so it stays too. And you *will* learn how to use a gun. I need a backup I can count on."

He took a step closer and his voice had a soft, dangerous edge. "Kindergarten is over, DJ. As we say in Mississippi, if you want to play with the big dogs, you have to get off the porch."

I hated him. My fingers itched to grab his knife and poke it in his arrogant back, which would be easy since he'd turned away to look at the door.

"We'll need to patch over the missing glass. I have a small sheet of plywood in my trunk that will work, and I need to bring in my stuff. Which room will be mine? Needs to be downstairs." He turned back to look at me, unaware that I'd been considering how he might enjoy a nice cup of tea laced with horsetail and birch oil to make hair grow out his ears.

I searched his face for any sign he might be joking. I didn't find one. "You've been working on police cases, so you must have been staying somewhere." Competition for unflooded housing was fierce among relief workers and would only get worse as more people returned to the city.

"I've been driving in as needed from my family's place in Picayune," he said. When I didn't respond, he added, "Mississippi, about an hour north of here. I've been based in Jackson, covering the Southeast for the FBI's prete force, but they're putting me in New Orleans full time now. It's too far to commute every day, so I need a place to crash."

Pain began throbbing behind my right eye again. "Since when does the FBI have a preternatural force?" Gerry had never mentioned it. I would have remembered.

"Officially, it doesn't."

Right. I tried to shake off the exhaustion settling over me. The room spun when I closed my eyes more than a blink. "Fine. You can stay here tonight and find a place tomorrow. There's a daybed in the office right off the kitchen." I watched as he arranged his weapons in a line on the sofa table. A tad obsessive, our enforcer.

I pointed at the device he'd been looking at earlier. "What was that gizmo you had before, the one that looks like a cell phone?"

Alex handed it to me. It had a larger screen than a phone, and no keypad. A glowing red ball blinked rapidly in the center of the screen.

"Tracker," he said. "Special enforcer issue. Helps us detect magical energy, sort of like a homing device. I'll have to calibrate it so your energy doesn't interfere with anything coming in from the Beyond. You're all that's showing up on it now that Lafitte's gone—it's how I knew he was here. The Elders are supposed to send us a bigger one in a few days."

Great. I'd been reduced to a blinking red dot. I handed it back without comment, shuffled my bloody feet to a nearby chair, and flopped. Never mind the upholstery. The energy I'd used fighting Lafitte was catching up with me, not to mention the stress of Gerry's disappearance, the horror of seeing all the Katrina destruction, and the appearance of the enforcer. I closed my eyes and waited for the sensation of vertigo to pass.

A few minutes later, I heard chairs being pulled across the

floor. I flinched and cracked an eye open as he positioned one facing me and sat in it. He pulled another chair alongside him.

"What are you doing?" Did I really want to know?

He opened a black case he'd set next to his chair and pulled out wet wipes and a long pair of tweezers. My first aid kit, which I guess he'd found rummaging through my kitchen. It had been a popular spot for plunderers today.

He handed me one of the wet wipes. "Here, use that on your face."

I didn't argue. It felt good after the heat and the blood and the plaster and the floor. My cheek felt swollen and throbbed in sync with my headache. I'd probably look like an abuse victim by morning.

"You need to get that glass out of your legs. Put them here." He grabbed an ankle and yanked it onto the chair next to him. What was it with guys pulling on my ankles today?

I jerked it back. "I can do it myself, thanks. Go away."

He lugged my leg back in place, holding it immobile with one hand, and stared at me until I quit squirming. "It'll be easier if I do it. If you'll shut up and sit still it won't take long." He began tweezing slivers of glass from my skin.

He only had my right leg immobilized and seemed to have forgotten I had another one. I raised my left foot to push him away but in one smooth motion he grabbed that ankle and pinned it too. Bully.

"I assume you're mainstreamed," he said, tugging on a slice of red glass embedded deeply enough to make my eyes water when it came out. The stained-glass panes had been red, blue, green, and gold. Made for a colorful leg.

"I'm mainstreamed as a risk-management consultant for Tulane University."

He paused, tweezers in midair, and gave me a skeptical look. "Which is what, exactly?"

"Minimizing insurance and lawsuit liability. It's a cover."
Well, not entirely, but I could almost see a neon sign above my
head flashing the word *geek*.

He snorted. "Hope they don't have to call you too often.
You can't seem to manage your own risks very well, much less
anyone else's."

I'd have kicked him if I had access to my feet. Instead, I
watched him pick out the glass for a while, then closed my eyes
again and let him go at it. At least I'd shaved my legs this morning, so I was spared that humiliation.

The sound of hammering startled me from a doze. How
long had I been asleep? I couldn't believe I'd fallen asleep with
an assassin hovering over me with tweezers.

Alex had already put the first aid kit away, found my tool-
box, and was nailing a piece of plywood to my antique cypress
door. I groaned in defeat. I'd do damage control on the house
tomorrow. Tonight, as long as he left me alone, Mr. Fixit could
do whatever charged his chain saw.

To give him credit, he offered to finish cleaning up. It was
almost six p.m., my head was pounding, and my arms sported
blackening bruises in the shape of Jean Lafitte's fingers.

I got a few things from the truck and unearthed a couple of
fluorescent lanterns from the back of the pantry, one for each of us.

I yawned. "Guess I should reestablish my security wards.
Storm tore them down."

Expressionless, Alex stared at me and tossed the grenade up
and down, catching it without looking.

"Then again, I guess you can handle anything that comes
along."

I sidled out of the parlor and left him alone, heading upstairs with my headache, a cereal bar, and a lantern. The enforcer should be a sufficient security system for one night.

SATURDAY, SEPTEMBER 17, 2005 "Today in New Orleans, a traffic light worked. Someone watered flowers. And anyone with the means to get online could have heard Dr. John's voice wafting in the dry wind, a sound of grace, comfort and familiarity here in the saddest and loneliest place in the world."

—CHRIS ROSE, THE TIMES-PICAYUNE

CHAPTER 11

I woke to stillness, a new New Orleans reality. Birds no longer sang in the trees; they'd either flown off in their own hurricane evacuation or been blown to Ohio. The streetcar lines had been destroyed, so no sounds of rumbling metal broke the quiet. River traffic hadn't resumed, so no foghorns boomed through the riverside neighborhoods. The evacuation hadn't been lifted, so little traffic moved on the streets. The soundtrack that ran behind life in New Orleans had fallen silent.

My bedside clock remained blank and dark, and the house already felt steamy. I lounged in the throes of half sleep for a minute or two before thoughts of Gerry and my new partner jolted me awake. I groaned and buried my face in the pillow. I was stiff and sore. The list of body parts that didn't hurt was shorter than the ones that ached.

I had washed off most of the blood last night using bottled water and sterile wipes from the first aid kit, and then had fallen asleep without pulling back the covers. I was seriously overdue for a shower.

I peered cautiously into the tub and turned on the water.

The plumbing knocked and complained, but after a few spits a steady flow streamed out of the faucet. It looked like water, which was a positive sign. I wet my fingers and held them to my nose. The water didn't smell bad—or no worse than usual. I'd read online at Gran's that you could probably use it for bathing without boiling it first.

The *probably* part was scary. Almost as scary as the herds of tiny gnats that had begun swarming out of the drains. A local academic had identified them as "coffin flies." Ick.

For now, however, grime trumped health concerns in my post-Katrina version of rock-paper-scissors, and I braved the shower. Maybe the coffin flies would drown.

The soap lathered and the shampoo got sudsy, but nothing else felt right. Jean Lafitte and the enforcer had diverted my attention last night, but now Gerry's disappearance claimed its place of priority. My heart felt too large for my chest, the effort of filling and releasing air from my lungs too ponderous. My memories before I'd come to live with Gerry existed only in fragments. The clear memories, the deep ones that formed the bedrock of my every thought, every movement—he lived in all of them. I didn't know how to spend my days without having him at least a phone call away, where he'd been every minute for the last eighteen years.

I stood in the tub, staring at the tile, water cascading over my head and running down my body in rivulets. It had covered my feet before I even realized I'd dropped the washcloth. I bent down and pulled it out of the drain, and then scrubbed it across my face, not sure if I was wiping away tap water or tears.

This wasn't accomplishing anything. I swallowed down the bad thoughts, the ones that kept whispering *he's gone*. I'd focus on what I could do today and let tomorrow take care of itself. Today, I'd go to Gerry's house. I'd call Tish and tell her about his disappearance. I'd see if I could find a datebook in his study and start making a list of his recent contacts.

When he came home, I'd do whatever he asked me to do and be happy for it. I'd never bitch about pixie-retrieval again. I'd debate arcane issues and laugh with him and appreciate the normalcy of it. We'd figure out a way to help New Orleans recover from this mess. When Gerry came back, everything would be okay.

And the sooner I found him, the sooner Bullet Boy could be on his way back to Jackson. He was probably downstairs now, planning target practice, leafing through a copy of *Guns & Ammo*, and thinking of ways to undermine me with the Elders.

I towel-dried my hair and opened a window, wishing for a rain to cool things down. Ironic how dry it had been since Katrina, as if the city had used up its quota of water for the rest of the year. I left the window open, figuring it would be safe enough during the daytime, at least for a while. I wasn't sure how Jean Lafitte had found out where I lived, but it should be a week or two before he was strong enough to cross over from the Beyond again.

That had been some fight—my first real physical battle. Despite Alex's late arrival, I thought I'd done pretty well considering I didn't have any advance warning and was magically unarmed. The smoke bomb was a stroke of genius. I couldn't wait to tell Ger—

I forced myself to finish the thought. *I couldn't wait to tell Gerry.*

I dug out a pair of black shorts and a lightweight sleeveless top that set off my eyes. Then, realizing I'd done it so I would look presentable to the chiseled war machine downstairs, I tugged it off and pulled on a black tank that washed me out, but would be cooler. If my partner was wearing all black again, we'd look like a goth matched set.

I pulled my damp hair into a ponytail to keep it off my neck and stuffed my makeup bag in a drawer. It was too hot to try and cover my bruised face. Besides, it matched the cuts and bruises on my arms and legs. The enforcer could think what he wanted. I was the soul of indifference.

I tugged on white socks and Nikes—no more bare feet for this wizard—and padded into the library, stopping to mourn my poor, violated door. With damaged houses in town numbering in the hundreds of thousands, the home-improvement warehouses would do a killer business as soon as the power came back on. I wondered if there was time to buy stock in Home Depot before the rush hit. Then maybe I could retire and spend my days hiding from Jean Lafitte.

I strapped my watch on my wrist and did a double take at the time—almost ten a.m. I'd lost nearly half my day already, buried in sleep. First things first, though. I threw a cushion in the middle of the library floor and set lavender and vanilla candles on either side of it. I stuffed my earbuds in, turned my iPod playlist to chamber music, and pulled out the magically treated rubies I used for grounding. I needed to be in control when I went in Gerry's house today.

He always told me empathic skills were both a blessing and a curse. So far, I was taking his word on the blessing part. Oh, being able to ferret out a liar came in handy, but sometimes believing the lie was less painful. And in a situation as emotionally charged as going to Gerry's ravaged house? I could only hope my preparations would keep me from turning to Jell-O and embarrassing myself.

After a quiet half hour, I put everything away, prepared to fend off emotional assaults. Well, almost. I pulled out bottles of dried acacia and hyssop and refreshed my mojo bag, then stuck it in my shorts pocket. Now I was ready.

Next on the agenda: food. I went downstairs and stopped in the office to make sure the landline phone was still out of commission. I'd have to see if local towers were repaired enough to call Tish on my cell. Funny that calls to and from the Elders didn't seem to have problems going through. I stared at the day-bed. Alex's briefcase and arsenal were neatly arranged on top of it, but it didn't look slept in.

"About time. Thought I was going to have to drag you out."

I jumped at the smooth-as-pecan-pie drawl coming from behind me, and turned to see New Orleans's new *cosentinel* leaning against the office doorjamb, a coffee cup in one hand and what looked like a bagel in the other. His black T-shirt had an outline of two canoers with the words *Paddle faster. I hear banjos.*

"Cute," I said, pointing at the shirt. "I didn't think you had a sense of humor."

He gave me a sly smile. "I have an excellent sense of humor. You just haven't said anything funny."

I sidestepped him and went into the kitchen, where a huge pile of MREs—military freeze-dried Meals Ready to Eat—had taken up residence in one corner, each wrapped in identical mud-colored plastic with the entrée name stamped on front. On the table sat a notebook and pile of papers.

"Looking for an apartment?" I asked.

"Paperwork." He thumped his pen on the notebook. "Lafitte was an unauthorized kill, so I have to explain it in triplicate to the head of the enforcers and the Elders. You know, about how I came in and had to save my new *partner*, who was unarmed and rolling around on the floor with the big bad pirate while wearing not much more than good intentions. It'll make a great water-cooler story back at headquarters."

Jerkwad. I ignored him, grabbed a bag of Cheetos off the counter, and ripped it open. I dug out a fluorescent-orange fried stick of perfection and crunched on it while I pondered the idea of Alex, my supposed equal in this partnership, filing paperwork with people who outranked me on the magical food chain. I'd need to file my own report to the Green Congress, asserting his gross overuse of violence, and copy the Elders on it as well. Alex wouldn't out-bureaucrat me, by God.

He snatched the Cheetos out of my hands, pulled out an MRE that said *Cheese & Vegetable Omelet*, and ripped off the top. "You need real food. If you're going to be my partner, you should at least be moderately healthy. There was nothing to eat in this kitchen but junk." He handed me a jar of instant coffee, a bottle of water, a mug, and a battery-operated mug warmer. I eyed my warm Diet Barq's with longing.

"Food nazi." I leaned over and retrieved the Cheetos bag from the trash. I considered my lack of domestic skills a badge of honor and, besides that, who the heck did he think he was? "I eat out a lot. Didn't really even have to clean out my fridge before I evacuated."

"Well, at least we don't have to drag it out to the median," he said, fiddling with the MRE. "When I was out running this morning, I saw at least one dead refrigerator on every corner."

I'd seen them as I drove in yesterday, and most were either duct-taped shut or had rotten food spilling out. Two weeks of ninety-degree weather without electricity had turned them into maggot factories.

I spooned some coffee into the mug, stirred in the water, and set it on the warmer. "We call them neutral grounds, by the way, not medians."

"Whatever." He walked to the table and shuffled through the papers, pulling out the sketch of the symbol from the voodoo murders. "I found this same symbol on the sidewalks in front of several houses this morning. Where can I find out what it means? We need Internet access."

This town no longer had electricity or safe drinking water. Internet access was probably way down on the recovery priority list.

I took the paper and looked at it again. "It could be a gang tag, but it's awfully detailed. The gang tags I've seen are simpler than this." I turned the sheet, looking at it from different directions. "I can give you the addresses of some of the voodoo places in town—they sell supplies for rituals, although I haven't heard of anybody using this kind of black magic in decades. And there's the Voodoo Museum down in the Quarter. Of course, nothing's open right now since the evacuation orders are still in effect. You really think this symbol has anything to do with our breaches?"

"I'm not sure, but I thought I'd send it in with my report to the enforcers."

"No, why don't I include it with my report to the Green Congress?" I would not be one-upped in the Report Olympics, at least not until I figured out what Alex Warin was up to.

A hint of a smile crossed his face. "Fine. We'll both report it."

We stared at each other until the MRE omelet got hot. I sat in a chair at the old chrome and red Formica-topped table I'd found at a yard sale and looked at my military meal: the rubbery omelet and hash browns with bacon-like chunks in them, plus some saltines, a candy bar, and a packet of Dijon mustard. Whatever military genius devised these meals obviously hadn't had to eat them. Maybe the mustard was for the crackers, and the candy was to get rid of the lingering aftertaste of everything else.

I dug in anyway. The texture caused a gag reflex at first, but I was hungry enough to push past it.

"Love a woman with an appetite." Alex sat at the table opposite me, arms crossed, watching me eat.

Sarcastic cretin. I glared as I chewed, but it was halfhearted. I hadn't eaten more than a cereal bar in almost twenty-four hours. I didn't need to be skipping meals. I couldn't look for Gerry if I got sick.

"How was the daybed last night?" I asked. He was way too big for that frilly little single bed. "It didn't look like you used it."

"I stayed in the living room, on one of the sofas," he said. "I wanted to keep an eye on the doors."

I rolled my eyes. "Of course you did. Kill anything?"

"No. I thought I smelled mold, though. Sneak any dead pirates in your bedroom window?"

Now he was just being petty.

"Thanks for breakfast," I said. "Now, when are you leaving?"

It was like pulling hen's teeth, as Gran would say, but I finally weaseled enough information out of Alex to find he'd made arrangements to take an apartment in the French Quarter over a bar that belonged to his cousin Jacob. I wondered why he hadn't moved there in the first place. Either he saw me as a damsel in distress who needed a big bad protector, thought he might get a taste of eye candy, or had some other agenda, like sabotaging me with the Elders during this so-called probationary period. Maybe all of the above.

I had a thought. "Is Jacob an enforcer too, or a were?"

Alex frowned. "Jake is probably the least magically inclined person on God's green earth." He didn't offer more, so I didn't ask.

I finished my breakfast in silence, then trashed the MRE wrappings. I wondered how many months it would be before things like mail and garbage pickup would resume. I already had a pile of street and yard debris the size of a small car in my side yard.

"I'm heading to Gerry's this afternoon if you want to go," I said. I thought it was a generous offer, an olive branch of cooperation and goodwill.

He looked up from his report. "I think we should call the Elders to see if there are any breaches they want us to check out first. Besides, Lakeview's still flooded. You planning to swim?"

I looked at Alex, his pen poised over that damned report like the Sword of Damocles. Screw it. "You check on breaches. My top priority is finding Gerry. The Elders might be ready to write him off, but I'm not."

He leaned back in his chair. "The Elders aren't writing Gerry off. They're taking his disappearance very seriously."

Yeah, right. "You don't seem in any hurry to help look for him."

"Wasted effort. If Gerry is alive, what makes you think he wants to be found?"

Of all the idiotic . . . "You think he's playing hide-and-seek for the fun of it? At a time like this?"

Alex laid the pen down. "Look, I read his file as well as yours. Gerry's had his issues with the Elders. He doesn't like the way they run things. I'm just saying maybe he has his own reasons for disappearing at this particular time, and I'm not sure walking around his empty house will tell us anything useful."

Understanding finally slapped me on my bruised cheek. "You think he's disappeared deliberately so he can, what, enact some devious plot against the Elders?" My blood pressure soared. The nerve of this guy. His gall knew no bounds.

Alex shrugged and stuck his papers in a manila envelope. "It's a possibility."

"You don't know what you're talking about." Gerry was a complainer but he wasn't a traitor. He thought the Elders were bureaucratic idiots, but he also drilled every magical law into me like gospel.

This big jerk wasn't going to help me find Gerry. He wanted to *catch* Gerry. Big difference.

"Fine," I said. "You flit around town running errands for the Elders like a good little soldier. I will look for Gerry myself."

He sealed the envelope and stuck it in the back of his notebook. "I repeat: How do you plan to get into Lakeview?"

Like it was any of his business. "I'm calling Tish—Gerry's girlfriend—to get contact info on some of her coworkers from the Port of New Orleans, and see who's in town with a boat. If I find a boat, I'll get in."

"She's a wizard?"

I nodded. "Green Congress, an engineer. She's as worried about Gerry as I am." And would snatch Alex bald when she found out he suspected Gerry of disappearing on purpose.

Alex looked at me a few seconds, drumming his fingers on the table. "I might have a quicker way." He pulled out his cell phone and hit a speed-dial number. "Jake, do you . . . Damn." He clicked the phone shut and tried the call again. And again. Fourth time was a winner.

"Jake has his dad's boat and can meet us in Lakeview about one thirty," he said when he ended the call.

"What's this *we* business? I thought you had breaches to find."

He stood up and stretched, rolling his head side to side and popping his neck. "Partners, remember?"

Like I could forget. Still, it solved my boat problem and gave me an hour to unload the rest of my stuff from the truck. Jean Lafitte had thrown me off schedule. Without a way to get ice, the perishable herbs were going to have to be trashed, but I lugged everything else upstairs.

Alex helped, pausing to look at the mangled library door. "What happened here?"

"Jean Lafitte happened," I said. "My house has sustained more damage in the last twenty-four hours than in the whole last century."

He raised an eyebrow at the aluminum pan that still lay on the floor, coated with ashes. "Do I want to know?"

"Homemade smoke bomb. It got me away from the pirate. Well, for a while."

He fought to keep the serious look on his face. "You really do need a gun."

Yeah, and I had lots of ideas on what to do with it. I grabbed the pan and set it on the worktable without comment.

He continued his inspection of the library, pausing to look at jars and amulets, plants and powders, occasionally asking questions. Fine, let him snoop. I had nothing to hide.

It was clear from his comments he was pretty well-versed in magic, but then again, I guess he'd have to be.

"Have you worked with a lot of wizards?" I asked as he scanned the titles in the shelf where I kept most of my personal spellbooks.

"A few—all Red Congress," he said. "Enforcers usually get pulled in last, when the wizards have done all they can, or else we get called when the Elders need something taken care of fast. Red wizards don't have all this stuff."

I smiled. "No, physical magic is pretty straightforward. No bells and whistles. I like to think ritual magic is more flexible, though."

He stopped at my worktable and ran a hand along the dark mahogany wood beginning to turn red with age. Since I had been gone for a while, the table was mostly empty except for a layer of dust and a large wrought-iron cross I'd found in an architectural salvage yard and paid a local welder to put on a stand. It kept me centered, reminded me who was really in charge when things got crazy.

"I like this." He fingered the cross. "I used to not buy into my family's religious beliefs—thought I was too smart for it. But the more evil I see, the more I realize it has to be offset by an ultimate good, or else there's no point to it."

Sheesh. Talk about a hot- and cold-running enforcer. Just when I decide he's an Elder-toady conspiracy theorist, he turns into a philosopher.

I made a concentrated effort to read his emotions, opening up my mind to anything that might drift my way, but got nothing except a light magical buzz from the magic-infused herbs in my library. Maybe the renewed mojo bag and grounding was blocking him.

"Stay out of my head—it's invasive," he said, giving me a sharp look.

I opened my mouth to tell a big, whopping fib of denial, but stopped myself. He'd caught me. "Sorry," I said. "I just can't figure you out. How did you know what I was doing?"

"Enforcers learn how to put up mental blocks and recognize when someone's trying to get in. You're the first empath I've met, but some pretes can play serious mind games."

"So you were shielding yesterday." No wonder he'd been such a blank, although he could still be a soulless freak. Jury remained out on that one, although I couldn't imagine a soulless freak with eyes the color of dark chocolate.

I didn't have to be an empath to interpret his tight smile. "You bet I was. Took a lot of concentration, too. I wasn't planning to come in with such a bang."

No kidding. "You do know Jean Lafitte's not really dead, right?" I asked, not sure how often—if ever—enforcers came up against the historical undead. "All you did was send him back to the Beyond, slow him down a little, and make him even madder."

He shrugged. "No problem. I'll just kill him again."

CHAPTER 12

Truth be told, I'd rather have gone to Gerry's house alone, at least this first time. Not just because of the inevitable onslaught of memories, but so I could really look around without Alex watching me. Despite a couple of hints that a decent guy might lurk beneath all the cold iron and hot ammo, we didn't have the same agenda. I wanted to find Gerry, and he wanted to find out what Gerry was up to.

I'd be watching Mr. Warin, and not just because he was easy to look at.

"I'll drive," he said, heading toward the small parking area behind my house. It had enough space for both my truck and the vehicles belonging to the young couple who owned the dark-green shotgun house next door. I figured I'd seen the last of Bill and Eileen. She was pregnant, and their business had flooded. They had nothing to come back to.

I looked at the spotless Mercedes sitting next to my dusty Pathfinder. Black, of course. What a surprise.

"Do you really want to take your nice, shiny Batmobile into the flood zone?" The thing reeked of money and frequent, loving hand-washings. Apparently, assassins got paid better than deputy sentinels. Bet you didn't see Alexander Warin buying cheap Winn-Dixie rum to save a few bucks.

"It needs washing anyway."

"Okay, your choice." I stuck my keys in my backpack and headed for the Mercedes. I'd never ridden in one anyway—it might be my only chance. Besides, despite all my preparations, I wasn't sure how seeing my childhood home in ruins would hit me. Even driving to Lakeview would be stressful. Might as well let him handle that part.

I settled into the buttery soft seat—black—and strapped myself in. It still had the new car smell to it. "So, why aren't you driving some big studly truck with Playboy Bunny mud flaps?"

"Why aren't you riding a broom?" he muttered to himself as he crossed St. Charles into the flood zone and began winding his way through side streets, dodging swaying power lines and weaving through haphazard piles of debris.

He turned onto a street that hadn't been cleared very well and stopped the car. A boxy white washing machine rested in the middle of the pavement, surrounded by limbs and leaves. We stared at it in silence a few seconds before Alex backed up and headed down another street.

"Turn right up here and the next left, and it'll take you all the way to Lakeview." It finally occurred to me that he was lost, and God forbid a man should ask for directions.

He grunted and turned right. "I knew that."

Heh. I shook my head and looked out the window, staring at the ruins. My hometown, my own wasteland of stony rubbish and broken images. I needed someone to share my horror with, to lie and tell me it would be okay. I needed Gerry.

I thought the devastation in Mid-City had given me a good idea of what to expect from Lakeview, but I was wrong.

Alex's FBI badge eased us through two checkpoints, and as we got closer to the 17th Street Canal, the mud on the road began to thicken. So much for the spotless car.

Still cursing under his breath, he pulled to the roadside on Canal Boulevard and stopped. We sat a moment and looked at the sea of brown and gray that coated everything in front of us— mud. Wet mud, dried mud. Mud on trees, on cars, on houses. Mud on top of mud.

Alex sighed and reached into the backseat, handing me an oversize tan plastic bag with a blue Dillard's logo on the side.

"Aw, a present, and my birthday's not until February."

He almost smiled. "Well, I saw these and thought you'd look hot."

I either had to joke or cry, and Alex's strained expression told me he felt the same way.

I opened the top of the bag and peered inside, pulling out a pair of clear rubber galoshes, the kind little kids used to wear over their shoes on rainy days. Except these would come up to my knees. Great. Clear rubber go-go boots.

"I'm touched, but you shouldn't have." I looked at them again. "Really."

"Put them on. We're going to have to walk a few blocks. I'm not going to risk getting my car stuck in this." He retrieved a pair of more dignified shrimp boots for himself and opened his car door, sliding them on before hitting the ground. "And don't get mud in my car."

Sure, no problem. Grimacing, I slipped the boots over my Nikes before getting out. Good thing. When I stood up, my feet sank about an inch into what I could only hope was mud. It smelled like a lot of other, less savory ingredients had been mixed in. I coughed, sneezed, and trudged my way after Alex, struggling to pull my feet far enough out of the muck to move them.

A weathered black and silver Dodge pickup towing a small motorboat pulled up behind us, and Alex circled back to greet the driver. I couldn't see who sat behind the crusted and dirty windshield, but Alex stood at the driver's window and pointed down the block where the boulevard disappeared into floodwater.

The truck pulled ahead, maneuvered a deft U-turn, and backed toward the water. Alex motioned for me to follow. By the time I lurched my way to the truck, he and the pickup driver were sliding the boat down the trailer ramp.

Sweat trickled down my neck, and if I hadn't been afraid of being poisoned by toxic sludge, I'd have made like a pig and wallowed in the mud to cool off. I kicked at a fire hydrant, trying to jolt some of the heaviest sludge off my boots, and heard a soft laugh behind me. With a final kick that sent a spray of brown gunk flying, I turned to see what was so funny. I needed a laugh.

A man leaned against the side of the pickup with his arms crossed. He was a few inches shorter than Alex, maybe just shy of six feet, with sun-streaked blond hair that reached his collar and a sleeveless blue T-shirt and khaki shorts. His tanned legs between the bottom of the shorts and the top of sturdy black shrimp boots were scored with scars, bad ones, as if whatever made them meant to do serious damage.

He'd been grinning when I turned around, flashing a heart-stopping set of dimples, but when he saw my eyes linger on his legs, the grin eased into something more wary.

I smiled and squished over to introduce myself. "I'm DJ Jaco. Thanks for letting us use your boat."

The dimples returned as he took my hand in a firm grip. "Jake Warin. Actually, it's my dad's boat. I was running rescues after the storm, but there's nobody left to rescue now." He had the same Mississippi drawl as Alex, only softer around the edges. New Orleanians sounded more like New Yorkers than Southerners.

Nobody left to rescue. I looked over my shoulder at the corpse of Lakeview. Not a tree or a blade of grass was alive here.

"Oh God, I'm sorry." Jake ran a hand through his hair. "Alex told me your uncle was missing. I'm sure he got a ride out and is waiting for the mayor to tell folks they can come home."

I turned back to look at him and managed a smile. "I hope so."

Alex splashed up to join us. "You met?"

"We did," Jake said. His gaze trailed to my feet and his smile grew wider. "Nice boots."

"Thanks. It's a fashion statement."

Alex shook his head and sloshed back toward the boat, sending waves to the top of my fashion statement. "Time to go. Meet us back here at five thirty."

Jake did a pretty good Alex impression at his cousin's retreating back. "Guess that's my cue to leave. Alex said you didn't need any help." He looked back at me with eyes the color of amber. "I hope you find your uncle."

I nodded and turned to follow Alex. I hoped so too.

Walking in the floodwater was easier than the mud, and it had washed most of the gunk off my boots by the time I half-fell into the boat. Alex started the motor and steered us toward Bellaire Drive, which ran alongside the breached canal all the way to the lake.

"So, what's Jake's story?" I had to talk loud to be heard over the chugging of the motor.

Alex gave me an inscrutable look. "Why?"

"Just curious. I noticed the scars."

"Ex-Marine. Got hurt in Afghanistan. Don't let the laid-back, country-boy act fool you. He's one tough SOB."

Whatever that meant. We rode a couple of blocks farther

before the engine started bellowing like a tortured animal and died, leaving us surrounded by an ocean of gentle sounds. The chop of a helicopter in the distance. Water lapping at the side of the boat. Alex trying to restart the motor. Our own breathing.

Empty houses rose around us like a surreal architectural city of the dead—except for a healthy-looking rat swimming past. I flinched and wrapped my arms around my middle.

It took a few tries, but Alex got the motor started again. It didn't sound happy as it gamely churned through the murk. Only ten or so blocks to go. There were no water rings on the houses now, at least not on the one-story places. The water had been over the eaves, and I tried to imagine it two weeks ago, escaping from home on a boat like this one, floating so high, knowing your whole life lay immersed beneath you.

I squinched my eyes halfway shut to block out the images, but I couldn't shut out the chalky smell. It permeated everything.

"Where's the house?" Alex asked.

"Another block, on the left. Two stories—balcony off the top floor." I mentally ran through the list of neighbors as we motored down the block. Grumpy Dr. Michealson, house totaled, hot tub in palm tree. Old Mrs. Finney, first floor flooded, hole in roof. The Zellners next door, nothing left to save.

And Gerry's house. My home until a few years ago. A big chunk of the brick veneer on the south wall had been sheared off and Gerry's old BMW remained upended. Otherwise, everything looked intact. No holes in the roof. Gerry wouldn't have needed an ax; he could have blasted his way out.

The double driveway in front wasn't visible under the black water, but Alex steered the boat slowly toward the house until we scraped concrete. The motor belched one final protest and died again.

He got out to secure the boat, but I couldn't stop looking at the house. I was seven years old again, sitting in the backseat of my grandfather's car, having just seen the expanse of Lake Pontchartrain as we crossed into the city, so wide I thought it must be the ocean. I'd been spellbound by the exotic landscape, the tall buildings, the size of the place, all the cars and people and sounds and smells.

I wanted to look at it, and then go home. I didn't want to live here with a stranger. I didn't understand why my grandparents didn't want me. But the man, Gerry, had stood in the door, smiling and telling me he was glad to meet me. He was the first person I'd met in my seven years whose emotions didn't bombard me, and being with him was peaceful.

"You okay?" Alex's voice brought me back to the still water and the empty houses.

"Fine." I took a deep breath, which made me cough again, then climbed out and headed for the front door.

"Wait." Alex opened a duffel bag in the front of the boat. "Jake brought this stuff. We need to use it." He pulled out big yellow rubber gloves, white strap-on face masks to cover our mouth and nose, and goggles.

"That's overkill." I shook my head and turned back toward the house.

He grabbed my arm. "You're the one who wanted to do this today, so at least do it right. There's no medical care here, and God knows what's in this water." His mouth twitched. "Although if you get sick I can do good sponge baths."

"I have two words for you: sexual harassment." I snapped the white mask on as I headed for the door.

When I reached it, I stopped, my breath caught in my throat. The symbol Alex had copied from the crime scenes, the one he'd seen on his jog this morning, shone faintly in red from beneath the shallow water covering Gerry's top doorstep. I shivered despite the heat.

Alex swore when he saw it, then splashed to the houses on either side of Gerry's and studied their entrances. "Nothing on those," he said, pulling the tracker off his belt and turning it on. "It's reading faint magical energy here—had to be recent because it usually dissipates quickly."

"Did you adjust it so it wasn't reading me?"

"Yeah, this is someone else—or some*thing* else." He frowned and walked back to the door. "It's definitely stronger at the house. Do you have a key?"

I gave him a withering look and pushed the front door open. "None of the locks held." I'd noticed open doors on most of the houses along the way. There was little left in Lakeview to steal, and no one to steal it.

I stepped inside, sliding and skating on the mud-covered tile of the foyer.

"The signal's a little stronger in here." Alex walked past me into the short hallway leading to Gerry's living room.

I stopped and took a cautious breath. I smelled mud, dry-wall, mold—the source of the chalky odor. I hadn't let myself think it, but deep inside, part of me had been afraid we'd walk in and find the stench of death. The house smelled awful, but no one had died here.

My shoulders sagged in relief. He couldn't be in the house, injured, or the Elders would have detected his energy field. So we were looking not for a body, but for clues.

I held out my hands, palms up, and closed my eyes, feeling the air with my senses. Gerry's wards were gone, as mine had been, but there was a tingling trace of energy similar to what I'd felt in my own house when Lafitte was upstairs. No way that infernal pirate had come back from the Beyond so quickly.

Coughing, I went down the short hallway into the living room, where Alex already walked carefully, holding the tracker. The tan carpet had turned black and squished inky slush with every step. Sometime during the flooding, Gerry's refrigerator had floated into the living room and had come to rest on its back, thankfully still closed, and the water-swollen mantle hung at an odd angle over the fireplace. But the mold was worst, a forest of it growing up the walls in a purple, black, and green visual cacophony Jackson Pollock would envy.

I'd tried to mentally prepare for this visit, hoping to keep tears and hysteria at bay. It hadn't occurred to me that I'd just feel numb. Maybe a person's brain could only take in so many horrific images before it gave up and filed everything away to process later. I'd have a lot to process later.

I veered off the living room and climbed the stairs to the second floor. At the landing halfway up, before the steps took a ninety-degree turn to the right, I stopped short again. "Alex, come here." My voice sounded calm; inside, I was screeching.

Our symbol again, this time painted in red on the wall along the landing. If I'd had any doubt before, I didn't now. This was no gang tag.

Moving silently, Alex edged around me and reached up to touch it, flecking off a piece of red and sniffing it. "Looks more like blood than paint. Not necessarily human, though."

I stared at it a moment, then led him up the stairs, barely daring to breathe. We stopped at the top and listened. I could see the slow, red pulse on the tracker as Alex held it in front of him.

He cut left toward the bedrooms and I walked straight, stopping at the open door of Gerry's study. I caught a quick movement from the far corner and felt a cold energy. Pinpricks of fear ran up my arms.

From the rear wall, a pair of smoky gray eyes stared back at me for an instant, then disappeared.

CHAPTER 13

I remained stuck in place for a few seconds before self-doubt started churning. Had I imagined the eyes, the movement? I walked around the room, looking at the spot from different angles. Maybe it had been some trick of light, a play of afternoon shadows.

"I haven't seen any sign of Gerry, and there's no evidence of a struggle up here." Alex came in from the hallway minus his boots and mask. "I took a sample of the blood to have it analyzed. Could be animal."

I shushed him. "Try your tracker in here. I thought I saw something."

He circled the room, holding the device in front of him, and finally stopped in the corner where I'd seen the eyes. "I don't know. Might be a little stronger here but if there was something, it's gone now. What did you think it was?"

I pulled off my own mask and eased my feet from the boots, although we'd already left black footprints everywhere. "Just a flash of movement, and eyes watching me from the wall by the bookcase. And I felt a different kind of energy when I first walked in."

"Energy like it was Gerry? Or like something else?"

"Don't know. I can tell it's there but not what it's from."

Alex touched the back wall, running his hands along the bookshelves, then checked the tracker again. "The signal's not stronger here than anywhere else in the house. You sure it was eyes? We know something was here earlier, but the movement could have been a rat."

I put both hands against the wall, feeling for the light prickle of magic. Alex was right; it was almost gone. But it hadn't faded completely, and rats didn't have a magical punch. Maybe some of my books on voodoo would help us identify what the drawings meant. Homework by candlelight.

On the left wall of the study hung a flat screen about three feet across and two feet high. I walked over to look at it, wondering if I could get it to work.

"What is that?" Alex asked.

"Gerry's tracker—sort of the industrial-strength version of the one you have. If something gets summoned from the Beyond, a map pops up on the screen with the location. I thought maybe it could show when something had been here."

He studied it, feeling around the edges. "How do you turn it on?"

"I'm not sure. I always thought the Elders powered it from their end." I placed my hand on the screen and willed a jolt of energy into it. It lit and buzzed briefly, then went black again.

"We should take it with us." He tried to pull the screen from the wall, and swore as it shattered and turned into a pile of crumbled glass.

"Nice," I said. "What a muscle monster."

"I didn't pull on it that hard." The enforcer actually blushed.

"It was probably warded to keep anyone from taking it." I headed back to the desk. "It doesn't matter. I doubt it would work for anyone but Gerry and my physical magic isn't strong enough to power it."

I pulled open the top drawer of Gerry's desk, glancing at the back wall to make sure no more stray eyeballs showed up. Alex began pulling books from the shelves.

"Don't worry about the books yet," I said. "See if there's anything in the attic we need to take out today. Sensitive material, anything overtly about magic or having to do with the Elders or Red Congress business. If you aren't sure what something is, it's probably better not to touch it. Let me come and look first." I wasn't sure it was wise to let Alex loose in Gerry's stuff before I had a chance to dig through it, but at least the attic was unlikely to have anything recent.

Plus, I wanted the study to myself. If we were going to find clues about what happened to Gerry, they would be here. Every time I'd scried him after the storm, he'd been in this room and usually at this desk.

I had one other thing to look at first, though. As soon as Alex dropped the attic ladder in the hallway and climbed out of sight, I walked to the far corner of the room and pulled up a small area rug. The transport we'd set up between here and Gran's house was still there, but an edge of the circle had been smudged out. The break was too clean to be accidental, so I added it to my list of mysteries.

I knelt beside the transport and put my hand on the chalk line, but that's all it was now—just a drawing. I'd have to do some research and find a way to tell if the transport had been used. Obviously, Gerry hadn't rerouted it to go somewhere else because it had been broken from this end. I replaced the rug, careful not to disturb it.

I returned to Gerry's desk and began sorting through papers, occasionally checking the back wall for activity. Each drawer had been stuffed with documents, and I marveled at the sheer chaos of it. This was an awfully messy desk for a person I'd always considered a bit of a fussbudget. Gerry collected antiques, considered himself an aficionado of fine wines, and alphabetized his books by author. His desk drawers looked like they'd been organized by a squirrel.

Bills, letters, receipts. Correspondence, newspaper clippings, photocopies of photocopies. I'd have to take it all home to sort later. Nothing screamed *suspicious*.

Alex thumped down the attic stairs. "Nothing looks out of place up there, but lots of stuff will need taking out eventually. I did find some empty boxes we can use." He walked in the study with an armload of flattened boxes and a rectangular leather case. "This was the only thing I wasn't sure about."

I set the case on Gerry's desk and opened it to find a wooden staff about two feet long, heavily carved with odd, unfamiliar symbols. I'd never seen it before, so Gerry must have had it stashed in the attic awhile.

"Did you run the tracker on it?" I asked.

"Yeah, and it's reading a little juice, so I didn't want to touch it."

I ran my hands along the wood. Red sparks spurted from its tip as I pulled it out of the case. It grew warm in my hand, and I traced my fingers along the unusual carvings—runes, maybe?

"You really think you should be doing that?" Alex leaned over the desk, propped on his elbows.

"Touch it and see if it does anything for you," I said. "It feels pretty harmless."

He looked at me suspiciously, then reached out and touched one finger to the wood. When he was sure he wasn't going to burst into flames or sprout horns, he added a few more fingers and ran his hand over the marks. "You never saw Gerry using it? Don't Red Congress wizards use wands or staffs?"

I shook my head. "Some do, but Gerry never liked them. He has a ring he wears for channeling occasionally but he can focus his magic without it." I returned the staff to the case and closed the latch. "We definitely take this thing with us today, though. As for the rest, let me pick the most sensitive to take now, and anything that might give us a clue to where Gerry is. We'll have to come back for the rest once the water's down enough to bring in the Pathfinder—if we haven't found him by then."

I stuffed all the papers into a box while Alex began sorting books into *take now* and *take later* stacks. I did my best to separate the task from the fact that we were dismantling Gerry's house as if he were never coming back.

The oddest things stirred memories. A pipe in a desk drawer conjured the image of Gerry sitting in the living room chair downstairs, puffing away on it as he tried to get the hang of smoking. Tish teased him about it till he finally admitted he liked the idea of being a pipe-smoker better than actually smoking one. The first year I drew a salary from the Elders, just after getting my Green Congress license, I'd bought him a Meister-stück pen for his birthday. It lay on the desktop, and I picked it up, rubbing the resin and gold surface with its etched nib. He'd fussed at me for spending so much on it, then I'd caught him admiring it when he thought I wasn't looking.

The memories knifed through the numbness and made my eyes burn. I stuck the pen in my pocket, moving to open the window and let in some air. Crying was for people who had time to be self-indulgent and I didn't, not right now.

I watched a helicopter hover eight or ten blocks north at the levee breach, long pieces of metal hanging suspended beneath it. The Army Corps of Engineers was scrambling to shore up the collapsed floodwall, and already people were wondering how much of this mess had been caused by the hurricane and how much by bad engineering. The Mississippi and Southeast Louisiana coasts had been devastated by the hurricane. New Orleans had drowned.

I turned at a noise behind me. Alex had taken my place at Gerry's desk and was trying to pick the lock on the bottom file-cabinet drawer, the only one I hadn't gotten to.

"Wait." I nudged him aside and pulled out the top drawer of the desk, reaching underneath and retrieving the key Gerry kept taped to the bottom.

He rolled the chair back so I could open the drawer. Inside were small leather books—dozens of them. I picked one up, nose wrinkling at the slightly musty smell, and flipped through page after page of Gerry's small, looping script. Journals. Each entry was dated, and several were illustrated with sketches of antiques and artifacts he'd bought. Maybe the weird staff was in here somewhere. I'd take these home and save them for him.

"Is there an entry for the day Gerry disappeared?" Alex leaned sideways in the chair and looked over my shoulder.

I examined the dates on the spines. "No, the most recent one ends last December. There are some gaps, though. The others must be stashed somewhere else." Maybe if we found his last diary entry, it could prove Gerry hadn't gone rogue. I should be able to look for him without also having to defend him, damn it.

Alex leaned back in the chair, scanning the desktop. His voice was casual. Too casual. "You *will* show it to me if you find it, won't you?"

Distrustful oaf. "Of course. I'd hate to make you file a report with the Elders that I'd withheld information on Gerry's disappearance."

Alex frowned. "I'm not the enemy, DJ."

I stood up and turned to sit on the edge of Gerry's desk,

facing him. "But you're not just here to be a sentinel either, are you?"

He looked at me steadily. "I'm here to be a *co*sentinel—to help you, not replace you, unless you really can't do the job."

Which he would decide, of course, the jackass. I knew more about sentinel work than this pseudo mobster ever would.

"I'm also here to investigate what happened to Gerry. It's part of what enforcers do. The FBI training isn't just an act."

"You really think he disappeared on purpose, that he's done something underhanded and, what, now he's figured out a way to hide from the Elders?"

Alex sighed, pushed the chair back, and chose his words. "I think Gerry has a history of opposing the Elders, and they think this storm could have given him an opportunity to act on his beliefs. Maybe he did something, maybe he didn't. That's what I'm here to figure out. If something happened to him, and he's de—" He stopped with the word *dead* halfway out, but it wasn't like I hadn't thought it myself.

"If he's in trouble," he said, "we need to know that too."

"But you don't think that, do you—that he's in trouble?"

Alex gave an impatient snort. "I think if Gerry didn't go rogue, he's probably dead. I'm sorry to be so blunt. But if he was injured, the Elders would still be able to detect his energy field."

The numbness returned, and my voice felt hollow. "You don't know Gerry like I do. He complains a lot, I'll give you that. He might even play the rules a little fast and loose, but he wouldn't set himself against the Elders. He just wouldn't."

I didn't have to ask what the Elders would do to Gerry if they decided otherwise. Treason carried a death penalty. Even humans didn't tolerate sedition, and they were a lot less rigid than wizards. That's the way it worked, and Gerry knew it. He wouldn't take the risk.

Alex reached for my hand but I snatched it away and stuck it in my pocket, fingering my mojo bag more out of habit than need. He could shield his emotions as well as Gerry.

He leaned back in the chair again. "DJ, I like your spirit. You're smart and loyal, and the fact you held off Lafitte as long as you did shows you can think on your feet. You might even be dangerous if you could shoot. But you have to at least consider all the possibilities where Gerry is concerned."

I might buy a gun just to use at times such as this. "I will be open-minded if you will."

He considered it. "Fair enough."

We worked a couple more hours in tense silence, sorting out the study, and I moved on to Gerry's bedroom. None of his clothes appeared to be missing. If he'd gone on a trip, he had packed light. He also hadn't taken his toothbrush or razor.

When I got to the far side of the bed, I stopped and stared at the floor. The interlocking circle and triangle of a transport had been drawn on the polished wood in dark powder. The symbols were unbroken, as they would be in a permanent transport, or at least one that had been used. I stuck my hand in the field of energy that would have been created had the symbols been infused with magic recently, but felt nothing. The powder was fine and black, and I spread a little on my index finger, careful not to disrupt the figures. I held my finger to my nose and smelled smoke. Ash.

"What does that look like?" I asked, holding up my finger as Alex came up behind me.

"Looks like charcoal, or ash maybe," he said, squatting and rubbing a pinch of the powder between his fingers. "What do you think it means?"

"Ash is used for some magic, but it's not a good conductor. Doesn't last long enough."

I paused, wondering how much to tell Alex, whether to

share information that might make Gerry look bad. But we'd agreed to find the truth, whatever it might turn out to be.

"There's something else," I said. "I don't know if you realize it, but the Elders recently changed their recommendations for ritual summoning, dispatching, and transports. Before, we used circles for everything, so if you found a circle it wouldn't tell you what it had been used for. This interlocking circle and triangle is used as a transport and nothing else. But there's no magical energy coming off it now. It's closed, but I don't know if it has been used."

Alex studied the figures. "Would the energy dissipate if the transport was used but there was no one behind on this side to break it? Like if he went somewhere alone and didn't return?"

"Eventually." I eyed the transport again. "But like I said, ash isn't a good conductor. An ash transport would lose its traces of energy a lot faster than something like sea salt or iron." Of course, Gerry knew that. If he used a transport of ash, he wanted his trail to disappear fast. If I could come to that conclusion, I was sure the enforcer could too.

Alex raised his head and looked sharply toward the door, then stood and left the room.

I met him in the doorway as he returned carrying an armload of ear-flattened, hissing, chocolate-colored feline. I'd forgotten about Gerry's cat.

"Sebastian!" I reached out to pet him, happy to see any tangible sign of Gerry. At the sight of me, his ears flattened even more and he exposed a mouthful of sharp, pointy teeth. You'd think I had kicked that cat at some point in its wretched life, but I swear I had treated it only with kindhearted affection. Well, and periodic indifference.

"It's okay, boy," Alex said, smoothing out Sebastian's fur. The big cat began to purr and relaxed in Alex's arms. Traitorous ingrate. "There was a huge bag of food and plenty of water set out for him in the other bedroom. He must have been hiding under the bed when I was in there before."

Sebastian's slightly crossed blue eyes settled on me in a baleful glare. Still, Gerry had loved him, and he'd been through a rough couple of weeks. I reached out to rub behind his ears. He loved it when Gerry did that. All I got for my sympathy was another hiss, a show of teeth, and a scratch on the back of my hand.

"Okay, I tried," I said, annoyed. "He's all yours."

"Jake's allergic to cats, so you'll have to figure out a way to get along," Alex said. "There's a carrier in the other room and I'll put him in it. Once you get him home, you two are on your own."

Sebastian and I looked at each other, doubt written on both our faces.

While Alex went to put the cat in the carrier, I sat on Gerry's bed, a high four-poster covered with a simple dark-green duvet, and tried to figure out my next steps. The room smelled like Gerry, like his aftershave and cologne, a familiar undercurrent beneath the odor of mold. I traced a finger along the seams of the duvet and wondered how this could be happening.

I needed to talk to Tish next, to get another opinion from someone who knew Gerry well. Then I'd start researching the weird symbols we'd been finding, and would have to do it the hard way. No electricity, no Internet. Before dark, I also needed to replace the wards on my house. Eventually, Jean Lafitte would come for me again.

"Got it all solved?" Alex watched me from the doorway, a bland expression on his face. For once, I'd really, really like to read someone else's emotions.

"No," I said. "I was trying to decide what to do next. We need to find out what those symbols mean." I didn't mention Tish. Talking to her was personal.

He came in the room and sat on the bed next to me. "I have to ask you something."

I raised my eyebrows.

"Has Gerry ever asked you to do anything you thought might be a little off? Could you have helped him do something wrong without realizing it?"

I stared at him. Oh my God, did he really think that? Did the Elders think that? That I was either corrupted myself or too stupid to know I was being used?

"No, I have not helped Gerry do anything *off*." Well, the Lafitte seduction scheme had been questionable on his part and stupid on mine, but still.

Alex looked back at the transport. "I've told the Elders that whatever's going on, I don't believe you're involved. But I had to at least ask you."

My voice gathered heat. "And after knowing me less than twenty-four hours you think I'm not involved because . . . ?"

"Because I can tell how much you believe in Gerry and think something bad has happened to him." He shifted on the bed and looked me in the eye. "Nothing personal, but I don't think you're a good enough actress to fake that much concern."

I had done very little magic today and Alex was an emotional void, but my muscles ached and my limbs felt heavy. Stress. I didn't want to have to defend Gerry. I surely didn't want to have to defend myself. I wanted to curl up in a sweaty ball and go to sleep on Gerry's bed. Alone.

Instead, I walked out of the bedroom and returned to the study, sitting at the desk to pull on my dirty boots. I stuck the wooden staff case under my arm, grabbed a bag of cat food in my left hand, clutched the handle of Sebastian's carrier in the other, and headed downstairs. I heard Alex calling after me, saying he'd box up a few more things and be out soon.

Hope he wasn't packing more than he could carry, because I was taking my tired body and my new cat home to think. I squished through the living room and foyer to get outside, set the carrier and staff in the boat, pushed it away from the curb, and looked at the motor, trying to remember how Alex had started it. Didn't you just pull a cord or something, or was that a lawn mower?

"Damn it, DJ, stop!" Alex hopped out the door, pulling on his boots. "I'm just doing my job."

"Whatever." I didn't want to hear any more about *his job.*

"I'm going back in for that last box of papers. Stay there." He splashed back toward the house. "And don't even think of trying to ditch me. I have the boat keys."

Boat keys. Who knew? Another emotional outburst spoiled.

We rode down Fleur de Lis and back toward Canal Boulevard with no noise but the chugging motor. Jake had already returned and backed the boat ramp to the water's edge. He sat on it, waiting, looking nice and friendly and agenda-less. He hooked a line as Alex killed the motor and we got out, then pulled the boat toward the ramp.

He looked from me to Alex and back again. "Lovers' quarrel?"

I frowned and glared at Alex's back. Lovers? How *had* he explained our relationship? Neither of us answered.

Jake grinned as he and Alex got the boat secured. He walked with a limp, as if the most badly scarred leg, his right, wouldn't quite bend the way it should. It didn't seem to slow him down.

"If you wanna ride with me, I'd be happy to take you home," he told me, ignoring his fuming cousin.

"She's with me," Alex snapped.

The hell I was. "I'd love a ride, thank you."

I settled my backpack and Sebastian's carrier in the bed of the pickup, snatching my hand back to avoid a well-aimed set of claws that swiped at me from the carrier vents. I tugged off the boots and got in the passenger seat of the truck, holding the staff in its case. Alex's car door slammed, and his wheels spun on mud before he gained traction and peeled off with a dramatic, messy splatter. Heh.

Jake's dimples deepened as he opened the driver's side door, watching over the top of the truck as Alex left. "You just made my day, sunshine. Not many people can get under my cousin's Teflon coat like that. What did he do?"

"I'd just had enough of his sparkling personality for one day." Guilt started setting in. He had only done his job, after all. I didn't have to like it, but I also didn't have to take my frustrations out on him. I was angry at the situation, not at the enforcer. Well, sort of.

I sighed. "I probably overreacted. Now you'll be in his doghouse too."

Jake laughed as he took a corner slowly, making sure the boat could clear the narrow street. "No big deal. We've spent most of our lives butting heads. This is normal."

We reached a security checkpoint. The officer waved at Jake and motioned us through the intersection without making us stop.

"Old friend," Jake explained. "Where's your house?"

"Nashville and Magazine—you know the area?"

He nodded, and we drove in easy silence till we cleared the second checkpoint.

Jake cleared his throat. "I don't mean to stick my nose in your business, but how long you and Alex been an item? He's been down here off and on since the storm consulting on cases with the NOPD, and he usually kisses and tells. I'd remember if he had a girlfriend in town."

Definitely should have ridden with Alex. "Uh," I said. "We've been together awhile. But not that long."

He smiled. "Whatever you say."

I was such a bad liar. "Okay. Not long. We met pretty recently, in fact." Like, yesterday. "Is he always so . . ." I searched for the right word. Grumpy. Stubborn. Monosyllabic.

Jake raised his eyebrows. "Intense?"

That worked. "Yeah, is he always so intense?"

"It's an act." Jake chuckled. "He works hard at that tough-guy thing. Alex is a marshmallow underneath all the crap. You've just gotta dig for it."

"Hmph." Jake hadn't seen the grenade-toting, pirate-killing side of his cousin, obviously.

We spent the rest of the drive to my house in comfortable conversation. I described my evacuation, minus the magic parts. Jake told me about the damage his and Alex's families had in Picayune, what it was like riding out the storm at his bar, the Green Gator, and some of the things he'd seen running rescues out of Gentilly and Lakeview and the Lower Nine.

Jake Warin was open and talkative and way too charming. Uncomplicated. Untainted by the Elders and their political machinations. By the time we got to my house, I'd fallen for the dimples and the amber eyes enough to accept a dinner invitation, time to be determined by Katrina recovery. The storm shaped everything now, even a dinner date. We had to wait till a restaurant opened, or at least till the electricity came back on.

Jake didn't mention my boyfriend Alex, and neither did I.

I smiled as I climbed out of the truck and said good-bye. He'd helped me step outside myself and distracted me for a few minutes, an unexpected pleasure in what was shaping up to be a frustrating day.

"Oh, wait." I stuck my head back in the passenger window. "You'll probably see Alex before I do. When he gets back to his room at the Gator, tell him I'm sorry I overreacted."

Jake laughed. "He isn't staying at the Gator, but I'll tell him whenever I see him."

He waved and pulled away, leaving me to wonder what the enforcer was up to.

CHAPTER 14

By the time Alex showed up at my house an hour later, a box of papers under each arm, I'd mentally chastised myself for leaving him and had sworn to be more cooperative. For one thing, we had to work together, like it or not. For another, I wanted him to share information with me, which meant sucking it up and letting him do his job.

I hate it when life forces me to be mature.

After Jake dropped me off, I'd reestablished my wards. I filled seven small pouches with a mixture of protective herbs, infused each one with magic, and planted them in a rough circle around the house. Then I walked the circle, connecting the energies and repeating the safe word that would drop the wards. I chose *Lafitte* as my safe word, a reminder of why I needed protection.

Raising the wards depleted what little energy I had left. When Alex pulled his mud-splattered car into the driveway at dusk, I was sitting on the back stoop, trying to muster the strength to take a shower.

He dropped the boxes and a bag of cat litter next to me with a thud and turned to leave.

"Wait," I said to his back. "I'm sorry, okay? I know you have to look at all the possibilities and I'm the one who works with Gerry. Your asking if I helped him . . . well, it took me by surprise. I'm sorry I overreacted." No point in waiting to apologize. Crow is a dish best served warm.

He looked back at me, dark eyes softening as he opened his car door. "We both had a long day. See you tomorrow."

Guess we'd discuss why he lied about his living arrangements another time.

By eight, I'd taken my second shower of the day, hopefully drowning another generation of coffin flies, and had lugged the lantern back downstairs in search of dinner. I stashed the pile of nonperishable food I'd brought from Gran's—Cheetos, crackers, chips, tuna—in the cabinets, then studied the dozens of MREs Alex had brought with him last night. I'd kill for something cold, but I doubted there was a single ice cube in Orleans Parish.

I dumped some cat food and water in bowls for Sebastian, who'd been giving me the stink-eye from beneath the kitchen table since I'd let him out of his carrier, then opened an MRE for myself. Meatloaf and mashed potatoes, vanilla wafers, cocoa mix, and jelly. Military menu planners are either crazy or sadists, but the self-heating element was genius.

Between bites, I dug my cell phone out of my backpack to call Tish. She had driven from Houston to Bogalusa a few days ago to help her family clean up storm damage, but made me promise to keep her up to date on Gerry. They had been together a long time, but didn't seem interested in even living together, much less getting married. Whatever their relationship dynamic, it seemed to work. She was about ten years younger than him, which put her in her mid-forties, and was a smart woman who'd taught me a lot of ritual magic Gerry didn't know. We'd developed my grounding ritual together, and she helped me repeat it till I gained the focus to do it consistently.

On my fifth try, I finally got a call to go through.

"Thank God. I've been trying to get you since last night— it's hit and miss with any five-oh-four area code," she said. "What's the news on Gerry?"

"He's just gone, Tish. I don't know what to think." I filled her in on the trip to his house, then backed up to tell her about the visit from Jean Lafitte and the arrival of the new co-sentinel.

We sat in silence a moment while she processed it.

"Do the Elders and this enforcer really think Gerry went rogue?" she finally asked. "Do they have any proof other than his reputation for being a curmudgeon where their policies are concerned?"

I thought about my conversations with Alex. "No proof, at least nothing I've been told. But they seem to believe he's either gone rogue or he's . . ." I couldn't say *dead*. My throat closed around the word.

"Tish, do you think there's any way they're right about him taking some kind of action against the Elders?" I hated to even ask the question but I guess, like Alex's question to me, it needed asking.

Long silence. "I know Gerry's unhappy the Elders hold such iron control over the borders to the Beyond. He's felt that way a long time, but . . ." She trailed off, then started again. "I can't see him acting on it. He crossed the Elders once and paid a heavy price for it. He wouldn't do it again."

Huh? "What do you mean?"

Tish gave a short laugh. "I'm not surprised Gerry never told you—it wasn't his finest hour. He was in Edinburgh during the Wizards' War in seventy-six. He fought for the Elders, of course, but you know Gerry. He wasn't shy about telling them they were handling it wrong, that they should relax the borders instead of fighting the pretes. They finally shut him up by sending him to New Orleans as sentinel. Important job, but about as far from the halls of power as one can get."

Hmph. I'd asked Gerry once why he'd come to New Orleans. He'd talked up the city's appeal as one of the world's greatest supernatural hot spots. No mention of it being a punishment to keep him isolated from the decision making.

No wonder the Elders were suspicious. But the wizards who had openly sided with the vampires and other pretes in that war had been executed. More reason for Gerry *not* to have betrayed them.

"What do you think happened to him?" I asked.

Another pause, then a quiet voice. "What are officials doing with the bodies . . . the people they're finding who died during and after the hurricane?"

Oh God, I hadn't thought of that. "All the hospitals in Orleans Parish flooded. A makeshift morgue has been set up in St. Gabriel—I think that's just outside Baton Rouge." Few, if any, of the bodies had been identified. Hundreds had already been found in New Orleans alone, and more were being found every day. "I'll find some way to check."

"I wish I could come and help you, honey."

"I know. I'll be okay." I knew Tish's elderly parents, who were mundanes, had lost their home and she was trying to get them resettled in a trailer, plus straighten out their insurance. Her brother had his hands full with his own home loss in Ocean Beach, Mississippi. Finding Gerry—and exonerating him—would be up to me.

We talked awhile longer before the signal failed and we got disconnected. My few bites of military meatloaf sat like concrete in my stomach. I pushed the rest of it around the plastic container for a while before giving up.

I had pulled a notebook from my kitchen drawer and started sketching out the symbol from Gerry's house when I heard a scratching sound at the back door, followed by a bark. I peered out the window, but it was über-dark outside, the kind of dark city dwellers forgot about until the electrical grid went black. Surely a looter—or Jean Lafitte—wouldn't bring a dog.

I held up the fluorescent lantern and opened the door, *eek*-ing like a girl as something big and solid raced past me into the kitchen. Sebastian, puffed out like a brown dandelion, shot off the top of the fridge and into the parlor.

"What the . . . ?" I stared at an enormous golden dog with a shaggy coat, floppy ears, a big grin, and a tail that plumed over his back. A black and pink spotted tongue lolled out the side of his mouth. Too bad my wards didn't work on dogs, although this one looked about as dangerous as the Taco Bell Chihuahua.

I held a hand out for him to sniff, then scratched the top of his head. "Where did you come from?" I felt around his furry neck for a collar but came up empty.

I knew from news reports that thousands of newly homeless dogs roamed the city streets. Their owners had evacuated without them, earning their own place in the fiery pits of hell, or they'd gotten separated during the storm. This one looked healthy. If he'd been on the street almost three weeks in these conditions, he must have a talent for scrounging. He didn't seem feral.

Not that I was paranoid or anything, but I didn't want to take any chances that this wasn't a real dog. A girl can't be too careful. I put a hand on either side of his head and closed my eyes. He pulled away at first, but finally stood still while I tried to feel his energy. He gave off a little buzz, but nothing more than he'd get from crossing my wards. Certainly not enough to be a prete.

Then he stuck his big baby-blanket of a tongue out and licked my mouth. Yuck, and no way. I'd just acquired a cat that hated my guts. I wasn't ready for a French-kissing dog.

"You can't stay here," I said firmly, opening the door wider so he could leave. I got behind him and tried to push him out but he dug his toenails into the wooden floor and wouldn't budge. It was like trying to prod a balky mule, not that I'd dealt with any balky mules myself, but I'd seen the carriage drivers in the French Quarter coaxing and begging their beasts to cooperate without much luck.

The dog yawned and trotted farther into the kitchen, resting big paws on the edge of the table and grabbing my plastic MRE container with his teeth. He was after my meatloaf.

"Wait a minute, buddy." I stood stupidly at the door for a while, looking from dog to yard, but finally surrendered. "Okay, I'll give you something to eat, but: You. Are. Not. Staying. Here." I punctuated each syllable with a pointed finger as if it would make him understand me better.

He grinned and wagged his tail, spotted tongue hanging askew. He must have some chow chow in him. And maybe golden retriever. And pony.

I scraped my leftover meatloaf onto a saucer, added some tuna, and set it on the floor, then put down another bowl filled with bottled water. I spotted Sebastian back under the kitchen table, spearing the invader with a malevolent glare. Or maybe he was looking at me.

The dog gobbled the food, sucked down the bowl of water, and padded off into the parlor, followed by Sebastian.

"Hey!" I shouted, taking the lantern and following them. The dog stretched out his considerable length on one of my sofas, head propped on the arm and one paw draped over the edge. A fine, clear stream of slobber trailed down my custom upholstery. Sebastian jumped on the back of the sofa behind him and curled into a ball. He liked the dog better than me. That was truly insulting.

I tried the front door, opening it and making clicking sounds with my tongue. The dog rolled his head around and grinned at me from the shadows, his teeth picking up a gleam from the lantern. Unyielding, I opened the door wider and pointed outside.

He sighed, the weight of the world on his furry shoulders, and slouched past me out the door, flopping in a heap on the front porch.

"Fine, stay there if you want." I locked up and headed back to the kitchen, but not before I heard the soft thump of the dog settling against the door. In the lantern light, I saw a bit of golden fur poking between the door and the threshold. For the first time since returning to New Orleans, I laughed. I laughed so hard it brought tears.

Then the laughter left, the tears stayed, and I sat in the middle of the floor next to my fluorescent lantern. I cried for Gerry, for New Orleans, and for myself. I didn't know what to do for any of us.

MONDAY, SEPTEMBER 19, 2005 "Tough-as-nails survivor had only a jug of water: Rescuers find him 18 days after storm."

—THE TIMES-PICAYUNE

CHAPTER 15

Sunday had been a how-to in frustration, raising more questions. Monday, I hoped to get answers.

I'd called the St. Gabriel morgue a dozen times on Sunday, but either got no answer, had been disconnected, or spoke with yet another tired-sounding official trying to be polite. The last one said he was very sorry but I would have to be patient. More than six hundred bodies had been brought in so far from Greater New Orleans. He took Gerry's name and physical description and my phone number, but promised nothing.

I'd tried using hydromancy again, to no avail, then refreshed my mojo bag. Finally, I got the bright idea that I'd try to summon Gerry, even though I'd never heard of anyone summoning a wizard—or anyone else this side of the Beyond, for that matter. Ghosts, demons, vampires, the historical undead, yes. If I tried and it didn't work, big deal. At least I was doing something.

I gathered up some of his things to use in the summoning ritual: the pipe, a picture of the two of us taken at JazzFest year before last, one of his journals, and the Meisterstück pen. Pulling aside the throw rug in my library, I chalked in a circle and placed his belongings at north, south, east, and west. I used a small lancet to prick my finger for a few drops of blood to place on the circle and fuel the magic. Thankfully, summoning was one of only a few rituals requiring blood. Finally, I settled on a floor pillow and tried to clear my mind of everything but Gerry.

At first I thought it was working. A dark mist gathered inside the circle, tried to thicken and solidify, then dissipated. I attempted a second summoning, and a third, but couldn't even get the mist back.

Alex had showed up at lunchtime, bringing hamburgers and fries he'd found somewhere in neighboring Jefferson Parish. They had electricity. Ice. Air conditioning. Maybe even Internet service. I was jealous.

"Peace offering," he'd said, holding up the bag when I opened the door.

I smiled, feeling magnanimous in the face of fast food. "I should be the one making a peace offering, but I'll take the burger."

"It's cold, but I got tied up on the way back. Did you hear about the murder?"

It had been all over the WWL newscast I'd heard on my battery-operated radio. Another soldier on security detail had been found dead that morning in Mid-City, complete with the voodoo-ritual candles and dead rooster. That made three dead, and the media was in a lather about a serial killer. Not only was there a whackjob at large, but the murderer was preying on the soldiers in town to help us.

"You got called in?" I asked. "Anything supernatural about it?"

Alex shook his head and rattled a few loose fries out of the bag. "Not that I know of. The NOPD detective who's heading up the investigations, Ken Hachette, is a friend of mine. Well, a friend of Jake's, technically. They were in Afghanistan together and co-owned the Gator till Jake bought him out last year. Anyway, he called me in to help with the cases."

I chewed in silence a moment, savoring the grease, before I could ask, "Did you see the crime scene?"

He nodded. "I didn't see the symbol anywhere, but the area was a mess. Flood zone. Ken didn't know I was in town, or he would've called me earlier. I think I'm going out there later to look around again. See if the symbol got covered up."

"So we still don't know if we're dealing with a crazy human or a crazy prete." I savored my fries and didn't care that they were cold.

"Oh, I've been meaning to show you this." Alex opened his briefcase and pulled out a book on elven magic. "It's one of Gerry's. Did you know the staff we found was made by the elves? Or at least it fits the description in the book. Apparently, these elven staffs choose their owners. They're useless to anyone except whoever they've chosen."

That staff was downright creepy, but then again, I'd always thought elves were creepy with their mental magic and secretive ways—not that I'd ever met one. I supposedly had elves back in my gene pool somewhere, but the whole race had flittered off to the Beyond eons ago and kept to itself.

"This is going to sound bizarre, but I swear that thing moves," I said. "Almost gave me heart failure when I first noticed it, then I thought I was hallucinating. But it happens a lot. It travels from room to room." I'd been handling it a little, trying to figure out why it reacted to me, either turning warm or shooting out red sparks.

Interest lit Alex's face. "The book says they can do that— they will follow their owner. Well, the book calls it their master."

I smiled. "Except I'm not an elf, remember. It can't have claimed me as its *master*."

I flipped the book open to a page he had dog-eared and started reading.

"I saw in your file that you had elves on your mom's side of the family," he said, making me wonder what else was in that file. "Maybe you have enough for it to claim you."

"I doubt it. From what I've read, they can do really subtle mental magic. I'm about as subtle as a tank."

"You have a point." Alex shoveled the final quarter of his burger in his mouth and ignored my squinty-eyed look.

I turned back to the book. "It might help to know what those markings on the staff mean—they look similar to the ones in here. After I eat I'll go upstairs and get it, compare the runes."

"You won't have to," Alex said, pointing. The staff stood propped against the door facing. Earlier, it had been on my work-table upstairs.

After lunch, I identified most of the carvings, but they were less than illuminating. Just a series of runes for unrelated words, as near as I could tell—wind, time, earth, power, immortality, fire. Things creepy elves might like, but I did not.

Alex hadn't been the only one doing research. I had been trying to identify the voodoo symbols at Gerry's and other houses. I'd pulled a couple of reference books from my library and had started slogging through them, but the work was tedious. Oh, to be able to Google *weird voodoo-related graffiti*.

⸙

By Monday morning, I was no closer to figuring out Gerry's whereabouts and was running out of things to try. Still, visiting the morgue probably wasn't the brightest idea I've ever had.

First, I got rid of Alex, telling him I had cramps and wanted to rest. Mention cramps and guys get a panicked, deer-in-headlights look and develop a sudden urge to go hunting or drink beer. Like hormones might be contagious. Too bad they're not. The world would be a more equitable place. Or more violent. It could go either way.

He headed off to look for breaches or do something manly with the *friend* he claimed to be staying with once I'd pried out an admission he wasn't living at Jake's. He'd been vague. Probably, his friend was tall and buxom and dumb as a box of rocks. I reminded myself that the enforcer's love life didn't concern me, and that the annoyance I felt was strictly professional.

Whatever he was doing, it was happening without his tracker, which I'd lifted from his briefcase.

I took the chameleon potion I'd prepared Sunday night and dressed in khakis and a tan T-shirt. True invisibility isn't possible, but the potion works pretty well in a pinch and the neutral clothing should blend with the industrial-tan walls of the makeshift morgue. I knew the wall color because I'd asked during one of my phone calls. People will tell you anything if you are inquisitive and don't mind making a fool of yourself.

I also pulled out the magicked medical ID I'd been flashing at nice National Guardsmen all over town and an equally phony press pass I'd used on sentinel business a few years ago to gain access to the New Orleans Saints' locker room in the Superdome. A stray siren had developed a penchant for tailbacks, and an NFL play-off berth was at risk. If the Saints were having a good enough year to be in contention for the play-offs, no siren better stand in their way. One of the badges might get me onto the morgue grounds, and I had the potion for backup.

As I cranked the Pathfinder, I spotted Gandalf trotting around the corner. Yes, I'm a sucker and had kept the dog. In less than forty-eight hours, I'd given him a name, constructed a makeshift collar from a luggage tag, and turned an old length of clothesline into a leash. When stores reopened, I'd buy him the real thing. He was even sleeping in my bedroom.

He barked and ran toward the truck when he saw me getting ready to leave, so I opened the passenger door and he hopped in. He filled up the seat and spilled over the gearshift.

"So, boy, we're going on a field trip," I said, scratching the top of his head between his ears, which made him zone out in some kind of doggy stupor. I liked having a dog. He let me speak my mind, and never talked back or argued. He thought I was the smartest, coolest person on earth, and didn't cast judgment because I didn't have a lot of experience and couldn't shoot a gun. He liked to share my junk food, protected me while I slept, and didn't eat as much as one might think. The stupid cat even liked him.

Best of all, he had no emotions I needed to protect myself from and I could babble at him to keep my mind off where I was going and why.

"I wish you were my partner," I said. He grinned at me and drooled on the passenger seat. "Yeah, I know, really. It would be great. I can't get a read on Alex, and that drives me crazy. You're easy to read. You're a sweetheart."

Another good thing about dogs. You can sound like a complete idiot when you talk to them because dogs don't care. Dogs love idiots.

Gandalf stretched his body around the gearshift and laid his head on my thigh. I stroked his soft fur and sighed.

"Now, don't get me wrong. Alex is easy on the eyes. Sexiest thing I've seen since Jean Lafitte, in fact." Gandalf whined and licked my arm, and I pondered the sad state of affairs that the first sexy man I thought to compare the enforcer to was an undead pirate who might or might not have tried to kill me.

"Then there's his cousin, Jake. He has these killer dimples and he even asked me to dinner. Do you *know* how long it's been since I had a date?" I could have told him, had he asked. Two freaking years, that's how long. Wizards don't get out much.

Gandalf raised his head and looked at me with what I imagined was concern for my sanity.

"I agree," I told him. "I'm babbling." I was trying not to think too hard about where we were headed, and what I might find there. As badly as I wanted to find Gerry, I did *not* want to find him in the St. Gabriel temporary morgue. The longer it took to locate him, the more I feared no happy ending was possible.

I stroked the dog's silky ears and drove the rest of the way in silence.

Getting to St. Gabriel was an easy hour's drive; getting into the morgue proved tougher. Guards blocked the only entrance to the parking lot of the old warehouse that now housed New Orleans's dead, and a chain-link fence ran around the perimeter of the property.

The guards were firm. "No media, ma'am. No visitors. Definitely no dogs." I should have tried the doctor's badge first. Stupid. I'd just wait till the next shift came on duty.

I drove down the highway to a small truck stop, waiting for the guards to change shifts. I hated to leave Gandalf in the car but he couldn't go inside, so I left the windows down. A slice of pecan pie later—well, okay, two slices plus a hamburger for Gandalf—and I was ready to try again.

The evening-shift guards were no pushovers, either, and wouldn't go for the medical ID without an authorization from the Louisiana medical examiner's office. I decided to abandon the front-door tactic, parked a block away from the warehouse, and went for Plan B. With Gandalf chuffing beside me, I tucked my hair under a gold Saints cap and circled to the back of the property, following the railroad tracks that ran along the perimeter. Just a girl walking her dog. Dusk descended slowly over the light-industrial area, making everything look as gray as the concrete parking lot.

I found a good spot, dropped my bag beside Gandalf, and told him to stay. He whined, but sat next to the bag. I had the chameleon potion in my pocket, and as I climbed the chain-link fence, I was glad I'd opted for my Nikes instead of boots.

The guys on TV detective shows make fence-climbing look a lot easier than it is. By the time I'd lugged myself to the top and slid clumsily over, the best I could do was drop down the other side, landing on my butt in a bank of loose pea gravel. I hoped Alex's tracker wasn't broken. Gandalf whined again as I picked gravel out of my palms.

I drank the chameleon potion, wrinkling my nose at the bitter taste, and crept to a back door that had a window inset. I wore a small amulet that could provide a light source when it got dark, but for now I could still see.

I shrank against the wall as two men exited the door, heading toward a small side parking lot. Before the door clicked shut behind them, I was able to slip inside. Finally, a lucky break.

I didn't expect anything to come from it, but I pulled Alex's tracker out of my pocket and turned it on. The little LED screen turned green, and then a red dot began blinking in the center. There was something magical here, or at least I thought that's what the light meant. I couldn't exactly ask for a lesson after pilfering it.

Staying close to the walls and hoping the potion helped me blend with the institutional tan, I edged down a hallway that opened into a cavernous warehouse.

The work of the St. Gabriel morgue played out before me like a bad horror film that should have been shot in grainy black and white. Heavy-duty plastic coated the concrete floor, and on the plastic lay bundles I knew were bodies, waiting to be processed for their turn in the coolers till their date with the DNA sampler rolled around. The smell, antiseptic with an underlying tinge of decomposition, assaulted my nose and lungs, and my bare arms goose-pimpled from the cold. The AC must have been set on fifty degrees. People with clipboards and masks scurried around, looking purposeful and efficient as they strode in and out of hallways, across the main room, and back again.

I reached in my pocket and fingered my mojo bag to help dull the overwhelming sense of depression that drifted off the workers. I leaned against the wall, my stomach churning and nausea making my pecan pie poise for a bitter return. My limbs felt heavy, like they always did when I'd sucked in too much of a bad emotion. I couldn't stay here long, even with all my preparation.

Clearly, I hadn't planned this very well. Why did I think I'd be able to slip in and, one by one, slide nicely preserved bodies out of freezer cases until I confirmed that none of them were Gerry? This place was running 24/7 and no way was I going to see anything helpful.

I plastered myself against a wall, a good distance away from the activity, and pulled the tracker out again. The red light blinked faster than before. Frowning, I held it out and watched the light as I turned it to different spots in the room. There. It had definitely sped up when I held it to my left.

I scanned the area. Two hazmat-suited workers were squatting next to one of the bodies. One of them must be the source of the magic. The worker facing me had been writing on a clipboard but suddenly looked up and scanned the room. His eyes stopped on me, and I froze. No way he could see me. Unless he wasn't human.

He said something to his coworker and stared in my direction a moment longer before heading toward a door in the back. He looked back at me—it had to be at me—and jerked his head for me to follow. Maybe I needed to revise my chameleon potion recipe.

I walked slowly along the wall, not wanting anyone else to

notice me, and slid through the doorway behind the man. It opened to a small office with a single desk and two chairs. The door closed behind me, and I turned to see Mr. Hazmat taking off his hood.

"Who are you?" he said, squinting at me and frowning. "I can't see you clearly—you're hazy. But I can tell you're a wizard."

I had about a half second to decide whether to tell the truth or pretend to be a grieving citizen. As Alex had duly noted, I'm not that good an actress. "I'm a Green Congress wizard, here looking for a missing family member."

"Good luck," he said, setting his hood on the desk and adjusting the collar of his white coveralls. "We don't know who any of these people are, we're understaffed, families with missing people are frantic . . . It's a mess." He squinted at me again. "I'm Adam Lyle, Yellow Congress."

Click. Now I got it. "You're telepathic," I said. "I couldn't figure out how you knew I was there. I didn't know we had any Yellow Congress wizards in this area." It was the smallest congress by far, with wizards specializing in mental magic.

He nodded. "Yeah, wizards have a different mental signal than most people. I'm used to shutting humans out, but you came through loud and clear. And I'm not local—drove in from Houston to help."

"You're a doctor?"

He smiled. "Psychiatrist, actually. But they're too understaffed here to be that picky."

"A psychiatrist who can read thoughts. That must make you really effective." I didn't want him in my head, not one bit. No wonder Alex shielded so hard around me. Talk about an invasion of privacy.

Adam laughed. "I only get general signals from a person unless we're touching. Take you, for example. All I can really tell is that you're a wizard and you're telling me the truth, or at least the truth as you see it."

I introduced myself then, and gave him a highly edited version of my truth, ending with a physical description of Gerry. "He went missing a few days ago. This seemed like a logical place to look."

He shook his head. "There's no way to tell. Even if you narrow it down to victims who are white, middle-aged males." He sighed. "All I can tell you is no one with any magical aura still active has been brought in when I was here, and I've been here a lot the last ten days."

It had been a long shot, but I was still disappointed. I found a pad on the desk and wrote down my name and phone number. "Will you call me if any wizard turns up?"

He stuck it in a zippered pocket. "How'd you make out during the storm?" It had become the ubiquitous question around town among the few citizens who'd returned.

"Not too bad—just wind damage," I said. "I was Uptown, in the lucky twenty percent."

"I have a couple of friends, Blue Congress, who live in that area. They both teach art at Tulane." Blue Congress wizards were the artists and creatives in our world. Blues and Greens usually mainstreamed as academics.

"Have they come back yet? I've been wondering how many wizards were in town." You never know. We might need backup.

He picked up his clipboard and hood. "No, they're gone till the end of the year. I'm staying in one of their houses and keeping an eye on the other. Everything is fine except for some weird graffiti painted on their doorsteps. Same thing on both houses, but not their neighbors' places. I figure it's gang-related."

The hair on the back of my neck stood at attention. "What kind of graffiti—what does it look like?"

He gave me a curious glance and shrugged, then took out a pen and used a page from his clipboard to draw a rough illustration of the symbol I was seeing way too much of.

"You know what it means," he said—a statement, not a question. "Well, I'm getting an energy spike from you anyway."

"I don't know what it means but I've seen it a couple of other places, too. Can you give me the names and addresses of your friends?"

He wrote the information down and handed me the paper. "I put my phone number on there, too. If it turns out to be something my friends need to know, call me, okay? They're both teaching at other schools the fall semester and don't plan to come back till the university reopens, probably in January."

We left the room together, then I sneaked back to the exit and out the back door. Gandalf stood and wagged his tail when he saw me. After making sure no one was in the parking lot, I hauled myself back over the chain link, snagging my shirt on the top of the fence.

As overjoyed as Gandalf was to see me, ripped shirt and all, I didn't chatter at him on the drive home. What did those symbols mean? I had to find out. And I wondered if I had stumbled on the pattern we had been missing.

I pulled off the road at a gas station, dug my cell phone out of my pocket, and scrolled to the call log from the day Gerry went missing. *Congress of Elders.* I pressed send.

TUESDAY, SEPTEMBER 20, 2005 "Day 22: The official death toll in metropolitan New Orleans—736."

—THE TIMES-PICAYUNE

CHAPTER 16

The Speaker of the Elders hadn't been pleased to hear from me at midnight Edinburgh time, but he'd gotten me what I needed. When Alex showed up Tuesday morning, I was already scanning a printout of every wizard in the New Orleans metro area, along with addresses and emergency contact information. Only two other wizards were currently in town besides me and Adam Lyle, and both were of the elderly Blue Congress variety. Probably not much help if we needed it—talk about people who were useless in a fight. I circled their names anyway.

"Lafitte." Alex muttered the safe word to cross my wards and came in the back door, all dressed in—surprise—black. "Couldn't you have picked a better password?"

"Why are you using it anyway? The wards only work on pretes."

"Seems like a good habit." He opened the cabinet and pulled out a couple of protein bars, then poured a cup of coffee.

"Don't you have food at your *friend's* house?"

"No." He shoveled half a protein bar in his mouth and grabbed the list from the table in front of me. Looked like somebody got up on the grouchy side of his friend's bed this morning.

"What's this for?" He sat at the table and slid the list of wizards back to me. I described my visit to the morgue, conversation with Adam Lyle, and suspicion about the symbols.

"It's probably a coincidence," I said. "But I think it's worth checking out some of the addresses on this list, just to see if these symbols are marking only the homes of wizards. Maybe wizards are being targeted, and whoever's behind it did something to Gerry."

Alex eyed me over his coffee cup. "You shouldn't have gone out there by yourself. Where'd you get the list?"

"I didn't go by myself. I took my dog. Anyway, I called the Elders on the way back and the Speaker sent a courier with the list—got here around four a.m."

Alex leaned back in his chair, and I imagined I saw grudging respect on his face, or maybe it was wishful thinking. "Good job, Sherlock. We should split the list and do some cruising around today. "

"I know. I'm hoping this gives us a clue about Gerry." I fidgeted with a coaster. "The longer he's missing, the more I'm afraid this isn't going to end well. Maybe I was naïve to think it ever could have." Maybe I was naïve to be opening up to the enforcer.

"We'll figure this out. If he's out there, we'll find him—I promise."

We both knew it wasn't a promise he could keep, but it made me feel better to hear it.

I took the Uptown list and Alex took Broadmoor and Mid-City. If wizards' homes in those areas were all marked and we couldn't find the symbols on other homes nearby, it seemed safe to assume wizards were being targeted. Then we'd just have to figure out who was doing the marking, and why.

I drove through Uptown one neighborhood at a time, beginning at the big bend in the Mississippi River at the triangular area called Black Pearl and moving outward in a widening arc. I had twelve names on my list, and none of them were in town.

I found the first address, parked the Pathfinder, and walked the block end to end, both sides of the street. Only the wizard's house, a small pink shotgun with ornate gingerbread trim, had been marked with the symbol, spray-painted in white at the foot of the stairs leading to the front door.

The pattern held throughout my list, and I headed home with the beginnings of a headache. It didn't matter how long it took. I would find the meaning of that symbol today. If all wizards' houses were marked with the same symbol we found at Gerry's, that made Gerry a potential victim, not a rogue. A rogue wouldn't target his own house.

Alex probably wouldn't get finished with his list until noon, so I had an hour to kill. I pulled out a few references I thought might help in researching the symbols, then did some necessary domestic chores I'd been putting off, namely laundry, which had to be hand-washed in a sink full of questionable water and hung around the bathroom. I really missed electricity.

No point starting my research till Alex came back, so I decided to sweep off the leaves and branches from the hurricane that still littered my porch. In front of my house, traffic had started picking up on Magazine Street—mostly construction workers and soldiers. That, plus the fact that my parking space was in back, meant I rarely used my front door. I sure hadn't used it since it got covered in plywood after Jean Lafitte's visit.

Manual labor distracted me from Gerry and wizard conspiracies for a few minutes before I saw it: the symbol of rectangles and stars, painted on the sidewalk in red at the foot of my front steps. I sat hard on the top step, staring at it. I hadn't seen any other red symbols today—they'd all been white. The only other red symbol had been at Gerry's.

I'd been sitting there several minutes when from behind I heard Alex walking through the house. "I'm out front."

"You were right about the—" He stopped, then sat on the step next to me, deflated. "Shit. How long has it been there?"

"I don't know. I never use the front door, so it could have been here since right after Lafitte came to visit. Did you see any red symbols today, or were they all white?"

He thought a moment. "All white, I'm pretty sure. And you were right. It's only wizards' houses that are marked. And now this." Alex looked worried. Enforcers shouldn't look worried.

"We've got to find that symbol."

We grabbed a quick MRE for lunch, then settled on the living room sofas with all the reference books I could find on voodoo history and symbology. I'd been going through the largest dictionary almost two hours before I found a similar mark. Instead of the cross and rectangles, it was made up of two large intersecting Vs, with stars coming off it at six points. I held the book toward the window to more easily read the small text: *Vévé or symbol of Ayizan, the voodoo goddess of commerce.*

"Holy crap. I think it's a symbol for one of the voodoo gods, not one of the rituals. We should have thought of that." I slammed the book and ran upstairs to the library, Alex following close behind.

"New Orleans voodoo wasn't based on the traditional African religion, but a version that developed in the West Indies," I said, scanning the assortment of books on deities until I found one on the Haitian Vodou pantheon. I settled on the love seat and started flipping through it. "They have a different set of gods."

Now that I knew what to look for, the search took less than five minutes. "Here it is," I said, reading. "It's the vévé, or symbol, of the Haitian Vodou god Baron Samedi, and is used to invoke him or offer sacrifices to him."

"Is there a chapter on Samedi?" Alex looked the name up in the African book, but it wasn't there. "We need to find out all we can about him."

He moved to the love seat beside me, close enough to read my book and distract me with his presence all at the same time. I jerked my mind from broad shoulders to the book's index and began to flip pages.

Samedi was a popular guy. "He's the god of the dead, or of the crossroads between life and death," I read, scanning through the descriptions. "He's the leader of a group of loa called the Barons. Looks like a skeleton in a top hat and tails. Wears dark glasses with one lens missing. He seems to thrive on sex and debauchery."

Great. Sounded like a guy that would be popular in New Orleans, or at least in the touristy areas.

I scanned another couple of pages. "Followers believe Baron Samedi is the god that determines who lives and who dies, and is the head of the Vodou gods who are linked to magic, ancestor worship, and death. Believers don't consider him evil, just capricious."

Alex reached across me to lift a page and better see the illustrations. "I don't believe in voodoo gods, but some murderous SOB obviously does. If it weren't for the wizards' houses being targeted I wouldn't think this was supernatural at all, but just a nutcase."

I stared at the book's drawing of the vévé. "I don't believe in those gods either, from a religious standpoint. But as far as the Beyond goes, what we believe doesn't matter. The fact that a lot of people *do* believe is enough to make him real. And voodoo supposedly still has an active presence in parts of New Orleans. Certainly did in its past. And the fact that wizards' houses are being marked means it has to be supernatural."

"So, you think the undead Marie Laveau has come back with some agenda like Lafitte did, and is making sacrifices to this Samedi guy?" Alex leaned back on the love seat and stretched his legs, one heavy, black-clad thigh running alongside my leg.

Sure was hot in this house.

I got up and paced the library. "Marie Laveau would make sense. She's by far the best-known voodoo practitioner who ever lived here. But why would she be killing soldiers? Since she's marking their houses, why not kill wizards?"

We stared at each other.

Alex was already punching a number into his cell phone. "I need to talk to Ken again—let him know these symbols are showing up on houses. I'll leave out the wizard part. Maybe they can at least put some patrols out at the addresses where the wizards are in town."

Including mine. I doubted the cops had the manpower for extra patrols, or that it would do much good, but I slid a pad and pen in front of him anyway.

He stared at the notes after ending his call. "Our symbol was painted at the scene of all three murders—they finally uncovered it on the sidewalk in the last one. Ken says they don't have any leads, and they're frustrated. The dead soldier this last time was from somewhere in Texas, no ties to the local voodoo community that anyone has found. First victim was from California, second from Virginia."

"Do the police know what the symbol is?"

"No, they made the voodoo connection because of the candles and the dead roosters. Second murder also had a kind of altar set up with a bottle of rum on it. Ken's best guess is that the murders are some warped kind of blood sacrifice, maybe an appeal to the gods for hurricane relief."

I huffed. "Why kill the soldiers who are helping us, then?

The sacrifice part sounds right, but what does it have to do with wizards?"

"Any chance the soldiers were wizards?"

I didn't think so, but it warranted another call to the Elders. I was beginning to think we needed our own Elder hotline.

WEDNESDAY, SEPTEMBER 21, 2005 "The east bank of New Orleans may not have safe tap water for up to two more months, Sewerage & Water Board officials revealed Tuesday, further jeopardizing plans to begin a staggered repopulation of un-flooded Uptown neighborhoods . . ."

—THE TIMES-PICAYUNE

CHAPTER 17

The murdered soldiers were not wizards, but the Elders were "concerned that spillover from the breaches with the Beyond might be inadvertently impacting the nonwizarding population." Which was a bureaucratic way of saying they didn't want human cops dragged into anything related to magic. So in true Elder fashion, instead of doing the expedient thing and send-ing us out to track down the voodoo bad guys, they told us to sit tight while they rattled some red tape.

Great. *That* would help find Gerry. To stay busy till the magical desk jockeys got their horses lined up, I began sorting through the boxes filled with Gerry's books and papers. At the bottom of the third box, stuck between *The Way of All Vampyres* and a tome on wizarding history, was Gerry's last journal.

I thought about calling Alex, but the citywide dusk-to-dawn curfew had already gone into effect and he'd headed back to wherever Alex went at night. I'd eaten dinner, checked my wards, showered, put on a tank top and shorts, and settled in the library. Gandalf snored in front of the fireplace and Sebastian watched me suspiciously from atop my worktable. Calling Alex would ruin our little picture of domestic bliss.

I turned to Gerry's last journal entry, September 13, the day before he disappeared.

Helicopter noise driving me mad, but rescuers finally stopped pressuring me to leave. They dropped water and military rations for me this a.m. Interesting visit from Beyond. Levees not the only hurricane breaches!

That was it. No sense of fear or urgency. Obviously, he didn't have to leave in search of food. Whoever visited him from the Beyond must be behind his disappearance, and maybe was somebody he'd dealt with before since he wasn't upset. To me, that said Jean Lafitte or Marie Laveau—and Marie personified New Orleans voodoo. Besides, I'd have lifted something from Lafitte's emotions when we'd played tussle on my living room floor if he'd been involved in any shenanigans other than his own lust for vengeance—or, well, just lust.

Marie, though, also had approached Gerry in the past, looking for an inroad back into modern-day New Orleans. Maybe after the hurricane, she came back, offered Gerry a deal, and then double-crossed him. Then he'd gone into hiding to get away from her and figured out some way to make himself undetectable.

It was all speculation, but I hadn't heard a better theory yet.

I was still pondering the possibilities the next morning at breakfast. I'd dropped my wards, let Gandalf out, and was sitting at the kitchen table reading Gerry's journal and celebrating the return of electricity and air conditioning when Alex waltzed in the back door, my neighbor Eugenie hanging on his arm and every word out of his mouth. He was in dark and dangerous flirting mode—something he hadn't used on me since our first meeting, thank God.

Eugenie had been playing with her hair color again and was tugging at blue-tipped spikes with the hand that wasn't latched on to Alex. Her shorts were too tight, her top too low-cut, and her laugh echoed through the house. I wrapped my arms around her in a hug because I had missed her so much. Whenever she thought he wasn't paying attention, she'd look meaningfully at Alex and raise her eyebrows. I ignored her.

Someone pounded on the front door, startling all of us.

"I'll get it," Alex said. "Probably the National Guard again." Soldiers had been coming by several times a day since Monday, telling us to evacuate in advance of Hurricane Rita. The storm had grown to Katrina proportions in the Gulf, and the New Orleans civilian population—not counting journalists—was estimated at fewer than fifty. Alex had taken to pulling his FBI badge out to get rid of them.

Eugenie planned to leave again this morning, headed back to Shreveport until Rita blew through. She'd just sneaked into town long enough to check her house.

"Honey, my roof is trashed worse than the Quarter after Mardi Gras. Water came in everywhere upstairs," she said. "My insurance guy says it'll be a month before he can even come out and look at it."

I held my breath, hoping she wouldn't call on my supposed expertise in risk management to assess her insurance company's liability. Since the cedar hadn't done any damage to my own roof, I'd decided not to bother filing a claim.

She had more important things on her mind. Eugenie loved romance and was still fixated on Alex. She lowered her voice to a conspiratorial whisper. "Where did you find that great big pretty man? You been holding out on me."

The sight of Alex had apparently pushed most of her

insurance concerns aside, and I wondered what he would think about being called pretty. Probably pull a gun on her.

"He's just a friend. Came down from Picayune to help me clean out Gerry's house."

Eugenie's green eyes narrowed. "Darlin', anybody with that nice little butt ain't friendship material. Besides, he don't consider *you* a friend. Says you two been seein' each other."

I scowled in the direction of the front door. "Oh, did he?"

"Now, DJ. Don't blow it. That one's a keeper, and you've gotta admit your track record with guys is, well, sorta pathetic."

She was being kind. It was worse than pathetic. "Yeah, well, we'll see."

We did a quick comparison of evacuation horror stories, and she won for most horrific. She'd been stuck for a month in a two-bedroom house in Shreveport with her Junior League sister, her pontificating attorney brother-in-law, their five-year-old-going-on-twenty twin daughters, and a pair of yappy mini schnauzers.

"I was a big hit with the girls after I gave them my makeup bag. Plus, it made my brother-in-law so mad his face turned purple."

A pang of sadness hit me, listening to Eugenie talk. It felt so normal, like nothing had changed. But everything had changed.

After a few minutes, Alex returned from answering the door and sent Eugenie into a virtual swoon, especially since I'd let it slip that he was an FBI agent. He wore a cream-colored shirt with the sleeves rolled up to his elbows, and tight jeans worn to a light blue in all the right places. It was the first time I'd seen him out of basic black, and I had to admit he could be a keeper except for a few control issues and that bit with his secretive personal life. And the grenades.

"Who was at the door?" I asked. "Another evacuation warning?"

"Yeah." He dug in his briefcase and fished a protein bar out of his never-ending supply. If Eugenie was going to crush on Alex, I needed to warn her about his tendency to turn monosyllabic without notice.

"So, Alex honey, what does a big FBI agent keep in his briefcase?" I swear Eugenie batted her eyelashes at him. See, that was the difference between us. I sneaked around and plundered through his briefcase when he wasn't looking, and Eugenie just asked him. Maybe my distrustful nature was hampering my love life.

He gave her a smoldering look. "If I told you, I might have to shoot you."

"I bet you have a real big gun." She flashed a dazzling grin his way.

I was going to barf.

He did the slow, lazy smiling thing guaranteed to make her feel warm and fuzzy the rest of the day, and poured himself some coffee.

I had pilfered through his briefcase the day I stole the tracker, so I knew the only things in there were a cell phone, a box of protein bars, a couple of knives, some ammo clips, and a gun. A moderate-size gun.

Eugenie finally got tired of flirting and headed across the street to pack for Shreveport. As soon as the door closed behind her, Alex went into the living room and came back with a large cardboard box. In large, flowery script, it was addressed to "Drusilla Jaco and Alexander Warin, Sentinels." In the return address space was one word: "Elders."

"Where did that come from? It was at the door?"

"No, that really was a soldier telling us to evacuate, but you got a call from the Elders while I was in the other room—your cell was on the coffee table. They sent this to the transport in

your library." I'd left the courier transport open the night they
sent the list of wizard addresses. One never knew when a transport to headquarters might come in handy, especially these days.
Edinburgh might make a good place to hide from Jean Lafitte.
Or Marie Laveau.

Alex pulled out a penknife to cut the box open, and we
peered inside at what looked like a large light table, the kind
used by photographers and graphic designers. Only there was
no plug.

"What is it?" Alex asked.

"The screen on it looks sort of like Gerry's big tracker.
Maybe it's a smaller version."

Alex held up his hands. "I'm not touching it. I broke the
one at Gerry's house."

I lifted it from the box and took it to the office desk. We
stood on either side of it, waiting expectantly. Nothing happened.

"Maybe I have to activate it. I might have enough juice since
this one's smaller." I touched the edges of the screen and willed a
bit of magical energy into it. Within seconds, it lit from below
and a series of dark lines began forming an image. It was like
holding an oversize Etch-a-Sketch while someone operated it
from underneath, only in blazing color.

"Glad mine runs on double-A batteries," Alex said, leaning
over to look at the screen. "What are we looking at?"

"A map of New Orleans." I looked at the familiar crescent
shape of the Mississippi River as it wound through the city. The
map marked each of the seventy-two distinct neighborhoods, including current flood levels and habitation. In Uptown, my house
popped out in purple, the magical version of YOU ARE HERE.

Alex dug in the box, pulled out a folded sheet of paper we
had missed earlier, and read it aloud.

Now that most areas have been drained of floodwater, please begin investigating temporal or lateral breaches between New Orleans and the Beyond, as time permits. Blinking signals will indicate breaches. Until permanent repairs are made, please note that most signals will be false alarms.

"Wonder why they didn't send this earlier?" Alex asked.

"Maybe the breaches are mostly in areas that were flooded and we wouldn't have been able to get to them," I said, looking at the map. "Or maybe there were so many false-alarm breaches they thought it would be a waste of time."

He moved beside me, shifting the screen to look at it more closely. Red stars had begun popping up on the map, and all of them were blinking.

"Good grief. All those are breaches?" I counted the blinking stars—sixteen of them. The stars were bigger than the street names so I couldn't tell their exact location. Using my index finger, I stabbed at one in frustration. With a soft whirring noise, a portion of the map rose from the grid. The blinking light disappeared and in its place was an address in the Central Business District.

Alex wrote down the address on a notepad while I punched the second blinking star: a spot in the French Quarter. We wrote down all sixteen addresses. One was in Lakeview—Gerry's house.

"I want to check Gerry's first," I said. "We can tell from your portable tracker if it's the old one from whatever showed up there after the storm, or if it's new."

Alex set his notepad down and stared at me. "What are you talking about? How do you know for sure anything showed up after the storm?"

Oops. I'd meant to tell him about finding Gerry's most recent journal. I really had. Eugenie had distracted me. "Gerry

had a visitor the day before he went missing. That's all I know."
I went back in the kitchen and brought it to him.

"Why didn't you call me?" He frowned as he read the last
entry. "Are you sure this is all you found?"

"Yes." I turned to go upstairs for my backpack. He wasn't
the only one who could converse in single syllables.

I'd planned to spend the morning calling the last people
Gerry had talked to before he disappeared—I'd pulled their
names from the journal. Instead, I'd check out a few breaches
with Alex and see if I could wipe the suspicious look off his
face.

I slid small vials of salt and mercury in my pocket, then
checked the contents of my backpack: premixed potions for camouflage and immobilization; elixir of magnolia root and liken-
grass for memory modification; and duct tape and WD-40.
Anything magic couldn't fix, duct tape and WD-40 could.

My nerves jittered as I gathered my supplies. This is what
I'd been waiting for, wasn't it? The chance to prove I could
handle runs on my own? Oh God, *please* don't make me have to
be rescued by the enforcer.

I took a few deep breaths, grabbed my bag, and got downstairs just as Alex came in the back door. I stopped and gawked.

He'd slipped on a black sports jacket and was checking the
clip on a big black pistol. Not the little one from his briefcase, but
the one from our first meeting. I had no idea where he'd been
hiding it. He probably had weaponry stashed all over my house.

He slid the pistol into a shoulder holster under the jacket
and picked up the shotgun he'd used to blow Jean Lafitte back
to the Beyond. Finally, he clipped a tracker onto his belt—must
have been a duplicate, because I still had the one I'd stolen from
him hidden in my dresser. Just because I didn't see any grenades didn't mean he wasn't carrying.

Not in my town. "Whoa, cowboy," I said, holding up my

hands. "We're just checking things out, not blasting our way into the Beyond."

If Alex thought we were storming into Lakeview or the CBD, guns ablaze, he needed a reality check. Mollycoddling preternatural interlopers like my favorite undead pirate could be tedious, but it was better than blowing their heads off. Besides, there was no point in overly pissing off the undead, just on principle. For one thing, you never knew when they'd come back.

Plus, discretion is an important part of this business. Nothing would attract the attention of real cops, not to mention the nervous young National Guardsmen swarming all over New Orleans, like a big Mississippi boy wielding deadly weapons in broad daylight. They were understandably jumpy, and they might shoot Alex before he could whip out his FBI badge.

I tried to explain all this.

Alex didn't care. "We try it your way first, but this is what I do. Live with it." His expression dared me to argue.

I wasn't sure which worried me more—going into a potentially volatile situation with him or without him. Not that I had a choice. "Come on, then."

I scowled at him as I walked out the back door and headed for the Pathfinder. I was driving; he was riding shotgun. Literally.

CHAPTER 18

Nothing much had changed at Gerry's except we could get there without a boat, and I wasn't nearly as squeamish about getting mud on my vehicle as Alex. I cringed as I walked across the living room, trying not to stir up the odor of swamp crud soaked into rotting carpet. I stood next to the pass-through into the kitchen and studied the living room wall. In two days, the mold had visibly advanced in its march toward the ceiling. I'd left my mask hanging around my neck when I walked in, but now snapped it over my nose and mouth.

Alex's tracker screen remained blank as we walked through the rooms. It was just another empty, flooded house full of muck and memories. I looked closely at the transport in Gerry's bedroom, looking for any clue to his visitor. Nothing.

Back outside, we studied the remaining addresses and decided to visit the unflooded areas first, where more people were around who might be impacted by an active breach.

First up, the CBD, where we found an undead Huey Long pontificating in Lafayette Square before a gaggle of camo-wearing guardsmen and four or five sweating cleanup workers in stripped-down hazmat suits. He'd wandered in, obviously thinking he could do a better job than the current politicians in cleaning up the post-hurricane mess. I figured a lot of folks would agree with him.

I'd convinced Alex to leave the shotgun in the car, and we managed to lure Huey away from his audience and dispatch him to the Beyond under the pretense of sending him to the governor's mansion in Baton Rouge to take over the cleanup efforts. He'd probably be back as soon as he figured out we'd led him down a primrose path straight to Old Orleans.

Then we headed to the French Quarter, where we found a goblin sitting in a corner bar on Decatur, downing Jack Daniel's. I wondered where he'd gotten money to pay for it.

His dark skin was leathery and wrinkled, gray hair long and plaited into pigtails that trailed down the sides of his neck from beneath a red bandanna do-rag. He looked like a really decrepit Willie Nelson and glared at us with beady black eyes as we approached. Alex finally forced him to cooperate with the threat of a cold iron blade.

"I don't know why you bothered," I said. "He just wants to get drunk, and goblins don't like to fool with humans unless they're serving alcohol. The breaches are obviously standing wide open. He'll just come back."

Alex looked at the next breach address and grimaced. "It's the principle."

We got in the Pathfinder to head for another blind date with the Beyond in a different part of the Quarter. "We have real work to be doing, and this feels like busywork," I groused, slamming on my brakes to make way for a speeding Hummer.

"There's not a lot we can be doing about Gerry without more information," Alex said. "We need to at least check these breaches out."

Maybe he didn't know of things we could be doing, but I

did. "Well, I've been thinking . . . maybe I should try to summon Marie Laveau."

Alex slammed his foot on an imaginary brake pedal on the passenger side as I dodged a Jeep. "Watch where you're going. And don't summon anybody. Don't even think about summoning anybody."

"Why not? Marie Laveau, or some of the voodoo followers, are involved in all this somehow. Why not just ask? Even if it isn't her, she might know something. I'll even let you shoot her." If all else fails, dangle the promise of violence in front of him.

Alex let out a breath as I parked on Royal Street. "Look, the Elders said wait so we wait. Whatever this voodoo thing is, it might be in violation of an existing treaty and they'll want to explore that first. Sending us after Marie Laveau would be a last resort."

Somehow, our positions had been reversed. He was playing the politician and I was advocating violence. We might not be good for each other.

I let it go. I didn't need his permission. If I wanted to summon Marie Laveau, Jean Lafitte, or Elvis, for that matter, it was no concern of his.

The next address given us by the magic box, as I had decided to call the Elders' new mode of communication, was at Royal and St. Louis. In normal times this was a busy corner, with the massive old Royal Orleans hotel, framed by Antoine's and Brennan's restaurants and an assortment of specialty shops carrying everything from collector porcelain dolls to antique firearms.

Today, like the rest of the Quarter, it was mostly deserted. A couple of stray locals who'd refused to evacuate for Rita wandered down the street, and police officers buzzed in and out of the eighth-district station on Royal. We had our pick of parking places, unheard of in the Quarter pre-Katrina.

Next time I'm having a chat with the Elders, I'm going to suggest improvements to their reconnaissance methods. Too much guesswork. We didn't know if we were looking for a demon from hell or a rampaging politician, assuming there was a discernible difference. Alex's tracker headed us in the right direction but didn't tell us what we were looking for.

Finally we heard him, a lone cornet player sitting on the curb of St. Peter Street in front of Preservation Hall. Since the early 1960s, it had been the Mecca of traditional New Orleans jazz. I'd heard Katrina had battered its roof, scattered the musicians, and shut it down indefinitely.

I recognized the musician immediately—Louis Armstrong, with his close-cropped hair and a face that looked like it had done more laughing than frowning. He wasn't laughing now. A few soldiers and bohemian Quarter residents gathered around him, their faces solemn. More than a few wiped away tears, but the set of their jaws was hard. We'd all mourn for a while, but at the end of the day we were a tough lot, and we'd survive.

At the end of the song, the cornetist bowed his head, and the onlookers applauded.

The streetlights flickered on to signal nightfall, drawing an even bigger round of applause. Electricity! It felt like a luxury, even though the juice had been back on a couple of days in the Quarter and Uptown. I'd never take it for granted again.

Louis got to his feet, and we waited while several people crowded around him. He handled the attention like someone who was used to it.

"Yeah, I hear that a lot," he told a young couple marveling at his resemblance to *the* Louis Armstrong. "We mighta been related back in the family somewhere—you never know 'bout those things."

He pulled a white handkerchief from the breast pocket of his black suit and wiped his face with it. The temperature hovered around ninety, but he didn't seem to mind despite the old-fashioned suit and bow tie. After making people cry with his music, he was now teasing them into laughter.

Louis was one smart cookie. If he'd come back claiming to be the memory-fueled version of the city's most famous musician, we'd be doing damage control. Instead, he was charming his new fans without ever saying who he was or what he was doing here.

Finally, the last of the crowd wandered away, and Alex and I introduced ourselves. He squinted at me and gave me the patented Armstrong grin. "Never did meet a wizard before, I have to say. But I figured somebody would know if I just came wanderin' out of the Beyond."

"Mr. Armstrong, exactly how did you get here?" Alex asked. "Did someone summon you from this side, or send you from the Beyond?" We weren't sure if our historical undead were just stumbling into the breaches or coming across intentionally. No questions about the goblin's motive. Goblins followed the alcohol.

"Call me Pops," he said. "Everybody does. No, I came on my own. I wanted to see what happened in the hurricane." Louis's gravelly voice sank to a whisper as he nodded toward Preservation Hall. "Never thought I'd see this place closed down."

"Can we buy you dinner?" I asked, earning a startled look from Alex. I wasn't sure if he was shocked at the invitation or the idea that the historical undead, unlike garden-variety ghosts or other undead like vampires, could eat, drink, and (if Jean Lafitte was any indication) engage in all kinds of human activities. The only thing they couldn't do was die—at least not unless everyone forgot about them and took away the memory magic that fueled them.

Besides, I had an ulterior motive—I thought Pops might be able to tell us how riled up the scarier denizens of the Beyond might be.

The only open French Quarter restaurant we found was on Esplanade, a small mom-and-pop dive already crowded with off-duty guardsmen. They were bellied up to the bar three bodies thick, snagging bottles of cold beer as fast as the bartender could open them.

Once we'd gotten a table and ordered burgers—the only thing on the chalkboard menu—I touched the legendary bandleader on the arm. "Louis, how did you get here? Did anyone help you?"

Louis took a big sip of soda and smacked his lips. "Man, that's good." His smile faded. "Old Orleans is buzzing about the hurricane and how easy it is to come across now."

Old Orleans lay like a thin veneer between modern New Orleans and the rest of the Beyond. Most of the historical undead lived there, plus anybody else from the Beyond who wanted a change of scenery. It was a free-for-all zone for preternaturals and a dangerous place for mortals to wander, or so I'd heard.

"Are there people in Old Orleans involved with voodoo?" Alex asked. "Do you know if Marie Laveau is there?"

Louis took a bite of his burger and nodded. "She's there all right. But I got nothing to do with her. She don't mess with me, and I don't mess with her."

A kernel of a plan nudged at my brain. "But you play in clubs there, right?" I asked. "And you hear things?"

"Yes, I play. And I guess I could hear things but I mind my own business, you know what I mean?"

I chewed my lip and pushed my burger away. Suddenly I wasn't so hungry. I wondered how close the Elders were to repairing the breaches and doubted the Speaker would give me a straight answer if I asked. To find Gerry and see how he fit in with the voodoo puzzle, I'd have to do it myself.

"Louis, would you like to stay in New Orleans awhile?" I

asked. "Maybe play a little music?" From my peripheral vision, I saw Alex's eyebrows meet in the middle of his face.

"I would, Drusilla," Louis said. "But where would I stay? And where would I play?" He chuckled at his own rhyme.

I slid my gaze to Alex, who was giving me his most intimidating stare. It didn't work. "Any ideas? Can Louis stay at Jake's since you aren't living there?"

He clenched his jaw and pulled his phone out. I could practically see the wheels turning in his head: the good little soldier wondering what I was up to, if the Elders would approve of it, and figuring the answering was probably no. He made the call anyway. I think I was winning the bad influence contest.

While Alex called Jake, I filled Louis in on the basics of cell phones, which he found fascinating. If we had time, we'd have to show him the Internet.

"Okay, I think we've solved the problem," Alex said, snapping the phone shut. "Louis, how would you like a few days at the Green Gator? My cousin Jake owns it, over on Bourbon Street. He just reopened. You could play there at night, and he has an apartment upstairs you can stay in."

Louis raised his eyebrows. "What's the catch?" Louis hadn't been born yesterday, after all. There's always a catch.

CHAPTER 19

It took some convincing, but Louis finally agreed to be my spy. I had no doubt Alex would go running to the Elders as soon as he got a chance.

"I told Jake your name was Jackie Williams and you were a Louis Armstrong impersonator," Alex said as we got back in the Pathfinder and headed for Bourbon Street.

Talk about an understatement. I wasn't too concerned about anyone finding Louis suspicious, though. Ordinary people don't know there's magic in their midst and will go to great lengths to explain away things they don't understand. This just might work. Louis would play the Gator at night and live upstairs at Jake's, but would keep tabs on the Beyond during the daytime and report back to us.

"Don't get involved in anything yourself," I said. "Just tell us anything you hear involving voodoo practitioners or gods—or wizards."

He sat in the front seat, studying the storefronts as we drove through the Quarter. "Oh, you don't have to worry about me

getting involved, no ma'am," he said, laughing. "I want nothing to do with those people."

I had a feeling his definition of *those people* differed from my
dad's and Gran's.

The Gator was open, and we headed in to get Jackie Williams squared away with Jake. The lone bartender, Leyla, stood
behind the long wooden bar that ran along the left side of the
room, tossing long black hair over supermodel shoulders the
color of café au lait. She gave Alex soulful cow eyes as he introduced us. He winked at her and got a giggle in return. Oh,
please.

Jake walked in from the back hallway and I knew just how
Leyla felt.

He nodded at Alex, shook hands with Louis, and gave me a
smile that made my heart speed up. What was it about this guy?
The dimples were nice, but I thought the biggest attraction was
his high normal factor. He was simple and safe and plain-vanilla
human.

Jake tossed a key to Alex. "Why don't you help Jackie there
settle into his room? I'll keep DJ company till you come back
down, and then Jackie and I can talk business."

Alex stopped just short of a snarl and led Louis toward the
back hallway. Jake got Leyla's attention and pointed toward
the back. She nodded and flicked a cool, appraising glance at me
before turning back to the bar.

A small stage on the right held a piano and bench, and an
old-fashioned jukebox in the corner pumped zydeco music to
the small crowd already filling the scattered tables. Mostly cops
and soldiers, judging by the haircuts.

"Let's get away from the jukebox." Jake put a hand on my
shoulder and guided me toward the far wall. He leaned close to
my ear so I could hear him. "You want something to drink?"

I shook my head and fought the urge to make cow eyes and giggle.

From the front of the bar, one couldn't see the three back booths tucked in a little area set off from the main room and muffled from the worst of the noise. I slid into the last booth on one side of the table, and Jake took the other side. I noticed he kept his right leg almost straight when he slid into the booth. That one definitely hadn't healed right.

I waited for him to say something, and laughed when he seemed to be waiting for me to start. "I'm not very good at small talk," I said, feeling every bit the geeky social misfit I was.

"Okay, let's start with easy things." He smiled. "You're a native? You talk like a native."

I wasn't sure he meant that as a compliment. "You mean I speak Yat?" Secretly I was pleased. I liked the local accent, its nickname taken from the universal local greeting, *Where y'at*. "My family in Alabama would come after you with a shotgun for saying such a thing."

"Alabama." He grinned. "I like Alabama. Alabama and Louisiana make folks in Mississippi feel good about ourselves—y'all always keep us from ranking dead last in stuff like literacy and life expectancy."

I laughed, but couldn't argue with him.

We talked easily for a while. I gave the short explanation of risk management, the perfect cover occupation because either people don't understand it or find it boring. He talked about the ins and outs of running a business in the French Quarter, and of growing up in Picayune.

He reached across the table and took one of my hands, turning it over and tracing his thumb across my palm. "You and Alex. Am I gonna be stepping on any toes if I ask you out?"

I curled my fingers around his thumb. "Alex and I are just friends. And you already did ask me out, remember?"

Speak of the devil. Alex and Louis rounded the corner and stopped next to the booth. I tried to pull my hand away but Jake held on, watching his cousin.

Alex didn't react. "Let's go. Jackie needs to talk to Jake about his performing schedule."

He was quiet on the walk back to the Pathfinder. I waited for him to bring up the whole Jake handholding thing.

"This is really not a good idea." He finally spoke up after I'd driven two blocks.

"Jake is none of your business."

He looked at me, frowning. "I wasn't talking about you and Jake, although that's not a good idea either. I was talking about using Louis Armstrong as a spy."

Oh, that. "What the Elders don't hear from you won't hurt them."

"You don't think they'll know?"

I shrugged. "Maybe, maybe not. They can't tell which breaches are being used and which ones aren't. All I know is they're dragging their feet playing politics instead of looking for Gerry. Plus, three soldiers have died, and there's some voodoo threat to the wizards in town. At least we're *doing* something."

He gazed out the window. I barely heard him mutter, "Maybe so."

While Alex pondered his own moral duty to the Elders, I pondered Jake and Alex. And Leyla. Tall, pretty Leyla whose gaze followed Alex around the room like a heat-seeking missile. Not that I cared. Still, I'd be better able to do my job if my curiosity were satisfied.

"So, Alex, why don't I drop you off at your friend's place instead of going all the way to my house to get your car? I can pick you up in the morning."

"No, go on to your house. I might need my car tonight."

We were already out past curfew. I knew a lame excuse

when I heard one. "Why don't you want me to know where you live? Because you're living with Leyla?"

He stared at me, his face glowing a little green from the dashboard lights. "Huh? I barely know Leyla. Why would you think I was living with Leyla?"

"So who are you living with? Why is it such a big freaking secret?"

Silence. Eyes straight ahead. Brain racing like a hamster on an exercise wheel.

"It's not such a hard question, Alex."

Finally, he sighed. "You aren't going to like it. But that voodoo symbol in front of your house worries me and I never know when you're going to do something crazy like go to the morgue."

Doing crazy things beat doing nothing. "What does that have to do with where you've been living?"

"I've been living with you. You just didn't know it."

I blinked.

"Gandalf," he said.

"What about Gandalf? You haven't even seen Gandalf."

Alex took a deep breath. "I *am* Gandalf. I'm a shapeshifter." He still didn't look at me, even when I ran the Pathfinder onto a sidewalk and jerked it to a stop a foot from a trash pile the size of a small office building.

I stared at Alex's profile, and the line of dominoes began falling. Alex and Gandalf were never around at the same time. Alex had ties to the were community, which a shapeshifter probably would. He always used the password to cross my security wards even though I told him humans didn't need to. The reason Gandalf seemed to listen so well was because he had Alex's brain.

I'd picked up a buzz of energy around him before, but there had always been something else to blame it on. I shut my eyes and sent out my empathic senses, and there it was—that light aura of magic I'd been blaming on wards and magical herbs. What an idiot.

I banged my head on the steering wheel. How many nights had that freakin' dog been sleeping in my bedroom? How many secrets had I told him? I groaned in mortification. "Please tell me you didn't understand all those late-night heart-to-heart talks I've been having with Gandalf."

Alex looked sheepish, in a canine sort of way, then grinned. Oh yeah, *now* the man grins. I didn't even know he had teeth.

"I know you think I'm hot." Then the grin faded. "Of course, you think Jake's hot, too, and Jean Lafitte, who's not even alive. You're really screwed up, you know that?"

I couldn't even look at him. I might have to put in for a transfer. I might have to change my name, abandon magic altogether, move back to Alabama, and marry a pig farmer. My grandmother would be thrilled.

He turned serious. "A lot of enforcers are either shifters or were. You were stubborn and wouldn't let me stay with you, so I figured I'd give you a more palatable form of protection." He shrugged. "It seemed like a good idea, although I kept waiting for someone to ask why I kept having to shower at the FBI offices or wander up and find me naked on your porch since it's the only place I can find to shift back."

Too much information.

I could be calm and mature about this. I assumed an air of casual curiosity. "Can you only turn into a dog, or other animals as well—a cow or a bat or something?"

"A *cow*?" Alex looked offended. "Most shifters have a particular form they take. Mine has always been a dog."

I didn't know whether to laugh or beat him over the head with the elven staff, which I just noticed had made its way to my backseat. I needed to figure out what that thing could do, other than be creepy.

This was a sad turn of events. I had really grown attached to Gandalf. He was a lot easier to get along with than Alex, and he didn't play with guns.

Another reality hit me. "So you're telling me you don't actually have a place to live and we just gave Jake's spare apartment to Louis Armstrong?"

He gritted his teeth. "Look, part of my job here is keeping you safe to do *your* job, and I can't do that living in the Quarter." He gave me his half twist of a smile that had become a lot less sexy now that I knew it also belonged to my canine confidant. Make that my *former* confidant.

"You know, it's kind of a possessive pack thing, too."

I'm sure my face turned purple. Thankfully, it was dark. "A *pack* thing? Like, we're members of a pack? I didn't think shifters had packs. Don't even tell me. You're the alpha, right?"

"You missed your turn."

I had cranked the Pathfinder, pulled back onto the street, and had, indeed, missed the turn to my house. I noticed he hadn't answered the alpha question, but decided to leave it alone for now. I couldn't handle any more revelations tonight.

Finally, I had to be practical. Even twenty-four hours ago, I wouldn't have considered a bodyguard. Today, with Gerry still missing, a voodoo vévé painted on my sidewalk, someone targeting wizards on my turf, and an undead jazz musician as my spy, opening my doors to a lying, dirty dog of a shapeshifter sounded reasonable.

Alex moved in.

THURSDAY, SEPTEMBER 22, 2005 "Category 5 Rita has N.O. nervous; [Mayor] foresees a much smaller city."

—THE TIMES-PICAYUNE

CHAPTER 20

Call Tish and report that there's nothing to report. Check. Call Adam Lyle at St. Gabriel to confirm there's nothing new. Check.

Call last appointment Gerry had in his journal before Katrina. Check. Lester Meadows, sentinel of Appalachia, was about to retire and said he'd called to see if Gerry would recommend me for his post. He'd been disappointed when Gerry told him I wouldn't be interested. This was all news to me.

Call next-to-last appointment from journal: check. Selena Milette, a minor mage who wanted to take the exam for Blue Congress, said Gerry was an arrogant sonofabitch like all wizards.

Call third-to-last appointment: Elder Willem Zrakovi, head of the wizards for North America. No way. Not ready for career suicide, though I did wonder what they'd talked about.

Then I was stuck, and Alex was stuck with me. Everyone had been hustled off the streets and ordered out of town in advance of Hurricane Rita, another killer storm with a wimpy name. She was headed for east Texas or western Louisiana but if she turned sooner rather than later, we'd get clocked again.

People had learned a lesson from Katrina. No casual "maybe I will, maybe I won't" attitudes about evacuating. This time, the few people in town had run like gazelles, except for me and Alex.

I tried one last time to get him to leave, sharing Gerry's philosophy about sentinels splitting up during hurricanes. It was annoyingly like the conversation Gerry and I had at Sid-Mar's two days before Katrina, with the roles reversed. Karma sucks.

"You need to at least go to your folks' house in Picayune," I said, explaining the bits about hell breaking loose and weakened levees. He was unloading his stuff in my office, including weights and cases of protein bars and lots of black clothing.

"It's different this time," he said. "I'm going to stay at your place, and we know it didn't flood here. Even if the levees give way again, we'll be okay."

"Not all the levees broke, remember. If the Mississippi River levee breaks, this house will be somewhere in the Gulf of Mexico. Take the cat to Picayune, at least."

"Not leaving. Give it up." He pulled an iron out of a box. "I can use your iron so I don't need this, right?"

An iron? Was he kidding? God made knits so people didn't have to iron. "I don't own an iron. And I don't need protecting, just in case you're staying out of some misguided macho thing."

He smirked. "I'm staying because I wouldn't trust you not to move to a new address while I was gone. Not that I couldn't find you now that I have my tracker back. Quit stealing it."

Damn. Wait. I'd hidden it in my underwear drawer. "You were pawing through my dresser," I said, eyes narrowed.

"The black bikinis are sexy."

"Glad you liked them. You'll never see them again."

I helped him hang the new library door and install a new dead bolt, thanks to a home-improvement store that had finally opened in Jefferson Parish. Then we spent the rest of the afternoon reading, inhaling all the information we could find on the Baron Samedi and both Marie Laveaus, mother and daughter. Afterward, I sorted a few more of Gerry's papers while Alex read through journals, starting with the most recent and working backward.

We decided to compare notes over dinner.

"Here's my big scoop," I said. "Remember I told you Jean Lafitte mentioned a new partnership before you blasted him?"

Alex nodded, chewing on a slice of vegetarian pizza he'd gone all the way to Metairie to find. I had pepperoni. "So?"

"So, guess who Monsieur Lafitte allegedly had an affair with a couple hundred years ago?"

"Why, are you jealous?"

I took a bite of pizza and wrinkled my nose at him. Our relationship seemed to have devolved into bickering one-upmanship, but at least it was mostly good-natured.

"Marie Laveau," I said. "Don't know if it's true—they would barely have overlapped in their years in New Orleans, and she was ten or twelve years younger than him. But there's so much conflicting information about when either one of them actually got here, it's possible. Laveau and Lafitte. Maybe they're together again."

Alex frowned and picked up a mushroom that had fallen on the table, popping it in his mouth. "When's the earliest you think Lafitte could be strong enough to come back from the Beyond?"

I pointed to a wall calendar hanging from the side of the kitchen cabinet nearest Alex. "Tomorrow, the twenty-third. I've circled it in red."

"How sure are you?"

I shrugged. "I don't have a lot of experience with revenge-seeking members of the historical undead. But from what I've read, if you send them back violently, they need from one to two weeks to recover full strength. Tomorrow makes a week since you shot Lafitte, and I figure since he's probably the most powerful of the historical undead in New Orleans he'd need the minimum. The second-strongest is probably Marie Laveau. Everyone here knows who both of them are." Especially Lafitte, who had a town and a national park and a bayou and God only knows what else named after him.

"So maybe Marie Laveau really is our murderer," Alex said. "But what would the link with Gerry be, and the wizards?" He paused. "Do you think Gerry would work with her?"

Deep breath. He's just testing theories. "No. What could it accomplish? I think he caught her coming through a breach and she did something to him."

Alex had stopped eating and drummed his fingers on the Formica tabletop. It was his one nervous habit. "If your theory is true, you realize Gerry's probably not alive. If he were injured or being held somewhere against his will, the Elders would know about it—they'd be able to detect his force field unless he's figured out some way to evade their trackers."

I toyed with a slice of pepperoni. He wasn't saying anything I hadn't thought a hundred times. "I don't want to think he's dead. But he's been missing a week now, and I'm running out of ideas."

Alex got another slice, and we ate in silence a few minutes. My pizza had lost its flavor.

I pulled out some foil to wrap it up so I could eat the leftovers for breakfast. Alex had finished his.

"You want the rest of mine?" I asked.

"No way. You're going to end up wearing that pepperoni on your hips."

Did he think I was too hippy? I wasn't hippy. "Snob," I said, wrapping the pizza. It would make a great breakfast. Then

I asked, "Did you find out anything interesting in Gerry's journals?"

"I found some stuff on the staff from his attic. You need to read it."

We went in the living room, and Alex handed me a journal with the page marked. "You read. I'll shower."

Before I began, I flipped over a page to see how long the entry was. At the end of Gerry's neat handwriting on the next sheet was a drawing he'd done of a wooden staff. Not *a* staff, but *the* staff.

Below the illustration, which he'd drawn in meticulous detail, complete with all the odd runes, he'd written *Elven Staff, from the Last Age*. I tried to remember my elven history lessons with Gerry: Elves had gotten fed up with humans and gone in a snit to their own corner of the Beyond. What was its name . . . Elfheim. So I guess this staff was from the period just before they took their elven toys and went home, minus at least one stick of wood. Gerry had bought it at an auction.

Worked with the staff far into the morning, he had written. *I had hoped, with elven blood myself, I might be able to wield it, but it doesn't respond to me. Perhaps the child can use it when she gets older.*

That was weird. I didn't know Gerry was of elven descent too, only that he was really interested in them. Was I the child? I looked at the date on the entry: 1985. Couldn't have been me, then. I would have been only five and still living in Alabama with my parents. I'd have to ask Tish who the child might be.

I looked around the room and there the staff was, leaning against one of the bookcases. I'd accepted that it was always going to follow me around like a puppy. It only seemed to happen in my personal space, though—the house and the car. So far, it hadn't followed me to the Gator or back to Lakeview.

I picked it up and felt the warmth spread through it. Was that the kind of response Gerry was hoping for? I tapped it against the edge of the coffee table and tried sending a tiny pulse of magic into it. Red sparks flew from the tip, smoke puffed from the table, and I smelled charred wood. Oops. I waved the smoke away, coughing, and found a charred place the size of a quarter.

"What's burning?" Alex wandered in from the office wearing a pair of loose jogging pants and a towel around his neck.

"Uh." Talk about eye candy. I pried my wanton gaze away and pointed at the table. "I was trying out the staff."

"Damn." He touched the burn mark and pulled away a sliver of charred wood. "Have you ever been able to do anything like that before?"

"Please. I'm Green Congress. I was exhausted after churning enough heat to set off my little Jean Lafitte smoke bomb."

"Did burning up your coffee table tire you?"

"No." Hmm. If I could learn more about the staff, and how to use it, maybe I wouldn't need the shooting lessons Alex kept threatening me with.

FRIDAY/SATURDAY, SEPTEMBER 23–24, 2005 "Flooded again: Breach in Industrial Canal inundates Lower 9th Ward, Arabi . . . Latest hurricane washes away signs of renewal."

—THE TIMES–PICAYUNE

CHAPTER 21

Storm preparation time. Again. I spent Friday morning moving plants, using a strengthening charm on the windows, and going through my grounding ritual just in case. I still had the cypress tree on my roof from Katrina. Maybe Rita would blow it off.

Alex put his FBI badge to use and came in at midday with another cache of MREs, a generator, enough gasoline to blow Louisiana off the map without a hurricane, a half-dozen gallons of water, and way too many boxes of ammo. My kitchen looked like a survivalist camp.

Jake arrived an hour later with a pickup load of supplies, adding to the warehouse ambience my first floor was beginning to acquire. I wasn't sure if Alex had invited Jake to ride out the storm with us or if Jake had invited himself. Alex's scowl made me think the latter as he grudgingly helped Jake cart in even more MREs, a cache of batteries for the radio, and at least three cases of beer. At this rate, I'd be dining on military grub and drinking Abita till I hit middle age.

He also brought a deck of cards, poker being a Warin hurricane tradition. "You think you're up to playing with the masters?" Jake motioned me to a seat between him and Alex at the kitchen table.

"I won't be able to keep up with you guys, but I'll do my best," I said, confident I'd beat the crap out of them. I had learned from a master; Gerry was one hell of a poker player. I might not be a good liar but I could spot a poker tell in a flash, even without using my empathy. All I had to do was lay back a few hands and pay attention, then go for the kill.

"What should we play for?" I asked. "Pennies? Dimes?" I wasn't rich enough for dollars, not being a Bourbon Street bar owner or a shapeshifting assassin.

Jake and Alex exchanged knowing looks. I was about to be had.

"Truth or Dare Poker," Jake said. "Whoever has the lowest hand has to answer a question or take a dare from the person to his right."

Oh, boy. Why did I think they'd done this before? "Okay, but I'm not doing raunchy, on questions or dares either one." I could see this easily getting out of hand. I slumped into my chair and wondered what laying back the first few hands would cost me. There was only so much truth I was willing to tell.

I stuck to my plan, watching Jake first. He ran his fingers through his hair, then ended up with the low hand. Nervous gesture. He was going to be an easy read.

Alex sat to his right. "Have you ever been arrested?"

A muscle flicked in his jaw. "You know damn well I have, Alexander. I got two DUIs and a revoked license back in 2003."

Maybe this wasn't such a good idea. They weren't going to play raunchy. They were going to play mean.

Jake dealt the next hand, and I watched Alex, looking for a

tell. He was inscrutable, didn't even do his finger-drumming thing. He also won, and I ended up low. I gave Jake my best pleading, be-kind-to-me look.

"Let's see, short stuff. What would I like to know about you?" He leaned his chair back on two legs and flashed one perfect dimple. "If you had to be locked in a secluded cabin for a weekend with one person in this room, other than yourself, who would it be?"

Dark brown eyes watched me from the left, amber ones from the right, cross-eyed blue ones from the top of the refrigerator. Thank God. "Sebastian," I said, pointing. He hissed at me. Not technically a person, but close enough.

I asked Alex who his first kiss was (Silvie Hollinsworth in first grade, which got a howl from Jake), the last lie he told (that he needed the generator for FBI business), and his worst habit (being stubborn. Duh).

Alex let up on Jake after the arrest question and asked him his worst childhood memory (being whipped for dismantling the cash register in the family hardware store, then having to work off the repair cost). He took the dare on telling the worst joke he'd ever pulled and had to mime his most embarrassing date. Apparently, he'd fallen asleep and gotten slapped. What came in between, I wasn't sure.

I had to fess up to never skinny dipping (I am a city girl, after all), my worst fear (zombies, only Jake thought I was joking), and then I got the question that ruined the whole game: What do you want most?

I wanted to find Gerry.

We decided to quit playing and have a beer. By the time the electricity died again, we'd all retreated to different parts of the house to read or nap.

The next morning, Rita blew in. Wind howled around the

corners of the house, sounding like an inhuman scream, and I watched out the window as slanting rain pooled into a river along Nashville and Magazine.

About noon, I took the lantern in the kitchen to fix MREs for all of us. We each had the Cajun Rice and Sausage meal, which included side dishes of cheddar-flavored pretzels, a toaster pastry, and raspberry jelly.

It could have been romantic considering the handsome men sitting with me at the kitchen table had they not spent the entire meal engaged in a debate over the not-inconsiderable merits of the 9-millimeter semiautomatic (better accuracy, less recoil) versus the .38 snub nose (lightweight, foolproof) for personal self-defense—namely, my personal self-defense. I had no idea what they were talking about.

Jake, who knew only that I had some nebulous relationship with his cousin and was missing an uncle, apparently didn't find the subject of my needing a gun the least suspicious. Gotta love the South.

I shook my head, threw the MRE packaging away, and went into the living room to read more of Gerry's papers while rain continued to pound the windows. I curled up in an armchair and a pattern soon emerged. Gerry would go on a job, then use his report to the Elders as a platform for pointing out how things would be better if they'd relax the borders between the modern world and the Beyond. He'd had a lot of vampire cases in the last year—many more than I realized—and recorded several instances where he'd been contacted by various leaders from the Realm of Vampyre, the vamps' part of the Beyond. He'd even had a couple of meetings with one of the vampire Regents, who were like Elders with fangs.

He wrote about contacts with various members of the were community and some of the fae leaders. Gerry had his hands in a lot of political pots, but nowhere did any reference to voodoo appear.

I set the papers aside and tried to reconcile this newly emerging picture of Gerry with the man who raised me. The one who'd taken me in and made me his family, but would change the subject if I asked about his real relatives. Who'd taught me to follow the rules, yet fought to change them. Who'd encouraged me to use my Green Congress skills, yet held back on helping me develop whatever physical magic I had. Who'd been so fascinated by elves and his elven heritage, yet never told me it was something we shared.

I burrowed deeper into the chair, closing my eyes and listening to the rain and the cutthroat Warin poker game that had resumed in the kitchen with lying, cheating, name-calling, and betting.

"I bet Dad's boat you can't win three hands in a row." Jake sounded cocky.

Outrage from Alex. "You can't bet Uncle Eddie's boat. You don't own it."

"I have it, dude. You know what they say about possession and the law."

"It doesn't apply to wagers."

I smiled. They sounded like kids. Probably had been doing this their whole lives. I tuned them out and let myself be lulled by the sound of the rain.

". . . DJ?"

I stirred, hearing my name as if from a distance.

Jake's soft drawl said my name again, but I realized he wasn't talking to me. I blinked and pressed the stem on my watch to illuminate the dial. I'd lost a half hour. Must have fallen asleep.

"So, let's get this clear." Jake's voice carried from the kitchen.

"Next high hand gets first dibs on DJ and the other one clears the path, right?"

I gritted my teeth. They were betting on me? Unlike Uncle Eddie's boat, I could fight back.

Alex's voice, in an exaggerated whisper. "No way. I got here first. Nobody invited you. You can take your Marine Corps, camo-wearing ass back to the Quarter."

I got to my feet, walking quietly to the kitchen, and stared sharp, pointy knives in Alex's back. Jake saw me and flashed a grin, and I had an embarrassing urge to let them play the hand and see if he won. But I hated to let myself be reduced to the status of a motorboat.

"Oh, I don't think so, Cuz," Jake said, gaze trained on me. "What you want to have ain't the same as what you think you got."

I eased across the kitchen to throw away my Abita bottle and gave Alex a hard thump on the head as I went by, startling him. On the way back, I put a hand on each of his shoulders, leaned over, and whispered, "Sexual harassment."

He at least had the decency to look guilty. Jake laughed, so I gave him a glare too. As near as I could tell, he had started it. Before I could think of a scathing comment for him, his cell phone rang. A few seconds later, so did Alex's.

Jake's call ended first. "As much as I'd like to play that hand, I've gotta go."

"What happened?"

"Me too," Alex said, ending his call. "Will you be okay here by yourself for a few hours?"

The boat and a couple of strong backs were needed just west of Houma, where a Warin cousin was slogging through his house in waist-high water, trying to salvage anything he could. This hurricane season just wouldn't end.

After Jake left to extract the boat from a garage space he'd rented outside the Quarter, Alex pulled an FBI windbreaker from one of his bags. "I hate to leave you here—it sounds like Lafitte's a threat from this point on," he said. "Say the word, and I'll stay."

I shook my head. "No, you go. I'll check my wards as soon as you leave." I handed him the keys to the Pathfinder. "It's not up to your usual standards but it's better for weather like this. Good ground clearance."

He took the keys and smiled. "I'll be back tonight." He still looked undecided, so I pushed him toward the door.

From the kitchen window, I watched him pull the hood up on the jacket and splash toward the Pathfinder. He'd left the keys to the Mercedes on the counter. I smiled and picked them up, rubbing my fingers over the soft leather of the key case and hanging them on the hook where I kept my own keys.

The rain had slacked a lot since earlier in the day. I checked the wards on the back door, running my hand along the door facing and feeling for the slight resistance, then took the fluorescent lantern and walked to the front door. I squinted through a narrow gap in the plywood.

Movement in front of the pizza place across the street caught my eye, and I strained my eyes to see through the drizzling rain, which was bringing on dusk earlier than usual. For a moment, no more than a blink, I saw a tall black man on the corner wearing a top hat, dancing around a cane on the sidewalk. He wore sunglasses in the rain, with one lens in and one out. He stopped and grinned at me, waved, then disappeared, leaving nothing but rivers of rainwater.

I could feel my heart thudding in my chest. The figure hadn't been Marie Laveau. It looked like the illustrations we'd seen of Baron Samedi.

CHAPTER 22

My hands shook as I rechecked the wards on every door and window. They were strong wards. Neither Samedi nor Jean Lafitte should be able to enter. But just in case, I took the lantern upstairs and locked myself in my library.

I considered calling the Elders, but what could I tell them? That I saw a voodoo god dancing on the sidewalk in front of Marinello's Pizza? That Jean Lafitte maybe had an affair with Marie Laveau a couple of centuries ago, therefore they were now in the midst of some nebulous anti-wizard conspiracy? That, somehow, all this might be related to Gerry's disappearance?

No contacting the Elders—not yet, anyway.

I knew Alex would come back if I called him, and that realization stunned me. Our relationship had gone through some changes in the last week. Something to ponder later.

The shrill blare of a car horn outside made me want to fly out of my skin, and the crunch of metal-on-metal sent me running to the window. I pulled the curtain aside and looked out at a pair of soldiers standing beside their respective Jeeps, arguing.

Light rain reflected in their headlights—the only lights on the darkening street. I pulled the curtain back more and looked a little farther, toward Marinello's. Nothing but shadows and rain.

I paced around the room awhile, thinking about Gerry and Marie Laveau and Baron Samedi, the puzzle of it gnawing at me. And was Jean Lafitte involved with them, or was he an isolated problem?

Scanning the bookshelves, I retrieved the volume on the first Marie Laveau, the one who might have dallied with Lafitte when she was very young. I hadn't been able to summon Gerry, and I didn't have the guts to summon Jean Lafitte or Baron Samedi. But maybe I could talk to the voodoo queen.

To do the summoning, I needed four items related to her. I cut out an illustration of her from a book of local history, then read for other ideas. She loved jewelry, so I unlocked the library door and pulled a pair of gold bracelets from my jewelry box in the bedroom. Next, I ran downstairs and got the bottle of rum Lafitte had drunk from, and added to it dried red peppers from the spice rack—a ritual offering for voodoo ceremonies. Finally, I locked myself back in the library and chose red and gold candles to appeal to her power.

Moving an area rug aside, I carefully drew a summoning circle in chalk not far from my Elder transport, and covered it again in sea salt for extra strength. I looked at the setup a moment, wondering what I should ask her and whether she'd tell me what I needed to know. Most pretes were bound by the blood of summoning magic to answer questions truthfully. The historical undead could lie through their immortal teeth.

Scanning my supply shelves, I pulled out a plastic case divided into small compartments originally meant to hold nails and bolts. I kept magically infused gemstones in it. Most truth amulets contained red agate, so I chose one from the box and set it inside the circle. Then I placed the summoning items at the four compass points, and pricked my left thumb with my silver knife. As the blood hit the circle, I called her. "I summon Marie Glapion, also known as Marie Laveau."

Almost immediately, I felt the power spring up, forming an invisible containment cylinder. I backed away, knelt on a cushion, and waited. It took a couple of minutes. I was about to give up when a mist formed inside and gradually took on a feminine shape.

The historical undead always came back at their most powerful age, or the time they'd been at their most famous. Jean Lafitte looked to be in his early thirties; Marie Laveau was a bit older, maybe forty. She was at least a head taller than me, with skin the color of caramel. Gold hoop earrings caught the light as she swept a strand of thick, dark hair over her shoulder and knelt inside the circle to get a better look at me, dark eyes flashing. I thought about hiding. This idea was making my morgue visit seem sane.

"What do you want, wizard?" Her voice rose and dipped in a musical patois that made me think of palm trees and hot West Indies winds. Her long red skirt brushed the sides of the circle, and she reached her hands toward me, palms flat against the cylinder.

"I want to ask you questions, and you are bound by my stone to answer truthfully." I struggled to keep my voice even and calm. Something about her made me want to go blubbering behind the sofa.

Marie stood and looked around till she found the agate next to her feet, and gave me a calculating look, a half smile on her face. "Clever. I repeat, wizard. What do you want?"

I took a deep breath. "Why is the vévé of Baron Samedi marking the homes of wizards?"

She smiled coyly, and knelt again. "Most wizards are enemies of those in the Beyond. We all want to know where our enemies live."

Obtuse. Try again. "When you say 'we,' do you mean the followers of voodoo?"

"No."

"Are you speaking of only yourself?"

"No."

Grrr. Avoid yes-or-no questions. "Who considers the wizards his enemy and wants to know where they live?"

"All of us, wizard, from Vampyre to the City of the Gods. We are all your enemy."

That was scary, not to mention unhelpful.

"Are you leading a revolt?"

"I am but a follower, wizard. You would do well to stay in your nice little home and not meddle with things too large for you."

Okay. She didn't deny a revolt, even implied it. "Is Baron Samedi on this side of the Beyond?"

"Samedi is the god of death and life. He is everywhere."

Useless. "Are you working with a wizard?" God, Gerry. I'm sorry I even had to ask that question.

"No."

Rephrase. "Has anyone in the Beyond been working with a wizard since the storm?"

"I have to answer truthfully, as you say. But only if I answer at all. I tire of your questions." She clamped her jaws shut and stood again, looking down her nose at me.

I stood and paced around the circle. "You and Jean Lafitte," I said. "I hear you had quite the romance."

The comment took her by surprise, and she turned to watch me as I walked. "I did not know the pirate in my human life. But . . ." Her voice rose in astonishment. "You must be the one I heard about, the one who got the better of him. Yes, I see it on your face. . . . Ayeee." She began to laugh, a rich and musical sound punctuated by the tinkle of bracelets on her arms. "The pirate Lafitte is not happy with you, little one, but he will tell you that himself soon enough."

Uh-oh. "What do you mean?"

She continued to laugh.

"What does he have planned?"

A smile. "I will talk no more, wizard. Keep me here as long as you like, but you cannot make me answer."

I pelted her with a dozen questions more, and continued to be met with silence. For a while she remained standing, silent, bright-eyed, amused. I plopped down on my cushion and thought about leaving her there all night just for spite, but the smile on her face gradually grew harder, and her expression angry.

She knelt, created her own circle within mine, and began chanting in a rhythmic lilt: "Madame Brigitte, behold the lash which this wizard has cut to strike you with. I bring it to you that you may teach her the lesson she deserves." She took two small sticks from a pocket hidden in the folds of her skirt and placed them in an X on the side closest to me.

It was damned creepy, whether you believed in it or not. "Here is the woman I pray you to torment," she chanted, and I felt my magical containment falter. It needed more blood to keep her from tearing it down and coming after me. It wasn't like she was telling me anything useful. She was just giving me plenty of material for future nightmares.

I grabbed my silver knife, sliced across my thumb, and dropped blood on the circle again. "Marie Laveau, I release you back into the Beyond." I hoped my pronouncement didn't sound as rushed and freaked-out as it felt from my end. She smirked at me as her image faded.

Once I was sure nothing was left in the circle, I broke the binding and collapsed in an armchair. My head pounded and I felt like I'd been hit by the two Jeeps down in the street. I'd sliced my thumb too deeply, and blood coated my left hand.

I picked up the elven staff, which had moved itself into the library sometime during the day, and it seemed to make the headache better. Even the soft steady light of the fluorescent lantern hurt my eyes, so I turned it off, letting the darkness wrap around me like a blanket. I held on to the staff and curled up on the love seat to think, trying not to bleed on the upholstery.

I knew it was a dream as soon as it began. One of those weird, lucid dreams, where you don't really get scared because you're aware on some level the monster in the closet is only a dream monster, only in this case it was a dream Gerry.

I walked through a long, downward-sloping corridor. The floor was dark cobblestone, worn smooth as if by centuries of footsteps. Flickering gas lanterns cast geometric shadows on the slate-gray masonry walls. I could touch the sides of the narrow passageway on either side of me as I walked. Above, I saw the night sky peppered with bright stars, yet the thick, musty air didn't feel like it was outside.

In the dream I wore a red tank top and jeans, the same thing I'd worn all day. My skin pimpled with cold, and I wished I could dream up a sweater.

At the end of the corridor, I reached a heavy door of gleaming dark wood with an ornate brass knob and key plate.

A circular stone room lit by two gas lanterns lay on the other side of the door, its only furnishings two facing chairs like ancient thrones, with tall backs and silk-covered seats. One chair was empty. Gerry sat in the other, waiting for me.

I wanted to run to him, throw my arms around him like I did when I was little, but he looked somber. The last time I'd seen that look, he'd just caught me doing hydromancy. He'd lectured me with passion about the laws of magic and why they were important.

He looked distinguished, aristocratic, his silver hair pulled

back in a short ponytail, his green silk shirt—a gift from me—
rustling as he shifted in his chair.

"Sit down, Drusilla. We have to talk." He rarely called me
Drusilla, always said it was an old-fashioned, sentimental name
that didn't fit me. If he called me Drusilla, I was usually in trouble.

"You should not have summoned Marie Laveau," he said.
"I can't protect you if you prove yourself too strong. You
mustn't call attention to yourself."

My fingers dug into the arms of my chair. "Gerry, where
are you? I've been looking for you. The Elders are looking for
you."

A hint of his old smile. "Yes, I imagine they are. I don't have
much time, so listen to me. Drop the search for me. If you act as
if you believe I'm dead, the Elders will too. They're taking their
cues from you."

"But I don't think you're dead. I'd feel it if you were gone.
I'm working to find you—just tell me what happened. Tell me
how to help."

He smiled at me, finally. "Trust me enough to do what I
say, and let me go."

I didn't know how to answer.

He looked behind him as if someone outside my field of
vision had spoken. "Have you been to my house?" he said,
turning back to me. "You need to find the journal and the staff.
You—"

"DJ!"

A pounding noise brought me to my feet, and I was back in
my library, my breath coming in gasps. A dream. It had been a
dream.

"Are you in there? Open up!" Alex pounded again.

I stumbled to the door, groggy, and turned the dead bolt
latch, stepping aside to let him in. He smelled of rain and sandalwood.

"DJ?" He sounded uncertain, and flipped the light switch
out of habit. It surprised both of us when the overheads came on.

"I'm okay. Just a bad dream."

"Why were you here in the dark with the door locked?" He
saw the throw rug tossed in the corner and walked to the circle.
"What have you done?"

"You aren't going to like it."

"Obviously."

I looked at my watch—nine fifteen. "Have you eaten dinner? I haven't. Come downstairs and I'll tell you." I wanted to
process what I'd seen and heard before I talked about it. Part of
me still felt caught in the dream.

He caught my arm as we left the library. "Are you hurt?"
He turned my hand over, inspecting it. The blood had dried,
the cut closed up.

"No, let me wash it off. I'll meet you downstairs."

We heated MREs out of habit and sat at the table, eating in
silence. He watched me take every bite, waiting to pounce.

"How are things in Houma?" I asked, pushing my plate aside.

"Fine. No more stalling. Who did you summon?"

I filled him in on seeing Baron Samedi in the rain, then the
frustrating interview with Marie Laveau.

When I finished, he propped his elbows on the table, fingers steepled in front of him. I waited for him to start the bar-
rage of name-calling, but he was buried in thought.

"You realize the implications of this?" He slumped back in
his seat.

I nodded. "It sounds like someone, maybe the Baron, is
trying to build up power, maybe even working with other pretes
like the vampires. Is that feasible?"

"It's not only feasible, it's happened before," Alex said. "The
war in seventy-six saw several prete groups band together, but
in that one, the fae sided with the wizards and the vampires

stayed neutral. They're the most powerful groups in the Beyond except for the elves, who never get involved, so the wizards ended up winning. She didn't mention the fae, did she?"

"No. But why Samedi? Why would he be the ringleader—even among the old gods, he wouldn't be the strongest. If there was some organized prete uprising, wouldn't the fae queens or the vampire regents be pulling the strings?"

"Unless Samedi has a powerful ally on this side. Marie didn't answer the question about Gerry. Even if it backfired on him, he could have helped set it in motion—whatever it is."

I started to tell Alex about the dream, then decided against it. It was just a dream, nothing more. In fact, it was surprising I hadn't dreamed of Gerry before now.

Alex dug his cell phone out of his pocket and placed a call. We really did need that Elder hotline.

MONDAY, SEPTEMBER 26, 2005 "Thin line separates hope from hell: Jeff getting back on its feet, but Orleans flat on its back."

—THE TIMES-PICAYUNE

CHAPTER 23

I sat in the Pathfinder on Magazine Street after a junk-food run, drumming my fingers impatiently while stewing over my new position in the Elders' doghouse. After his phone call, Alex had told me Willem Zrakovi was furious at me for summoning Marie Laveau on my own. Then Elder Zrakovi called and told me himself. He was deeply disappointed in my insistence on taking things into my own hands. That stung.

You'd think the Elders would appreciate knowing a bigger conspiracy might be afoot, one that went beyond a missing sentinel, some voodoo symbols, and an angry pirate. But no. I had disappointed them. Deeply.

After my Elder wrist-slapping (Alex assured me that Zrakovi would have chewed me a new one in person if he'd truly been that upset), I'd spent most of the day turning my house into a virtual Bastille against the French pirate. Charms, hexes, potions. Anything I could make up ahead of time and have at the ready. I wasn't going to be caught unarmed again. I went through my grounding ritual twice and made up a second mojo bag. Couldn't hurt to have a spare.

I was so jumpy Alex got nervous and insisted we go ahead with plans to get the tree off my roof. Since I thought the tilting cedar might make an easy ladder for Jean Lafitte to climb in my bedroom window, I agreed. For the past week, I'd haggled with different tree services, trying to negotiate a reasonable price. Once Alex heard my lowest estimate had been from a Bobcat driver who wanted $4,000 to take it down, the Warin clan decided to do it themselves.

I'd heard the Winn-Dixie on Tchoupitoulas had reopened a couple of hours a day, and I was out of Cheetos. Otherwise, I wouldn't have left the house. For a largely unpopulated city, this little unflooded stretch of New Orleans was beginning to feel crowded, and I wasn't sure where Jean Lafitte might show up. Of course, it was also possible Lafitte wouldn't come back for revenge at all and I was wasting my paranoia.

Jake's old Dodge pickup was already parked beside the house when I got back, and I snickered when I saw he'd added a hood ornament from a Jaguar—no doubt to irritate Alex, whose freshly washed Mercedes had been moved out of the driveway and parked across the street. I parked behind Jake. I'd hate to waft any road dust Alex's way.

An extension ladder rested against the back of the house, and Alex and Jake stood at the foot of it, looking up while a tall, rangy guy poked around at the eave line. When I joined them, the man descended the ladder and introduced himself. Don Warin was one of Alex's three older brothers—as tall and dark as Alex but with shorter hair and minus the enforcer physique. He looked at me with naked curiosity.

"Oh, Mama insisted I come and help," he said when I thanked him for driving all the way from Picayune. He grinned and stuck his hands in his pockets to give me the once-over, and his Mississippi accent was thick as cane syrup. "We didn't think we'd ever see a gal get her hooks in my little brother. I have to report back."

He looked at Alex. "Mama wants to know when you're bringin' her home for dinner?"

Uh, that would be never. I gave Alex a glare I hoped he interpreted correctly as *Not happening. Ever.*

His mouth curved in a smug smile.

Alex and Jake kept their one-upmanship to a minimum in front of Don, and I left them to their business. If they wanted to insist tree removal was man's work, who was I to argue?

I pulled out another box of Gerry's stuff. Saturday's dream hadn't been anything dramatic like an omen or a telepathic message, but he had told me to find the staff and a journal, so I might as well make sure I'd found all the journals.

A loud bump from the roof jarred the house.

"Watch where you're putting your big feet!"

"Then get the hell out of my way!"

"Would you two shut up for once?"

I wasn't sure how much the sawing, banging, and cursing on my roof had to do with my cedar tree.

I opened the box and decided the first thing I should do is sort the notebooks from the correspondence, invoices, receipts, and bank statements, then see if any of the notebooks looked like a journal. If I dreamed of him again, I'd have to teach him a few things about organizing documents.

I sorted awhile, then noticed the elven staff propped against the door that led into the office. Last night, it had been in the library. I went in the kitchen and stuck my head out the back door to make sure the Warin boys, or at least the non-shapeshifting ones, were keeping themselves busy. Coast clear. I returned to the living room and picked up the staff.

As always, it grew warm under my touch and a few sparks burst from the end. On a whim, I pointed it at the ceiling fan turning lazily overhead and shot a tiny bit of magical will into it, just to see if I could speed the fan up. If I could figure out how to use and control this thing, it might help me increase my physical magic.

"Ack!" The fan sped up all right—after a few seconds, it spun so fast it wobbled on its stem, and black smoke poured out of the motor. The smoke detector began an ear-splitting screech before I could race to the wall switch and turn the fan off.

By the time Jake and Alex hurried in the back door with Don close behind, I had stashed the staff under a sofa cushion and stood underneath the fan wearing what I hoped was a perplexed expression. My hand still tingled from the transfer of energy, but I didn't feel drained at all. I was beginning to like this staff. I just needed to figure out how to harness it without burning my house down.

"Must be a short in the wiring," I announced somberly as they came to a halt beneath the fan, which was still puffing rings of noxious black smoke. The air smelled of scorched electrical wiring.

"I've installed a million of those things we've sold at the store and I ain't ever seen one do that." Don took off his Picayune Maroon Tide baseball cap and scratched his head.

"We'll pick another one up for you at the store and put it in," Jake offered, while Alex frowned and looked at me skeptically.

"Thanks, Jake. I'll pay you for it, of course."

His dimples were deep enough to dive into. "I'll come up with a special price for you, sweet pea." I didn't think his price involved money.

Don stared at Jake, eyebrows raised, then looked at Alex. Clearly, if I was supposed to be Alex's woman, hell-bent on a course to meet his mama over family dinner, Jake had stepped over the line of common decency. Let them figure it out; I wanted no part of it.

Don and Alex headed out to finish the work, but Jake stayed behind. He closed the door behind them and turned to look at me, hanging an arm of his sunglasses in the front of his T-shirt.

"Darlin', I'm getting mixed signals about you and Big Al." His eyes looked like honey, and I wondered if our dinner date was still going to happen. I sure hoped so.

"Big Al and I are, uh . . ." I paused. What were we? I couldn't say we were working together or I'd have to lie and tell Jake I was involved in law enforcement. I winged it. "We are friends, like I said. Nothing exclusive. He really has been helping get my uncle's place cleaned out."

His expression softened. "I'm sorry about Gerry. They never found him, did they?"

"Not a sign." I paused. "It's been hard. He raised me. He's more like a father, really."

He nodded. "I've lost people that way, when it's sudden and you don't have a chance to say good-bye. The questions eat at you. Even if you know what happened, you still ask why."

We sat at the kitchen table. "You talking about Afghanistan? Alex told me you'd had a rough time of it."

Jake stared out the window. "Yeah, half my unit got killed. You start questioning why some people die and others live. You feel guilty because you're one of the so-called lucky ones. You ask what it is you're supposed to do with your life to pay for having survived it. Sometimes you wish you hadn't survived it. If you think about it too much, it can eat you alive." He looked back at me, and I could see traces of the ghosts that haunted him.

"Don't suck down all the hurt, DJ. It'll catch up with you in a bad way."

I blinked back tears and stared at the table. I wasn't going to let myself start crying because once that dam was opened I might never get it closed. "I don't know how to let it out and still keep going," I said. "How did you do it?"

He laughed—a sharp, bitter sound. "You don't want to do

it my way, sweetie. I drank too much and shut out everybody that cared about me. Talk to a friend, a relative. Somebody."

I looked out the window too. There was nobody.

Alex saved me from having to answer by stomping back inside, so full of anger and jealousy he wasn't even trying to shield it from me. I wiped away a stray tear before he saw it.

Or maybe not.

"What's going on?" Alex looked at me, ignoring Jake.

I cleared my throat and avoided Alex's eyes. "I was just asking Jake how Jackie Williams was doing at the club."

"Packing them in." Jake leaned his chair back. "It's crazy how that guy looks like Louis Armstrong, sounds like Louis Armstrong, knows all the Armstrong songs. I don't know where he came from—he doesn't talk much. But I'm not complaining. If we try to cram any more people in we're gonna get called for a fire-code violation."

Don joined us for a few minutes but had to leave for Picayune. The Twin Spans were still down so he'd have to drive the Causeway, twenty-six miles straight across the middle of Lake Pontchartrain. I thought any bridge so long you lost sight of land had to be dangerous.

"Yeah, Alex, guess it's time for us to take off, too." Jake didn't want to leave me with his cousin. A serious Warin competition was heating up and I was the bone of contention.

"I'm already home. Moved in with DJ just before Rita hit." Alex gave his cousin a big, doggy grin.

I gave Alex a look that would send lesser men to their knees, begging forgiveness. He ignored it.

"Is that so?" Jake contemplated this new bit of information and cocked his head at me. I couldn't read his expression and had sworn off taking cheat-peeks at his emotions. A little wave of anger hit me anyway. "Well, then. I guess I'll see you lovebirds later."

He grabbed his keys and walked out, letting the door close a little too hard behind him.

I thought about trying the elven staff on Alex. "I liked you better when you were a dog."

"Don't get involved with Jake, DJ. Right now he needs to think we're a couple, unless you're ready to introduce him to the historical undead."

I needed to just swear off men. I'd done without one this long anyway, and they were way too complicated.

CHAPTER 24

As long as Alex and I were posing as a couple, we might as well go to dinner. A few restaurants had opened in Jefferson Parish, and anything that wasn't an MRE, a sandwich, or a protein bar sounded like nirvana. We'd just reached the outskirts of Metairie when Alex's cell rang.

"It's Ken, from the NOPD," he said, flipping the phone open. The conversation was brief.

"Another voodoo murder." Alex clipped the phone back to his car's visor and took the next exit. We turned around on Veterans and headed back toward New Orleans.

"Where did it happen?"

"In Lakeview—another National Guardsman."

"Is Ken going to let you look at the crime scene?" *You* meaning *us*.

"I'm not officially on the case yet, but we need to see it anyway."

We dodged military checkpoints and went back to the house first so I could get my backpack. I ran up the stairs and into the library, hopping around as I tried to simultaneously pull on my boots and find magical items that might help us sneak into a muddy, roped-off neighborhood with no electricity and lots of cops. At least most of the post-Rita floodwaters had finally drained out of Lakeview.

I procured the ingredients for a variety of spells, stuffed them in my backpack along with my mojo bag, and slipped a light-emitting obsidian amulet around my neck. As I headed toward the door, I tripped over the elven staff, which had placed itself in my path. The thing's ability to track my movements was downright unnerving.

"Oh no you don't, buddy. I'm not ready for you yet."

I took the stairs at a fast clip, sliding at the bottom as I rounded the corner. Alex hadn't been idle, either. He was nestling his biggest handgun into its shoulder harness beneath a black jacket, and I saw a couple of knives strapped inside the coat. It didn't bother me a bit. In fact, I hoped he had the grenade and the shotgun loaded for undead pirates and voodoo gods.

We drove the five miles back to Lakeview and parked next to the mountain of storm debris on Pontchartrain Boulevard.

"How far to the crime scene?" I asked, watching the glow on the horizon from the lights in Metairie. Everything on the Orleans side of the 17th Street Canal was dark. Across the narrow canal, on the Jeff Parish side, life buzzed almost at pre-storm levels.

"I'm not sure, just that it's on Fleur de Lis, a few blocks from the levee breach. We'll have to walk in from here and stay hidden. Everybody's twitchy. They might shoot first, then worry about who they're shooting at."

I dug in my backpack, handed him a piece of peppermint candy, and took one for myself.

He raised an eyebrow.

"To keep us from coughing. We didn't bring masks and we're trying to be quiet. This will help."

We climbed out of the car, closing the doors softly to avoid being heard, and walked west toward the canal. I tripped over something in the dark—a board or tree limb, or at least I hoped that's all it was. Alex caught my arm before I went sprawling. Light reflected from the corner of Fleur de Lis, so we approached slowly, peering around the edge of a house at two policemen with light sticks, stripping crime-scene tape across neon yellow sawhorses. Red flashing lights reflected on the police car windows from the ambulance parked a block on the other side of them. The surrounding streets were empty and silent and very dark.

"How's your pitching arm?" I whispered, opening my pack and feeling around for three small bags of powder. "I want you to throw these bags one at a time in different directions, as far as you can, away from the crime scene. Then we'll slip over there."

I also handed him a small vial of fluorescent green liquid. "Before you throw, drink this."

"What do they do?" He looked at the vial and the bags, frowning.

"Camouflage and fireworks. Just do it."

Alex shrugged, tossed back the vial of liquid with a grimace, and threw each of the bags in succession, far into the night in different directions. When each bag landed, an explosion echoed through the neighborhood and sent off flares that illuminated the ghostly, empty houses and reflected off small ponds of remaining floodwater. The guardsmen and police shouted as they jumped in vehicles and headed toward the noises.

Alex and I slipped past the barricades and ran toward the house nearest the ambulance. At least Lakeview had lots of empty buildings to hide behind. The bitter taste of my own chameleon potion lingered in my throat. The police and EMTs ahead of us might think they saw movement but we should be well hidden. Unless, of course, one of them was a telepathic wizard.

By the time we'd run the long block, I had to sit on an over-turned tree to catch my breath. Alex wasn't even breathing hard, damn his healthy, protein-shake-drinking hide. I could almost see him biting his tongue to keep from making a smart-ass comment.

Once I could breathe, we crept along the side of what used to be paved roads. Now, as near as I could tell, they were covered with a thick layer of sand. You'd never know asphalt lay underneath. I hadn't been this close to the breach.

I injected a little energy into the obsidian amulet to help us see without attracting attention, but it wasn't enough.

"Oof." Alex grunted and hit something, then I ran into his back. We'd collided with the side of a house, a big one, skewed diagonally in the middle of the road where it had washed off its foundation. Working our way around it was treacherous. I gasped as I tripped again, and ran my hands lightly along the edges of jagged wood, trying to feel my way around the building slowly without impaling myself on anything. Creating a bigger light source was too risky.

Finally, we got within a few yards of the crime scene, and the emergency lights made it easier to see from our vantage point behind an empty house. "Let's split up, move around, and see what we can. Meet back at that house in the road in fifteen minutes," Alex whispered.

I stared as he pulled a handgun and three knives out of hiding places in his clothing, thrusting them at me, handles first. Then he peeled off his jacket and shirt, folded them quickly, and laid them on the ground. Shoes came off next, followed by pants and briefs. Flashing red lights bounced off his body.

"Uh." I couldn't think of anything else to say. *Hot damn* seemed inappropriate given our situation.

He raised an eyebrow. "Stop gawking. I'm going Gandalf on you."

"Right." I knew that.

Alex knelt and the air shimmered around him. Within seconds, my old buddy stood in his place. The shift had seemed effortless. Weres suffered through their change, all cracking bones and reshaping skeletal systems. Lycanthropes might be tougher, or so I'd heard, but shapeshifters had a more pleasant time of it.

"We'll meet back here in fifteen. Guess you can't wear your watch, so just wing it," I said. Alex's Rolex lay atop his stack of clothes. I picked it up and slipped it on my arm, above my Timex. Life wasn't fair.

Gandalf ran north of the police cruisers and out of sight, so I edged to the left, heading toward the ambulance. I squatted behind a pile of debris and peered around it. A young guardsman lay on a stretcher, his chest rising and falling with rasping breaths. He'd been gutted, and the EMTs worked to secure his spilling organs enough to get him in the ambulance. Another body lay on the ground, covered. Dead. Two of them this time. On cop shows, they call that *escalation*.

My gag reflex tried to kick in, and I closed my eyes and willed it to pass. I eased around the ambulance and tried to see the crime scene through the ocean of legs. A movement caught my eye and I saw Gandalf prowling the opposite side of the circle. He seemed to have a better angle.

"Hey, buddy." A cop standing at the edge of the onlookers spotted Gandalf and reached down to pet him. Gandalf wagged his tail, gave his best doggie grin, and moved into prime viewing position. Suck-up.

Alex had given me his tracker before he shifted, and I pulled it out of my jacket pocket and checked the signal: a faint pulse. I closed my eyes and let my mind empty so I could feel the energy around me: magic, faint and dissipating. We were too late again. Whatever did this was long gone. All I could tell was that it was the same cold, liquid energy I'd felt that first day at Gerry's.

I worked my way around the ambulance to get closer to the wounded soldier, kneeling behind the rear tire. A man wearing a conservative suit and an expressionless cop face squatted beside the stretcher as EMTs hooked up monitors and worked to stabilize the victim. Stress tightened the skin around his eyes as he watched the emergency techs work. He didn't look like he smiled a lot.

"Detective Hachette, you might as well leave." The EMT who seemed to be in charge, a woman with a headful of braids and a take-no-prisoners attitude, looked up from working on the injured man and glared at the detective. I took a closer look at Ken Hachette, former Marine buddy of Jake's and former co-owner of the Gator. He looked to be in his early thirties, and was of African-American heritage and serious demeanor. He'd been the one feeding Alex information about the murders.

"Has he been conscious?" Ken leaned toward the stretcher, looking at the soldier's face. I crept a little closer, grimacing as my knee hit an empty can. The detective's sharp gaze shot in my direction, hesitating a second as it passed over where I knelt, hopefully looking like anything other than a short, blond wizard-in-hiding. He turned back to the soldier, holding up a hand and signaling the EMTs to wait.

"We've got to get him to the hospital *now,* detective. He's not going to be talking to anybody for a while." The EMT bullied him aside, clearing a path to the rear of the ambulance. "In fact, he'll be lucky if he makes it. Somebody sliced this boy up good." She blocked my view of the techs as they raised him carefully.

"Where you taking him?" Ken asked the second EMT, a pale young man who looked like he should be at a library, working on his calculus homework. He seemed in danger of either fainting or throwing up.

"Goin' to EJ," the woman said. East Jefferson General was across the parish line, only a few miles and a civilization away from this wasteland. "He needs the Big Charity trauma unit, but it's probably shut down for good after the flood."

I stole away from the ambulance as she crawled inside with the soldier, then slinked behind police squad cars, trying to stay as close as possible to Ken in case he talked to anyone else. But he got in a light-colored sedan and sped toward Metairie, ahead of the ambulance.

I crept back to the rendezvous point, and Gandalf trotted in a couple of minutes later. He shifted back, pulled on his pants and shoes, threw on his shirt and shoulder holster, and carried his jacket. We retraced our steps to the car, not talking till we got there.

"What did you find out?" I said, panting as we buckled up and headed back toward town.

"One guardsman from North Carolina dead, his throat cut. The other one gutted—you saw him. They don't think he'll make it." His expression was still and serious. "It's such a waste."

"Could you see any of the crime scene? I couldn't get close enough."

Alex nodded. "Same as before. Dead chickens, candles. The symbol—what did you call it, the vévé? It was drawn on the side of the house nearest the body. Any signs of magic?"

"Dissipating, as usual."

We fell silent as we drove back into the small section of New Orleans that had working streetlights, and I squinted at the brilliance of them after the blackness of Lakeview.

"It's only nine," Alex said. "We've already broken curfew, and they don't seem to be enforcing it anyway. Why don't we go to the Gator, get something to eat? Jake's staying open till eleven now. They don't serve anything except fried stuff, but it beats another MRE."

I thought fried stuff sounded great. "And we need to talk to our spy. He hasn't reported in lately." In fact, he hadn't told us anything useful yet at all. But Louis seemed to be enjoying himself, Jake was making a ton of money, nobody was getting hurt, and—so far—the Elders hadn't busted me.

The Quarter was getting more crowded by the day, mostly with soldiers and reporters and construction workers. No one else had anyplace to live, so the daily traffic in and out of the city was a nightmare. Jeeps and pickups lined Bourbon Street near the Gator, so we parked a couple of blocks away on Royal and Alex pulled his coat back on to hide the gun. Had it only been a couple of weeks since I'd chastised him for carrying too many weapons? Boy, had my tune changed.

We'd almost reached the bar when I realized I'd left my cell phone in my backpack. "Give me your keys. I need to go back and get my phone." One never knew when the Elders might call. "Go on in and order me an Abita. It'll make Leyla's day if you go in without me."

Alex rolled his eyes and tossed me the keys. "Dark or amber?"

"Surprise me."

I headed back to the car, enjoying the breeze as it came off the river. The air finally had a touch of coolness to it. I loved fall in New Orleans, the one time of year when climate control was optional.

I retrieved my phone and headed back toward the Gator. I'd just reached the alley next to Jake's building when a man stepped out of the dark and clamped a hand over my mouth. I wriggled against his arm as it locked around my waist and tried to bite the fingers pressed hard against my lips. It didn't do much good—he was strong. He dragged me the length of the alley and into a dark area behind the bar I hadn't known was there. Calling it a courtyard would be too generous.

I tasted blood as I finally managed to nip his hand and jerk away from him. He responded by shoving me to the ground. My face hit the dirt before I could break my fall.

My attacker said something in French and grinned. I couldn't understand the words, but I knew the score. When faced with a guy who spoke French and was dressed like Yul Brynner in *The Buccaneer*—bad pirate garb, in other words—I pretty much knew who he worked for. He was a young, greasy-haired blond, and hadn't seen a dentist in a while. Maybe never.

I eased my cell phone from my pocket and managed to punch speed-dial three and send before he kicked the phone from my hand and clocked my chin with the toe of his boot.

I rolled into a fetal position, moving my jaw back and forth to make sure nothing was broken. God, I hated pirates.

I got a foot underneath me and rose to my feet, backing away from him and rubbing my chin. He was a very happy boy. I knew because I'd left my mojo bag in the car and could read him like a map.

"Where's your boss?" I asked, trying to ease my way around him toward the back door to the Gator. I'd worry about whether or not it was locked when I got there.

"Boss?" Pirate Bad Teeth cocked his head and grinned.

"Yeah, boss. Jean Lafitte?"

The grin widened. Lafitte should offer his hired help a dental plan and some personal hygiene classes. I struggled to remember some rudimentary French. *"Où est Lafitte?"* Not that I wanted to see him, but at least he could threaten me in English and he didn't smell bad.

Bad Teeth didn't want to talk. He motioned with his hands for me to come to him. Yeah, like that was happening. I made a run for the door but he caught my arm as I went past, and my forward momentum took us both to the ground.

I clawed at him and got a forefinger in his eye, which accomplished nothing except to make him bellow and raise a fist to hit me. I closed my eyes and tried to shield my face with my hands, waiting for the blow. It never fell. One second he was on top of me, and the next he was flying backward, courtesy of Jake.

Alex dragged him into a dark corner of the alley, while Jake jerked me to my feet and hustled me in the Gator's back door.

A gunshot brought us both to a halt.

CHAPTER 25

I turned and tried to head back out, but Jake stopped me. He pulled a key ring from his pocket, slid off a gold-colored key, and put it in my hand.

"Top of the stairs, to the right. See about your face. I'll help Alex."

I wanted to make sure Alex wasn't hurt. And if Alex had shot someone from the Beyond, I didn't want Jake to see a pirate's body disappear into the ether. But I couldn't say that. I nodded.

He touched my cheek with his fingertips and went back out.

I drooped against the wall for a few seconds, fighting a wave of dizziness, then pulled myself up the stairwell that rose off the back hallway. The sounds of the crowd, Louis singing, beer bottles hitting tabletops—all of it blended into a single wall of noise.

The second-floor landing was a small rectangle with dark wood floors and doors opening off each side. I stuck the key in the door on my right and took a look at Chez Jake. It was so not Alex. Not a set of weights, an iron, or a protein bar in sight. Just an old collection of furniture that probably came out of his parents' garage, a fancy sound system, and a shadow box displaying a Purple Heart and a Navy Cross.

I didn't stop to snoop, but headed through the bedroom and into the bathroom. A bruise was already forming, a turquoise smudge on my chin, visible even through the dirt. I opened a couple of cabinets, found a washcloth, and cleaned up as best I could. I didn't know what else to do for it.

"That's not going to be pretty come tomorrow, darlin'." Jake stood behind me with a grim expression, watching me in the mirror.

"What happened?"

"Come on downstairs. I need to close."

I gave him the key and followed him into the hallway and down the stairs. "Is Alex okay?"

"He is."

Turning monosyllabic under pressure seemed to run in the family.

Jake stopped in the tiny kitchen and talked to the cook, got Louis's attention and slashed a finger across his throat, then leaned over the bar to talk to Leyla. The band stopped mid-song and Jake got onstage, giving everyone ten minutes to finish their drinks. "Sorry to cut it short tonight folks, but it's a family emergency. Hope you'll come back tomorrow."

People began moving toward the door. I sat on a barstool and waited while Jake and Leyla rushed the stragglers out, then Leyla grabbed her purse from under the bar and made her own exit.

Before the last customer left, Alex returned from the back. His jacket wasn't even wrinkled. I raised my eyebrows and he pantomimed a shot to the head. Guess Lafitte had one less undead pirate at his disposal.

Leyla left without closing the door behind her. I walked

over, flipped the OPEN sign on the door to CLOSED, and locked the door with the thumb latch.

Alex had cleared one of the tables and motioned me over with a jerk of his head. My lip felt rubbery and heavy and my head throbbed, but we needed to do some damage control with Jake. I hoped memory modification wouldn't be necessary. I didn't want to scramble around in Jake's head, plus I didn't have the energy to slog back to the car to fetch the potion from my backpack.

Jake went behind the bar, pulled out a bottle of Four Roses, and brought it to the table along with some glasses.

"He's really upset," Alex whispered. "He's bringing out the good stuff."

Jake sat opposite Alex. "Start talking. Do I need to call the police?"

Bad idea. Plus, their buddy Ken was busy with a murder tonight, possibly two if the wounded soldier didn't make it.

"It's taken care of," Alex said. "Forget it happened."

Jake poured a couple of inches of bourbon in each glass, took one, and shoved the other two in the center of the table. "That's gonna be kind of hard with sunshine here looking like the loser in a prize fight." He reached out and turned my chin toward him. I tried not to wince.

"What did he hit you with?" Jake studied my face with the look of someone who'd seen his share of injuries. Almost clinical.

"His boot," I said. "He was kicking my phone away." Speaking of which. "I need to get my phone."

Alex reached in a pocket and slid it toward me. "I found it. Where was he?"

"Hiding in the alley. He was waiting for—" I almost said *waiting for me,* but Jake wouldn't understand why I'd have a nautical stalker. "Waiting for someone to attack."

I grabbed the glass of whiskey and took a sip. It burned all the way to my empty stomach. Alcohol was probably a bad idea. On the other hand, it might make my chin hurt less. I poked my tongue at the inside of my bottom front teeth to make sure they weren't loose.

"He try to rob you?" Jake wasn't giving up.

"I guess that's what he had in mind." Not such a lie. I'm sure he would've robbed me of something. Some dignity. Probably my freedom. Lafitte might want revenge but I still didn't think he wanted me dead. Of course, I'd been wrong before.

"Like I said, let's forget about it." Alex said. "DJ and I need to go."

Jake stared at him. "You don't seem real upset about shooting a guy dressed in a bad pirate suit behind my bar, Alex. For that matter"—he turned to me—"neither do you. So how 'bout you tell me what's going on?"

Alex cleared his throat. "I don't know—"

"Just don't even start with that *I don't know* bullshit." Jake kicked at the table, making the glasses rattle. Coils of his anger and frustration slithered over my arms like snakes. I shivered. Why-oh-why hadn't I stuck my mojo bag in my pocket instead of leaving it in the backpack?

"I know you aren't just down here helping Drusilla clean out her uncle's house. For one thing, you're not the manual labor type. And at this point, seeing as I suddenly have a dead-ringer for Louis Armstrong playing inside my bar and a dead pirate behind it, I think I have a right to know what's going on. So don't sit there and tell me you don't know."

At this point, I could have been floating around with a lampshade on my head, playing maracas and singing show tunes. Alex and Jake were having a full-tilt stare down. This was a Jake I hadn't seen before. Under that laid-back charm and all the dimples, he had a hard inner core. All I saw now was the Marine, or what happened to the Marine after life slapped him around too hard.

When I'd first met them, Alex had called Jake a tough SOB and Jake had called Alex a marshmallow. I'd thought they were deluded. Now I thought they knew each other pretty well.

The marshmallow broke first. He blew out a sigh, leaned back in his chair, and stretched his neck with a series of audible cracks. One of his stress habits. He'd be thrumming his fingers on the table next. "Okay, fine. DJ and I are working together on a case, a tough one, and I'm sorry you got caught up in it."

He looked at me briefly, as if to warn me to keep my mouth shut and play along. No problem. My lips were zipped.

"I can't say any more right now, except I'll try to keep it away from the Gator. When I can explain it to you, I will." Alex locked eyes with Jake, waiting to see if he'd buy it.

Jake rested his elbows on the table and studied his cousin for what seemed like a day and a half. "Fine. For now. But as for me and the Gator, don't change what you're doing. For whatever reason, it seems important for *Jackie* to be workin' here. I'm drawing good money off him. Just warn me if anything's going down I need to know about. And for God's sake, don't get Leyla or the band involved in anything. It's too hard to find employees right now and I don't want them getting hurt or scared off."

Jake shifted his gaze to me.

I couldn't decide whether to try and look contrite, scared, or defiant. I settled for blank-faced.

"When this is over," he said, "we're all gonna sit down and have a chat about what's going on—not just what happened tonight, but all of it."

Alex looked relieved at being let off the hook, at least temporarily. Come to think of it, I felt pretty relieved myself. I had already envisioned having the little speech that goes something like, *Sorry, Jake, but the world isn't exactly what you thought it was.*

The monsters you believed in as a kid are real, and your cousin just killed one behind your bar. Oh, and he can turn into a dog, and I'm a wizard.

We might be forced to have that conversation down the road, but not tonight.

Jake pushed his chair back and stood, signaling an end to his part of the conversation. When Alex told him again not to call the cops, he nodded, went behind the bar, and started clearing out the cash register.

Alex and I headed for the front door. As I passed him, Jake motioned for me to stop. He propped his elbows on the bar and reached over to pluck a leaf off my shirt. "You sure you're okay?"

I nodded and tried to smile, but Jake's emotions were freaking me out a little. His anger and frustration had been replaced by a heady dose of adrenaline and envy. Part of him had liked the rush of tonight's drama and wanted to be part of it.

CHAPTER 26

I walked down the stone corridor once more, and again I knew it was a dream. The corridor had changed. The smooth stones along the walls were rutted and chinked as if someone really strong had taken a mallet to them. Chunks of rock littered the pathway. Only one in three gas lanterns burned, so the shadows fell heavy and long. The door at the end of the passageway creaked when I opened it, hinges coated red with rust.

I walked into the room and saw Gerry waiting in the same chair as before. He wore a dark sweater I'd never seen, and his hair was down. His eyes were intense, and his mouth tightened in a straight, grim slash.

"You aren't making it easy for me to protect you, Drusilla. You're drawing too much attention to yourself."

When I first came in, I'd thought he was angry. But he was scared. I could feel his emotions, which I rarely could with Gerry. Plus, this was a dream, right?

"Protect me from Jean Lafitte?" A bit late for that.

He stood and paced the edges of the room. "It's bigger than Jean Lafitte, girl. Defend yourself against Lafitte if he comes after you, but don't do more. Stay away from anything to do with the Beyond."

Gerry came to a stop in front of my chair. He leaned over me, his face close to mine. I smelled Ralph Lauren aftershave, and his aura crackled over my skin. He was one step shy of panic. "Tell the Elders you know I'm dead. Have a damned memorial service if you want to." He pulled away and returned to his chair. "Just stay away from this, DJ, and keep the enforcer out of it too if you don't want him killed."

I sighed. "I hate these freaking dreams."

"This is no dream, and you best not treat it as such. Did you find the staff?"

"That thing is dangerous."

He smiled for the first time. "You can use it then? I had hoped . . ." He trailed off. "Don't let anyone know you can use it, or they'll try to exploit you, Elders and elves alike. It's important."

"Fine, I can't control it anyway. Gerry, what can I do to bring you home? If this isn't a dream, if you're still alive, tell me where you are."

"Pretend I'm dead, for now at least. Did you read the journal?"

"Which journal? There are three dozen journals."

"Nineteen-ninety—"

The dream ended abruptly as a car alarm echoed through the neighborhood. I tossed until my legs were twisted in the sheets, trying to go back to sleep, to continue the dream. Finally, I just flopped on my back and stared into the dark.

A journal from the 1990s, then. That narrowed it down, although I still didn't know what I was looking for. Or would I just be wasting time?

Okay, so these dreams didn't feel like the ordinary Freudian brain-dumps, where a bicycle meant sex and your first-grade teacher on a bicycle meant you needed therapy. These dreams, or visions, or whatever they were, had too much information in them I couldn't pull from my subconscious because I didn't know it to begin with.

Once I accepted that, the next step came more easily. I crawled out of bed and went into my library. Boxes of books sat everywhere, and another stack of loose books was piled on my worktable where Alex had been sorting them.

The journals had gotten scattered. I had some of them downstairs but some were still up here, and I still wasn't sure we'd found them all. I began dragging boxes of books aside and digging through them. I winced as a heavy volume on the history of dragon lore fell off the table and crashed on the floor like a boulder. I hoped Alex was a heavy sleeper.

Apparently that wasn't in the enforcer job description. Only a few seconds passed before I heard him climbing the stairs. He appeared at the door wearing low-slung jeans and a rumpled frown. In other circumstances, I'd have stopped to admire the view.

"Insomnia?" His frown deepened as I replayed my dream.

I tried to be dismissive. "I know it's probably just a dream—it's normal that I'd dream of Gerry."

"Are you sure? Did you and Gerry ever communicate mentally?"

I snorted. "The only people with fewer psychic powers than Green Congress wizards are Red Congress wizards."

"Well, we're up now," he said. "Why not at least take all the journals to one place and pull out the ones from the nineties?"

We gathered them up and took them to the kitchen table, sorting out ten journals dated between 1990 and 1999. I opened one, running my fingers along the lines of tiny print. A bunch of little leather books representing the sum of a man's life.

Alex reached out, took the journal from me, and set it on the table. "We can do this tomorrow. Between the pirate and the dream, you've been through enough tonight."

The pressure of unshed tears built behind my eyes, and I turned to go back in the living room, not wanting him to see me awash in my own pool of self-pity. He reached for me again, and gathered me into a hug, holding on even when I stiffened and tried to pull away. I didn't grow up around touchy-feely people, and didn't know how to let him in or even know if I wanted to. Finally, I let myself rest my cheek against his chest and inhale the scent of soap and sandalwood aftershave, comforting yet exotic.

He leaned in, his lips hovering over mine, hesitant. I kissed him, whisper soft, and he took the invitation. The hard muscles of his back bunched as he lifted me to sit on the counter. He trailed his fingers over my face where the bruise ached, then wedged his body between my knees and kissed me again, his hands holding me against him, mine sliding around his waist. I reached out to him with my mind and felt his want, his protectiveness. The worry and fear of the day melted under his warmth. Scent. Taste.

I finally pulled away, my voice ragged. "We can't do this."

It was two a.m., and both of us were vulnerable. Alex's feelings for me were all mixed up in his rivalry with Jake, and I didn't know what I wanted. We were just learning to work together. Maybe we were even becoming friends. Anything else had Big Mistake written all over it. It would be so easy to do but so hard to fix.

Alex backed away, looking rattled, and I eased myself off the counter. We busied ourselves piling the journals from the nineties in one box, and the rest of the journals in another. I took the small box to the living room. He stayed in the kitchen.

Not that we were avoiding each other or anything.

TUESDAY, SEPTEMBER 27, 2005 "City tries again to bring life to shattered area . . . Most of N.O. unlivable; Louisiana death toll 864."

—THE TIMES-PICAYUNE

CHAPTER 27

I read past dawn, but still hadn't found anything by the time Alex left on an emergency job for the Elders, checking a new breach that had popped up in Lower Plaquemines Parish, southeast of New Orleans. It would require a boat, an FBI badge to gain access to the hurricane-decimated area, and possibly guns. I elected to stay home.

We ate breakfast together, making polite conversation but avoiding eye contact. I had done my grounding ritual before breakfast, covered my bruised face with makeup, and had my mojo bag refreshed and in my pocket. I didn't know if Alex felt awkward after our late-night kitchen make-out session, but I did.

"What time will you be back?" I asked. "The construction guy from Picayune's coming down to look at Gerry's house about lunchtime."

He'd just finished cleaning the big pistol on the coffee table and was strapping on a Kevlar vest. "Not sure—it may be hard getting in there without the local deputies wanting to tag along, or it may be a cakewalk. No way to know. Eugenie's home—why don't you get her to keep you company? Maybe wait on going to Lakeview. Lafitte's going to try again."

Yeah, and no telling how many pirates he had running around looking for me. My encounter with Bad Teeth had rattled me. I knew Lafitte could come back, but hadn't realized he might have a whole crew of undead pirates with him. They weren't famous enough to have a long shelf life outside the Beyond, but Bad Teeth had created a lot of trouble in less than ten minutes.

Still, I couldn't sit at home and hide behind my wards, and besides, I had a plan that didn't include Alex. "I need to get this over with," I said. "Besides, the construction guy's probably already left Picayune. It's too far to make him drive for nothing."

Alex holstered the pistol. "Be careful. Take the elven staff with you, at least. You can set fire to anyone who tries to hurt you."

He almost smiled, and we almost looked each other in the eye. I breathed a silent prayer of thanks that the Big Mistake hadn't happened.

As soon as Alex left, I retrieved the journal I'd been working on before breakfast. I was at 1997 and working my way down. A lot of the entries were in the form of angry diatribes against the Elders, mostly Willem Zrakovi and Daniel Ciro, head of the Red Congress—Gerry's boss.

The journal entries didn't tell me anything useful about Gerry's whereabouts or current problems but did give me some insights into his views on magic policy. How had he felt so at odds with the Elders and yet spent so much time teaching me the importance of following the rules? Or maybe I had been so self-absorbed I didn't observe the differences between the talk and the walk.

I glanced at the clock and cursed. Time to head to Lakeview. I gathered my backpack, complete with a few extra items I'd added this morning, then grabbed the elven staff. "You get to go this time, Charlie." If it was going to follow me around like a pet, it might as well have a name.

This construction friend of Don Warin's was doing me a big favor by driving down to look at Gerry's house. Between Katrina and Rita, crews across the Gulf Coast from Mobile to Port Arthur had waiting lists longer than Santa on Christmas Eve. At least I didn't have to sit around and wait for insurance adjusters—Eugenie was on her second. She had buckets all over her attic to catch rainwater.

I parked behind Gerry's upended BMW and coughed as I got out of the Pathfinder. With the return of hot, dry weather after Rita, the thick layer of mud had dried and cracked in the blazing sun, creating a pattern that looked like alligator skin. I dragged the mask out of the car and hung it around my neck, and dug another peppermint out of my backpack.

A heavy-duty pickup already sat in front of the house. It had probably once been white. Now it was covered in mottled shades of brown and gray like everything else. A short, beefy guy with red hair and an open, friendly face full of freckles climbed out to meet me, and he wasn't alone. I'd recognize his companion's dimples anywhere.

Jake introduced me to Rick the construction guy as *Alex's old lady*. He even managed to do it with a straight face.

"Yeah, Donnie told me Alex found him a woman and settled down. Never thought I'd see it," Rick said, giving me a jovial once-over but obviously seeing no need to address me directly. "She met Norma yet?"

"Not yet. They're still enjoying their domestic bliss," Jake answered, as if I weren't standing next to him. "Hate to spoil it by bringin' Aunt Norma into the mix."

I rolled my eyes, which was about all the protest I could muster after making out with Alex on the kitchen counter.

We slipped on our boots and masks and headed into the house. I'd been leaving my plastic go-go boots outside Gerry's door. Nobody had been desperate enough to steal them. Copper wiring was the hot ticket with flood-zone thieves these days.

Going inside put an end to any joking. The mold had continued to blossom since my last visit, barely leaving the house recognizable as the place I'd grown up in. Rick walked around with a clipboard, making notes. Jake occasionally pointed something out to him.

I squished around and got depressed at the talk of studs and drywall and mold penetration. Finally, I went out back, stripped off my crud gear, and sat on the deck, its wood dry and fragile—at least the half that hadn't already caved in. Eventually, it would rot like everything else. The houses on either side of Gerry's were deserted, windows broken out. Heck, every single house in Lakeview was deserted. Two square miles empty and ten thousand people homeless just in this one neighborhood. Then multiply it by dozens more neighborhoods.

There wasn't much left of Gerry here anymore except the upstairs furniture. Nothing from the first floor could be saved. I had taken all the books already and boxed up his personal stuff—clothes, shoes, even a few small furnishings—and stacked them up to take home with me a little at a time. When he came back, he could stay with me till his house was habitable again. At least that's what I kept telling myself.

Rick's heavy boots echoed through the open door as he tromped up the stairs to continue his inspection. Jake came out back, stripped off his mask, and stomped as much muck as he could off his boots. He eased himself to the deck beside me, favoring his right leg, and massaged his hand over the muscle just above the knee.

"It still hurts you, doesn't it?"

"Aw, no. I just use it to get girls to feel sorry for me." He bumped his shoulder against mine and smiled. "Is it working?"

I laughed and shook my head, thinking Jake Warin had to be the kindest, bravest man I'd ever met. After all he'd been through, all the pain he lived with every day, he was trying to cheer me up.

His smile faded. "Do you need help taking anything out of the house—you know, furniture or bigger boxes? I still have my dad's old Dodge." I'd thought the Dakota with the Jaguar hood ornament was his.

I sighed. I didn't want Gerry's furniture to end up on the curb with the piles of limbs and moldy Sheetrock—that hurt to think about. But I didn't have room for it, either. I wondered if he'd want it after losing the rest of the house, and figured the answer would be no. Gerry loved antiques but he wasn't sentimental about stuff in general.

"I'd like Gerry's desk eventually, I guess." He'd want that saved. Nothing from the bedroom. I still hadn't broken the ash transport circle and triangle there, but had pulled a rug over it. I'd do it after Jake and Rick left.

Jake looked around, his tawny eyes reflecting gold in the midafternoon sun. "This is a nice property. You could rebuild, you know. It's more land than you have in town, and once they get the floodwalls rebuilt it'll be safer. No way the Army engineers are gonna let this happen again."

I tried to see it from his viewpoint, but all I could think about was loss. It hadn't even occurred to me that if Gerry was truly gone, I'd probably inherit this. Or maybe Tish, unless he had some family members hidden away somewhere. It didn't matter.

"I don't want to live here again. I don't think I could."

Jake wound his fingers through mine. Holding hands felt nice. I could read his affection and concern and protectiveness.

No overriding urge to lock lips next to the breadbox. I leaned my head on his shoulder and we watched a pair of gulls sitting on the buckled floodwall, impervious to either us or the racket of the Army helicopters that still hovered over Lakeview.

He raised my hand and kissed the back of my knuckles, then released it and stood as Rick walked out the back door, clipboard in hand, mask around his neck. The rotting deck groaned under the weight of the contractor in his heavy boots, and a black trail of sludgy footprints followed him out the door. Back to reality.

"What do you think?" Jake asked.

I struggled to wrench my mind from Jake and focus on Rick. Rick was simple. Rick just wanted to fix Gerry's house. Rick wasn't interested in a relationship more complicated than wielding a hammer and collecting a paycheck.

He cleared his throat and looked at his clipboard. "Ms. Jaco, I know you hoped we'd be able to leave the upstairs like it was, but I'd really advise you to let us gut the whole thing." His light blue eyes radiated sympathy. I wondered how often he'd given this speech in the last couple of weeks.

"The mold has gotten into the upstairs walls, and I just don't think you want to risk not getting it all. The roof's okay, so we can strip it back to the studs, get rid of the mold and moisture, and then you can decide later what you want to do with it."

I wasn't surprised, but it still felt like a knife in the gut. I looked down at the rotting deck and wondered what Gerry would want to do—that made the answer simple.

"Go ahead and strip it down." We set a date for late October, the earliest Rick's demolition crew could get to it.

As soon as the guys left, I pulled the mucky boots on again and got my backpack out of the Pathfinder. I walked slowly through the downstairs, opening my mind to feel any magical energy that might be there. All clear.

Same thing upstairs. I ended in Gerry's bedroom, unrolling the rug carefully to expose the ash transport. I'd been doing my bedtime reading on magic reconstruction. It was a complex ritual with iffy results, but I saw no reason not to try it—only wished I'd found out about it earlier.

If the ritual worked, I would be able to see the last person to use the transport. It wouldn't tell me where the person had gone, but at least I'd know if Gerry was the one who'd used it.

I made sure the interlocking circle and triangle were still intact, smoothing out a couple of rough spots caused by moving the rug, then took out a small jar of ground ash roots and sprinkled them in a circle and triangle just inside the original. I shaped the new figures carefully with my fingers so they'd touch Gerry's original symbol at all points. Inside that, I traced the shapes again with dried ground ivy. The work was tedious; each layer had to touch the layer next to it, but not overlap.

Next, I took a vial of pomegranate juice and two small emeralds, and stepped inside the transport, sitting cross-legged. I spoke the words for invoking the magical reconstruction as I dragged a finger covered with the bright pink juice across my forehead. Finally, I took an emerald in each palm and made a fist, injecting small bits of magic into the memory stones.

Then I concentrated and waited. When my mind wandered, I'd bring it back to the circle. The room grew hotter, the light outside my eyelids brighter, but I didn't open them. Finally, I saw the room in my mind—not a memory but an image, as if I were viewing it from outside my body. I watched Gerry enter the transport. A tall black man stepped in next to him, a white skeleton painted on his skin. He wore a top hat and a tuxedo jacket.

The Baron Samedi was transporting out with Gerry, and they were laughing.

CHAPTER 28

I drove home in a daze. Alex had been right all along, damn it. Gerry had struck a deal with Samedi, gone somewhere with him willingly, and his plans had obviously gone wrong. Samedi was Gerry's mysterious visitor from the Beyond.

I couldn't deny Gerry's complicity anymore. Whatever had happened to him at Samedi's hand, Gerry had put himself in position for it to happen.

I pulled into my drive at four thirty and saw Alex's car already there. I sat in the Pathfinder a minute, taking deep breaths and fingering the mojo bag I'd hung around my neck with a cord. My chest felt tight, and I wanted to break something.

Gerry had been stupid. There, I'd been disloyal and thought it. I doubted anyone in the Beyond could be truly trusted, but the god of a minor religion, barely kept alive by people's fading beliefs? Gerry knew better, because he taught me better. I wasn't sure how I could be so worried about Gerry, and still be so pissed off at him. Right now, I'd like to find him so I could wring his neck.

Grabbing my backpack, I stomped to the back stoop, climbed the stairs, and stopped with my key halfway to the door. An ornate silver dagger protruded from the wood, where it was serving as a pushpin to hold an envelope in place.

Alex opened the door. "Why are you just standing . . . What's wrong?"

"Did you come in the back?"

"Yeah, why?"

I pulled the dagger from the door facing, handed it to Alex, and opened the envelope. Inside was a card signed *J Laffite* in an ornate, flowery script, along with a spent bullet. I wasn't sure why history had changed the spelling of the pirate's name to Lafitte but he'd apparently missed the memo.

I laid the bullet in my palm. "This look familiar?"

"Let's go back inside." As soon as we closed the door behind us and locked it, he took the bullet and examined it. "It's a .45, military issue. Looks like the kind I used on Lafitte."

"It's probably the *one* you used." I handed him the card and took the dagger, turning it over in my hand. Lafitte had gouged a hole in my plaster wall with one just like it, down to its wicked triangular blade.

Alex tried his tracker at the back door and got a faint, pulsing signal. "At least he didn't hang around waiting for you."

"He knew you were here."

"Maybe he's after me instead of you—I'm the one who shot him."

I considered that possibility. "No, it's me. Jean Lafitte and I have a bad history that began before you trotted in with your shotgun."

I pulled a soda from the fridge and went into the living room.

"And, by the way, you were right about Gerry all along." The familiar ache of magic settled into my muscles as soon as I hit the armchair. Not just magic, though. Too much stress, too little sleep, too many skipped meals.

"What are you talking about?"

I told him about the reconstruction ritual, about Gerry and Samedi heading off who knows where, practically arm in arm.

He sat quietly for several minutes and wouldn't look at me. "You know we have to tell Zrakovi."

I nodded and stared at the floor. "I just don't understand why he'd do it. Why he'd risk himself like that."

Alex remained quiet. I finally looked up at him, expecting either an *I told you so* or a show of sympathy. I didn't expect anger. His eyes were dark, and he tightened his hands into fists, then released them, then tightened them again. He looked like he wanted to punch something. Hard.

"Look, I'm sorry," I said. The last thing I wanted was to alienate Alex. He was the only ally I had now. "I know I shouldn't have done this when you weren't there—"

"I'm not mad at you." He got up and paced the living room, his voice low, words clipped. "If I could get my hands on Gerry right now I'd kill him."

I slumped against the back of the chair, unsure how to defend Gerry anymore. "You can't be surprised. This is what you suspected all along. He went rogue, or at least it's sure looking that way." Treason. Execution order. I was mad at Gerry, but I couldn't stand to see that.

Alex sat on the sofa next to me. "I guess I'd started to see him through your eyes. I can believe he'd risk himself for his ideals, but I can't believe he'd risk you. Any danger you're in is all on him."

He stretched his arm around me and squeezed my shoulder. I knew he wanted to comfort me, and I wanted to be comforted. But we sat there awkwardly for a minute and didn't look at each other. It was too soon after the counter episode.

"Have you eaten dinner?" I asked.

"No."

We headed for the kitchen, dragging out MREs. At the rate we were consuming them, we'd have to break down and start cooking in another week or so.

I filled him in on the house inspection, and in the interest of full disclosure, told him Jake was there.

"I'm not surprised. He worked with Rick in construction awhile after college, before he went into the Corps."

I decided the less discussion of Jake, the better. "What was your mysterious errand today?"

Alex grimaced. "A new clan of merpeople has moved into South Plaquemines, in a small community called Tidewater. They're mainstreamed in the fishing industry. After talking to the clan leader and the Elders, we decided to let them stay, at least until things settle down. The Elders have their hands full with the vampire regents and the fae right now. They don't have time to deal with mers."

"What are the vamps and fae up to?"

Alex shook his head. "Same old thing, I guess. They're using the storm and the temporal breaches as an excuse to reopen the whole subject of border oversight. I'm sure there are a lot of other prete groups watching to see what happens."

About seven, Alex got another call from Ken. The Voodoo Killer had struck again. Another guardsman, this time in Bywater, halfway between the Quarter and the Lower Nine. Five deaths now, plus the poor guy still barely hanging on. I wasn't sure how much more New Orleans could take before it imploded, or how long before the National Guardsmen would be drawing straws between facing the dangers of New Orleans versus Kabul or Baghdad—and who could blame them?

"Ken invited me to look at the crime scene before forensics gets in there," he said, strapping on his vest and shoulder holster.

"I know you will disagree, but I think you should stay here, behind your wards. Lock yourself in. Lafitte's already come after you once tonight."

If I sat here by myself all night, waiting for Jean Lafitte to show up, I'd go crazy. "I think I'll go to the Gator. Why don't you meet me there after you finish up?"

"Forget it." He pulled a jacket on over his vest. "That's one of the first places Lafitte will look for you, and you're less exposed here."

I blew out an exasperated breath. "I can't just sit here waiting for something bad to happen, Alex. I will go berserk." I'd be jumping at every leaf that hit the porch, every sigh of breeze that swept past the window.

When he flicked his gaze toward heaven and shook his head, I knew I'd won.

"Fine," he said. "But I'll drop you at the Gator on my way out and make sure you aren't hijacked by pirates."

"Give me five minutes."

I ran upstairs and reapplied makeup on my chin bruise. I also grabbed my spare mojo bag and stuck it in my pocket, and picked up the backpack. I wouldn't be caught empty-handed again. On the way out, I tripped over the elven staff, which had placed itself across the doorway.

I thought of Bad Teeth and his boot heel. "Okay, Charlie. You're going." I stuck it in the backpack. It poked out one side of the flap, but till I found a better carrier, it would do.

As soon as Alex dropped me off and I opened the door of the Gator, the noise hit me like a physical force. BeauSoleil was rocking "Zydeco Gris-Gris" on the jukebox, and most of the tables were already full of guys. It was a great time to be a single woman on the prowl in New Orleans, as long as soldiers and construction workers were your type.

Leyla spotted me at the door and nodded toward an empty

stool at the near end of the bar. By the time I climbed up, she'd brought a Diet Barq's. "Jake's meeting with a supplier," she shouted over the din.

I paid her for the soda. "Is Jackie upstairs?"

She nodded, and I wove my way through the bar to the back. My spy hadn't exactly been forthcoming with useful information.

Louis answered on the second knock, looked up and down the hall after letting me in, and relocked the door before I'd made it two feet inside.

"I heard on the news that another man's been killed." His eyes were wild, and his fingers twitched at the lapels of his dark suit.

I nodded and sat on the sofa, hoping he'd do the same. He was making me nervous. "You hadn't called, so I wanted to check in and see what you'd found out. You're not hearing anything about these murders from your sources in the Beyond?"

He finally perched on the edge of the armchair. "I'm not a very good spy, DJ. I only hear about things after they happen, or things that don't seem important. Like that pirate moving in down the street."

My breath hitched. "What?"

He nodded. "That Jean Lafitte. He's set up in the Quarter somewhere. Don't think he has anything to do with the murders. Although, with pirates, I guess you never know."

Holy crap. "What *do* you know about the pirate, exactly?"

He shrugged. "Only that it's someplace he knew from his first life, and he's got some guys with him."

Double holy crap. That could be just about any place in the Quarter.

Louis' shoulders sagged. "Like I said, I'm not a very good spy."

I barked out a laugh. "Maybe better than you know. Anything else you found out after it happened?"

"Nothing I can think of."

I stayed in Louis' room after he went down for his first set, thinking about Jean Lafitte sitting somewhere nearby like a big hairy spider, waiting for the right moment to pounce. That was just wrong. Why should I have to cower and sneak around my own town? I shouldn't have to be escorted everywhere by an elven staff or a guy with a gun.

Jean Lafitte was smart. He had a reputation for being ultimately loyal to only one person: himself. He could be bargained with. Surely I hadn't made him so angry he'd pass up a profitable business deal. Plus, I got the impression he was a player in the Beyond. I might be able to get information from him about Gerry.

I wasn't waiting for him to find me. I'd find him.

I took a cab home, greeted a grumpy Sebastian—oh, wait, that was redundant—and went upstairs to the library. I pulled the Elders' magic-box tracker to the edge of my worktable and leaned over it, studying all the blinking lights. I wrote down the five breaches in the French Quarter in a notebook.

Taking the list to my computer, I powered up and, thanking God for restored Internet service, Googled all five addresses. I had thought one of them might be the Lafitte Blacksmith Shop, where Jean Lafitte's brother Pierre had run the legitimate front for their smuggling empire. But it wasn't one of the addresses listed.

Two of the breach sites were open areas—one at Armstrong Park, the other at St. Anthony's Garden behind St. Louis Cathedral. A third was at an art gallery on Bourbon surrounded by businesses that had started reopening. The pirate wouldn't want to risk that much exposure.

Two possibilities remained: either a Royal Street shop selling French antiques or the Napoleon House on Chartres. Both buildings predated the pirate, and Jean Lafitte was definitely a

French antique in his own right. But antique shops were usually crowded with merchandise and wouldn't offer enough space for a comfortable pirate hangout.

That left the Napoleon House. The restaurant and bar was still closed, and there were big banquet rooms upstairs off a courtyard, well hidden from the street. It was a ballsy place to hide out, being across the street from the big Royal Orleans Hotel and a block from the district police station, but Jean Lafitte was a ballsy kind of guy. He'd like it that the cops were a block away and clueless, and he'd like staying in a place that had been built as a residence-in-exile for Napoleon Bonaparte, even if the emperor had never actually lived there.

I knew where to find Lafitte.

CHAPTER 29

I took inventory of my backpack contents, then slung it over my shoulder and headed downstairs. I clutched the elven staff in my right hand, not because I thought I could use it, but because it made me feel better. Tougher. Ready for another round with an angry Frenchman.

Stopping at the Gator again, I got some paper from Leyla and left Alex a note. If Jean Lafitte didn't kill me, Alex would. Either way, it shouldn't be a boring night.

A fine mist wet the streets, and I shivered in my lightweight sweater and jeans, walking close to the buildings both for warmth and camouflage. At the corner of St. Louis and Chartres, I stopped in the shadow of the Omni Royal Orleans and studied the Napoleon House. Its front door opened catercorner to the intersection, and the first floor containing the restaurant and bar was dark. I studied the second- and third-floor windows, but drapes or shutters blocked any light that might be there.

I wondered if the front door was locked. Lafitte's pirates would need to be able to slip in and out quickly. Looking around to make sure no one was nearby, I crossed the street and gently pulled on the handle. Locked, damn it.

I walked alongside the building down St. Louis until I reached the next storefront. No way in there.

Retracing my steps, I walked down Chartres on the other side and found a small wooden door, absent any signage, that was in the right spot to lead into the kitchen area or courtyard. I looked around again, then tried the door. It swung open and I stepped inside quickly, closing it behind me.

A dim light shone from somewhere in front of me, but it wasn't bright enough to keep me from tripping or help me get a read on my surroundings. I knelt and stuck the elven staff back in my pack, then slid open the zipper on the front, feeling for my obsidian amulet. I warmed the stone in my hand and willed a tiny burst of energy into it, enough to bring a faint glow.

I was in a narrow hallway that opened into the courtyard. A door to the right about halfway down looked as if it went into a storeroom. The path ahead of me was clear, so I stuck the amulet back in my pack and crept to the courtyard opening.

A soft light flickered from an open door upstairs, enough for me to take a better look at the layout of the courtyard. I'd been here a lot as a customer. The bartenders mixed a mean Pimm's Cup, the kitchen turned out great muffalettas, the sound system played classical music, and the ambience of shabby elegance made it a great place to pass the time.

I'd never looked at it from a siege standpoint, however. The long, rectangular dining room and bar stretched to my right. Around the courtyard sat tables with chairs propped on top of them, and several big banana trees. To my left rose a staircase of dark wood leading to a gallery-style balcony that stretched around the second floor. The third floor looked empty, but not the second, and a large room normally rented out for banquets and private dinners was the source of the light.

The banana tree opposite the room made a good hiding place, but didn't show me how many people were upstairs. Male voices spoke softly in French, a glass tinkled, a laugh echoed off the balcony. The smell from a cigar tickled my nose and mixed with the damp mustiness of the courtyard.

I chewed my lip, thinking. I hated to prance up the steps and walk into the room without knowing how many people were there, and how well they were armed. I wished I had the time and materials to do some hydromancy, but wishes . . . horses . . . beggars.

Finally, I formed a plan. It wasn't a good plan, more of the kitchen-sink variety: full frontal assault, mixed with a little seduction and, if needed, begging and pleading. Tears might be called for, assuming one of Lafitte's goons didn't shoot me on sight.

I checked my knife and staff, then took a bit of ground buckthorn and periwinkle leaves and placed them into a bottle of purified water from my pack. I gulped down about half of the translation potion, grimacing at the bitter taste.

Lafitte spoke fluent English but if he started chattering in French or Spanish, I wanted to understand what he was saying. The buckthorn brew should bridge any language barriers for a few hours. I hoped I wouldn't be here that long.

I pulled the elven staff out of my bag, took a deep breath, and marched up the stairs, making no attempt to be quiet. Since I had decided subterfuge wasn't going to work, I'd go the opposite route and see how far fake bravado got me. My boots clicked on the wooden steps and, as I expected, the aged floor of the gallery creaked when I walked across it. I couldn't have slipped up on them.

A short, red-haired man stepped out of the open doorway ahead and stared at me, green eyes opened wide in shock. He cursed in French; I heard it in English. Only bad thing about those translation potions was an annoying disconnect between ear and mouth, like watching a TV show where the sound wasn't in sync with the picture. He lowered a bayonet toward me but it was almost an afterthought. Guess I didn't look that scary.

"Captain Lafitte?" I figured that would transcend any language barriers.

The sentry raised his bayonet like a drawbridge and edged his black boots back to let me pass. He looked scared, but I couldn't feel his fear. My grounding and mojo bag were holding.

I stepped into the room, taking a quick look around at the drawn curtains that kept the dim candlelight hidden from the street, and at the two men sitting on either side of Lafitte. All gaped at me in shock over their brandy snifters. A wooden box of cigars sat on the table.

So we had Lafitte and three other pirates versus one little wizard. No problem.

Lafitte recovered first. His expression was careful, noncommittal. "You are always a surprise to me, Mademoiselle Jaco. Are you so foolish as to have come here alone?"

He leaned back in his chair, stretching his long legs and crossing them at the ankles. He wore a simple white shirt open halfway to his waist, and a blue jacket hung on the back of his chair. His dark hair was pulled back and tied at the neck with a blue ribbon. Very pirate couture.

I decided to start with the humble tactic, and tried to match his formal speech patterns. I'm all about respect. "You're looking well, Captain. I must apologize for the way things last ended with us. I don't choose to solve my problems with violence." Well, not with a shotgun anyway.

He pulled the shirt front aside a bit to reveal a pink scar. He was virtually healed. Even the scar would be gone in a few days. "I do not hold you responsible for this, although your friend . . . well, let us say it will be best if he is not with you this evening."

I nodded, glad I'd bypassed Alex. I wanted diplomacy to have failed decisively before the shooting began.

Lafitte rose and sauntered around the table toward me, graceful as a lion. I considered screaming and running past the sentry and back into the courtyard, but stood my ground out of nothing more than sheer stubbornness. I had sought him out, after all. I was a warrior. Warriors don't scream and run.

I could feel the power rolling off him as he came to a stop in front of me. It wasn't an empathic thing, just an aura powerful people had, intensity and confidence and arrogance so strong you could almost touch it.

He put a big hand on my shoulder, squeezing slightly, and pulled me, stumbling, farther into the room. "Sit with us, Drusilla." Sounded like the pirate and I had advanced to a first-name basis.

Like a gentleman, Lafitte introduced me to his companions, beginning with the bayonet-wielding redhead, Bouret, who'd reassumed his position at the door. I assumed he was a junior pirate flunky since he didn't rate a seat with the big boys.

The two men at the table stood as we approached: Pierre Lafitte, shorter, darker-skinned and heavier than his brother, and Dominique You, who looked like every clichéd movie pirate I'd ever seen, complete with a hook nose, a powerful build, and a look of amusement that made me shiver. Also thought by many to be a Lafitte half-brother, You had been Jean's most trusted soldier in his first life. Apparently in his undead life as well.

All of the men wore knives, but I didn't see any guns other than the one attached to Bouret's bayonet. They hadn't expected a fight tonight. Fewer guns was a good thing.

Pierre Lafitte moved toward the windows, and Jean shoved

me into the chair at the table, a little more forcefully than was necessary, I thought. Guess they weren't going to invite me for cigars and brandy.

I settled the backpack and elven staff against my chair, within easy reach of my right hand. Jean resumed his seat and eyed me expectantly, both amusement and lust washing over me, but not anger. That meant the seduction card might still be on the table, and if not, well, they could laugh at me all they wanted. I could be really amusing when I had to be.

"You know, Captain Lafitte, I expected you to be down at your old blacksmith shop. It's a bar now, but the building's still intact." Nervous babble. But it seemed too abrupt to just come right out and ask him to quit stalking me—oh, and if he'd heard anything about Gerry or Baron Samedi.

His laugh was sharp. "Surely you did not come here to discuss history or architecture, Drusilla." He smiled. "And surely you can call me Jean at this, how do you say, advanced stage of our relationship."

We had a relationship? I forced myself to look away from his glittering eyes and focused on his mouth. This was not a relationship I wanted to have. Well, it might be fun for a while but it didn't have a future. One of us was already technically dead and I didn't think I'd be well-remembered enough to warrant a magical afterlife outside the Beyond.

"I came here to ask you to forgive me for what happened earlier, and to offer you another partnership—a real one this time."

A slow smile spread across his face and he leaned back in his seat, gesturing for me to continue.

Dominique leaned forward in the chair opposite me, arms propped on the table, and gave me a steely look that made me think he might really, really enjoy a good round of torture. I could read nothing but aggression from him. No point wasting my womanly wiles on him.

I shuddered and looked back at Jean, glad I could observe their emotions without feeling them myself—so far.

Jean reached out to stroke my arm.

I slapped his hand away. "Business first." I'd keep the seduction option closed as long as I could.

He narrowed his eyes and chuckled. "And what do you think you can offer me now, Drusilla, other than a little playtime? You need my assistance much more than I need yours, especially since crossing into the city from the Beyond is so simple now."

Well, yeah, he had a point, but still.

He leaned back and raised his eyebrows, mouth quirked up at one corner. "But I will listen to your business offer. It should at least be entertaining."

I could do entertaining. "I'm the New Orleans sentinel now. I can get you concessions from the Elders to trade antiques for modern goods between the modern world and the Beyond, as you've wanted. As long as no ordinary people are made aware of it and no one is injured, of course. What I'm saying is that up to a certain point, I can look the other way while you do business— if you help me." I wasn't sure how well I could fulfill that promise should he go for it, but I'd sweat the details later.

He sighed and leaned forward over the table, pulling the red elastic band from my hair, loosening my ponytail and letting my hair fall around my shoulders. I thought I was going to have to slap his hand away again but he only stroked my hair once before settling back in his chair, looking at the elastic with interest and then sticking it in his pocket. Thief.

"And in exchange for this generosity on your part, *Jolie*, what would you want from me?"

"Forgiveness for my former actions," I said. "And information. When we first met, I got the impression you knew about the elves and the vampires, so I assume you make it your business to know what's going on in the Beyond."

He crossed his arms over his chest. "I find it only sensible to know the things that go on around me, *oui*."

"Then what I want is to learn what the Baron Samedi is doing, and if Gerald St. Simon is helping him."

He exchanged glances with Dominique. "Why do you think I have been looking for you, Drusilla?"

Uh, revenge. Or maybe not. My uncertainty must have shown, because Jean and Dominique laughed.

"I am not looking for revenge, although you certainly deserve it. No, Samedi sent me here to capture you and bring you to him, in exchange for much the same offer you have made—free rein to do business once the borders are under new control. So the question for me is, whose offer should I take? Why should I work with you instead of him?"

My mouth felt dry and I stuck my hands underneath my legs to keep them from shaking. Samedi wanted me? And had approached Jean?

I stiffened as Pierre came to stand behind my chair and reached over me for his glass of brandy. He leaned too close, but I didn't flinch. Big girls don't flinch.

"She would be much more enjoyable to bargain with than Samedi," Pierre told Jean, stroking a hand up my arm. Okay, now I flinched. He didn't match Jean's oozing power but he had a stronger dose of creepy.

"I agree that she could be most enjoyable." Jean said. "Of course, we can take *her* without taking her bargain, *oui*? As she once told me herself, she is but a woman."

Misogynistic brute. Jean and I stared at each other, both of us more calculating than angry. More a chess match than a duel. I'd done my research. The pirate had a ruthless side, but he also had his own warped moral code. Loyalty had been paramount to him. His men who broke the rules didn't have to worry about being caught by the authorities. They had to worry about Jean hanging them from the nearest cypress tree.

"You should work with me instead of Samedi because I'll keep my word. I won't lie to you or turn against you. I'll be a loyal partner."

Jean's left eyebrow rose a fraction as Dominique and Pierre barked out harsh laughter.

I shrugged. "Well, okay, the thing in Delacroix was a lie, technically. But I'm not lying now." I felt my bargaining position sink lower by the minute. I didn't have a moral high horse to ride.

I tried again. "Tell me what you want in exchange for information. If it is mine to give, I will."

He stood and walked to the outer window, pulling the shade aside a fraction to look out on the street. "I would want these things. Free passage to come and go into New Orleans as I choose, without interference from your Elders or your enforcers." He dropped the shade back in place and paced the room. "I want your assistance with my business dealings, as you offered before. Also, I want a house in the city where I can live when I am here." He walked behind my chair and leaned over, whispering, "Perhaps one near yours."

He wanted to be neighbors? Well, that would be fun.

"There might be more, but I would have to give it some thought. Can you offer me these things?" Jean half-sat on the table next to me so I had to crane my neck to see his face. Talk about a power position.

I thought about it, about how I could finesse it with the Elders. About whether I could live up to my part of the agreement without the Elders knowing it. About what the pirate would do to me if I didn't follow through.

"How do I know the information you give me is worth the

price?" I asked, mentally calculating if I could hold down a second job at McDonald's to pay rent on a pirate den in my neighborhood.

He bent down, smelling of tobacco and cinnamon, and smiled. "It will be a gamble, no?"

I took a deep breath and nodded. "I agree."

"*Trés bon.*"

Jean walked back to his seat. "I will tell you this first, *Jolie*. I had already decided not to take the Baron up on his offer to procure you for him."

Procure was an awfully nice way of saying *kidnap*. "What does the Baron want with me?"

Jean eyed me thoughtfully. "Perhaps I should not make a bargain with you, Drusilla. If you do not survive the Baron's attempts to gain power, our arrangement will not be worth much and I will have angered him for nothing."

"Then it behooves you to help me survive it," I snapped. He was either going to tell me what I needed to know, or he wasn't. Alex could show up at any time.

"The Baron wants to make a partnership with you to replace the one he made with your mentor. If you do not agree, he plans to kill you in order to gain your power. He will probably do so regardless."

Mentor. Jean knew about Gerry. I swallowed down the rising panic and tried to understand.

"What kind of bargain does he have with Gerry?"

Jean shrugged. "Your mentor wants the Baron to grow in power so he can force your Elders to change their laws. In order to help him do so, he has established ways for us to come and go at will from the Beyond through these . . . what do you call them?"

He gestured over his shoulder and I leaned around to see

the interlocking circle and triangle drawn on the shiny wood floor. My heart sank.

"An open transport," I whispered. Gerry was out of his mind.

"*Oui,* a transport."

I took a deep breath, trying to organize the questions and thoughts flying around my brain like leaves in a hurricane. "I still don't understand why you need Gerry's transport—the borders between New Orleans and the Beyond were damaged by the storm. I've seen Samedi, so I know he's crossed over at least once." Not to mention Jean himself and Louis Armstrong and whoever else wanted to trot across the borders.

"The damage between worlds is already being repaired and, even now, it is difficult to find reliable places to cross back and forth," Jean said. "But your mentor has solved that problem with his transports. Now, he is more useful to the Baron as a sacrifice. Blood spilled in his name gives him power, and now he wants yours most of all."

Jean shook his head. "You should have stayed quiet in your home and not become involved in this, Drusilla. I fear it will not end well for you."

Well, there was good news and bad news. The pirate didn't plan on killing me, but the voodoo god did. I still didn't understand why my blood would help the Baron more than Gerry's, unless it was the cumulative effect of two wizards. Double the blood, double the power.

I had an idea. "Will you help lure the Baron to me, so the Elders can fight him?" Samedi was stronger in the Beyond, where a wizard's physical magic was said to be weak and unpredictable. But on this side of the fence, he'd be no match for a strong wizard.

Jean gave Dominique a look of amusement. "Women

always ask for so much. Such things have not changed over time."

He huffed out a big, fake, put-upon sigh. "I will forgive your earlier betrayal, and I will answer whatever of your questions I can, in exchange for the concessions you agreed to earlier. I will not, however, cross the Baron so transparently as to bring him here, even if I were able. He has already grown powerful."

At this point, I'd take what I could get. "Fine."

Jean smiled, reached out, and pressed my chin between his thumb and index finger. I winced and jerked away from him.

"I am sorry my man marked your face," he said. "The younger ones, they do not have a great deal of sangfroid."

My translation potion interpreted that as self-control, and I had to agree Bad Teeth didn't have much of it.

He settled back in his chair. "What information do you want, *Jolie*?"

I thought a minute. I had so many questions I didn't know where to start.

"Has the Baron been killing the soldiers here, or is someone doing it for him?"

"Ah, so serious." Jean lit a small cigar. "Very well. *Oui*, one of the Baron's followers here in the city has been killing your soldiers on his behalf, for the blood sacrifice. Samedi does not think as you and I do."

Somehow I doubted Jean and I thought alike. At least I hoped not.

"He believes he does a kindness to your city by having his follower kill only those who are strangers here rather than your own citizens." He nodded at my snort of outrage. "As I said, he does not think as we do."

"And what about the signs marking the houses of wizards?"

"His followers will eventually kill those in the marked houses when they return to the city, beginning with your mentor, and probably you as well. From you and Monsieur St. Simon, he wants power. From the rest? Simply to rid himself of an annoyance. But, as I said, I have decided it is not in my best interest to help him. This is good tidings for you."

Jean stood, walked behind my chair, and put his hands on my shoulders, then moved them up to stroke my neck. He had really big hands. Strong hands. It occurred to me that he could wring my neck like a chicken if he wanted to. He leaned over and spoke softly, his breath warm on my skin. "Plus, killing you would be a waste, *n'est-ce pas?*"

I swallowed and sat very still. I'd quit thinking about the chicken-neck thing and had moved on to pondering his comment about killing my mentor.

"Is Gerald St. Simon still alive?" I held my breath, willing him to answer.

Jean squeezed my shoulders, then left to pace near the windows again.

"I do not know."

"Where is he? Have you seen him?"

Jean returned to his seat, poured a glass of brandy for me, and one for himself. "I have not seen him, only heard that he made a deal with Samedi after your hurricane. He set up ways for Samedi's followers to travel in and out of the Beyond, as well as myself and my men."

I took a sip of the brandy without thinking, then put it down as soon as the burn hit my throat. The old rule about taking candy from strangers should apply doubly to taking alcoholic beverages from undead pirates. Especially those you'd once tricked with doctored rum.

Gerry had helped Samedi for a while, at least, and there was a chance the Baron hadn't yet turned on him. Gerry was probably still alive and had figured out a way to block detection by the Elders.

"Do you know if he is still helping Samedi?"

Jean twisted his brandy snifter by its stem, swirling the dark amber liquid. "I assume so, but do not know. Like you, he wanted to make an agreement. Unfortunately, he chose the wrong creature with whom to do business. He was foolish to trust one of the old gods, especially one as lacking in influence as Samedi. The Baron is but a stalking horse for stronger powers in the Beyond."

I stared at him. Jean was getting downright chatty, and had finally said something worth hearing. Samedi was playing Gerry, but other groups were playing Samedi, or at least using him.

"If you think Samedi is so untrustworthy, why not help me?" I asked. "Our agreement benefits you more if the borders remain under the authority of the wizards."

Jean looked at Pierre a moment, then back at me. "One does not win battles by taking on opponents without the necessary strength to conquer them. I do not believe you can defeat the Baron alone, and your Elders have placed their focus elsewhere."

The Elders were busy negotiating meaningless treaties with the vampires and the fae so their stalking horse, a small-time voodoo god, could fly below the Elders' radar until he gained enough power to open the back door for everyone to stampede through. He'd do the dirty work, and they'd reap the benefits. I wondered how much of it Gerry knew, or if he'd knowingly backed David because he was sure Goliath wouldn't take the small threat seriously until it was too late.

Jean reached across the table and took my hand. I let him.

"I would like to help you more, Drusilla. I will not do as Samedi asks but, for the present, I also will not cross him further." His hand slid up my arm to my shoulder.

It might have slid farther had Alex not chosen this particular time to burst into the room, startling me and Jean both, as well as the three others. And the gun he pointed at Jean might have been effective if Bouret, bayonet at the ready, hadn't been standing just inside the door where Alex couldn't see him.

Diplomacy was about to bite the big one.

CHAPTER 30

I'd barely had time to register Alex's arrival and jump to my feet when Jean spit the word *parjure*—treachery—and backhanded me hard enough to knock me sprawling out of my chair. My temple met the edge of a side table with a wood-splintering crack, and I hit the floor on one shoulder.

I shook my head, trying to clear the pinpoints of light that danced in front of me, and heard a shot from the doorway. I tried to see where Alex was, but Jean grabbed my hair and jerked me to my feet. I think our relationship was taking a new turn.

He stood over me, eyebrows knit tight, one hand holding me in place by a fistful of hair. I aimed a knee at his groin and got a satisfying hiss of pain in return before he flung me back to the floor. My shoulder hit the table this time, but at least it wasn't the shoulder I'd landed on earlier. I like my bruises in matched sets.

From my prone position, I risked a glance toward the doorway. Bouret lay on the floor, and Alex and Dominique were throwing punches. Good. One less pirate, maybe, and Alex was still fighting.

Pierre remained near the window, knife out, watching both scenarios. Guess he'd go where he was needed.

"You were foolish to bring the enforcer here, Drusilla." I could feel Jean's anger all the way to his boots, which were in close proximity to my face. "Get up."

I rose slowly, shaking my head again to stop the room from spinning. "I didn't try to trick you," I said hoarsely, then propped against the table for balance and did a double take. The elven staff, which had rolled underneath me when my chair fell backward, now rested against the table next to my left hand. I eased toward it without looking away from Jean and managed to grasp the staff and tuck it behind me.

"I think you are a liar. This makes me rethink my position about taking you to Samedi," he said. "Pierre, let Dominique kill the man. What do you think we should do with our little wizard here?"

Pierre's brown eyes gleamed above a sly smile, but he didn't answer. Neither he nor Dominique had said much since I arrived, but then again, Jean yammered enough for both of them. I heard the grunting and crashing sounds of the fight continuing near the door, but didn't look away from Pierre.

I backed away from him with the staff still behind me. At least Bouret was out of commission. I wasn't sure what Pierre had in mind, but he was going to be my first target.

I raised the staff and pointed it at him. "Let us go, and I won't use this."

Jean chuckled. "What is this little stick, then? Should we cower from it?"

I tried shooting as much energy through it as I could muster. Without the staff, I might have been able to light a candle. With the staff, the small table between Jean and Pierre burst into flames. Okay, so I needed to practice my aim.

A spate of French flew from both brothers as they beat out

the fire. No doubt they didn't want their comfy pirate head-quarters and open transport burned down. A minor inferno wasn't the diversion I was going for, but I'd take it.

I raced for the door, shouting for Alex to run.

Dominique caught me by an ankle as I went past and sent me sprawling on the polished hardwood. Before I could scramble away, he hooked an arm around my neck and hauled me upright. My feet dangled in the vicinity of the floor but I didn't struggle much since he'd pressed one of the triangular blades against my throat.

Now would be a good time for Alex to ride to the rescue. I rolled my eyes to the left and saw him on the floor near the same spot where Bouret had fallen. He wasn't moving.

Oh God. I tried to keep my mind from spinning into a horrific tangle of fear and what-ifs. Maybe he was just unconscious. There might still be time to help him if I could suck up to Jean again or, even better, get to my backpack. First, I needed to get away from Dominique.

I bent my leg and kicked backward, slamming my boot into his knee with a satisfying crack. He grunted, removing the knife but tightening the arm around my neck till my breath came out in rasps and I fought for oxygen. Not the result I was hoping for.

"Bring her to me." The room was turning gray, and Jean's voice seemed to come from a distance.

Dominique shifted his choke hold into a rib-crusher as he slid his arm from my neck to circle my waist. I took a gulping breath, and my vision cleared.

He dragged me into the center of the room and tossed me to the floor near Jean. I'd been spending an awful lot of time on the ground lately, but at least this time I'd landed in a useful place—near my backpack. I curled myself into a ball facing it, and snaked a hand slowly to ease inside the front flap.

"Bouret est mort?" Jean's boots were inches from my head. One good kick and I'd be toast.

"Oui." Dominique's voice came from across the room. After he'd dumped me like a sack of dirt, he had returned to Alex.

"Et l'executeur?"

The executioner. Alex. I held my breath.

"Pas encore. Mais bientôt." Not yet but soon.

Alex was still alive, at least for now. My shoulders relaxed from a tightness I hadn't realized was there. I still had time to help him. My fingers shook as I blindly eased my right hand around the backpack's interior.

Serious hexes are illegal in the magical world. Black magic is right up there with treason in the list of offenses punishable by execution. I occasionally came across an obscure hex recipe in my reading, however, and if I ever got home, I was going to cook up a few—just for times such as these.

I located the potions I'd brought with me, wrapping my fingers around two vials at once and slowly extricating them. I thumbed off the top of the first one. I'd made a variety of non-lethal charms to use in tight situations since I seemed to be getting into them regularly these days, and had no idea which ones I held. I might make it rain. I might cause smoke. Whatever, it would have to do.

I groaned and struggled to sit up, shielding the vials in my right hand as I clambered unsteadily to my feet.

I'd faked the groan. The unsteadiness was real.

Jean stood in front of me holding the elven staff, eyeing my struggle without expression. "I cannot reach a conclusion about you, Drusilla. You stride in here alone like a brave warrior, then your enforcer sneaks in to kill us."

I kept my right hand hidden behind me, but rubbed the side of my mouth and jaw with my left. My fingers came away bloody. "I didn't intend any harm to you, Jean. My friend must have followed me." Yeah, because I left him a note. "He is protective and is trained to fight, much like your own men."

Jean tilted his head to study me as Dominique grabbed me from behind again, wrapping one arm around my rib cage and squeezing the shoulder I'd bashed into the table with his other hand. My breath caught at the pain and I couldn't stop myself from whimpering, but at least my right hand was still free.

Pierre finally spoke, rattling to Jean in French. The gist of it was that I was a conniving strumpet and that if Jean wouldn't turn me over to Samedi he should at least lock me up for them to enjoy later. Oh boy. The night just kept getting better.

Jean flicked his gaze to Dominique and nodded slowly. "We will do this, yes, so that she does not destroy our door to the Beyond. We will take her to one of the damaged houses near Barataria." He smiled at me. "We will visit you often, though, *Jolie*."

I moved fast, flinging the contents of the open vial over my shoulder into what I hoped was Dominique's face. He cursed and let go of me, giving me time to pop the top of the other vial and hurl its ingredients at Pierre.

Jean grabbed the back of my sweater before I could run, and hauled me back to him. "You are a witch." He watched his companions, irritation clear in his expression. Pierre had burst into gales of laughter, tears streaming down his dark cheeks. He'd gotten the laughing potion, apparently. Dominique stood rooted to the floor, frowning.

"Dom," Jean barked, cursing as the man looked at him blankly. "What have you done to him, witch?"

"His mind is clouded," I said, struggling in Jean's grasp. "He'll be back to his cheerful self in a few hours." I couldn't let the insult pass, so I added, "And don't call me a witch. A witch couldn't do this kind of magic." It was awesome, if I did say so myself.

Pierre had collapsed into one of the chairs, mucus and tears mixing on his face as he howled.

"I suppose my laughing brother too will recover in a few hours?"

"I don't want to hurt any of you, Jean. I just want to leave here and take Alex with me."

He jerked me around to face him, and I saw a glint of humor seep back into his dark-blue eyes. "Bah. You are a pox, *Jolie*. I will allow you to leave, and take your killer with you. How you get him out of here is your affair."

He let me go, handed me the staff, and stalked to the banquet table, resuming his position next to the cigars and brandy. "But you will honor our agreement, *oui*? And if you attempt to return and break our transport, I will find you again. Next time, I might not be so generous."

I held the staff to my side. I knew Jean wouldn't hurt me—not today, anyway—but he also knew I wouldn't hurt him. Damn. Our relationship seemed to have shifted from adversarial to . . . less adversarial.

Jean shouted for Dominique to sit down, and the big man walked toward the chair, wrinkling his brow as if trying to remember who he was. That was a fine confusion charm. I'd have to make up more for emergencies. Pierre remained in his seat near the window, braying.

I ran to Alex and knelt, rolling him onto his back. "Alex." I tapped his cheek and spoke louder. "Wake up!"

His eyes cracked open, narrowed, then closed again, and I let a wave of my own relief wash over me, along with his annoyance. Thank God. If he was conscious enough to be pissed off, he was going to be okay.

I dragged my backpack over and pulled out a bottle of hartshorn—aka smelling salts. Don't leave home without them. I held them under his nose, and his brown eyes shot open again.

"Umph." He waved the bottle away.

"Have you been shot?" The front of the Kevlar vest looked intact, but blood seeped beneath the lower right side of it.

"Stabbed," he said, breathing hard. "I shot the guy with the bayonet, but the other one got a knife under the vest. Lost the gun."

I jerked at the Velcro straps and pulled the vest and T-shirt away from the wound. Sweat beaded on his face, and his breathing was raspy. I probed the cut with my fingertips, trying to see how deep it was and if it would be safe for him to try to walk. It had already started healing around the edges. Shapeshifter genes.

"Umph!" Alex shoved my hand away and struggled to a sitting position.

"I'm going to call Jake. Do you think you can get downstairs with my help?"

He nodded, then froze as he spotted Jean watching him from the banquet table with malevolence. "Where's my gun?"

The man could barely talk and he wanted his gun. "They're letting us go. Just shut up and see how fast you can get on your feet."

I ignored his grumbling and kept an eye on the pirate as I dug my cell phone from my backpack and called Jake, giving him only the barest details.

Sliding the backpack straps over my shoulders, I turned back to Alex. "Can you make it downstairs if I help?"

He and Jean were still making Rambo eyes at each other, and his voice came out as half-Alex, half-growl. I hoped Gandalf wasn't about to make an appearance. "You're leaving him here?"

God save me from alpha males. "Yes," I snapped. "And so are you. Jake's on the way."

Alex pulled himself upright, thanks to a death grip both on

my bad shoulder and the wall. I tucked myself under one of his arms, took as much weight as I could, and helped him hobble to the door that led to the landing.

"*Bon chance,* Drusilla," said a soft voice behind me.

I looked over my shoulder. "Stay away from New Orleans till this blows over, Jean. It's not your fight. You don't want to make an enemy of the wizards."

He took a puff of his cigar and nodded. "Samedi will not give up. But should you survive this attempted coup, remember the bargain we made."

Like I could forget. I had practically agreed to be Jean Lafitte's modern-day sugar mama.

Alex and I made our way slowly down the stairs and out the hallway, using my amulet to light the way. Jake was already outside by the time we got there, standing against a red late-model truck. He didn't ask what happened—didn't say a word. He just pulled Alex's arm around his shoulders, half-carried him to the passenger door, and shoved him onto the seat.

"You coming?"

I shook my head. "I'll be there as soon as I can."

He gave me a grim look before pulling away.

I limped toward the Gator on foot, moving slowly in the shadows of the buildings. I needed the ten minutes of walking and the slap of cool night air to ponder what Jean had said. Samedi was on a power-grab, using a human murderer to make his blood sacrifices. And he was nearing his goal: to get enough power to stay in the modern world indefinitely, in defiance of the Elders. Gerry was alive and in New Orleans, or at least he had been when that transport was established. Samedi planned to double-cross Gerry, if he hadn't already, and eventually he wanted all the local wizards dead. Wanted me dead—or to be his new partner, which was worse. And the other pretes were using Samedi to do their dirty work.

I pulled Gerry's staff from my backpack, tracing my fingers across the runes. A couple of red sparks flew out as I touched it. Using that staff had felt amazing. I'd felt strong, powerful, without the energy drain of my own magic. I wondered what it could do other than setting tables and ceiling fans on fire.

All that euphoria had disappeared now. My head throbbed where I'd hit the table, both shoulders ached, and the longer I walked, the more new pains popped up.

A drop of blood fell on my hand, and I looked down to see more blood on the front of my sweater. It looked black under the streetlights. Add a freakin' nosebleed to my litany of injuries. Lafitte had really slapped the crap out of me. If he'd done this much damage backhanded, I'd hate to see what he could do with his fist. Maybe now that we had some nebulous relationship, I'd never have to find out.

CHAPTER 31

I didn't see Jake when I went into the Gator, but Louis was on-stage belting out his final encore. He missed a few words of "Do You Know What It Means to Miss New Orleans?" when he saw me, eyes widening with alarm. I gave him a thumbs-up and walked to the bar.

"You look awful!" shouted Leyla over the noise.

I gave her a limp wave as I eased onto a stool, wincing at the pain that shot down my back and into my hip. I wondered if there were any chiropractors in town.

After snagging a Diet Barq's and making a slow, careful climb up the back stairs, I knocked on Jake's apartment door. There was no answer, so I tried the knob and found it unlocked, opening into pitch-black. I stood in the doorway for a second, trying to decide whether to stay or leave.

A soft voice came out of the darkness. "Come on in, DJ." A click, and Jake turned on a small lamp next to the old, battered armchair where he sat, a rifle across his lap and not a dimple in sight.

I entered the room just far enough to close the door behind

me, then leaned against it. The soft lamplight harshened the frown lines creasing Jake's face, and he watched me without blinking. We seemed to be playing a game of chicken to see who broke first, similar to the stare down he'd had with Alex after Bad Teeth got shot.

"Well, hell." I groped the wall next to the door till I found a light switch and flipped it on. My patience for drama had about reached its limit.

Jake's face changed when the light hit me, from anger to surprise to concern, then back to anger. I was too tired to block out his feelings, so I knew all those emotions had run through him in quick succession.

"What in God's name have you and Alex been doing? I didn't get a good look at you earlier—you look worse than he does."

"You sure know how to sweet-talk a girl." I sighed and held on to my rib cage as I sat on the worn brown plaid sofa. The more time that passed, the more I hurt. A stabbing pain ran from my lower back to my right knee, and I suspected my face was swelling where Jean had bounced me off the table—either that or I was going blind in my left eye. I put the Barq's on the coffee table. It hurt too much to drink it.

"Is Alex okay?"

"He'll be sore for a while, but nothing serious. Used superglue on the wound. We'd have to take him all the way to Metairie to get stitches." Jake got up and rummaged around in the small kitchen off the living room. "Want a real drink?"

He came back with a bottle of Four Roses and a couple of glasses. A second trip to the kitchen yielded a dishcloth, a couple of gel ice packs, and one of those bulky first aid kits made for campers. I spotted a small mirror in the kit and picked it up to look at my reflection. Weary eyes stared back at me from above a purple, misshapen jaw on one side and a bloody, ragged cheek on the other. Not my best look, although the older bruise on my chin matched my eyes.

"Turn toward me."

"Easy for you to say. I think an eighteen-wheeler ran over my back." I managed to avoid whining as I twisted on the sofa to face him. The warm, wet cloth felt good on the noninjured parts of my face and sent new waves of pain shooting into the rest. His hands were gentle as he bandaged my cheek and sat back to survey his handiwork, then handed me the ice packs.

"One for your face, and the bigger one on your back," he said.

I sighed as the cold pack hit my back. "Feels good."

"Take those home with you and keep 'em in the freezer. I have plenty here for my knee. If you and Alex are gonna keep playing war games, you'll need them." He raked his fingers through his hair. "Don't guess you're gonna tell me what happened back there any more than Boy Wonder, are you?"

He didn't seem to expect an answer, just picked up the glass of bourbon and held it toward me. I shook my head. I could barely stand upright as it was. A shot of bourbon and I'd be spending the night on the brown plaid sofa.

Jake kept the glass for himself and leaned back, squinting a little as he studied me. "I've been thinking about you two. No way Alex is regular FBI. Even their field agents don't go in with the kind of gear he carries. I'm thinking more like special ops of some kind. He's been on the road a lot the last few years, and now he shows up here attached to you like a dog on a leash."

I choked at the irony, which made me cough, which in turn shot stabs of pain through my midsection. Jake interpreted my sudden inability to swallow as a cue that he was on the right track.

It was as good an explanation as anything I could make up. "You're sort of right, but I can't say anything else right now. I'm sorry. It's safer for everybody that way. You know the drill." He was a Marine. Surely the Marine Corps had a don't-tell-them-the-gory-details-for-their-own-good drill.

He growled in frustration. "I don't need protecting. Did it ever occur to you I might be able to help?"

I smiled a little, at least till the pain started, and reached out to stroke his cheek. He took my hand and held it against his chest. "Not going to let me in, are you?"

"I can't, not yet. But soon." I rested my head on the sofa back and closed my eyes. I meant it. If we made it through this, I'd tell Jake what I was and see if he could handle it.

"We need to leave." I jolted upright as Alex emerged from the bedroom, much improved since I'd last seen him. The stab wound was covered in a white bandage, and he wore an open flannel shirt that was too tight for him—Jake's, I assumed.

I squeezed Jake's arm in thanks, groaned as I hauled myself off the sofa, and followed Alex out the door, grabbing the staff from where I'd left it propped in the hallway. At least it hadn't followed me into the apartment.

"I'm parked a block down." Alex said as he eased down the stairs, not asking if I could walk that far. He crossed the barroom in long strides. Keeping up with him would require running, and there's no dignity in running after any man for any reason, injured or not. I let him march off to the car while I took my time, waving at Louis and Leyla on the way out.

Alex didn't speak on the drive home, or as we went inside, or as I started a pot of water for tea. Fine. He'd work up to it, then he'd yell at me. I had plenty of time.

By the time the water was boiling, so was Alex.

"Okay, let's have it," I said, throwing my hands up after he'd slammed his third kitchen cabinet drawer. I'd let him get it out of his system, then I'd tell him everything I'd learned.

He lit into me like Sherman burning Atlanta. "What were you thinking? You weren't thinking, that's what." He choked the words out. "My job here isn't just to help you run errands and dig up facts. It's to keep you alive. We're partners. What part of not running into dangerous situations alone without backup do you not get?" He proceeded along those same lines for another couple of minutes before he ran out of steam, flopped into a kitchen chair, and glared at me.

"How did Lafitte lure you to the Napoleon House?"

"He didn't. I decided to go looking for him."

Alex's face turned an alarming shade of red.

"I had the situation under control," I said. "Jean gave me a lot of useful information."

"Jean. You're calling him *Jean* now?" Alex took Jake's flannel shirt off and threw it on the floor. His stab wound didn't seem to be bothering him very much.

"We had reached an understanding," I insisted. "Jean wasn't going to kill me." Chain me up in the swamps and turn me into a pirate floozy, but no point in adding that part.

Alex threw up his hands and stalked out of the room, swearing. "Jean. She's calling him *Jean*." The last words I heard before he slammed the door behind him were "damn stubborn woman" and a couple of F-bombs.

Well, that went well. I followed him, at least as far as the door to the downstairs bathroom. The door was ajar. He'd pulled off the bandage and was examining his wound in the mirror.

I peered around his shoulder. Not only had the wound stopped seeping, but the edges had begun closing over.

He looked in the mirror and eyed me standing behind him. "So, what's this valuable information you got from *Jean*?"

"You better come back in the living room and sit down. It's going to take a while."

As soon as I'd gone through the story with Alex, he called the Elders and got sent past the Speaker and on to Willem Zrakovi. He put his cell on speakerphone.

The Elder didn't bother telling me how deeply I'd disappointed him this time.

After Alex gave the condensed version, Zrakovi said, "Let Drusilla tell me Captain Lafitte's exact words."

So I went through it again. Samedi using the killings to gain power, influencing a human follower to do the dirty work. His plans to kill the local wizards. Gerry setting up transports. Samedi's plans to kill Gerry and either co-opt or kill me. Jean's refusal to play along.

Zrakovi's silence went on several minutes. I opened my mouth to ask a question—namely, how the Elder thought Gerry managed to avoid detection—but Alex shook his head and held a finger in front of his mouth.

So we waited what seemed like a week. Elders move at the speed of glaciers.

Finally, Zrakovi spoke. "I need to confer with the Elders' council, and then I have a meeting with the fae leaders that will tie me up the rest of the day. Have a transport ready Thursday at nine a.m. your time. We will talk then."

Grit teeth. Another day of waiting.

"And Ms. Jaco?"

Ungrit teeth. "Yes, sir?"

"Stay at home."

WEDNESDAY, SEPTEMBER 28, 2005 "Nearly a month after the New Orleans area was devastated by Hurricane Katrina, residents are returning to some neighborhoods. . . . And as signs of life slowly return to the city, the search for storm victims is winding down."

—THE TIMES-PICAYUNE

CHAPTER 32

Alex got cabin fever before I did. By noon, he'd decided to head to the NOPD and look at the murder files again now that we knew the killer was a human under Samedi's control, possibly by possession. I also suggested he swing by the Gator to see if he could get information on the murders out of Louis. Our spy hadn't been a rousing success, but he had at least given me the tip that led to Jean Lafitte. He might know more than he realized.

Earlier, I'd arranged to meet Eugenie in Metairie to help her find a new refrigerator, but I called and rain-checked. I didn't want to explain my cuts and bruises. I'd been rain-checking her a lot in the last week. I hoped she didn't think I was avoiding her.

I finally pulled out Gerry's journals from the nineties again. I'd only gotten through 1997. I cranked up Irma Thomas on the iPod and eased my sore bones onto the sofa. By the time I'd read 1994–96, both Irma and I were in a stupor, so I limped to the bedroom. Sometime during 1992, I dozed off and drooled on Gerry's lengthy review of Anne Rice's latest vampire novel.

Finally, it was almost four p.m., and only 1990 remained

unread. Alex was still gone, and rain threatened to make my gloomy day complete. Not that Gerry's journals were all boring, but they made me think of him, and thinking of him made me sad and angry and confused.

My mind kept returning to the questions that hurt the most: Did Gerry know about innocent soldiers being sacrificed on Samedi's orders? I couldn't believe the man who raised me would stand by and let that happen. I had to believe he was unaware of it.

I went downstairs for a candy bar because I thought chocolate would ease me through the final journal. January 1990. Gerry stayed on a month-long tear about the Soviet Union's political activities and the end of the Cold War.

I got a second candy bar. February 1990. More of the same. I thought about another nap but made myself keep reading.

February 27, my tenth birthday. I smiled as I read Gerry's account of taking me to the Lundi Gras parades and remembered the fun we had. He'd taken me every year since I moved in with him, holding me above his head to get beads and stuffed animals off the Mardi Gras floats till I'd gotten too big. By my tenth birthday I'd have been screaming for my own beads and darting into the street between floats to snatch more.

DJ is growing up so fast, and looks more like Carrie every day. I see myself in her too. She's stubborn and, oh, what magic she has! Not just her mother's ritual magic but my physical magic, too. Elven blood from both of us. She's special, but of course a father would say that. Must bring her along slowly . . .

Pressure built behind my eyes as I reread the paragraph. He'd thought of himself as my father, even saw traits of himself in me. The journal entry showed a sentimental side of Gerry I'd never seen, and wished I had. And had he known my mom? It sure sounded that way.

I read the rest of the entry for that day, but it was just an accounting of our Lundi Gras. We'd bought cotton candy from cart vendors and gone to dinner at Bruning's up on the lakefront. Gerry had let me order softshell crab for the first time, then traded his shrimp for my crab when I refused to pull its legs off and eat them.

I kept going back to that earlier paragraph. Why hadn't anyone told me that Gerry and my mom knew each other?

Unplugging my cell phone from its charger, I called Gran, only half expecting her to answer. Wednesday was dinner night at church, and she was usually there when the doors opened, ready to socialize with the other Methodist matrons.

She picked up on the third ring, sounding out of breath.

We had our usual "how are you" conversation—nothing deep. I'd never been the granddaughter she wanted, and she'd never given me the emotional support I needed. We just accepted it and did the best we could. Maybe most families are like that, magical or not.

Then we settled into silence as she waited to find out why I'd called.

"I was reading some old journals of Gerry's." I struggled for the right words. "He wrote some things that made me wonder . . ."

"What is it, Drusilla? Just ask your question."

"Why did no one ever tell me Gerry knew my mother?"

She didn't answer at first, and only the sound of music playing in the background let me know she was still on the phone. I could picture her in the kitchen, music drifting from the old radio in the window over the sink. She always left it on when she did housework.

Gran sighed, a soft, unhappy sound, even from two states away. "You need to talk to your father. Can you come up here?"

"Gran, you know I can't, not now. There's too much going on and things are getting worse. Just tell me."

"It's not my story to tell."

I tightened my jaw, and it hurt. I didn't have the patience to spare her feelings.

"That's crap. Just tell me, bottom line."

She laughed, but sounded more sad than amused. "You sound like Gerry. Never mind the preliminaries—just out with it. Well, I'm telling you to call your father."

"Fine," I said through clenched teeth. "Talk to you later." I hung up before she had a chance to respond.

I could count on my fingers the number of times I'd called my dad. Gran had always been the go-between. Still, we'd connected a little when I was there a couple of weeks ago. I paced around a few minutes, ratcheting up my courage. I'd expected Gran to blow the question off and tell me I was mistaken, or maybe that Gerry and my mom had met one time. I hadn't expected "call your father."

Dad answered on the first ring. Gran had already gotten to him. "I've been waiting for you to call," he said, his voice slow and heavy. "I've been expecting this talk for about twenty-five years, but thought it was Gerry's place."

This *talk* was sounding scary. "Just tell me, Dad."

"I knew your mama growing up, all through school, did you know that?"

I swallowed my impatience. "I knew you were high-school sweethearts."

"We were. I didn't know about this magic business, of course. Didn't believe it at first when I did find out." He paused, and I heard the sound of liquid pouring into a glass. "We went our

own way after school, and I heard she went someplace in En-
gland. Later, I found out she decided she didn't want her magic
but had to go through this class first, something like that."

"Once you give up your magic, it's permanent," I said.
"They make you go through a class so you're sure about it."

Ice rattled in a glass, and I pictured him sitting in his house,
drinking iced tea while Martha bustled in the kitchen, getting
dinner ready. So normal.

"Anyway, she met Gerry there. Loved him a little, I guess.
But at the end of the summer she came home, said she didn't
want that life."

"And the two of you got married?" So she had known
Gerry. Had loved Gerry maybe.

"Yeah. But she was expectin' when she came back. I didn't
care that you were Gerry's, because you were hers, too."

My brain short-circuited, and I couldn't speak.

"Drusilla, you'll always be my daughter. I sent you to live
with your mama's parents because I just didn't know what to do
with the magic and I thought your grandmother would. Then
those Seniors . . . No, that's not right."

"Elders." My voice was faint.

"Those Elders insisted we send you to Gerry—he wanted
to raise you. We thought we were doing the right thing for everybody." His voice shook. "Honey, I hate to tell you all this on
the phone. Why don't I come on down there?"

He'd never before offered to set foot in New Orleans. I
swallowed hard. "I have to think about this awhile. I'll talk to
you soon, Dad."

Dad. I hung up. The phone rang back almost immediately,
but I couldn't talk anymore.

I stretched out on the sofa, welcoming the back pain because it kept me grounded, and went through the story of my

life, the one I'd grown up with. My father was Peter Jaco. He was nonmagical and my mom gave up her magic for him. When she died, he didn't want me and gave me to my grandparents. They didn't want me and sent me to Gerry.

I'd had it wrong my whole life.

CHAPTER 33

After a half hour of disconnect, almost like an out-of-body experience, I stuck the phone in my pocket and carefully stacked all the journals back on the coffee table in chronological order. Then I dusted the furniture and sorted the magazines scattered around the room. I ignored my protesting back and shoulders.

Gerry was my father.

I was seven again. I had been at his place maybe a week, and started having nightmares about being lost. He'd come to my room, wiped away my tears, told me about the world of magic I was a part of, one where people lived especially long lives, where I'd always have a family, where people took care of each other. He promised I'd never feel lost again.

He'd been wrong. The loneliness I felt now, had felt this last month, left me empty and rudderless. I struggled to breathe as my throat tightened. I'd spent my life pushing Dad away, blaming him, blaming my grandparents for not wanting me. Gerry knew I felt that way, and he still didn't tell me the truth. He let me hang my whole world on him.

I screamed and kicked at the table. The journals scattered on the floor, and a glass candleholder broke on the slate hearth. Hot tears threatened to escape as I picked up the shards of glass, watching the bright red blood well up on my fingertip where a sliver made contact. I picked up the matching candleholder, hefted its weight in my hand, and threw it against the wall as hard as I could. It chipped the plaster wall and bounced unbroken to the floor.

Sebastian meowed from the kitchen, demanding his dinner. I wrapped a napkin around my finger and plopped a can of foul-smelling cat food in his bowl while he wound his way around my legs—the first sign of affection he'd ever shown. "You're more Gerry's child than I am. At least he acknowledged you," I snapped at him, scuffing out of the kitchen and heading upstairs.

Maybe I wasn't being fair. He'd given me everything except his name and even then, maybe he thought he was protecting me. Why was I defending the bastard?

I crawled under the covers for a while, growing angrier. I was so tired of surprises and secrets. I wanted to be Eugenie, worrying about my leaky roof and my insurance adjuster, or Leyla, with legs a mile long and an uncomplicated job that paid the bills.

I had to get out of the house. I got up and inspected my face in the bathroom mirror, pressing a fresh bandage over the worst cut. I covered the rest with makeup while I figured out what to do with myself. No clothing or shoe stores were open, so retail therapy was out. I thought about walking across the street to Eugenie's salon for a haircut, but it would require explanations. My makeup job wasn't that good.

I grabbed my keys and headed to the truck. I could drive, just drive. I'd look at the ruins of my hometown and remind myself how much I had. How the hundred thousand people who'd lost everything would look at my life and wish they were me.

Dusk came and went. I'd been driving in circles for more than an hour when I stopped to let a Jeep pull in front of me and realized I had ended up near the Gator. I pulled into a parking place around the corner and sat in the dark, listening to the tick of my cooling engine. I wasn't sure what I hoped to find here.

No point in overthinking it.

I waved at Leyla, who stood behind the bar flirting with two off-duty guardsmen, judging from their clean-cut looks and short hair. Business was still slow this early on a Wednesday night. I looked around for Alex, but he was probably still at the NOPD or upstairs with Louis. Good. I didn't want to answer any question more complicated than a bar order, and as soon as Alex got involved, he'd badger me till I told him the truth. A truth I didn't want to discuss.

Leyla sauntered over. "Your face looks better. Wanna Barq's?"

"Makeup," I said. "No, Four Roses, straight." Jake's brand. Why not?

She shrugged and reached under the bar for Jake's private stash. She set the bottle and a glass in front of me and left it. "Looks like you might need more than one," she said over her shoulder, heading back for her guardsmen.

The first sip burned the back of my throat. In fact, it burned all the way down my esophagus and set fire to the lining of my stomach. I hadn't eaten since breakfast. I snatched a bowl of peanuts from a nearby table and set them in front of me as well.

Midway through my first drink, I felt my insides stop quivering. Four Roses was better than a mojo bag. I fed coins into the jukebox and picked out three BeauSoleil songs. I could pretend Michael Doucet was singing to me, one of my all-time fantasies.

When Jake slid onto the next stool, a quizzical smile on his face, I thought I'd never seen anyone so beautiful, all sun-streaked hair and amber eyes and dimples.

He propped his right arm on the bar, and his left rested on his thigh as he sat sideways on the stool facing me. He didn't say a word, just watched me with a half smile. His emotional signals came through loud and clear: He was amused, and he wanted me.

I needed to be wanted. I stroked a hand down his right arm and leaned closer to look at the bulldog tattoo on his forearm. "What's that about?"

He flexed his forearm. "Marine devil-dog. Marines are supposed to fight like dogs from hell. I reckon that's true."

I wrapped an arm around his neck, pulling him toward me.

He showed me the dimples, but his eyes were unreadable. "What's up, cupcake? How come you're drinking this early on a Wednesday evening?"

"Because I want to be somebody else tonight. I'm tired of feeling sorry for myself. I'm tired of being angry and sad and afraid." I put my hand on his arm, tracing the dagger tattoo on his left bicep below the sleeve of his Gator T-shirt, feeling the wiry muscle underneath the skin. "I want you to help me."

I leaned closer, pulling him toward me, and kissed him. He held back a moment, then circled me with his arms and pulled me off the barstool. His kiss was rough, hungry. The alcohol dulled my abilities to pick up his emotions, but I could tell enough to know we both wanted this, needed it. The whole damned bar could be watching—I didn't care.

His arms held me captive and I was one happy prisoner as he moved his lips along my jaw and scraped his teeth against the curve between my neck and shoulder. My heart kept time with the fast thump of the jukebox bass. Even if I hadn't been half-sloshed he would've made my head swim.

Way too soon, he broke off the kiss and leaned back, hands

on my waist, looking at me hard. He shook his head, reached around me for my half-finished glass of bourbon, and downed it in one swallow. "I am too damned noble for my own good," he muttered, then turned back to me. "I've tried losing myself in a drink, angel. And I've tried losing myself in another person. It don't work, and you and me deserve better for our first time."

I sat back on my stool and spun to face the bar. Spinning was a bad, bad idea. I'd never handled alcohol very well anyway, and the empty stomach made it worse. I gripped the edge of the bar till the room stopped tilting, then turned back to continue my attempted seduction of Jake, certain I could wear him down. He was on his cell phone, watching me with a trace of a smile. He ended the call, pushed the bowl of peanuts in front of me, and took away my bourbon. It was downright rude.

The depth of his betrayal showed up about a minute later in the form of Alex, who strode into the bar from the back, Louis tagging along behind him.

I jumped off the stool, took a second to make sure I wasn't going to fall down, and turned on Jake. "You smirking Judas. You called him? He's not my babysitter. You . . . I'm going to turn you into a toadstool. I'm going to put a curse on your . . . your . . ."

I think I got in at least one good punch before Alex grabbed me from behind and herded me toward the door.

I was spared the indignity of being physically hauled out by the simple fact that the day finally caught up with me. As suddenly as it had disappeared, sobriety returned, along with its best friends, headache and nausea. Deflated, I followed Alex to his car. Guess I'd get the Pathfinder back tomorrow.

"What the hell was that about?" Alex drove up Rampart Street toward Uptown, taking turns fast enough to make me think about barfing out his window, except it would take too much energy. "Jake said you were upset."

Exactly who was the empath here? I looked out the window.

"I thought you were going to stay home. What happened?"

I slumped down in my seat and watched the streetlights float past. I loved electricity. "I don't want to talk about it."

He frowned and looked back at the road. I hadn't grounded today and didn't have my mojo bag, so his wonky shapeshifter feelings came through faintly. He was jealous of Jake.

I looked out the window and concentrated on getting out of his head. Jealous. Good Lord, I didn't want to go there. I didn't want to go anywhere. In fact, I considered asking him to stop the car. My stomach rolled while someone in my head stabbed the back of my eyeballs with a fork.

Alex turned in the driveway and killed the engine. "Tell me what happened."

"Let's go in the house."

He made coffee and we settled on the sofa in the living room. My head pounded, and I made the story as short and unemotional as I could.

"How do you feel about all this?"

I always hated it when TV reporters stuck a microphone in the faces of people who'd just lost a home or a loved one, wanting to know how they felt. They felt like shit. They hurt, and they didn't know how they were going to get through the night. They wanted to scream and cry and hit the guy with the microphone.

I took a sip of coffee laced with sugar and real cream. "I feel stupid. I feel angry and betrayed. I want to hug Gerry, and then I want to kill him."

My hand shook, and coffee splashed on my lap. "Damn."

"Here." Alex took the mug and set it on the table, then wrapped his arms around me. My shoulders tensed, but he didn't let go. My world narrowed to this moment, the tick of the clock on the mantel, the tightness in my chest, the solid cocoon of his arms that felt like the only thing between me and the abyss of anger and regret I'd been teetering around all afternoon.

He rested his head against mine, his mouth near my ear. "Quit trying to be so tough, DJ. I'm here. I'm not leaving."

"Everybody leaves." The words slipped out unconsciously, but they rang true.

One arm circled my shoulders while his other hand stroked up and down my arm as if I were a skittish kitten he was trying to calm. I was frozen between my desire to escape today's hard truths and a hunger to take the comfort he offered.

Finally, my muscles began to relax. Inhaling his scent. Needing his solid presence. I'd thought his unwillingness to avoid hard issues was the last thing I needed tonight. Maybe I'd been wrong.

"I know what it's like to feel alone," he said, settling against the back of the sofa and pulling me snugly against him. I could feel his heartbeat through his shirt and his protectiveness as an emotional undercurrent to his touch. He wasn't trying to keep me out of his head for a change.

"I had a big family but I shifted the first time when I was fifteen. Scared me to death. I didn't have control over it at first. It would happen when I'd get upset or angry, so I had to learn to be unemotional and keep everybody at a distance. Shifting's not hereditary like your wizard's magic—nobody knows why it happens. I thought I was the biggest freak in the world for a long time."

I nestled into him and rested an arm on his chest, trying not to overanalyze the moment. "How did you figure out what was going on?"

"The Elders sent someone to work for my dad a few months after my first shift. He stayed there as a stock clerk for years, till

I got out of high school. Sort of like Gerry was to you, I guess. Someone I could be myself with, that I didn't have to put on an act for."

That sense of finally belonging somewhere. I'd found it at Gerry's as a child, and I needed to remember that. Maybe now that the truth was out, all of us could put the past to rest and start over. If Gerry had time for a new start.

I stayed there a long time, wrapped in Alex's arms, not feeling alone, and it was the best, most unexpected gift I'd ever received.

CHAPTER 34

Alex had fallen asleep by the time I finally pulled myself away from him. He mumbled and rolled on his side when I got up, one arm dangling to the floor. Watching him sleep, I could imagine the lonely, frightened teenager. I pulled off his shoes and spread an afghan over him.

Then I went upstairs to think. We were running out of time. Samedi was gaining in power, and would make his move soon. He'd already sent Jean to fetch me, so maybe he considered himself one little blond wizard's power short of being able to take on the Elders.

I sat in the library for a while, holding the elven staff. I needed to talk to Gerry, and the only conversations we'd been able to have since his disappearance had been through dreams.

If he could come to me in a dream, maybe I could go to him.

I took the staff in my bedroom, turned out the lights, and lay down. It was midnight, and as tired as my body was, my brain continued to race. Finally, I called on the exercises Tish had taught me early in our sessions on meditation, when we'd been trying to develop the grounding ritual.

I tensed my muscle groups one by one, then released them, starting with my toes and working my way up. I finished, and started over. Toes, tense, release. Ankles, tense, release. Calves . . .

I stood in the stone passageway, but it was dark. The gas lamps lighting the way in the earlier dreams were gone, and the dark was so black I couldn't see the walls on either side of me. The staff was in my hand. I squeezed it and held it in front of me, and the elven wood glowed and circled me in light.

I walked ahead, trailing my free hand along the rough stone wall. A twisted tree root that had risen through the path grabbed at my feet, causing me to stumble. More roots, as well as tangled, thorny vines, snaked through the passage walls, whose once-smooth stones were now more chipped and broken than before.

At the end of the passageway, the heavy door was missing and the opening yawned black and empty. I imagined some subterranean ocean in which I might drown if I stepped inside, but I went in anyway. The staff cast orange shadows on the walls of the round chamber,

Gerry sat in his chair, his mouth crimped into a thin line. "Sit down, DJ. This is the last time we'll meet—you have no idea what kind of risk you're taking."

His eyes shifted to the staff and widened. "Bloody hell. You *can* use it."

I sat facing him, clamping my fingers around the arms of my chair to keep them from shaking. I didn't want him to see my rage. Didn't want him to focus on my emotions and not the issues.

I struggled to see the man I loved through the layers of deceit. "Why didn't you tell me you were my father?"

"Ah." He leaned back in the chair and crossed his legs. "I wanted to, but I kept waiting for the right time. I certainly didn't want you to find out like this."

He searched my face. "You're properly outraged, I see."

I'd always wondered if the fierce grip Gerry kept on his emotions was strength, a defense mechanism, or just a stiff British upper lip. Whatever, it was maddening. "What did you expect? That I'd be blasé about being lied to my whole life?"

The staff, which I'd propped against the chair, emitted a burst of red sparks. It seemed to be channeling my anger.

He stared at it, then looked back at me and smiled. "You have the gift of old magic, elven magic—more even than I'd hoped. You are like me, you know. You're tough and resourceful and believe in fighting for your beliefs. You have your mother's face, but you're like me."

"I'm not like you." My voice shook and I gripped the chair arms harder. "I haven't betrayed the Elders. I haven't put every wizard in New Orleans at risk. I haven't sat by while innocent people were killed. Five men are dead, Gerry. Please tell me you didn't know about that."

"I didn't know at first, but concessions had to be made for Samedi to get the power he needed."

He wouldn't meet my gaze. "No one else is at risk now. You're only in danger if you keep trying to find me. I'm telling you again. Step away from it, let the Elders think I'm dead, and allow things to unfold."

God. He'd known about the murders. Five dead sons, brothers, fathers he'd seen as *concessions*. I had to make him understand his naïveté in thinking the killing was done.

"Samedi plans to double-cross you," I said. "He's trying to bring me to him, and then he plans to kill us both."

Gerry laughed. "You have it wrong, love." He leaned forward, excitement on his face. "Imagine what it will be like when this is over, when the Baron and I have opened the borders for everyone. The vampires and fae will back us; I've talked to their leaders. The Elders will be forced to cooperate.

Just think of the world we can make with science and magic coexisting."

I shivered at his words. Who was this man? His idealism had blinded him, and I didn't know how to get through. If he thought prete groups and humans could peacefully coexist in some mystical utopia, he was ignoring every lesson history had taught us.

He moved his chair forward till our knees were touching, and took my hands. "Did I do too good a job drilling the Elders' rules into you? Use your brain, girl. Think for yourself."

"Jean Lafitte said—"

He released my hands and sat back in his chair. "Jean Lafitte would lie to the Pope if it gained him an advantage. Surely you're not basing your ideas on anything said by that libertine?"

I didn't know what else to say. "Gerry, at least tell me where you are. If you're here in New Orleans the Elders are going to find you."

He laughed, and that familiar sound tore into me like a knife. "The Elders won't find me, and you need to stop trying. I'm sorry I waited too late to tell you I was your father in a proper way, but you have to let me go for now. We'll have plenty of time to catch up when this is over. Samedi's ready to make his move."

"Gerry, I—"

"I'll see you when this is over, DJ. Stay out of the Beyond."

I jerked awake, cold sweat beaded on my forehead. The bedside clock read three a.m., the witching hour. I sat up, still in my jeans and sweater, rehashing the conversation with Gerry. Why had he told me to stay out of the Beyond? Why would I even try to go into—

Oh my God. No wonder Gerry was off radar, and why he was so sure the Elders couldn't find him. He was in the Beyond, probably in Old Orleans. That had to be it. Why else would he mention it?

All my life, I'd heard about the dangers of going *over there*. Physical magic wasn't reliable outside the temporal world. Here, the wizards were the most powerful things around. There, we were just one more magical species in a world full of them. We weren't even the largest group—the fae outnumbered us, I knew, and the vampires came close.

I got up and tiptoed into the library, locking the door behind me. What should I tell Zrakovi?

Curling up in an armchair, I thought about Gerry being my father, insisting I was like him. I'd denied it, but in some ways he was right. I'd always thought he was the impulsive one, but it hadn't been Gerry who kept Louis Armstrong as a spy. He hadn't tried to wrangle a deal with Jean Lafitte. The difference was, Gerry had crossed a line. He'd let people get killed. I couldn't rid my mind of the gutted soldier lying on the muddy ground in Lakeview. Gerry had a hand in that.

An iron band wrapped around my chest, squeezing, and every lungful of air took an effort. I had to talk to Zrakovi in a few hours. If I told him Gerry was in the Beyond, that he was still conspiring with Samedi, I'd be signing my father's death warrant. If I kept quiet and the Elders didn't figure it out on their own, I'd betray everything I believed in, everything Gerry had taught me to believe in.

I wasn't sure I could live with either option.

THURSDAY, SEPTEMBER 29, 2005 "The names of the first of Louisiana's Hurricane Katrina victims to be identified were released Wednesday, but scores of victims may never be identified. . . . The 32 were the first of the 896 victims recovered so far to be identified by the state."

—THE TIMES-PICAYUNE

CHAPTER 35

I was still in the library with the door locked when Alex came looking for me about seven a.m. I'd done my grounding ritual twice. My mojo bags had been refilled with fresh herbs.

He pounded on the door, and I ran to unlock it before he flattened it and I had to buy yet another one.

"I hope you didn't summon someone else while I was asleep." He paced the room, wafting traces of sandalwood aftershave and soap and coffee behind him. My area rug was in its normal spot, but he lifted the edge to make sure I wasn't trying to hide anything.

I could hide a lot without moving a rug.

"I didn't summon anybody. I've just been up all night, thinking."

"Uh-oh." He smiled then, and I knew I'd made the right decision.

I patted his arm as I headed back to the sitting room. "Let me take a shower, then I'll come down and tell you what I've been thinking about."

I covered the worst of my bruises in makeup again. If this kept up, I'd need stage makeup to give me better coverage.

Alex had cooked breakfast—real eggs, bacon, toast. "Figured we'd need lots of protein to talk to Zrakovi this morning," he said, handing me a plate.

I didn't have an appetite, but knew I needed to force it down. Last night's dinner had been peanuts and bourbon. My diet wasn't helping me cope.

"So," he said, sitting at the table with a pile of eggs the size of a softball, "were you up all night thinking about Gerry being your father?"

"Sort of." I bit off a bite of bacon and promptly spat it into a napkin. "What *is* that?"

"Soy bacon. It's good for you."

I was unsure about many things in my life, but I was fairly certain God did not intend bacon to be made from a plant.

"Let me ask you a hypothetical question." I set the vile bacon travesty aside and chewed on some toast. "If you had to choose between protecting someone you loved and doing what you thought was right, what would you do?"

He put his fork down and frowned. "Why do I think this isn't hypothetical?"

I shrugged and took a sip of coffee, avoiding his eyes.

He cleared his throat. "Well. I'm assuming, in your imaginary situation, that doing both isn't an option. In other words, I can't both protect my loved one *and* do the right thing."

I shook my head.

He pushed the rest of his eggs around with his fork. "I'm not going to ask what you found out, or figured out. If you tell me, you know my loyalties lie with the Elders. You have to make your own decision, and I'll do my best to support you."

"Even if I make the wrong decision?" Would he support me then?

He gave up on breakfast and put his fork down. "I'll try."

I sighed. "I still have some thinking to do, and I need to call Tish."

I left Alex to clean up and went upstairs to ready the transport for Zrakovi. Then I made my call, telling Tish everything, start to finish. I could tell when she started to cry. I didn't ask Tish if she knew Gerry was my father. All that had to be set aside for now, all the who-knew-what-and-when.

She blew her nose, and I could visualize her squaring her shoulders. "I can't tell you what to do, DJ. Gerry's my one great love, but he's wrong about this."

"If I tell the Elders, we'll lose him."

She didn't say anything. She didn't have to. Either way, we'd already lost him.

I checked the transport, and waited for Alex to join me. A few minutes before nine, with no Alex in sight, an image appeared in the transport and solidified into a short, slender man with pale, thinning hair in a stylish cut. Bright blue eyes studied me from above a prominent nose. I stared back at him. I didn't know proper Elder etiquette. Should I kiss his ring? Genuflect? Somehow I thought Zrakovi would be older, taller.

He raised his eyebrows and crossed his arms across his chest, rumpling the jacket of his conservative black suit. "Well?"

Ack. Stupid. I'd created a closed transport, not an open one, so he couldn't move until I broke the circle. I smudged it open with my foot.

"In these times, you probably should have asked to see identification," he said. "But the closed transport was a good idea."

"Well, a paranoid one. You never know who might show up these days."

He laughed.

Willem Zrakovi walked around my library, nodding as he perused book titles and peered into shelves, scanning the long rows of neatly labeled glass containers.

Alex wandered in with one of his foul protein drinks. He choked at the sight of the wizard, and collapsed in a fit of coughing.

The wizard looked over his sizable nose and nodded. "Mr. Warin."

"Elder Zrakovi," Alex croaked.

Zrakovi turned back to me with a warm smile—he certainly beat the Speaker on people skills. "Forgive my manners, but I am always fascinated to see another wizard's work space, especially of the Green Congress. Yours is most impressive. I am Willem Zrakovi. I apologize that we haven't met in person earlier, but these are difficult times."

I pondered whether one should offer refreshments when entertaining wizarding royalty, but decided against it. He could afford his own snacks.

"Elder Zrakovi." I wasn't sure how to begin, so I pointed to a seat. I'd take my cues from him.

He looked out the window briefly before sitting in one of the library armchairs. I took the chair facing him and decided he must originally have been a Green Congress wizard himself. He wore an enormous emerald ring on his left ring finger. Jewelry's a dead giveaway on a wizard. I'd have more emerald jewelry if I could afford it.

He cleared his throat. "Drusilla, I understand you obtained some information both from summoning Marie Laveau and meeting with Jean Lafitte. You've been very busy."

Zrakovi didn't know the half of it. "I've also gotten some additional information by doing a reconstruction of a transport I found in Gerry St. Simon's house. And from a sort of lucid dream." That sounded really stupid now that I'd said it aloud.

He looked taken aback, and Alex stifled a smile from his perch atop my worktable.

"Your mentor taught you to be creative in your magic use, I see," Zrakovi said drily.

I grimaced. "Look, sir, I know keeping Louis Armstrong as a spy was kind of unorthodox, but . . ."

Zrakovi held up a hand to stop me. "I wasn't referring to Mr. Armstrong. That was an unusual means of gathering information, but I thought it quite clever. Obviously, that tactic wouldn't work with just any of the historical undead."

Zrakovi looked at me a few seconds before continuing. "Why don't you tell me everything you've learned."

CHAPTER 36

With a silent apology to Gerry and a prayer that I'd be able to live with my decision, I spilled my guts. About Gerry's cheerful departure with Samedi in the transport. About Jean Lafitte's contention that the vampires and fae were using Samedi as a stalking horse to test the waters in overthrowing the Elders. About the first two dreams in which Gerry and I had communicated. Even about the traveling elven staff.

"And there was a third dream last night, which I initiated," I said, glancing at Alex. He looked surprised, but nodded his encouragement. "Gerry is alive."

I stared out the window, seeing nothing, willing myself to stay calm and see this through. "He's in the Beyond, I believe, probably in Old Orleans. He is still backing Samedi. I tried to warn him that he was going to be double-crossed but he didn't believe me."

"Damned arrogant fool," Zrakovi snapped, getting to his feet and beginning a rapid back-and-forth pace in front of the windows. "He wouldn't try to work through channels, wouldn't consider the idea he might be wrong. And Samedi. Of all the creatures to trust . . ."

I waited, eyes on the floor. Even with a grounding and two mojo bags I felt the sizzle of Zrakovi's anger.

"Tell me about these dreams." Zrakovi pulled his emotions under control and sat down again. I still wished I could move farther away from him, to escape his intensity.

"I thought they were just dreams at first. Alex suspected they might not be. But last night, after I learned—" Did I want to even get into the daddy business? "After I learned some personal information about my relationship to Gerry, I decided to try and instigate another dream myself. And it worked."

"What did you find out about your and Gerry's relationship?"

I blinked. "Uh, that's he's my biological father. Did you know that?" Of course the Elders knew that. They wouldn't have had my grandparents send me to Gerry at random.

"I thought he'd have told you by now." Zrakovi frowned and fiddled with his cuffs. I bet I knew what his poker tell would be. "I realize the personal cost of what you're telling me. I admire your courage."

I looked at the rug, which had a spot on the corner that was coming unraveled. Courage. What a joke. I wanted to run out the library door and keep running.

"So." He got up and paced again. "As you suspected, you were not having dreams, Drusilla. Dream magic is an elven skill. A few Yellow Congress wizards can do it, but not many."

Alex and I exchanged startled looks and he tilted his head in the direction of the library door, where the elven staff had propped itself against the wall.

"You have elven blood from both biological parents, which is rare," Zrakovi said. "You've shown some skill at elven magic since you were a child. And now the staff." He shook his head.

"I don't know what that means. We shall have to do some research."

I took a deep breath. "What do you know about Baron Samedi? Why does he want me?"

"Like many of the gods in the Beyond who have fallen out
of favor in modern society, Samedi resents his fading powers—
voodoo has virtually become a tourist attraction in New Orleans, and the loa hate that. Samedi has been consigned to the
Beyond for a long time now, and to come back, he has to build
up his power with blood sacrifice. A wizard's blood would be
very attractive to him, especially a powerful wizard."

"But I'm not powerful." I could barely handle a simple summoning. "I just don't get it."

"It's the elven connection," Alex said. He'd been silent till
now, but he hopped off the worktable and came to sit on the floor
next to my chair. "That's what he wants, isn't it? Gerry can't give
him that."

"I think that's probably true," Zrakovi said. He walked
back to the window and looked at the empty street for a few
minutes.

Finally, he returned to his chair. "I think you've rightly de-
duced that Gerry is still alive and in the Beyond. His magic
wouldn't work properly there, so it's a huge risk for him to take.
He's forfeiting most of his power, but it would allow him to
help Samedi in secret."

I stared at the rug again.

Zrakovi leaned forward so I'd have to look at him. "I've
known Gerry a great many years, since long before you were
born. He's always hated that the Elders kept such rigid control
over the Beyond. I have no doubt that in any agreement with
Samedi, he thought he was doing the right thing. But what he
has done is, in our world, unforgivable. You understand that,
don't you?"

I pulled my legs up in the chair and wrapped my arms around my knees. "I do."

Alex was finding his shoelaces fascinating, but sensed me watching him. We locked gazes. He looked miserable. I only hoped if the Elders found Gerry, they wouldn't make Alex be the one to kill him. Surely the Elders would do that deed themselves and not turn it over to an enforcer.

"What happens next?" Alex's voice was strained.

"You do nothing," Zrakovi answered. "Now that we know what is going on, let us handle it."

He stood, and Alex and I followed suit. "I'll contact the full Congress of Elders to secure a warrant that will allow us to detain Samedi and strip him of his power, but it's a political issue and will take a couple of days," Zrakovi said. "If he is interested in you either as a pawn or a sacrifice, Drusilla, he will try to pull you to him. Stay where you are, behind your wards, and let us do our work."

"Excuse me, sir," Alex asked. "But how long will it take the Elders to repair the damage between the Now and the Beyond?"

Zrakovi sighed and shook his head. "I don't know. We're trying to monitor and repair hundreds of breaches along the Gulf Coast from the two hurricanes. In the meantime, we're encountering resistance from many groups within the Beyond who see this as an opportunity to make inroads back into the mundane world. Now at least we know they're trying to keep our attention away from Samedi and Gerry." A trace of anger had returned to his voice.

He stepped back into the transport and nodded at me. I filled in the edge I'd wiped out earlier and fed energy into it. As he faded in a shimmer of light, Zrakovi said five words that echoed Gerry's: "Stay out of the Beyond."

Alex and I stood silently for a few seconds, then I flopped back in my chair. "Sit here, he says. I don't want to just sit here and wait.

Maybe if Gerry knows the Elders are onto them I can talk him into backing down, staying hidden in the Beyond. I need to get in touch with him again." I doubted I'd be able to sleep for a week, much less bring on some weird elven magical dream on demand.

"You absolutely do not need to get in touch with Gerry." Alex leaned over the chair and got in my face. I glowered at him. He knelt, a hand on either arm of my chair so I couldn't move, and his voice was firm. "Look, I know you love Gerry no matter what he's done, and you want to try to summon him and warn him to stay where he is. Am I right?"

I gave him a blank face.

He shook his head. "You have to do what Zrakovi said and keep a low profile till this is over. If Samedi finds a way to get to you, you're as good as dead."

He paused for a moment. "And you'll get me killed, because I'll have to try and save you."

I rubbed my temples with my fingers and shut my eyes, willing it all just to go away.

"How much do you know about the Wizards' War of Nineteen Seventy-six?"

I looked at him in surprise. "I know there was a group of rogue wizards who went up against the Elders. And I know Gerry fought in it—and he fought for the Elders." I didn't see his point. "Why?"

"It started a lot like this, only without the hurricane. Actually, I read about it in one of Gerry's books. One of the ancient gods from the Beyond took advantage of an ambitious wizard who let him come and go freely. Over time, he was able to draw dark wizards and other mages to his side. They finally launched a full-scale assault against the Elders. The only reason the wizards won is that they were able to draw the fae to their side, and the vampires stayed neutral.

"That might not happen this time."

CHAPTER 37

We went to the Quarter to get the Pathfinder, then I drove home while Alex picked up lunch. He didn't want me to go since I was unofficially under house arrest, hiding from the Baron Samedi.

I'd been thinking about the transport in the library, which made me think of summoning circles. I could summon creatures from the Beyond as long as I knew their true name. Could I summon Gerry? I had tried just after he'd gone missing and it hadn't worked, but maybe he hadn't been in the Beyond then. Maybe now it would work.

After lunch, I left Alex working on reports—enforcers must spend half their time doing paperwork—and went back to the library. I'd stacked Gerry's books along the walls as a stopgap measure until I had time to blend his collection with mine, and I crawled around the edges of the room, scanning titles. I pulled out a bulky leather-bound volume with thin, parchment leaves edged in gold. *The Book of Summonry* had been a prize in Gerry's library. He'd bought it at a wizard's auction in Europe about a decade ago for enough money to feed a small nation for a month.

It was a seventeenth-century original, and I'd never actually seen Gerry read it. He always said possession was its own reward.

"What's up?"

I jumped like I'd been hit with a stun gun. Alex lounged in the doorway with a suspicious look on his face. Sebastian twined around his legs, eyeing me with malice.

"Finish your reports in triplicate?"

"Don't change the subject. What are you doing?" Alex could read me way too well. "And did you know this was here?" He'd picked up Charlie the elven staff, which had made its way to my worktable.

"That thing just flat-out gives me the crawling creeps, but it was pretty cool using it against the Lafittes because it doesn't drain my energy like my own magic does."

"Nice try. Now, what are you doing?"

"I want to try and summon Gerry."

Alex banged his head against the doorjamb. "Did you listen to a single word of what Zrakovi said?"

"If I can get him back here, you can arrest him."

Alex tensed. "Are you insane? I know you're feeling guilty about feeding Zrakovi information on Gerry, but you know what will happen if he's arrested, don't you?"

I looked at the floor, then back at Alex. "I do know. But at least he won't be slaughtered by Samedi. At least he'll have a hearing. Maybe the Elders will strip him of his power but let him live."

Alex shook his head. "Do you think Gerry would want to live that way?"

Maybe not, but at least it would be his choice.

"Let's just try it," I said. "It might not even work. If it does, and he wants to stay and face the Elders, he can. If he doesn't, then at least he'll know the Elders are onto his plans. He might try to save himself and get away from Samedi."

Alex looked at the floor and his shoulders sagged. I knew I'd won. "Let me get my gun, just in case you get him and he agrees to come in."

Gerry was Red Congress and could zap a gun out of Alex's hand faster than Alex could even think about shooting, but I didn't say so. If Gerry turned himself in, he wouldn't fight.

Sunshine didn't seem to fit the mood for summoning, so I closed the library curtains and kept only one lamp on. I swept away the Zrakovi portal and took out my jar of salt. Then, on impulse, I set it back on the shelf and instead picked up a jar of cold iron filings, which were stronger.

Alex returned with a pistol in a shoulder holster—not the monster handgun he'd lost at the Napoleon House, but the smaller one he'd been trying to teach me to use. He watched as I formed the circle, leaving about six inches open.

"What are you using?" He touched the metal filings, careful not to break the circle.

"Iron, for extra strength. Just in case something has Gerry's full name and can answer to his summons. With all that's going on, you never know." I looked at his gun. "What kind of ammunition do you have?"

"Standard issue. Wizards are basically the same as mundane as far as ammo goes. Do I need something specialized?"

"I have no idea."

"Well, good. Now I feel better." Alex hopped up on the worktable and watched as I placed two purple candles at noon and six o'clock just outside the circle, and two gold at three and nine. I lit the candles and turned off the lamp. I wanted all the energy directed toward the circle.

Between the candles, I placed the items I'd used to try and summon Gerry before: the pipe, the picture of us from Jazz Fest, one of his journals, and the Meisterstück pen.

"Have you ever seen one of these done?" I asked.

"Only once, during training. I've done lots of transports, but by the time I'm called in, the summoning's over and things have gotten out of control."

"I know you know this, but just a reminder," I said. "Don't break the energy field for any reason, even with a bullet. It might look like Gerry but not really be him. If it isn't Gerry and something else manages to show up from the Beyond, we don't want it running loose. It can't leave the circle."

He nodded. I could feel his tension, so I fingered the mojo bags in my pocket for a minute, breathing deeply—only to have the sound of Beck's "Loser" come blasting from somewhere in the vicinity of Alex's jeans.

Talk about a mood killer.

"Sorry." He retrieved his cell phone and looked at the screen. "It's Ken. Might be about the murder cases. Hold on and let me take it."

He walked into the sitting room to take the call, so I closed my eyes and focused on Gerry. I could probably do the ritual better without Alex's anxiety mucking up the works anyway.

I fixed Gerry's face in my mind, took my place on the cushion next to the circle, and pricked my finger with a lancet. "I summon Gerald Michael St. Simon," I said quietly, letting several drops of blood hit the iron filings.

I waited. Twice, a shape began to materialize but faded. I concentrated harder, pricking my finger again and adding more blood to the circle. I heard Alex come back into the room and stand behind me, but kept my concentration.

"DJ," he hissed. "Open your eyes."

A figure had finally materialized, but it wasn't Gerry. Wasn't even pretending to be Gerry. It was a tall, powerfully built man, a white skeleton painted on his dark skin. He wore a top hat and a tuxedo jacket over a bare chest. Around his neck was a strand of dead frogs. At least I thought they were dead until one kicked a feeble leg and let out a hoarse croak. I stood up and stepped back, looking into the smoky gray, twinkling eyes of the Baron Samedi.

He bowed his head briefly in greeting. "Good evening, wizard. I had hoped our first meeting would be in the Beyond, but since you called my good friend Gerald Michael St. Simon, I couldn't resist answering." His voice was deep and melodic, hypnotic, yet carrying with it dark tones that called up images of pain and blood and sex. I felt his power crawl across my skin, but no emotions. My empathic skills didn't work on Samedi. Probably a good thing.

I felt myself being drawn in by his gaze, and broke eye contact.

"Don't look him in the eye, Alex," I whispered.

"Oh no, Alex, do look at me. Look at me closely, and I can show you one of my powers. You see, I know how you will die, both of you." Samedi laughed, a sensual, earthy sound.

Alex didn't respond. I could only hope he had the good sense to keep his gaze on the floor and his hands away from the gun.

"Where is Gerald St. Simon?" I asked. "Is he still alive?"

Samedi smiled at me and I felt his allure. I could walk through the transport, and he would take care of me. I heard his voice in my head. *I'd always keep you beside me. I'd never leave you.*

"DJ, step back!"

Alex's voice wrenched me back to reality. I jerked my gaze to the frog necklace, my heart pounding. Samedi had almost sucked me in.

"Your father . . ." I flinched at that reference to Gerry. "Oh yes, little elfling. I know he is your father. His death will give me a lot of power, but you." He smiled broadly. "You could bring me to my full power, either through your death or by joining with me. It is your choice."

So Jean had told me the truth about Samedi's plans—talk me into an alliance and kill me later, or just go ahead and kill me sooner. Either way, I ended up dead and Gerry couldn't be helped.

Samedi caught my eye again, and smiled. "You could bargain for your father's life. If I have you, I do not need him. He is old and weak, and you have power you do not even understand."

So people keep telling me.

The seductive glamour flowed off Samedi. My knees weakened, and I wanted to crawl toward him, to ask him to take me. I forced my eyes away from him again, and focused on the miserable, frightened eye of one particularly large frog. Its tiny nostrils flared as it struggled to breathe, and a fine stream of blood ran from its pierced side to pool on the floor.

"What is it you want me to do?" My voice came out in a whisper.

"Come to me, and I will tell you." Samedi reached for me, but Alex took my arm and tugged me back from the circle.

"I'm okay," I lied. "Let him play his games."

Samedi laughed again. I heard a window break behind me as the sound penetrated the room, but I kept my eyes lowered.

You will come to me soon, wizard—you and your enforcer. His voice was in my head again. *Perhaps you think your father deserves to die, as punishment for working with me. But I have a new friend with me now, too, one you might wish to save.*

Wagging his fingers in a parody of a wave, Samedi's image faded as quickly as it had appeared, leaving behind something small and shiny. Since he hadn't been the one I summoned, he apparently didn't have to wait for me to release him. I made sure his energy field had faded before reaching out a shaky hand to break the circle.

"DJ, we have to leave. Jake's missing—it's what Ken was calling about." Alex's voice shook.

"What?" I turned to stare at him, my heart dancing crazy rhythms.

"We've gotta go. I'll tell you on the way."

"Let me grab whatever Samedi left in the circle and we'll go."

I bent over and picked up the silver chain Samedi had left, and a chill of fear sped through me. Oh my God. Not just a chain—U.S. Marine Corps dog tags. The name stamped on the first line was Warin.

I handed it to Alex, whose face paled as he turned and headed for the stairs.

I pulled out my backpack and grabbed the four potions I had left from my Jean Lafitte escapade: mist, arctic, sleep, and torch. I stuffed them in my pockets. None were lethal, but they'd have to do. I knew physical magic didn't work right in the Beyond, but maybe potions were different. I got a couple of cords and strapped the elven staff to my thigh, then hung both mojo bags on another cord around my neck.

By the time I got out the back door, Alex had already pulled his car onto the street and was waiting for me, thunderclouds on his face.

He lurched the car away from the curb before I had the door closed.

"Tell me what Ken said."

"Leyla got to work and couldn't find Jake. She finally went upstairs and his door was open, blood everywhere, no sign of him. Louis is locked in his room and won't answer the door. She knew Jake and Ken were tight, so she called him instead of going through 9-1-1."

"So we're going to be dealing with the police?"

He shook his head. "I told Ken to hold off till I checked it out and called him back."

I pulled out my cell phone. "We need to call the Elders."

"Don't waste your time. I know what they'll say." His

knuckles had turned white from his choke hold on the steering wheel. "They'll tell us to sit back and let them handle it. Jake will be dead before they make a decision."

I pulled out my phone anyway and hit 2 and send. It was a sad state of affairs that I now had the Speaker of the Council of Elders in Gerry's former spot on my speed-dial list. The Speaker didn't answer, however. It was Zrakovi himself, sounding unhappy.

"Drusilla, we just received a breach alarm from your address. What is going on?"

I forced myself to breathe. I needed to sound calm, even though what I felt was more akin to hysteria. "I tried to summon Gerry, to convince him to turn himself in. Baron Samedi showed up instead. He has taken Jacob Warin, Alex's cousin, into the Beyond. Jake is a mundane. He can't defend himself. We have to go in there and—"

Zrakovi cut me off. "You will do nothing, Drusilla. Do you understand me? Given the number of wizards we have available, if we charge in without securing the alliances of other, stronger groups, we'll start a war we can't win."

His voice had risen to a shout, but I couldn't respond. How long since Samedi had taken Jake? What had they done to him?

"Do I make myself clear?" Zrakovi's voice made the phone vibrate. No more Mr. Nice Wizard.

"Crystal." I hung up on him.

"Told you." Alex didn't even ask what Zrakovi had said.

We were silent on our drive to the Gator, each lost in our thoughts. Jake was tough, and he'd try to fight them not knowing what he was up against. But he'd probably be kept alive as long as Samedi thought him a valuable hostage.

This was my fault, and I had to fix it.

CHAPTER 38

My nerves skittered as we walked into the Gator and saw Leyla behind the bar. She left her customer mid-order as soon as she saw us.

"I had to open today. Jake's gone, and it looks like something bad happened up there." She looked as if she'd been crying.

Alex gave her a curt nod and strode toward the back hall-way.

"What should I do?" Leyla watched Alex disappear into the stairwell. "I called Jake's friend, the detective, but the police haven't shown up."

"Ken called Alex—he's FBI. He can handle it," I said. "Can you run the place alone? Or do you have a friend who can come and help you?"

She nodded.

"Then business as usual. Close early if you need to. We'll find Jake."

"But—"

I ran toward the back and left Leyla to cope as best she could.

I found Alex sitting on Jake's sofa upstairs, looking stunned. The apartment door had been battered, and upended furniture littered the living-room floor. Blood. A lot of blood.

"He's gone. Looks like he put up a big fight." Alex picked up a CD case from the floor near his feet and threw it at the wall hard enough to break the case and dent the Sheetrock.

"Did you ask Louis what happened?"

"He said a giant snake with a human skull floated down the hallway a few feet off the floor, followed by a couple of guys Louis has seen hanging around South Rampart in Old Orleans. Not Lafitte's people. It happened early this morning. Louis ran in his room and locked the door. He heard what sounded like a fight, then nothing. He didn't even know Jake was gone."

A slow-birthing horror grew inside me. "God. This is my fault. Oh dear God." I sat on the sofa and tried to breathe.

"How?" Never had a single syllable sounded so hopeless.

"Louis. I brought Louis here. It was like hanging a neon sign over Jake's head that he was tied to this whole mess." Jake was a brave and honorable man, and I couldn't bear the thought that I'd gotten him mixed up in this.

I got to my feet and began pacing. "We need to make a plan. We have to go after him."

"You talked to Zrakovi. I know what he said—to stand down. He's looking at the greater good and all that crap I was spouting at you this morning." Alex looked as though the greater good had kicked him in the gut.

We stared in silence at the blood soaking into the hardwood floor, till I couldn't stand it any longer.

"I'm going after him. I know it's a long shot, but I have to try. Jake's only there as bait because Samedi wants me—it's why he left the dog tags in my summoning circle."

Alex looked at the floor and didn't answer.

"I'll use the transport site in Gerry's bedroom, assuming it will take me wherever he went," I said, heading toward the door. "But I need you to stand watch at the transport and pull Jake and Gerry out if I'm able to send them back. Then call the Elders or the ambulance—whichever is appropriate."

Alex followed me to the door and grabbed my arm. "Forget it. You're not going to the Beyond. It's too dangerous and chances are good you won't save either one of them. You'll just get yourself killed." I could feel Alex's fear as well as his conflict. He was torn between following orders like the good soldier he'd been trained to be and going after Jake himself. He was breathing hard and his eyes had taken on a reflective quality that made me think he was close to spontaneously shifting. His control was shot.

I pulled my arm away from him as gently as I could. "I know I'm overmatched, but I have to try." I gave him a wry smile. "I am Gerry's daughter, after all."

I headed across the hall, Alex on my heels. "You're not going in there alone."

"I don't plan to go alone," I said, pounding on the door. "I'm taking Louis with me."

CHAPTER 39

By the time Alex, Louis, and I reached Gerry's house, the sun had turned to orange fire over the lakefront. We didn't bother with masks this time, but our boots still sat outside the door and we slipped them on. No point in going into the Beyond covered in sludge. A couple of plastic grocery bags tied around his ankles provided protection for Louis, who wasn't happy about any of this. We dumped the boots as soon as we got upstairs.

Gerry's portal remained beside his bed, and I walked around it carefully, reinforcing it with iron filings so it would remain open. I handed the jar of leftover filings to Louis and told him to put it in his pocket.

"What's the plan?" Alex and Louis stood side by side, watching me.

I took a deep breath. "Louis and I go in. He can help me find information and stay hidden as long as possible. You stay here and wait for Jake or Gerry—both, I hope—to show up. If I'm not back a half hour after they come through, break the transport." I paused, then added, "If none of us shows up by dawn, break the transport and call Zrakovi."

Alex frowned. "What about you?"

I chuckled. "I hope I'll be right behind them but if I'm not, break the transport anyway. It can't stay open." I held up a hand to silence his protest. "This might be a one-way trip. But either way, Samedi won't win."

That's about the only part of the plan I had figured out. In case things went badly, if the only way to get Jake and Gerry out was for me to stay with Samedi, I had stuck a vial of lifesbane in my pocket. A quick sip and I'd be dead. Ironically, Gerry taught me about it so I wouldn't stumble on the combination of herbs by accident. I might die tonight, but I was going on my own terms.

I'd done some reading in Gerry's books on power-transfer and blood sacrifice, and since I was a wizard, Samedi would have to kill me himself in order to take my powers. He couldn't order a flunky to do it like he had the human soldiers. If I took my own life, it wouldn't do him any good. The thought of ruining Samedi's plans gave me a load of satisfaction. Not that I'd be there to enjoy the show.

I turned my back before Alex knew I'd seen the sheen of tears. The internal war he waged between duty and loyalty and his love for Jake was tearing him apart. Too bad love and duty didn't always overlap.

I took Louis's hand and stepped into the transport with him. I had just touched Gerry's staff to the symbols and begun softly saying a prayer for guidance and protection when I felt an arm snake around my waist. Alex pressed against me in the transport as it lit like a ring of burning coals and a shimmering cylinder rose around us. It was too late to get him out of there, but I elbowed him hard in his rib cage for good measure.

A flash of light blinded me and I struggled to breathe as the compression of air and time pushed on us from all sides. Powering a transport with the elven staff sure felt more powerful than my usual puny efforts. I closed my eyes against the fierce glare until my eyelids relaxed and I could feel the light subsiding.

"We're here." Louis tugged at my sleeve. I opened my eyes, Alex loosened his grip on my waist, and we stepped out into the Beyond. I had a new appreciation for how Dorothy and Toto must have felt landing in Oz, except I'd be overjoyed at the sight of a wizard and a couple of witches—even wicked ones.

I looked around me at quiet, cobblestoned streets and familiar French Quarter architecture. Wherever we had landed, it was secluded and definitely New Orleans. Make that Old Orleans.

And dim. I looked at my watch and punched the stem to light the dial. Five p.m. "Why is it so dark?" I whispered to Louis.

"It's always nighttime in Old Orleans," he whispered back. "We never see the sun. We go from sunset to dawn, then back to sunset. Always full moon too, so there's always loup-garou around."

Why had no one ever bothered to mention this? I'd have brought a flashlight. "Do you know where we are?"

Louis looked around and cocked his head, listening. "Lower Quarter. Looks like over toward Rampart."

We headed toward the closest corner. Gas streetlights flickered on the sides of buildings. The jangle of a dozen competing jazz tunes floated in from our left, and the air smelled of fried onions, stale beer, and rotting oysters—not so different from the Quarter's modern cousin.

I got the jar of iron shavings from Louis and quickly traced out a transport. We'd landed in an unmarked breach and might never find it again, plus I wasn't sure how to power something I couldn't see. I willed some magic into the new transport, and other than a faint popping sound, nothing happened. Guess that rumor about physical magic not working in the Beyond was true. I tried again using the elven staff, and was relieved when I felt the pulse of magic spread around the symbols.

The signs at the nearest corner read Burgundy and St. Louis, and I tried to fix the layout of the Quarter in my mind. "Louis, how much attention will we attract walking around Rampart?"

His eyes looked ready to pop out and roll down the sidewalk. "You can't go strolling down Rampart Street, no ma'am. Alex could, but not you. Human-looking women attract a lot of attention here."

I scowled, trying not to think too much about what kind of nonhuman women might be gallivanting around Old Orleans. "Well, I can't just stand on the street corner. What the—"

Alex peeled off his hoodie and threw it at me. At least I knew what he was up to this time, so I wasn't rendered speechless as he handed me his T-shirt, holster, and gun.

"Put them on, pull up the hood. Use the shoulder harness." He continued to strip. "Louis, man, hang on to my pants." Louis's mouth hung open, but he held out his hand automatically and took the jeans Alex handed to him.

Louis gasped as Alex knelt, the air shimmered, and big golden Gandalf stood in his place. Louis gaped at him until Gandalf body-bumped him toward Rampart. Then he mumbled something incoherent and took off at a quick pace. I bet Louis wished he'd never met us.

I had to hurry to catch up. I threw down the T-shirt and holster but slipped on the hoodie, which fell to my knees and covered the staff strapped to my thigh. I stuck the gun in my back waistband and hoped I didn't shoot my own ass off.

I pulled the hood over my head and kept pace with Louis, Gandalf between us. The barrel of the big handgun dug into my skin, and I wondered if I should have even kept it. My shooting lessons with Alex hadn't progressed past load, release safety, and aim.

Louis's gaze shifted toward Gandalf every other step. "Did you know he could do that?"

I patted the dog on his head, which hit me about waist level. "Oh yeah, I knew. He's actually nicer this way." Gandalf curled his upper lip.

The Quarter might smell the same, but this Rampart Street wasn't anything like the modern version. These days, or at least before Katrina, it was the edgy and dangerous outer wall of the tourist zone. Undercover narcs hung out on street corners hoping to make deals. Some really good old restaurants were in the area, but you locked your car and watched your back when you went in.

Old Rampart was hopping. The time period looked, well, timeless—an odd amalgam of jumbled eras. Napoleon meets Jay Gatsby meets George Jetson. No wonder Jean Lafitte was so well versed in modern customs.

Flashy neon lit the streets, and scantily clad women—not human, I assumed—hung out of windows and doorways, advertising their favors. A tall, dark-skinned woman with yellow hair tugged on my sleeve as I passed her. "C'mon, little boy, I'll take you on a ride for a little gold."

Little boy was good. If I looked like a little boy, the oversize hoodie was doing its job.

Before we'd gone half a block, I staggered and fell against the side of a storefront, struggling to stay on my feet. Gandalf nuzzled my waist and I put a hand on his head to steady myself.

"DJ, what's wrong?" Louis looked scared. Hell, Louis *was* scared. The woman behind us was angry. A man edged his way around us. He was anxious, on the verge of panic. A vampire was tracking him, and he didn't know how to hide from her.

"I can't block out emotions all of a sudden. I'm pulling them from everybody." I leaned against a building and closed my eyes, wrapping my hands around the mojo bags and focusing on my heartbeat, on the simple act of expanding and contracting my lungs. It helped a little.

Gandalf nuzzled my hip.

"I'll manage." I patted his head. Breathe deeply. Mind blank.

He chomped down on the edge of the hoodie and started pulling me in the direction we'd come from.

"No, Alex." I yanked the jacket away from him. "We have to do this. Louis, let me take your arm. Try not to feel anything."

Good luck with that. I was freaking him out.

I walked slowly, my arm locked in Louis's, Gandalf behind us. Even here, Louis was famous. Bouncers and hawkers outside the clubs greeted him as he passed, and that dropped his fear level lower and made it easier on me as well. My head pounded with the emotions hitting me, and my lungs constricted.

Finally, Louis slipped into a club called Beyond and Back. I followed him in the front door, head down, while Gandalf slunk into an alleyway beside the building.

"Sit in that corner and keep your head down," Louis whispered, pointing me toward an empty table in the back. "There's a door into the alley if you need it."

He went in search of a chatty bartender while I took a chair against the wall and looked from beneath the hood at the motley assortment of patrons who seemed disinclined to mind anyone else's business—probably a good idea in Old Orleans. A lot of them appeared to be drinking heavily, which numbed their emotions. I liked numbed emotions. I relaxed a little.

Not all of the bar patrons even tried to look human. I shivered when a very slim, very pale, very handsome man's black eyes lingered on me. He was hungry. I slipped farther under the hood when he moved a couple of tables closer. He was still staring when a dark-haired woman approached him, nibbled at his earlobe, and tugged on his arm, pulling him toward the door. He grinned at me before turning away, the tip of fangs visible against his lower lip. I shuddered and looked up as Louis sat opposite me.

"Bartender's a friend of mine," he said. "Only thing I could find out was some big ceremony's going down at St. Louis Number One. Thing is . . ." He looked around and spoke more softly. "Thing is, that's normally something lots of folks would want to go to. The voodoo have big parties all the time at the river and they have huge crowds 'bout every night. But folks are scared of the party tonight 'cause it's at the cemetery. I'm thinking that's where the old skeleton man is."

If Samedi's power lay in creating and controlling the dead, hanging out in a cemetery made sense. Good grief. I hoped I wouldn't have to deal with zombies. They were slow and stupid, as a general rule, but also wicked strong and had no self-preservation instincts, so you couldn't scare them or back them down. Forget the gun. I should have borrowed some of Alex's grenades.

The city's oldest cemetery, St. Louis Number One, was only a few blocks away. I edged out of my seat and slipped out the back door into the alley, Louis close behind. Gandalf waited at the door.

The elven staff grew warmer against my leg, as if it knew what was coming. I had the feeling Charlie was getting ready for something, or maybe it just picked up on my tension. I put a hand on it to see if it was vibrating, and all the noise in my head stopped. Just stopped. No emotions trying to filter in, nothing.

I loved this staff. If I ever met any elves, I'd have to thank them for making it.

We needed to scope out St. Louis Number One. "Are you still willing to help us?" I asked Louis.

He nodded, shifting Alex's pants to his other arm and not looking very happy about it. Neither was I.

"Stay hidden until whatever happens is over," I said. "If you can, help Jake or the older wizard—and Alex—get back to the transport at Burgundy and St. Louis. If you can't, don't worry about it. You've already helped us a lot."

"I'll get them there." Louis's jaw tightened. "I like Jake. He knew something was funny about me but he was always kind and treated me with respect. Besides, I figure me being at the Gator is what got him on that voodoo man's radar."

I swallowed my own guilt and tried not to think about Jake or Gerry either one, except as rescue targets. Going any deeper would turn me to a nervous pile of mush, and mush couldn't help anybody.

I turned to Gandalf. "How do you want to play this, Alex? Do you want to shift back?" The big dog looked at me, chuffed a noisy breath that sounded more equine than canine, and trotted toward the entrance to the alleyway. My little pony.

Thank God he hadn't listened when I told him to stay behind. I didn't want to do this alone, and he was the only one I trusted. We'd come a long way.

CHAPTER 40

The post-Katrina levee breaches flooded St. Louis Cemetery Number One, the oldest of New Orleans's "Cities of the Dead." Legend has it people are buried in aboveground tombs in New Orleans because the water table is so high a heavy rain could wash bodies out of the ground. Legend also says the water-table thing is an old wives' tale. Take your pick.

Another, more recent legend says you need to visit the cemetery in groups because criminals bent on robbery and mayhem lurk behind the crypts. Frankly, a normal criminal would come as a welcome relief.

I looked around curiously as we crept along the cemetery's outer walls. In modern New Orleans, the huge Iberville public housing project sat near the cemetery, trapping poor families in substandard housing for generations—at least before Katrina flooded them out.

Iberville hadn't made it to Old Orleans. Rows of multistoried wooden buildings with raised sidewalks and balconies spilled shouts and laughter and jazz from down the block. The scene came straight out of Storyville, the red-light district that occupied these streets at the turn of the century. Well, except for the people (maybe they were people) in modern clothing and the horses, streetcars, and automobiles from all eras jamming the intersections.

The area around the cemetery entrance was deserted, but I jumped as a gunshot echoed to our west.

"Prob'ly a card game gone wrong," Louis whispered. "Happens here a lot. Or dwarves. Dwarves shoot at anything that moves."

I tried not to think about gun-toting dwarves.

We finally reached the entrance to the walled-in cemetery, and Louis looked cautiously around the open gate. Electricity, probably fueled by some kind of spell, had made it to Basin Street, but not inside the cemetery. The grounds were lit by gas lanterns on black wrought-iron posts. In the flickering light, the jumble of tombs topped by crosses and angels threw shadows like skyscrapers angling across the narrow paths. A brighter light beckoned us farther into the grounds.

As we slipped from the shelter of one family crypt to another, I saw famous names from New Orleans history—former politicians, musicians, plantation owners, and pirates. But it was the cluster of people gathered near the light, singing and shouting, that I focused on. They had their backs to us, and I motioned for Louis to stay behind while I slipped in closer. Gandalf whined softly and loped off at an angle. I lost sight of him in the dark.

The scene looked like a scout meeting in hell. Flames from a bonfire shimmied in the center of facing rows of crypts, and a trio of young, dark-haired men sweated as they pounded out a hypnotic rhythm on small drums. Around the fire danced Marie Laveau, dressed in a short shift made from sewn-together red handkerchiefs. Circlets of bells on her wrists and ankles jingled as she moved and sang softly in a patois I couldn't un-

derstand. In her arms was an enormous black mamba, the ritual
snake of voodoo.

A wave of nausea crawled through me. Hunger, lust, rever-
ence, excitement. A jumble of emotions floated off the crowd.
My limbs felt heavy, and I reached to touch the staff. It all
disappeared except the nausea, probably caused by the seesaw
from emotional overload to emotional void. I liked the void a lot
better.

A movement behind Marie caught my attention. Standing
guard around the gathering were two wolves, both a deep,
rusty red and as big as Gandalf. Loup-garou, the rogues of the
werewolf world, the ones who wouldn't allow themselves to
be mainstreamed. Their yellow eyes reflected the dancing firelight.

The small crowd around the voodoo priestess was spellbound, swaying slightly, entranced. I remembered the seductive
pull of Samedi's voice. It wasn't hard to understand how they'd
gotten sucked in. *Hand on staff. Peace.*

I edged around to get a better look, tightening the hood
around my face, then froze. Gerry sat atop a low, wide tomb,
watching Marie and smiling. Twenty feet from him, tied to a
tall, post-like headstone, was Jake. Gerry was ignoring him.

A cold sweat broke out on my body and my hands con-
tracted into fists. Collateral damage. Change by revolution
never comes without someone getting bloody, and if you looked
at the big picture—like Gerry did from his standpoint, and the
Elders from theirs—Jake was an acceptable loss.

I looked at Gerry through a blur of tears. *I'm not like you.*

He turned in my direction and his gaze shifted to me. I
held my breath as he frowned, cocked his head, and watched
me a moment before turning back to Marie.

Either he hadn't recognized me, or he was pretending. Either way, safe to breathe again.

I walked around two women with their hands crossed over their chests, swaying to the drumbeats, and found a spot where I could get a better look at Jake but still stay toward the back of the onlookers. I swayed a little with the emotion of the people around me, trying to blend in. I reached down to touch the staff, but kept swaying. Just one of the faithful, waiting for something to happen.

Jake was propped upright, mostly. Ropes bound his knees to the marble column and his hands had been secured behind it. His head slumped forward but he appeared to be supporting his own weight. I breathed a sigh of relief. He was alive. So far, so good.

He shifted his head slightly to the right, watching something behind him. I squinted, and caught a quick view of gold fur. Gandalf was working the ropes with his teeth, trying to free Jake. So far, the wolves hadn't spotted him. If they scented him, I hoped he'd smell like canine rather than human.

A scream from the crowd riveted my attention back to Marie Laveau, who had fallen to the ground, stunned. The black mamba rose vertically as if standing on its tail, and the blasted thing had to be at least seven feet tall. The crowd backed away from the fire as the air around the snake shimmered and changed form. Their momentum carried me back with them.

The Baron Samedi had arrived at his own party.

Women shrieked; several fell to the ground. I wasn't sure where the worshipping ended and the fainting began. As long as the people in front of me stayed put, I didn't care.

He was a sight to behold. Like his incarnation in the safety of my library, Samedi stood tall, wearing a top hat, bow tie, and tails, black pants and red cummerbund, but no shirt. The frog necklace had disappeared so the skeleton painted on his body gleamed white in the firelight against his dark skin.

He reached down to a cage I hadn't noticed earlier and pulled out a squawking rooster, hanging by its feet from his right hand. It struggled, all bristling feathers and snapping beak. He swung it over his head a few times, laughing in that melodic voice that had hypnotized me earlier, and slung it into the fire. The rooster screamed as it ran around the circle in flames, causing the spectators to retreat farther. The smell of singed feathers assaulted my nostrils and increased the nausea. *Hand back on the staff.*

Several onlookers began running toward the cemetery gates, and before I realized it, the circle had thinned until there were only two rows of people between me and the main attraction. I pulled the hoodie as far as it would go over my face. It knocked out my peripheral vision so I couldn't keep track of how Gandalf was progressing in his attempt to free Jake, but at least it provided me a little more cover.

Unburdened of his rooster, the Baron straightened his bow tie and brushed off the cuffs of his tuxedo jacket. "Greetings, my followers, especially you, my dear Marie." He turned to smile down at the voodoo priestess, who sat on the ground at his feet. The imperious demeanor she showed while dancing with the snake—and taunting me in my library—had been replaced by a look of rapture.

Samedi's voice, as when he'd talked to me, vibrated with the cadence of old New Orleans, soft and lilting, with French and Spanish influences. Sensual, but deadly.

The people in front of me murmured and shifted restlessly. Several more slipped toward the exit, leaving a trail of fear that sent my hand reaching for the staff.

I wanted nothing more than to run out of the cemetery with them, but that wasn't an option. I was *so* not cut out to be a hero. A hero wouldn't shake and feel like throwing up. A hero would whip out a staff or a gun and take charge of the situation. I picked the tallest guy still among the onlookers and wedged in behind him.

Smiling as Samedi blathered on about how powerful he was becoming, Gerry looked relaxed and pleased with himself. I couldn't reconcile the Gerry I loved with this man who could sit smiling while Jake suffered. As soon as Gandalf freed Jake, I would slip out the gates and then decide what to do about Gerry. Jake wasn't here by choice. As much as it hurt, he had to be my priority.

I shifted my gaze to check on Gandalf's progress when I felt a hand on my back. A woman pushed me forward as she tried to get a better view. Muttering at the interruption, the tall man in front of me stepped aside, and I found myself in the front row. I had a clear view of Samedi.

He also had a clear view of me. I jerked my head downward, pulling my face as far into the hoodie as I could, but I felt the weight of his gaze. Imaginary ants crawled across my scalp, and a cold tingle marched up my spine, even with my hand on the staff.

"Our guest of honor has arrived!" Samedi's voice was a delighted singsong of rhythm. "Join us, won't you, little wizard?" I backed up and turned to run—right into the arms of Jean Lafitte.

Not again.

"A pleasure to see you, *Jolie*." Lafitte's dark-blue eyes shone, and I got a close-up view of the full lips and scarred jawline before he spun me around and propelled me forward. Traitorous wretch.

"Our deal's off, turncoat." I struggled as he forced me toward the center of the circle, in front of Samedi. I dug into his hands with my nails and wished he'd put a body part close enough for me to bite.

"You said you'd stay out of this, you jerk." What a fool. Trusting a pirate. And not just any pirate. Freakin' Jean Lafitte.

I finally pulled away from him, leaving him holding the oversize hoodie.

"Caution, *Jolie*," he whispered. "You are safer with me."

Yeah, like I'm trusting him again. I circled the fire, keeping the flames between me and Samedi. The old god's smile was so broad it barely fit on his face.

I pulled Alex's gun and pointed it at Samedi in a two-handed stance that probably looked cool, but had a far more practical purpose—the pistol was so big I couldn't hold it otherwise. I remembered to release the safety but didn't know whether the gun was still loaded with regular ammo or whether it even would work on a voodoo god, assuming I could hit him. I heard the rustle of feet as the few remaining onlookers decided they had something better to do with their evening. Marie Laveau slipped into the shadows as well. I kept the gun trained on Samedi.

"No need for violence, Drusilla, plus your little gun will not hurt me." Samedi's voice was a smooth-tasting poison—felt nice going down, then you were dead. "I have promised your old friend Monsieur Lafitte his own time with you before our business begins, is that not right, Jean?"

Maybe discounting Jean had been a mistake. I glanced back to where I'd last seen him and flinched as an arm slid around me from behind. He jerked me against him, reaching around to pull Alex's pistol from my grasp and toss it on the ground. Dominique You emerged from the shadows to retrieve it. The look he gave me wasn't friendly. Great. At least one of Jean's hench-pirates was present and feeling vengeful.

"What happened to the bit where I was safer with you?" I elbowed Jean hard in the ribs, but all it got me was a hiss and the business end of a knife pressed below my ear.

I hadn't handled the staff in a while, and Jean's emotions filtered through my defenses. Nerves and fear. Jean was afraid of Samedi, which I did not find reassuring.

"*Mais oui,* Baron. I would have my time with her." Jean's

breath was hot in my ear as he pressed the point of the knife into the side of my neck and flicked it. I felt a quick, sharp pain and a thin trickle slither toward my collarbone. I shuddered as his tongue licked the blood from my skin.

He nibbled at my neck and whispered, "You shouldn't have come, *Jolie*. I had to take your gun, but Samedi hasn't seen the staff and I know what it can do. However, I hope your aim has improved." He bit my ear hard enough to make me yelp.

Samedi prowled the edge of the clearing, watching us, eyes bright. Laughing and singing, enjoying his role as voyeur.

This was a ridiculous three-ring circus, and it was time one of the onlookers got off his butt and helped.

"Gerry!" I screamed at him, and he jerked his rapt gaze from Samedi to me. I'd never seen him look so vacant. He blinked twice and frowned, like he thought he'd seen me before somewhere but couldn't quite remember who I was.

Finally, insight hit me like a mallet. Gerry had been enthralled. No wonder he'd just smiled vaguely while everything went to hell around him. Samedi's seductive voice had almost lured me into my own summoning circle. Gerry would have been even more vulnerable working with the Baron in the Beyond, away from his magic.

How much of Gerry's behavior had been done under Samedi's influence? Had the old god kept him so zombied out he couldn't think or act on his own? Or was I still trying to make excuses for him?

Didn't matter. Right now, I had to reach him.

"Gerry, keep your eyes on me and think," I said, keeping my voice level. "Look at what's happening here. More innocent people are going to be killed."

He shook his head, trying to shake the cobwebs loose. "DJ? I told you not to come here." He looked back at Samedi, who caught his gaze and held it. Damn.

Gerry smiled. "You can join us, daughter. You'll make us stronger."

God, he was lost. Completely and utterly lost.

I felt Jean at my back. "Focus, Drusilla," he whispered. "You must focus on the Baron."

Samedi stepped between me and Gerry. "Your father is right. Will you be my partner now, or my sacrifice?"

He raised his arms to the side and began a slow, sinuous dance, chanting in an unfamiliar language. Maybe the freak was singing to me, or trying to hypnotize me. Thank God I hadn't had time to guzzle a translation potion.

Avoiding Samedi's eyes, I looked back at Gerry, who stood up and motioned for me to come to him. Jean held me firmly in place, but he needn't have bothered. I felt safer with the pirate now, which was a sad, sorry state of affairs.

And I'd owe the pirate one really fine house if we made it out of this.

"You must decide what you want to do," Jean whispered as he nibbled at my neck again.

"Tsk, tsk, Jean." Samedi chided the pirate with a grin that caused Jean to take a step backward, dragging me with him. Apparently, whispering wasn't on the list of freedoms he'd been granted to enjoy at my expense.

"Pardon, Baron." Jean gave Samedi a big grin. "I was overcome with passion."

Oh brother. Still, I had to admire Jean's cool. He might be afraid of Samedi, but wasn't showing it. Of course, he'd had a few centuries to practice his technique.

Samedi turned to Gerry, who was talking with a sense of urgency now, gesturing toward me.

A spark of hope ignited. Maybe Gerry had snapped out of the enthrallment. Maybe he could still control Samedi and salvage this mess.

"You dare threaten me, wizard?" Samedi laughed and signaled to one of the drummers, who set his instrument aside and pulled a knife from his belt. He didn't speak, but the menace was clear.

Gerry paled and slung an arm toward Samedi. I'd seen the move hundreds of time. He could fling enough physical magic to kill—at least injure—anything that got in his way.

Except it didn't work. Samedi stood still while the magic passed through his body and dissipated. His laughter echoed around the cemetery and raised goose bumps on my arms.

Gerry backed up, his gaze darting from Samedi to me.

"Bring her to me, Jean." Samedi turned his back on Gerry, confident his magic was useless.

Jean had lessened the pressure of the knife to my throat, but still held me firmly against him. I could feel his rage building. Anger with Samedi was fast outweighing his fear, and surges of it pulsed across my skin where he touched me.

"You have seen both of our guests tonight, your father and your young man." Samedi spoke to me but gestured toward Gerry and Jake like a game-show host displaying the grand prizes behind doors number one and two. Door number one, Jake, still hadn't raised his head, and I'd lost sight of Gandalf. He was out there in the shadows, waiting for an opening. At least I hoped he was.

Door number two, Gerry, stared at the ground. His shoulders rose and fell with the force of his breathing, and he lifted his gaze as if he could feel the weight of my eyes on him. I saw reason returning, thoughts starting to coalesce. And horror freezing his features. God help me, I'd almost rather he remain in his clueless state than see him paralyzed by guilt and fear, knowing his powerful magic—the thing that defined him—was useless.

Maybe he could help, or maybe he'd lapse back into enthrallment. I couldn't wait to find out. *Jake* couldn't wait.

"You don't want them, Baron. Let them go, and I won't fight you." My voice sounded a lot braver than I felt, maybe because of my Jean Lafitte energy snack.

I heard the pirate hiss behind me. He didn't like my tactic. Neither did Gerry. He labored to his feet, weaving precariously.

Samedi clicked his teeth in delight. "So you want to make a deal with me?" He put a finger to his mouth and rolled his eyes heavenward. "The problem is that I do not think one little elfling such as yourself is a fair exchange for both a wizard and a human."

He paused again in a pantomime of indecision. "I think an equal exchange is fairer. You choose which one shall have his freedom—your father or your young man—and which one will die. Deciding who lives and dies is usually my task, but I will share that power with you tonight. You will find it intoxicating. It is my gift to you for agreeing to be my partner."

Talk about a warped worldview. I looked at Jake's slack form, blood in his hair, and then at Gerry, who weaved on his feet and watched me in dismay. I was paralyzed. How could I possibly make that choice and live with the consequences?

With a hand signal from Samedi, one of the red wolves crept closer to Gerry, while the other, the bigger one, approached Jake from the side and nipped his arm.

Jake's head snapped up, and Gandalf sprang from the shadows behind him, teeth bared. He'd been hanging back, waiting to see where he'd be needed, and I felt a surge of love and fear that left me breathless.

Wolf and shifter tangled in a snarling ball of fur and fangs before breaking apart and racing into the darkness. A high-pitched yelp followed by a howl raised my own hackles, and then the wolf came trotting back to sit by Jake, blood dripping from its muzzle.

I choked on a scream. It didn't mean Alex was dead, I reminded myself. He was tough, and he was smart.

Jean squeezed my arm so hard the pain revived my focus. "Breathe deeply, *Jolie*," he whispered. "You will have to fight."

Jake raised his head and stared at me from a bruised, bloody face.

I closed my eyes and looked at the ground. Alex. What had I done?

I had done nothing. That was the problem.

CHAPTER 41

Jean eased the staff from its makeshift holster and settled it into my right hand, wrapping my fingers around it.

"It is time, Drusilla," he whispered.

Warmth from the staff radiated through me and cleared my head. My heart pounded, and my blood raced hot and wild. I could feel every sensation on the surface of my skin.

I stepped away from Jean.

Gerry made a hesitant move toward me. "DJ, get out of here," he said, his voice strained but sounding more like the Gerry I knew. "Run to the Presbytere—there's a transport there. Go home. Tell the Elders."

Samedi stood in place, looking amused as his eyes traveled between Gerry and me. "Wizards are fascinating creatures, struggling with their power and their feelings. You"—he looked at Gerry—"will not be saved by the Elders you have betrayed, while you"—eyes back to me—"will help me defeat them, either willingly or not."

"That would be not," I said, the staff vibrating in my hand. I dared a look into Samedi's eyes, and nothing happened. The staff seemed to be protecting me from his glamour, which meant its magic might work on him as well. I pointed it at him.

He laughed again. "Your magic does not work very well in the Beyond, wizard. Did you not see your father's pathetic demonstration? And you have not learned to use your old magic. Such a waste."

I felt a moment of doubt, but the staff sent electric pulses through my arm. It had plenty of power. I willed it to strike, and red ropes of flame flew from its end, so bright I had to squint against the light. The ropes shot past Samedi and wrapped themselves around the top of a tombstone three feet to his left. The marble exploded in a shower of flying rocks and dust—not exactly what I was going for, yet again. I really needed to work on my aim.

Samedi's eyes widened briefly when the rope trick started. By the time the tombstone exploded, he had disappeared.

I lowered the staff, irritated, and looked around. Samedi's helpers were gone now except for the two wolves that guarded Gerry and Jake. Still no sign of Alex.

I shifted the staff to my left hand, pulled one of the four small vials out of my right pocket, then popped off the top. Another Russian roulette of nonlethal charms that I prayed would work. For once, I was glad my magic was ritual rather than physical.

I had almost forgotten Jean behind me until he shouted. I spun in time to see the black mamba rising toward me, mouth open, fangs extended. I tossed the contents of the first vial as it struck, then rolled out of the way. A dark, poisonous mist hit the snake square in the fangs. It made a hissing sound, then vanished. I ground my teeth. The mist potion was gone now. Fighting Samedi was like trying to lasso smoke.

I crept from behind a tombstone and walked around the circle where the crowd had been, looking at shadows. I had another vial open in my right hand. How many forms did Samedi have? Snake, human. I knew there were more.

His human shape formed again on the other side of the fire. He had lost his jovial demeanor, and his smoky eyes had darkened to black pools. They weren't aimed at me, but at Jean, who'd come to stand at my right. I felt a presence on my left and looked around at Dominique, who flicked a brief glance my way before training his gaze back on Samedi.

"Jean, you are smarter than this," the old god said, his voice soothing, persuasive. "You would not side with the wizards against your own kind."

Jean's mouth was drawn into a tight line. "The wizards are arrogant, but you are *un mal bête*—evil. You are not my kind."

I handed the vial in my right hand to Jean and said, "Throw it if you get close enough." I pulled the next-to-last vial out and handed it to Dominique.

"What will it do?" he whispered in heavily accented English, taking off the top.

"I have no idea."

He exchanged a look with Jean and grinned, and they began walking in opposite directions, circling toward Samedi with swords in their scabbards and mystery charms in their hands, leaving me in the middle. The old divide-and-conquer strategy.

Samedi looked at all of us and laughed, pulling a long knife from his belt. He circled behind Gerry and his loup-garou guard, putting himself farther from the pirates who approached from either side.

Blooms of sweat had appeared on Gerry's shirt as his eyes moved rapidly from me to Samedi and back again. "We had an agreement, Baron. My daughter wasn't to be hurt. You agreed."

Samedi rested a hand on the side of Gerry's face and captured his gaze, and my father's body grew still. *My father.*

"Gerald Michael St. Simon, sacrifice your power to me,"

the Baron said softly, running a finger down the side of Gerry's neck. A wound gaped in the trail of Samedi's finger, and Gerry sank to his knees, blood washing his neck in crimson.

"No!" I didn't recognize the feral sound that came from my throat, but Samedi wasn't listening anyway. He raised his voice in a howl, and the wolves answered. The one closest to Jake sank its teeth into his right thigh and dragged him from the tombstone. The leg that had already been so damaged.

With Gerry out of the way, the remaining wolf looked from Dominique to Jean, and began slinking toward Jean.

"So it's me you want?" The pirate's grin shone in the firelight, and he pulled his cutlass from its leather scabbard, wielding the blade in his right hand and my potion vial in his left. "Come then, wolf. I have a taste of silver for you."

The loup-garou launched itself with a snarl.

Time seemed to slow down, each movement frozen in a series of moments. Jean saw the wolf coming and threw his potion as it struck. It left a ragged tear in his chest just before it froze, icicles of blood and saliva hanging from its mouth, frost covering its red fur. Jean rolled from underneath it as it fell. The arctic charm.

Dominique had rushed at the wolf attacking Jake and unleashed both the potion and his own silver blade. He had the sleep charm, and the combination of the sudden drowsiness and the blade took it down.

My final charm had to be the torch, and I rushed Samedi, getting as close as I could before throwing it. His top hat and coat burst into flames. He cursed and threw his arms out, then was gone again. I leaned against a tombstone, trying to catch my breath, and looked around for the snake.

Jean and Jake lay a few feet apart, both still, and Dom knelt next to his half-brother. Gerry hadn't moved since Samedi cut him.

A blow hit my right temple and knocked me flat, sending the staff on a graceful arc into the darkness. A turkey vulture, black as the snake, sat atop a crypt a few yards away, staring through crimson eyes.

Pain shot through my head and blood pooled in the dirt beneath me. I gulped in deep lungfuls of air to keep my vision from darkening. I'd have to faint later.

As I struggled to sit up, the emotions poured back in to join my fear. Dominique's anger, Jean's confusion, Jake's burning, agonizing pain. If they were feeling, they were still conscious. Nothing from Alex or Gerry, but I couldn't focus on them yet. Had to stay upright. Had to find the staff.

Which way had it gone? I groped around me in the dirt, keeping an eye on the vulture. Samedi's voice floated through my head, quiet and alluring, burying all the emotion. *You're alone now, little wizard. You have lost.*

The bird spread his wings and fluttered toward me, settling on the ground at my feet and morphing back into Samedi's human shape. I scrambled backward and hoisted myself to my feet using a headstone, reaching in my pocket for the lifesbane. I might not have saved anyone, but I wouldn't let Samedi win. As long as he didn't kill me, he still lost. I had to believe that. I pulled the tiny bottle of orange liquid from my pocket and smiled.

Maybe we were all acceptable collateral damage, every single one of us.

His eyes blazed as he realized what I held. "No . . ."

I popped the lid off the bottle and raised it to my lips.

Then I was on the ground, the bottle rolling away from me, and I scrambled for it. Something had barreled past me and I turned to see Gandalf, blood matted in his fur from snout to tail, with his teeth buried in Samedi's neck.

The old god screamed and struggled, then went still as he

morphed back into the mamba, striking at Gandalf but missing. Before he could strike again, Dominique tossed me the staff, which I turned on Samedi in one motion. I was too close to miss this time.

Sparks flew from its tip and the blinding crimson threads flowed out, wrapping themselves around the snake. I smelled burning flesh as Samedi screamed and morphed back into his human form again. I felt his power crumbling, burning to ash. Anger, then defeat, echoed on his face, and he faded into nothing.

I sat on the ground for a few seconds, smelling the damp earth and scorched flesh. Samedi wasn't really dead and gone. The Beyond doesn't work that way. But he'd been weakened, and it would take him a long time to regroup. He'd probably never have another opportunity like the one he'd just missed. I could only hope.

Gandalf had disappeared again, and so had Dominique. If they'd resumed their fight from the Napoleon House, I'd kill both of them myself.

I stumbled to Gerry and rolled him onto his back. He was unconscious, pale, his breathing rapid and shallow. I looked around for something to stanch the bleeding, pushing the anger aside and focusing on how much I loved him. I needed to get him out of here so we'd have time to settle our issues and see what was left.

I spotted one of Marie's scarves on the ground, folded it, and pressed it against Gerry's neck. He'd lost so much blood. The ground was muddy with it.

I half-crawled to a spot between Jake and Jean. Jake was unconscious, his breathing rasping but steady. One leg had been savaged, and bite wounds covered both arms. I touched him helplessly, not sure what to do.

Jean had managed to sit up. I turned to find him propped

against a crypt, the gaping tear to his chest already beginning to heal around the edges.

"Your friend will survive this, Drusilla. Dom has gone to find help."

I crawled over and sat next to him, taking his hand. "Thank you. I owe you one."

He chuckled, dark eyes gleaming in the dim light. "Yes, you do, *Jolie*. Perhaps more than one. When you—"

He fell silent as his gaze shifted past me to what must be the world's strangest second line parade heading toward us across the shadowy grounds. Dominique walked in front, Gandalf limping beside him. Behind them marched Pierre Lafitte, Louis Armstrong, and a motley band of musicians and pirates. New Orleans's immortal culture.

I closed my eyes in relief at the sight of Gandalf. I was even glad to see the surly pirate. They'd obviously reached some temporary truce.

Gandalf limped to Jake's side, sniffed at his face and whined, dropping into a pant beside him. He began shifting almost immediately, and I crawled to sit beside him as he curled into a ball and groaned.

"Talk to me, Alex." I smoothed his hair off his face and ticked through the injuries I could see. Deep shoulder gouge, and another in his thigh that had exposed muscle. Lots of blood.

"Unh." He pushed himself to a seated position and looked down at his thigh, and at the half-dozen bite marks across his chest and stomach. I'd already seen the ones on his back. "Shit. A few more minutes and I'd have been hamburger."

He was bitching too much to be dying. Hysteria and relief kicked in—until I saw Dom leaning over Jake.

My breath caught, then released in a *whoosh* as Jake moved his head and twitched a hand. He was still alive.

Dom leaned back and studied Alex. "The loup-garou bit Jean and your friend, and your shifting dog as well."

The *dog* grumbled something unintelligible as Louis came over with his pants and began helping him dress.

"I do not think it will affect Jean or the shifter, but that one . . ." Dominique jerked his head toward Jake. "You should watch him on the next full moon. If he lives, he will be loup-garou."

I stared at Jake in horror and stroked his shoulder. He moaned and turned his head toward me but didn't open his eyes. His lashes were dark against pale cheeks, and his blond hair was bloody and matted. I looked at the leg that always gave him such pain and couldn't tell where the denim of his jeans ended and the torn flesh began. It had been gnawed.

No one deserved this, but especially not him. He had walked through the hell of war already, and somehow managed to come out strong and decent and kind. And what had it gotten him? Pain and lies and the promise of a fresh new struggle in a world he couldn't imagine.

I took a deep breath and stuffed my feelings back inside. We had to get out of here before we attracted attention from the other denizens of the Beyond. The scent of blood alone would attract vampires or other loup-garou. There would be time for hysteria later.

"We need to get to the transport at Burgundy and St. Louis," I said, struggling to my feet. "They all need doctors."

"You too, my friend." Louis dabbed at my face with a handkerchief. I looked in confusion at the blood on my shirt, and wiped my hand across my nose. It came away bloody. A nosebleed. All this, and I had a freaking nosebleed. I'm sure there was irony there somewhere.

I felt dizzy again, but it was a regular kind of dizzy, from the buzzard's beak and blood loss. With the staff in my hand, my emotional walls felt strong and solid, and while I was tired, I wasn't nearly as exhausted as I should have been after using that much magic. I looked at the staff again, and I thought it purred.

Pierre Lafitte stayed to help Jean, but Dominique lifted Jake like he was no heavier than a baby—maybe a baby wolf—and one of the other pirates carried Gerry. Alex had managed to get back into his jeans and was able to walk on his own, albeit slowly. The wound in his thigh had already drenched the jeans scarlet, but his face had darkened from sheet-white to something just south of eggshell.

I fell in beside him. I wanted to tell him how worried I'd been, and how I wouldn't have wanted to survive this if he hadn't made it. I wanted him to know how important he'd become to me—as a partner, a friend, maybe more. I didn't know how to start.

Instead, I reached for his hand. His fingers curled around mine and squeezed.

"You okay?" I gave him a poor imitation of a smile.

He managed his own twitch at one corner of his mouth. "I will be."

We both looked behind us at Dom, carrying Jake. Alex's eyes met mine, and an unspoken promise traveled between us: We're getting him through this.

We finally reached the transport, sticking to side streets and bypassing the busy sections of Rampart. The transport was too small for all of us, so I took them across one at a time, using the staff for energy. My own magical battery was drained.

Gerry was in the worst shape, so I took him first, trying not to think about the way he was breathing—shallow, rapid breaths followed by what seemed like long stretches with no breath at all. Back in his bedroom, I pulled him outside the circle, stroked his cheek, then forced myself to go back.

As Dominique laid Jake inside the transport, he leaned close and spoke softly. "I do not share Jean's fascination with you, wizard. Should you hurt him again, remember that."

I didn't reply, but locked gazes with him as I fired up the transport. Great. Another immortal enemy.

I dragged Jake onto the bedroom floor next to Gerry, whose pulse was thready. Then I went back for Alex, my muscles aching.

When I got to the Beyond again, Dominique was gone. Good. I owed him one, too, but thought I might find his price too high.

Alex leaned on me heavily as we got ready to leave. He didn't talk, just grunted when I asked how he was doing.

I gave instructions for Louis to break the transport as soon as we were gone. "We wouldn't have made it without you," I said, trying to smile. I don't think I did a very good job of it, but he was a kind man and didn't judge.

"It's okay. I got to walk in the sunshine again," he said. "I got to play some music for a new bunch of people. I'm ready to stay here now. I'll break that symbol once you're gone, and that'll be the end of this spyboy's adventure."

I held on to Alex as I fed the transport one last ragged burst of energy from the staff.

When the light and pressure subsided, we stumbled into the bedroom. Gerry lay on the floor where I'd left him, but Jake had regained consciousness and managed to prop himself against an armchair with his eyes closed. His breath was ragged.

Gerry wasn't breathing.

I sat on the floor beside him, looking at his face, those so-familiar features. I wondered if I'd ever really known him, if we ever know anyone beyond what they're willing to show us. I leaned over and kissed his forehead, and tears tinged with my blood dropped on his face. I wished I'd known how to make this end well for him, or if he might have survived had I made different choices. I would have to live with that.

Alex had staggered to the bathroom, and I heard him rummaging around in the medicine cabinet. His injuries had worried me at first, but I kept forgetting about the shifter genes. He'd probably heal by morning. Jake was another matter.

I turned to him and found him watching me through half-closed lids.

"Hey, you're awake." I pulled a throw off the bed and crawled to sit beside him, putting pressure on his leg and telling a big old lie. "We're going to get you to a hospital—everything's going to be okay now."

He put a hand on top of mine, his strong, tanned fingers shaking.

His voice was little more than a rough whisper. "What are you?"

A month ago, I could have answered that question. Before the storm, before Gerry, before finding that blasted staff. Now I couldn't.

I whispered back: "I don't know."

FRIDAY, OCTOBER 7, 2005 "After the Storm: Louisiana death toll [to date]: 988 . . . Percentage of Entergy customers in the New Orleans metro area without power, Orleans Parish 59% . . . For now, only first-class letters will be delivered into the New Orleans region . . . Water on the east bank of New Orleans west of the Industrial Canal has been declared safe to drink . . . Limited medical care is available."

—THE TIMES–PICAYUNE

CHAPTER 42

I said good-bye to Gerry about a mile from the pile drivers and helicopters of the Army Corps of Engineers as they worked to piece the broken 17th Street Canal levee back together again. That was one big engineering Humpty Dumpty if ever I'd seen one.

The mud covering the grounds of the park along Lakeshore Drive had dried and cracked. I guessed eventually the brown and gray landscape of mud would give way to green shoots of weeds and grass. Life would go on, even in this land time seemed to have forgotten. The rest of the world had moved on but we wouldn't be able to leave Katrina behind for a long time.

The ground crunched as I walked to the edge of the water and looked at the mild blue waves washing on breakers of gray stone. In a small wooden box, I carried Gerry's ashes, thanks to a quiet cremation courtesy of the Elders. It had taken a week, but Zrakovi finally calmed down enough to talk to me and Alex instead of shouting. The powers-that-be weren't happy with either of us, and I didn't know what our future held. Zrakovi said we'd talk soon.

Right now, he didn't have time. The Beyond was in the middle of an uprising, and the Elders were fighting to retain control of the preternatural borders. Ironically, Gerry might get his wish about magic re-entering the world of humans, at least in New Orleans. Rumor had it several preternatural groups were already moving across, and the vampires and fae were running the negotiations. The elves were also said to be involved, and the Elders were making concessions.

The old gods of voodoo hadn't been invited to the negotiating table, and Samedi had been stripped of all power. His preternatural buddies had thrown him under the proverbial bus as an opening concession to negotiations.

Detective Ken Hachette had arrested a West Bank resident with a history of mental disorders after catching him setting up a voodoo ritual in Broadmoor. Souvenirs from every one of the dead guardsmen had been found in his house. The guy was probably as much a victim of Samedi as anyone, but I couldn't muster a lot of sympathy. He'd have a nice new home courtesy of the state of Louisiana.

I wished I'd handled things better, but whatever the Elders had in store, I wouldn't make excuses for saving Jake. As for Gerry, I'm wrapped up in guilt and grief and anger. I feel responsible for his death, and I miss him, and I'm angry with him. Given enough time, people say, everything heals. We'll see.

I wished I'd known more about my own abilities and their limits, and how I'd managed to use elven magic against Samedi. So do the Elders. The staff, Charlie, follows me around like a lethal, spark-spewing pet.

I wished I knew what kind of relationship Jean Lafitte thought we had now, and how he expected to be repaid for helping me. With the borders in flux, I had no doubt he'd be back sooner rather than later. I'd have to decide how to break it to the Elders that I promised the pirate a house and a business deal.

More than anything, I wished Jake hadn't gotten involved, but I wasn't sorry I'd met him or Alex. I don't know what kind of relationship we can have, any of us, not yet. Alex and I are waiting to see what the Elders say, and Jake is in a Metairie hospital, recuperating from a "wild animal attack" that supposedly happened in the flooded wilds of St. Bernard Parish. He won't speak to either his cousin or me. Alex says he's trying to come up with a rational Marine Corps–approved explanation for everything that happened.

Good luck with that. We'll have to talk to him before the next full moon. If he turns fanged and furry, he'll need our help.

I wished Katrina had never happened, that the city I love so much hadn't been so broken, its spirit so damaged, its naïve joy replaced by sorrow and cynicism and anger. Yet I know a lot of things I've come to love since the storm would never have been in my life without the pain.

Katrina took, and she gave.

I opened the box and said a prayer for Gerry as I flung his ashes into the calm, indifferent waters of Lake Pontchartrain.